The Castle of the Women

Alexander Lucie-

The Sicilian Novels

The Chemist of Catania

The Nymph of Syracuse

The Feast of the Dead

The Castle of the Women

Chapter One

After death, life.

When his wife told him that she was pregnant for the second time, Calogero di Rienzi had been disturbed, puzzled, surprised and then pleased. His previous wife had been killed in February, and he had only been to see his then mistress, Anna Maria Tancredi, some two weeks after that unexpected event, which had been the soonest he had been able to get away. On that occasion he had seen his new child Sebastiano and somewhat to his own surprise and hers, agreed that it would be best if they married as soon as possible to legitimise the newborn. Sebastiano had then been three weeks old. They had married on the day after Easter, which in that year, 2011, had fallen on Monday April 25th. It had been a very quiet ceremony, though it had been carried out by a Prince of the Church, the Cardinal of Palermo himself, who was, as Anna Maria described him, an old friend. Traiano had been there and so had Renzo Santucci. It had happened very early one morning in one of the side chapels of the Cathedral in Palermo. Then there had been a wedding breakfast at the Grand Hotel. (Traiano had sat next to the Cardinal, and they had got on famously.) Then the guests had left, and he had gone with Anna Maria to her flat nearby, where Sebastiano was with the nanny, and they had been alone, and that must have been when the second child must have come along.

He had not intended it and he had not expected it. After all, she was now past forty-five, and the first child, dear little Sebastiano, had been a huge surprise. But what would be, would be. He was very pleased. This would be his fifth child, and he wanted, naturally enough, another son. He was very pleased with his fertility. Every evening, from Catania, he would ring up Anna Maria, who remained in Palermo, to ask her about the progress of her pregnancy.

He was very glad he had married Anna Maria, even if the suggestion had come from her, because he liked her, he loved his new son, and he saw their alliance as deeply profitable. Of course, given that his first wife, Stefania, was hardly cold in her grave, and since her death had been a dramatic tragedy, he and Anna Maria had not made any announcement of their marriage as there was a certain degree of indecent haste involved. But one loses one wife, one finds another: that was his philosophy.

The shooting of his wife had largely concerned him because of the effect it might have on their children. Isabella, his eldest daughter, and Natalia, his second daughter, were, at the tender ages of not quite nine and five, old enough to appreciate the horror of seeing their mother shot in their presence, and her blood pooling on the pavement outside the airport arrivals hall. Renato, still a baby just past his first birthday, had been spared that. He would have no memory of Stefania. But the girls, they had been his first thought. The very night of the murder, his mother had come to stay, along with his sister Elena. He had been grateful, knowing that the children adored their grandmother and their aunt (not that he could quite understand why, but they did.) What he had not quite appreciated was the way his mother and Elena had not simply come to stay to help out on a temporary basis; they had come to stay with no intention of ever leaving. As a man, he understood the concept of territory, but he had not quite understood that women were similarly territorial. Stefania was gone, so her mother and sister-in-law, who had never liked her, had decided to lose no time in occupying her vacated space. It was essential that this was done quickly, before Stefania's blood relatives moved in. Stefania's mother did not have the advantage of being a widow, but her younger sister had no encumbrances, and had to be headed off before she made the move she was undoubtedly, in their mind, contemplating. Aunt Giuseppina was allowed, of course, to see the children, to take them to school occasionally and to babysit, all of which was curious, as she had never shown much desire to do anything similar before the tragedy. But the signora and Elena kept a watchful eye on her. They suspected, in the aftermath of the tragedy, that she was proposing herself as a second wife, neither of them having any idea of the actual second wife in Palermo.

These female machinations did not really bother Calogero overmuch. In the period preceding his clandestine second marriage, he spent most of his time in his office in the house where he slept on the sofa. He came out for meals which, given the signora's cooking skills, were remarkably good. The children came into him in the morning and the evening to play in his presence and to talk. His mother and sister were remarkably quiet when he was with them, thinking themselves in the presence of great grief.

In the quietness of the office, he received Traiano, generally at the dead of night. In the aftermath of the shooting, Traiano had proved his worth. As he had been the only person who had witnessed the shooting clearly – the killer had approached from behind, when the victim's back, as well as that of Calogero and the children, had been turned – he had muddied the waters by saying he could not be sure that Enzo had been aiming at Stefania, and could not swear that he had not in fact been aiming at Calogero but had missed, striking the wife instead. This was a useful ploy because it made the motivation of the killer even more opaque. Who had he been aiming to kill - the boss or the boss's wife? And the killer himself was saying nothing. He had never spoken before now except to his deceased brother, and it was pretty clear that he would never speak again.

This void, this silence, was filled by endless press speculation on the matter. Enzo was now incarcerated, presumably for life, in a mental institution, which was, in its way, tragic. The press also speculated on the death of Maso. Here, there were so many strands to the story, or the presumed story, to choose from. Maso had tried to kill Fabio Volta, who had killed him in self-defence. Fabio Volta had been briefly arrested and imprisoned, which had caused an uproar. After all, self-defence against young thugs was admirable, and did not the authorities recognise that Volta was a hero and liable to be killed in prison by some revenging criminal? So, Volta had been swiftly released. And of course that was what Maso, along with his brother was: a criminal, with the bedroom the two shared packed full of stolen electronic goods.

But why had Maso tried to kill Volta? Here the speculation grew fevered. It was assumed that Volta must have had something on Maso, and Maso must have been determined to silence him. It was at this point that the one thing that had worried Traiano more than anything turned out to be their salvation.

As soon as he had heard Maso was dead, Traiano had got in touch with Colonel Andreazza. He did this by calling the boy Paolo and then getting Paolo to send the Colonel a text message. Thus, when the Colonel came, he found Traiano, not Paolo, waiting for him in the back room of the pizzeria. Traiano had explained that he wanted the Colonel to get hold of and dispose of the laptop that had belonged to Rosario, which was in Maso and Enzo's bedroom, and which would surely be impounded by the police as evidence. The Colonel was only too happy to help, but by the time he paid a visit to the flat where Maso and Enzo's parents lived, his colleagues had got there first. Only later did he find out that it had been Volta who had urged former colleagues to make sure they got to whatever was in the bedroom before anyone else.

That the laptop had fallen into the wrong hands distressed Traiano, but in the end the story short circuited. It was assumed by the police that the laptop had been stolen from Rosario's flat by Maso and had not yet been wiped; there were lots of other stolen goods as well, but they had all been wiped and were untraceable. But this laptop linked Maso with Rosario who, though not classified as a missing person, nor the object of a murder enquiry, had not been seen since January. The laptop became proof that Maso had robbed Rosario and perhaps murdered him. It was already established that Maso was violent, as he had tried to murder Volta; perhaps the stealing of the laptop had led to a quarrel resulting in Rosario's death, and the emails sent from the computer subsequently had been designed to cover this up. And Volta had guessed this, so Maso had had to silence Volta. And when Maso had been killed, the crazy brother had shot Stefania di Rienzi (or perhaps had been aiming at her husband) blaming one of them for his death.

The police had come to interview Calogero and Traiano. With the grieving widower, they had tried to establish a connection with Maso. He was not forthcoming. Enzo had worked for his wife; Maso had been his sort of minder. But Calogero had no real memory of either of them. They had done some work in the office, which he rarely visited. They had done some work in the house, but he had been absent those days, he was sure. He took absolutely no interest in electronics and technology and did not even possess a computer or a mobile phone. He left all that to others. It was perfectly true, for they had told him that Maso had been a waiter at the pizzeria and it was quite possible he might have seen him there, as he did go there, for he owned the place after all. But he very rarely noticed who was waiting at table. He took their word for it that Maso was a member of the Purgatory gym, which he also owned, but he had never been there since it opened. It was true that Maso was a member of the gun club at Nicolosi, which he also owned and which he had never visited either. Of course, he knew all the boys in the quarter as he had grown up in Purgatory and never lived anywhere else; but why should he know Maso who was not from this quarter?

The police found Traiano much more forthcoming. Of course, he knew Maso. He had a job at the pizzeria, not that he did many shifts. He had not liked him. He was always trying to ingratiate himself. He was always hanging around, in the quarter, though he was not from Purgatory, or at the gym, or at the gun club. Well, not always hanging around, but hanging around more than was necessary. The reason was he had a bit of a thing going with one of the women of the quarter. Traiano was married, so he did not take an interest in these things, but the boys of the quarter did talk about such matters, and that was how he knew. Yes, he knew the brother who was seriously weird. He had advised Stefania not to employ him, but she was so soft hearted she had felt sorry for him. But he had had a bad feeling about Enzo from the start. Enzo, he had heard – as one does – from the brother mainly, who complained about it, was not sexually normal. He hardly ever came out of the bedroom the two of them shared, and he spent hours looking at violent pornography on his computer. Stefania was a very attractive woman, blonde, elegant, and perhaps if Enzo felt he could not have her, no one else would.

No, he did not know the name of the woman in the quarter Maso was seeing; it could have been any of a number of women, so he did not want to speculate.

As for Maso and Rosario, they would have met at the gym, and perhaps at the gun club. But he did not think they were especially close. As for Fabio Volta, the man whom Maso had tried to kill, he knew nothing of him at all.

And so, the story emerged: Rosario had been killed by Maso, who had been caught in the act of stealing his laptop. Maso had been killed by Volta in self-defence, after trying to silence Volta, who had known about his guilt. And the crazed Enzo, driven wild by grief, had killed the woman with whom he had become obsessed. The capstone to the story was provided by Colonel Andreazza who declared that the police believed Rosario to be dead, but were not seeking anyone in connection with his murder. Volta was absolved, as public opinion demanded. And Enzo was taken into psychiatric care and declared unfit to stand trial. Thus, the story unfolded.

This, at length, was what Traiano was able to report to his master as he sat in his secluded office, in the flat which was now dominated by his mother, sister and, to a lesser extent, sister-in-law. He was able to give Traiano several instructions. No one was to touch Volta. No one was to try and kill Enzo or to harm his parents. Enzo was a poor deluded man-child; as for Maso, who was to blame, Maso was dead. And Calogero knew that if anyone were to blame, it was himself for thinking Maso trustworthy. But he let that pass. Maso was dead, which was good.

Don Giorgio came as well. He sat with the women and children for some time, and was then admitted into the presence of Calogero. Knowing that Calogero had secluded himself from almost everyone, he was surprised to find him business-like rather than broken by the loss of his wife. He was struck by his lack of grief. He gave instructions for the delayed funeral of his wife, delayed because only now had the police released the body for burial. He wished her to be placed in the vault of the Church of the Holy Souls in Purgatory after a requiem Mass to take place early in the morning.

Don Giorgio understood this need for discretion, this desire to hide oneself away. The vault had not been opened for many years, but it could be done, and it was a well-known, if neglected, privilege of the members of the Confraternity that they and close family members could be buried there if they chose. He attempted to mention Rosario's name, but Calogero raised a hand to stop him, as if that were too painful to talk about. Calogero had one question.

'Where is Maso being buried?' he asked.

The priest had not known Maso at all, but he had heard the funeral was to take place in the parish of his parents, and then the coffin to be taken to the municipal cemetery. As he said this, he saw Calogero nod. Calogero had a horror of the municipal cemetery. It was run down, neglected, infested with criminals; the tombs were in some cases broken open and the ground littered with bones. That was where Turiddu was buried, not that he had ever visited the grave. It would do for Maso, but not for his wife. The vault, under the Church that he could see from his windows, was the best place for her.

Just as the lack of grief surprised the priest, it surprised Calogero as well. He felt nothing for his late brother; he felt very little for his late wife, shot in his presence, except a mild surprise that someone whom he had assumed to be a permanent part of his life should be so suddenly and unexpectedly removed from it.

Other people came in the days before and after the funeral. They too hung around in the kitchen being fed by the signora, talking to Elena and Giuseppina, being kind to the children. Among them were Renzo Santucci who had come from Palermo; among them too were Gino and Alfio. These, along with Traiano, were frequent visitors.

Gino had something particular to ask. He knew that this was not the right time, but he wanted to get married. Catarina was pregnant. It had happened as soon as he had got back from Hungary after Christmas. He wanted to get married on the first day don Giorgio would allow, which was Easter Monday, as it was now Lent and one could not get married in Lent. Calogero knew one could not get married in Lent, and gave his blessing. He himself would not be there, though he did not give the reason.

Gino was pleased to have the boss's permission. The wedding would give him something to think about. It would distract him from the gloom that had enveloped them all. Gino had offered to kill Enzo, wherever they had hidden him away, but the boss had forbidden this. Planning a wedding was an alternative distraction to planning and carrying out a murder. Alfio, his bride's cousin, felt the heavy atmosphere too. He was glad of the forthcoming wedding, but he also had plans for his own, now that his teeth had been fixed by the Hungarian dentist. He spent a long time in that kitchen receiving the ministrations of the signora, speaking to the children, while Gino was with the boss, or while he was waiting to be called in. He had known Giuseppina for some considerable time, though never known her well. Now seemed like a God-given opportunity to get to know her better. The same was true of Renzo. The signora seemed to have a particular liking for him, but more to the point, so did the signora's daughter. As Alfio advanced towards Giuseppina, so did Renzo advance more rapidly to Elena.

Traiano noticed this blossoming of young love. He also noticed the way both his mother and his wife, as well as Catarina, were swelling with their new babies. The boss had confided in him earlier that he intended to marry Anna Maria; so that meant four prospective weddings and, a month after the boss was remarried, four prospective babies. This involved, in its own way, a great deal of work, work on top of the usual tasks that arose in the quarter. All the women were to give birth in the period after the summer holidays, apart from Anna Maria, who was due the next year. All of these, and the courting couples, would be looking for some sort of recognition. That included his wife and his mother. And all of these people would expect him to take their requests to don Calogero. It occurred to him, not for the first time, that they feared the boss, and thus used him as an intermediary. Of course, for some of these, he was happy to do this; for others, less so.

Every morning, when he returned from his nocturnal activities, he slipped off his clothes and crept into bed with his wife, putting his arms around her and savouring her sweetness; as he began to make love to her, she would ask him the same question:

'Have you spoken to him about the flat?'

He assured her that he was waiting for the right moment to ask; that he hardly needed to ask; that whatever he asked he would get, provided the moment was right. But the moment had to be right. The poor man had just lost his wife and was, though no one else knew, about to marry another; he had a lot on his mind. But as he made love to Ceccina, grasping her warm soft breasts in his hands, he knew that she was not thinking just about him, but about the flat. The flat, this accursed question of property, had crept into the marital bed itself, the one place that he had always thought of as sacred.

Afterwards, she would get up, and he would watch her getting dressed. Then the children would burst in, Cristoforo now old enough to climb on the bed, and little Maria Vittoria. When they left, the peace would return and he would sleep, but these delightful moments with the family were ruined by the thought that Ceccina was thinking still about the flat, eaten away with worry that someone else would get it.

But who? Gino was someone he did not like or trust, though he felt a respect for his strength, his boneheaded physical strength. But if Gino was stupid, Catarina was clever. Alfio, if he was making up to Giuseppina, the boss's sister-in-law, the aunt of his children - would Alfio get the flat? Or would Elena and Renzo? (But they would surely live in Palermo.) Or what about Assunta and her husband? What about the signora herself? And what if the boss decided he did not want to move into the upper storey, still being restructured? But Ceccina was driving him mad, and he knew he would have to ask sooner or later. However, he decided to leave all this till after the wedding, the boss's wedding to Anna Maria Tancredi. A lot of things had to be left till after the wedding.

Once the ceremony in the Cathedral was over, once the wedding breakfast was consumed at the Grand Hotel in Palermo, and once Calogero had retired to her flat with Anna Maria, made love to her, had a shower and a cup of coffee, indeed while he was waiting for the coffee, he phoned Traiano at the hotel, telling him to come round with the car and take him back to Catania. She, his new wife, would understand, he was sure, that he could not be with people, just yet, for very long. She would forgive him for this very brief introduction to married life, and for the fact that, for the moment, there was no question of them living together or making much public fuss over their marriage. But he was sure she understood.

Where the boss would live, where the new wife would live, was the subject of much discussion in the car. When it came to getting people to do what you wanted them to do, Calogero had always taken the direct approach, exemplified by the knife (he did not like guns) or the fist, or bringing their heads down with force onto hard surfaces. But these domestic matters were different. You could not do that with women or with children, particularly not your own wife or your own children. He outlined a gentler plan.

'The house in Donnafugata is huge,' he said. 'We shall all meet up there for weekends, I think. It will be lovely in the hot weather. My daughters will like the pool, and they will get used to Anna Maria; I think the girls will like Sebastiano, as they adore all babies, especially Renato and your two. Perhaps you can come with Ceccina and the children. Then it will be allowed to dawn gradually on the children that Anna Maria and I are together; they may even get it into their heads that we should be together. Isabella and Natalia may sweetly suggest we get married.'

'But will you and Anna Maria live together?' asked Traiano.

'She has to be in Palermo for her work, and I have to be in Catania, though I am going to spend a lot of time in Palermo as well. And we can also spend time in Donnafugata; so, we will divide our time between the three places and coincide regularly, I am sure, though I cannot see Anna Maria spending much time in Catania with the Black Widow Spider in constant attendance.'

This was what he called his mother.

'Won't she go home?'

'She is useful with the children, and she is very stubborn,' said Calogero, not wanting to admit that he never quite knew how to deal with his mother. 'And she cooks and cleans, which is very useful.'

'The building work above you, how is that going?'

'The new flat? It should be finished by the late summer. Of course, one could not expect Anna Maria to live in Stefania's old place. The new place would suit her. It will have a lovely roof terrace. And leaving the old place might give me a reason to send the Black Widow Spider back to where she came from.'

'So, you are moving?'

'Yes. How big a fool is Gino, do you think?' asked the boss, suddenly changing the topic.

'A pretty big one, I think,' said Traiano. 'Why the sudden interest?'

'He came to see me, and so did that girl he is marrying. But they came separately. He told me that he was very keen to do some major jobs for me in Palermo, should the opportunity arise, and should I need them done. He wanted to kill Enzo but I said no. But he was fishing around for other work. He mentioned that as he was getting married, he might well need the money as well. He said that he and Renzo got on. Is that true?'

'He has been training Renzo in fist fighting in the gym. Do they get on? I doubt it. And if there are major jobs to be done in Palermo, I think you should reward Muniddu first before Gino.'

'Yes. But it is putting out feelers, isn't it? Bit of a cheek. Then the girl came to see me, saying that Gino did not know she was coming. That amazed me.'

'What did?'

'What she said. You paid her two thousand to seduce poor Rosario, didn't you?'

'I did. She was eager to do so.'

'And did she? Seduce him?'

'Not at first. But she did in the end. I am pretty sure she did.'

'Interesting. I remember at the time I had the idea of breaking up his engagement with Petrocchi's daughter. Well, Catarina came to me and said the child she is having is not Gino's.'

'Now I am amazed too. And what did she say next?'

'Oh, she was subtle. Please could I reward Gino with something nice and so on. The implication being that if I didn't, then she would, well, I am not sure what she would do. The implication was that I owed her something because she is the mother of my nephew.'

'And Gino is too stupid to realise that?' said Traiano. 'Of course, once the child is born, she could prove one way or another who the real father is. But Gino thinks it is his. He has been boasting about his impending fatherhood for weeks. Look, boss, I think she has overstepped the mark, though it may well be true that the child is Rosario's. I don't like the idea that she thinks she can blackmail you. Did she mention what she wanted in particular?'

'Yes. The flat, when I move out.'

Traiano concentrated on the road.

'We could get rid of Gino. I have never liked him. It is possible he put her up to this,' he said at last.

'No, he is too stupid. Besides he would go berserk if he knew he was not the real father. When you say get rid of him, what do you mean? He is Alfio's best friend and marrying his cousin.'

'I don't mean get rid of in that sense, though I would not mind at all. What I meant was we could send him to Palermo, permanently. He wanted to do major jobs there, where he is not known. Well, I suppose he would soon become known. But I could speak to her, and slap her down. After all, we have the upper hand. If we told Gino that she was not carrying his child but someone else's…'

'Speak to her,' said the boss. 'Tell her that I never want to hear any talk of a child of Rosario's again. And tell Gino that I have heard what he has said and that one day, one day we will use him. When the two old men, Lorenzo and Domenico Santucci, are dead, the agreement we have with them dies with them. We do not know when that will be. But when it happens, that is when we will wipe out all the males of the Santucci family.'

'All?'

'Yes, all. Renzo will kill his uncle Antonio. Antonio has sons, doesn't he?'

'Two, I think. They are still young.'

'Well, what do you do with vipers' eggs? Crush them. Then when Antonio is dealt with, we can take out Renzo.'

'But isn't Renzo going to marry Elena?'

'There is that,' said the boss, thoughtfully. 'We shall keep Renzo under review.'

Traiano was pleased to hear it. Renzo was far more of a rival than Gino or Alfio as far as he was concerned.

'Colonel Andreazza has been very useful to us,' said Traiano. 'Now he is getting fractious.'

'Meaning?'

'He wants more of what he has already had.'

'Then give it to him.'

'Understood. We might need to do something more to keep Paolo and his mother Beata sweet.'

'Who are they? Remind me.'

He did.

'I need Paolo to recruit some other boys for the Colonel, now that Paolo is getting too old for him.'

'Too old? How old is he?'

'I think he is twelve. They grow up fast round here.'

'Do whatever it takes. We need the Colonel onside. He has been, as you say, very useful. The people he sent to interview me were very pliable. He had tidied up a lot of loose ends.'

'I will see to it. I loathe the Colonel. You have never met him. Lucky you!' He judged the moment right. 'Boss…..'

'You want to ask me something,' he observed, knowing what it was.

'It's Ceccina. She is desperate to move somewhere bigger. The new baby. I don't get a moment's peace.'

Calogero hesitated. He was being asked a favour, and he knew that his was the very important currency in which he dealt, and that favours should not be dispensed too easily. But then he remembered the service that Traiano had done him. The ghost of his brother momentarily hung between them. He was unmentionable. But they both understood he was there.

'I always assumed that you would move into the flat when I moved out. And that you would have it. It is yours. Tell Ceccina. Of course, you own the flat you are in, don't you?' He was almost tempted to suggest that the current flat should be swapped for the new one. 'You can sell your current flat to Gino for a nice price. How about that? My current flat is yours; you can have the title deeds and we will get the accountants and the lawyers to fix it and make it look legal. Tell Ceccina to stop worrying. And when you sell your flat to Catarina, make it clear that you are doing her a favour, and that she needs to co-operate.'

'Understood, boss. Ceccina will be delighted.'

While the boss had been secretly getting married in Palermo, Catarina and Gino had been getting married in the Church of the Holy Souls in Purgatory. The boss had declined the invitation, which was understood, but everyone else was there. Traiano had been planning to make a late arrival at the reception, which he did, as the elaborate dinner was ending, congratulating himself that he had missed the boring Mass, the even more boring hiatus when the wedding photos were taken, and the orgy of overeating that was the wedding banquet. As he came in, tired from his drive from Palermo, having dropped off the boss, still in his smart suit, he saw his wife on the other side of the room, smiled and waved at her. He fought off the small children who immediately rushed to embrace him, and made his way to the top table to see the bride and groom.

Gino leaned back in his seat as he saw him approach, and Traiano wrapped his arms around his shoulders and kissed his cheek with fervour.

'I love your suit,' he said. 'Where did you get it?'

'Via Etnea. Catarina chose it.'

'It looks so good,' said Traiano. Then he turned to the best man, Alfio. 'Don't you agree?' he asked.

Gino smiled radiantly. Alfio, more intelligent, looked rather puzzled.

'And you look smart too,' continued Traiano. 'How is the new girlfriend?'

'She is not yet my girlfriend, boss,' said Alfio, looking across the room to where Giuseppina was speaking to her female friends.

'Make a move tonight,' said Traiano. 'The atmosphere is right. You'll see.' He turned to Gino, and lowered his voice, so no one could hear. 'The boss knows. We have discussed it. He knows what great work you have done in the past. He has not forgotten that. He knows that you will do great work in the future. He has you in mind for that. But just when, we are not sure. So be patient.'

'Tell the boss I am grateful,' said Gino.

He left him and went in search of the new wife. She saw him coming, read his intention in his face (he realised that she was clever) and moved away from her friends so she could speak to Traiano in private.

'Not a wise move,' said Traiano smilingly, 'what you said to Calogero. He does not like being reminded of his brother, and he has enough children of his own. If you bring that up again, Gino will hear of it and he will not be pleased. Let us just hope your baby looks like Gino and not like Rosario. Let's hope he or she looks like you.'

'You bastard,' she said, smiling in return.

'Yes,' he replied. 'I am a bastard. Correct. You are clever. Now, I know Gino's flat is small and not very nice. I am leaving my current house and will sell it to you for a very nice price. So, though I am a bastard, you need to keep me sweet, understood?'

She looked at the ground, then looked at him, mollified.

'Now, tell me something, my dear,' he continued. 'Is it Rosario's?'

'Yes.'

'You are sure?'

'Positive.'

'So, Gino is a complete fool?'

She shrugged.

'The boss wants Rosario to stay dead, understood? He won't even have his name mentioned. But I was Rosario's best friend, so… you see what I mean? You need to work out who your friends are and who your enemies are.'

'I just did,' she said.

He moved away. Lots of excited children, including his own, were mobbing him, and he finally made it over to Ceccina. He leaned over to kiss her as she sat at the table.

'Nice dress,' he said.

'I wish my sister had had a chance to do your hair before you came out,' replied Ceccina.

'I have been all day with the boss. Business. Secret business. Though you will all know one day. I have just told Catarina that she and Gino can buy our flat for a very good price when we move out.'

'When?' she asked sharply.

'End of summer, I reckon. When the boss's new place is ready and we get his old place.'

Her smile was radiant.

'When are we going home?' he asked with meaning.

'It is still too early. It's a wedding!' she replied, with a silvery laugh.

'Just remember that I am getting impatient,' he said, with a smile.

They were joined by Giuseppina, the late Stefania's sister. She did not have much resemblance to her sister, and had not dyed her hair blonde. The children had come too and were gathered around them.

'Do you think Aunt Giuseppina should marry Uncle Alfio?' he asked them.

Isabella was thoughtful.

'He is not very handsome,' she said. 'Unlike you, Uncle Traiano.'

'Not many people are handsome like me,' said Traiano. 'But I think Uncle Alfio is very smart, and I just told him so. He has had his teeth fixed, you know, which cost a lot of money and pain in Hungary. And we are at a wedding, when one thinks of marriage, when these things are in the air. But it is up to Aunt Giuseppina. I know that Uncle Alfio would be delighted.'

'He is sweet,' said Giuseppina. 'My parents know his uncle and aunt, Catarina's parents, so....'

But not Alfio's father, thought Traiano, who was in Piazza Lanza, last he had heard, with many years yet to serve.

Natalia was now tugging him by the hand.

'Uncle Traiano,' she said. 'Isabella likes Paolo.'

Isabella blushed and looked cross with her sister.

'Really. Which Paolo? There are so many. Is he here?'

'Natalia, be quiet,' said Isabella sternly.

'The one whose mother drinks crème de menthe,' said Giuseppina with meaning.

'I think I know him,' said Traiano. 'He is a messenger boy for your father and for me. Have you ever spoken to him?'

Isabella shook her head.

'Good,' said Traiano.

He gave Giuseppina a look.

'Their father is back, so do drop them off home whenever. I assume their grandmother will be waiting up for them. Then you can enjoy yourself with Alfio.'

'You seem very keen to make that happen,' she observed.

'And why not?' he asked.

He now saw Beata out of the corner of his eye. How on earth had she managed to get herself invited? Who had invited her? Had she come as someone's date? Wasn't she a former squeeze of the groom? He was quite, quite shocked. He looked around for the son. As he was condemned to be here for some time, he might as well do some work. He remembered that some of the male children had been out in the carpark of the hotel. He walked out and surveyed the dark scene from the steps of the building. There indeed, on the far side of the carpark, were a group of boys, sheltering behind a line of cars. He saw the tell-tale glow of a cigarette. He walked over, and as he did so, the boy holding the cigarette saw him and let the cigarette fall, a look a fear on his face.

'Grab him,' said Traiano, as soon as he reached the group of six or seven, which included Paolo. The smoking boy, who was the oldest of the group, aged about fourteen, was pinioned by the arms. At instructions from Traiano, who was now taking off his belt, he was placed against the bonnet of one of the cars. Everyone knew that the boss had a phobia about smoking, and anyone who was caught was likely to be severely punished. The boy began to whimper. His trousers were pulled down, exposing his tender teenage legs. He screamed as the leather of the belt hit his flesh, and hit him seven or eight times. Traiano then passed the belt to the other boys and they all had a go. If anyone was counting, they soon lost count of the blows. The victim then slid onto the tarmac.

'Is he from this quarter?' asked Traiano.

The other boys nodded.

'Then he ought to have known better,' said Traiano, putting his belt back on. He gave the boy a kick in the shins, and invited the others to do the same. They did so obediently, most of them, especially Paolo, with gusto.

'Next time, we will kill you,' said Traiano, with satisfaction. He walked away, having caught Paolo's eye.

'What is that young fool called?'

'Tonino,' said Paolo.

'Ah, yes, Tonino Grassi, I know him now. He has grown up, but not in a good way. Tell him to come and see me sometime next week if he knows what is good for him. If he wants to stay in the quarter.' They re-entered the building. 'How's the Colonel?' asked Traiano.

The boy looked at the floor.

'Do you want a beating too?' asked Traiano.

'No,' said Paolo hurriedly. 'The Colonel….'

'….is getting bored with you. Yes, I know. Well, that does not matter. We will find him someone else. Someone a little bit younger than you, perhaps. Someone better looking and more pliable. You find me someone like that, and he will be a very lucky boy, because he will make lots of money, just as you have. And if you find someone good, you will get a finder's fee.'

'How much?' asked Paolo with sudden interest.

'Five hundred,' said Traiano generously.

'And I won't have to see the Colonel anymore?'

'You don't want to see the Colonel?'

'No. Of course not. It is just the money.'

'There are more honest ways of making it. We will find you something.'

'Boss, you said when I was thirteen....'

'Yes, I remember. We will fix that. But first find someone new for the Colonel and get them prepared, if you know what I mean. Stress the money. The Colonel's generous. Now come here, give me a kiss and do not look so sulky. Remember what happens to sulky boys.'

The boy ran off. Then coming through the doors were the figures of his mother and stepfather.

'We are late!' she announced.

'Only by about seven hours,' he remarked, giving her a light peck on the cheek, and giving his stepfather a warm embrace. The night stretched before him, an endless expanse. All he wanted was to get away and go home, but that prospect seemed impossibly remote. Renzo Santucci was now approaching him, smiling. He smiled back. He quite liked Renzo. He wondered how serious the boss's thoughts were about wiping out the whole Santucci family.

'It's great, isn't it?' said Renzo. 'This sort of party. More fun than we ever had in Palermo. I am glad I came. Gino was very keen for me to come. Well, it is nice to please him, and it is nice to be here and see Elena as well.'

'One wedding brings on another.'

'You think?'

'Everyone thinks. I know the boss thinks so. I think he would like it.'

Renzo smiled. Traiano had touched a chord. He knew that only one thing mattered to Renzo, and that was pleasing Calogero. That was the slavish devotion which mattered, nothing else. Certainly not Elena. But she - he saw looking over to where she sat, surrounded by other women - was clearly eager to snare the man. Her hair had been done by Ceccina's sister. He was beginning to recognise her style.

'And she is keen too,' added Traiano. 'It all depends on you now.'

'To be the boss's brother-in-law would be a great honour. And, you know, it would unite the two families.'

'It makes perfect sense.' He lowered his voice. 'And you are going to need Calogero and his muscle when you take out Antonio Santucci. Though that only happens when his father and uncle are no longer here. And neither of them can live forever. And there is another thing,' he said, raising his voice. 'Alfio and Giuseppina are on the verge of getting together. That would give Alfio a little bit more importance than he deserves. You do not want him to put you in the shade. Giuseppina and Elena are almost always together, they see each other every day. They are friends, but rivals too. Elena does not want to be left behind.'

'She won't be,' said Renzo. 'I have been without a girlfriend since Christmas, and it's now Easter Monday. Time to do something about it.'

'Where are you staying tonight?'

'Your house, or had you forgotten? Certainly not in the boss's flat, with Elena's mother in the next room and three children waking up in the middle of the night. Actually, this is a hotel, isn't it? I am sure they have rooms.'

'Good idea,' said Traiano.

A few minutes later, he saw Alfio.

'Book a room here before they are all gone for the night.'

'What? Oh right, yes,' said Alfio.

This work done, sure to have won the undying gratitude of all parties, he settled into a chair. The boy Paolo came and sat next to him, and leaned his head against him.

'Who is the man your mother came with?' asked Traiano.

'One of the waiters from the pizzeria. His name is Amilcare.'

'I know him,' said Traiano, thinking of a youngish, rather shy man, whose main claim to fame was his ability to pick locks. 'Do you like Amilcare?'

'I don't mind him,' said Paolo, yawning.

By the time Alfonso, his stepfather, had joined him, Paolo was asleep. His head was resting in Traiano's lap. Traiano and Alfonso looked at each other.

'He should be in bed, so should my children, and so should I,' said Traiano. 'But Ceccina is enjoying herself. This sort of thing is what she likes. But for me it is work. This little boy seems to like me. His mother is a prostitute, so he is never properly looked after, particularly at night. He gravitates towards me.'

'Poor boy.'

'You think I am bad for him? Well, don't worry, I most certainly am. Children run wild in this quarter. They do not go to school; they play football in the streets and the square; they steal and all sorts of things. Then once in a blue moon, comes along a boy from the quarter who does everything right, and who goes to school and university, and says his prayers and goes to Mass, and becomes a lawyer and finds a lawyer's daughter to marry, despite not being good-looking. And then he is killed. The only success story in the quarter. Poor Rosario.'

'I had heard,' said Fofò. 'How does his brother take it?'

'He does not care at all. He cares very little about the wife as well. He expects to be loved but he does not love back. I think he likes his children, especially his sons. But he did not like Rosario. Rosario wanted to go his own way. He would not do as he was told. Poor Rosario. I miss him. I feel sorry for him being born here. Anywhere else, and he would have had a happy life. I am not so sorry for Maso and Enzo, those two brothers you photographed. One dead and buried and the other buried alive. What a fate! Enzo has lost the only person he could communicate with, and now he is imprisoned in his own silence forever. They will never release him. The parents must suffer too. But Maso is - was, someone who got what he deserved. I do not like Volta, but Volta was right to kill him. I am glad he did. Poetic justice for what he did to Rosario.'

'Rosario's mother and sisters?'

Traiano shrugged.

'It is as if he had never lived. They take their cue from Calogero.'

'And you don't?'

A tall, somewhat weedy youth was standing in front of them.

'Hi, handsome,' said Traiano to Amilcare. 'Have you come to collect this child off me? I would suggest you carry him without waking him up, but he is far too heavy. I had better wake him up.'

He poked Paolo in the ribs.

'Fuck off!' murmured the boy.

'What have I told you about swearing?' said Traiano sharply, slapping his face.

'Sorry,' said Paolo, tears springing to his eyes.

'One day I am going to give you such a beating,' said Traiano. But he gave the boy a hug and pushed him towards Amilcare.

'Take him to his mother, and take them both home,' he said.

'Yes, sir,' said Amilcare, taking the boy by the hand.

Seeing them go, Traiano relaxed.

'How is your baby?' he asked.

'Very well. How is yours?'

'Very well. Due at the same time as yours. Early September?'

'Ours is a little later. We only married in February.'

'They are married, you know. It is a secret for now, but it will come out.'

'Him and Tancredi?'

'Who else? They are not planning to announce it, just to let it seep out. It was this morning, in Palermo. You can tell Anna, as I am sure she will want to know. It was very early this morning in the Cathedral in Palermo. Then we had a wedding breakfast, then he went back to her flat, ostensibly to see the baby, Sebastiano, now two months old, and to seal the pact, I am sure. Then he phoned me and told me to pick him up and bring him back. He married her because of the child. Now he has four, two sons, two daughters. A nice number.'

'You will need to keep up.'

'I had three before the age of twenty,' said Traiano. 'A good start.'

'I will stick with one. We have Salvatore as well. And we have you.'

'You do, you do,' said Traiano.

By the time he got to bed, the sun had risen over the quarter, over Catania, over Mount Etna, over the Mediterranean Sea. People were getting up; the place was stirring. He was aware of this as he let himself into the flat, crept into the bedroom he shared with Ceccina, took off his clothes, being careful to hang up the smart suit carefully, and slipped into bed besides his sleeping wife. She always slept lightly, and he could tell from the way she stirred and the way she moved towards him, that she knew he was there. Gradually, her warmth enveloped him, and without opening her eyes, she spoke in a whisper.

'What kept you?' she asked.

'People, people,' he said.

He had had a long conversation with Renzo, far too long. Renzo had booked a room in the hotel and was on his way there, because Elena had gone up already. She had needed very little persuasion, a little to Renzo's surprise but not to Traiano's. Renzo, though intent on seeing Elena, still wanted to discuss the question of his uncle. It became clear to Traiano that he had already been discussing this with Gino, the one who was giving him boxing lessons, and that was why Gino had already approached the boss. Traiano counselled patience. Revenge was a dish best savoured cold, he warned. Too swift an action would look bad. One should act in cold blood. That ensured greater possibility of success and fewer mistakes. Besides, Antonio's father and uncle were still alive. But not for much longer, Renzo had pointed out. It was a good idea, he insisted, to make plans now. That guy over there, the one called Amilcare, knew everything about locks, thanks to his time in the University of Bicocca. The house in Castelvetrano was like a fortress, but Amilcare was able to get in anywhere, and then Gino could go in, and pop, pop, pop. When the aunt was out shopping. He saw it all. Traiano, too, saw it all. He wondered about the children, the ones who were Renzo's cousins twice over. But no one would miss Antonio Santucci, he was sure of that. A most unlamented man. It would be kindness itself to put an end to his miserable existence. But he changed the subject. What he wanted to know about was the immigrants. They needed more, and they needed them in the Furnaces, in large quantities. Palermo, said Renzo, would deliver. Then he realised that Elena was waiting for him, and hurried off.

'Renzo is spending the night with Elena in the hotel,' said Traiano to Ceccina now.

'Lucky him, lucky her,' said Ceccina. 'He is not so very handsome.'

'She is not so pretty. But he is very, very rich, and she is very greedy. It will make her richer than any of us, and richer than Assunta and richer even than the boss, perhaps. That is what she likes. Money.'

'You should not say that. She is my friend.'

'You know it is true,' he said.

After Renzo, he had spent time with his mother and his stepfather. This, he was able to discuss with Ceccina. His mother was beginning to show her pregnancy. Fofò - Alfonso - was very pleased with himself.

'I like Fofò,' she said. 'If you look like that when you are fifty, I shall be very pleased. Did you meet Gino's parents? They struck me as rather sad people. I think they have a hard life in Agrigento, perhaps harder than the life most have here. And did you meet the brother, Corrado he is called?'

'I spoke to him, for a bit, not long.'

'I could not believe he was Gino's brother. He is so nice, so charming. We all thought he was really nice. He is a stonemason. That is a good job, I think. Even Pasqualina seemed interested in him.'

'Talking of charming men, Alfio is spending the night in the hotel with Giuseppina.'

'Sweet Alfio,' she said. 'He has wanted a girlfriend since he was twelve years old.'

'Then I went to see the boss. His light was on, and I told him all this, and he was very thoughtful.'

'Good,' she said. 'And you sat in our future house. Now concentrate on what you are doing, and try not to wake the children.'

Chapter Two

'How was your time in jail?'

'Unpleasant, but mercifully brief. It was worse for Rosa, really. She panicked. Naturally, she thought that if they did not get me in the Cathedral Square, they would get me inside,' said Fabio Volta.

'We thought the same,' said the youngish woman who was called Chiara. 'When we heard the news, the news of your arrest, we made representations to the people down here. I am sorry to say they were ignored. So we went to the Viminal, in person, and though we were told to wait, well, we waited, and we saw the minister, eventually, and he listened to reason, made the phone call, and the rest you know. They released you. That is the way things get done in this country. Of course, there was a huge uproar about your arrest, but what really counts is the minister picking up the phone. And what matters is the right minister picking up the phone first, if you see what I mean.'

'If someone else had got to the phone first, you might be dead by now,' said the man called Silvio. 'I am assuming, of course, that whoever wanted you dead and sent that boy Maso wanted to finish the job. But perhaps not. Now that you are a public hero, perhaps you are untouchable. These people have a sense of public relations, as you probably know.'

'I am very grateful you got me out,' said Volta. 'I am very glad to be out.'

He waited for them to speak. Naturally, he owed them a debt of gratitude, and they clearly expected repayment. That was why he had agreed to the meeting and had suggested they meet here, in Taormina which, at this time of year, was full of tourists, the crowds of which helped to disguise this meeting of two men and a woman, who were not tourists, in this pleasant restaurant with its view of Etna on one side and of the sea on the other. The food was good too. He was eating spaghetti with prawns and garlic. After a near death experience, every mouthful was delicious.

'We want to get a sense of the shape of organised crime in Catania and how it relates to the organised crime in Palermo,' said Chiara who, despite her youth and her sex, was clearly the senior of the two. 'Like yourself, we are researchers. We start at the bottom of the pyramid and work our way up, all the way up, to Rome, to Brussels, to the places where the real power is. To New York, even. We have the same aim as you do. Except…'

'What Chiara means to say, and what I can say for her,' said Silvio, leaning forward in a spirit of male bonhomie, 'is simply this: We work for the state; we work discreetly; no one knows about us, and no one ever shall, partly because that would compromise our safety, and partly because we like anonymity. It is the way we work. The puzzle is something that fascinates us. We have been studying it a long time. Sometimes we make progress, sometimes not. Sometimes we are hopeful, sometimes we despair. Our work is very interesting. I live for my work. It cost me my marriage, and I regret that, but not too much, if truth be told. But when the great success comes, when, for example, Calogero di Rienzi goes to jail, it will be Sicilians who will take the credit. Not us. You. We know we are foreigners here, that we do not belong, do not fit in. But you, Fabio, you were born here, you worked here, you work here still. You know these people; you have met them. We study them from afar. No one will ever hear of us, but you, you will be famous; indeed, you already are. Your future career prospects in public life are rosy, if you do not mind me saying.'

'And what Silvio is not saying,' said Chiara, 'is that we need your help. The Italian Republic needs your help. Could you start by telling us whether you have any human intelligence inside the organisation led by Calogero di Rienzi?'

'Not any more,' said Volta with a touch of bitterness. 'My informant is dead. The brother, Rosario. He was a good boy. There was a leak; someone I assumed could be trusted. A policeman. Someone called Andreazza. We have no one on their side working for us. But they have Andreazza and numerous others, supposedly on our side, working for them. They pass things on; they do favours for them; they drop hints. Anything circulating in our police stations that they think they might like to know, they let them know. And they do favours. If they want it that there should be no patrol cars in a certain district at a certain time, it will happen. They pass the message along....'

'How?' asked Chiara.

'There is no paper trail; there is no electronic trail; no phone calls; no text messages, nothing like that. They use little boys as pigeons. The Purgatory quarter swarms with little boys, all willing to carry messages for a small reward. Catania is full of little boys hanging around on street corners, keeping a lookout for the boss, getting paid for their efforts, hoping to be made more use of as they grow up. So, we have no human intelligence and no electronic intelligence either. There is none to gather. They none of them have mobile phones or computers. Technologically, they live in the stone age.'

'Very clever,' observed Silvio.

'When it comes to communicating with Palermo,' continued Volta, 'that is done by word of mouth. They send someone by car, motorbike or train, or they visit in person. They buy train tickets with cash, naturally. If they stay in hotels, as I believe they do from time to time, either it is for some supposedly innocent reason as a cover, or they book in without booking in, leaving no record. Now, I know that Calogero is in league with the Santucci family, or what is left of them, but there is really little evidence that they have even met. They all stayed together at the Grand Hotel in Palermo over Christmas, but that was a huge party, full of children, and there is no plausible evidence that business was discussed, though it must have been. Everything is word of mouth; nothing is written down. And if you were to investigate the office in the building above the gym, you would find nothing untoward. That was where the late Stefania worked; that is where the sister, Assunta, now works. She is an accountant, as is her sister Elena. All above board, all perfectly legal. Except when it is not. But the secret of their success is to keep the two sides separate. The thugs and the accountants never mix. The thugs are in the basement, in the gym: Alfio Camilleri, Gino Fisichella and Trajan Antonescu. They are the main ones; there are others. Antonescu is the leader, because he is the most clever and the most dangerous.'

'About the murder of the brother, Rosario…' began Silvio carefully.

'If you think that was my fault, you may be right,' admitted Volta. 'Perhaps it was. But at the same time… The only person who could have got rid of the boss's brother was the boss himself. The order can only have come from Calogero. No one else would have dared move. He had a double motive. First, Rosario was talking to me. That was bad enough. But there was something else. Rosario told me, good Catholic boy that he was - good Catholic and innocent boy that he was - that he had had a brief affair with his sister-in-law. In Purgatory, nothing remains secret for long. If Calogero had known that, that might have been the real reason, and the fact that he was talking to me, the official reason, for his murder. It is true that Calogero was not particularly fond of his wife, but he would have resented her adultery with his brother enormously. A matter of pride. And the fact that he was obsessed with his brother. He would have seen that as the ultimate betrayal: Rosario loving her more than he loved him.'

'Did he have the wife killed? Was that a set up?' asked Chiara.

'That thought crossed my mind, but it cannot be. One would not hire so untrustworthy an assassin. The boy Enzo blamed Calogero for Maso's death, I suppose… it is generally supposed. Again, that is two brothers who had a very close, claustrophobic, relationship. Rosario used to talk about them. Maso used to complain that he never had a life because of

Enzo. Perhaps he had found one, and Enzo resented it. Whichever way, we shall never know.'

'You are right about Calogero not being over-fond of Stefania,' said Chiara. 'Even I was shocked. He was seen in the Cathedral in Palermo early on Easter Monday, well, leaving the Cathedral. It opened late that day, and Calogero and a group of people were seen leaving. Someone we know was waiting to get in – she is the cousin of that priest who is buried in the Cathedral, who was killed by organised criminals like Calogero. She did not know who Calogero was, but the sacristan was a friend of hers and told her there had been a wedding. We are in touch, and she told us. That is how things work; sometimes the most useful information comes this way. She is a good lady. Anyway, we checked the registers, both ecclesiastical and civil, and Calogero di Rienzi has married Anna Maria Tancredi. And the Cardinal Archbishop married them. Trajan Antonescu was a witness.'

There was silence while they contemplated this.

'I am not surprised,' said Volta at last. 'She is a very sexy, very rich older woman. Who would not want to marry her? She comes from a higher social class than he does, so he is marrying up. And they have a child, and he is very fond of children, very fond, especially of male children. And she has a voracious sexual appetite. That is well known. Years ago, well not so long ago, I knew her nephew, Fabrizio Perraino. An insufferable man. He got his jaw broken, and then ended up being disappeared on the Sunday of Violence, if you remember that famous day. Who took him out has never been clear, and it is very tempting to attribute all unsolved murders to Calogero di Rienzi - but it might well have been the Romanians - though his connexion to the San Lorenzo crime family was never that clear. Anyway, this offensive little prick, Perraino, used to boast that he was screwing his aunt, that she seduced him when he was eighteen, when his mother, her sister, was not looking. He was one of those always boasting about his conquests. Perhaps some jealous husband got rid of him. Whichever way, Tancredi is an asset as a wife. But at the same time, I am a little surprised. He has tied himself to her. She is, when all things are considered, more important than him. In addition, it may well shake up the delicate balance of things in Purgatory. She is from Palermo; she is not one of them. They may resent the incomer, the foreigner. People are like that. Particularly the other women. The children he has with Stefania may come to resent it. Keeping her as his mistress might have been the wiser course.'

'What other difficulties lie ahead for the San Lorenzo crime family, do you think?' asked Silvio.

'The same that lie ahead for all families. Squabbles, jealousies, especially jealousies about the division of the spoils. I am talking about the Catania people here, not the Palermo ones, of whom I know very little. But these people from Catania, from Purgatory, every Sicilian, everyone from Catania, will tell you that they are the worst sort of people. What this boils down to is that they are the very poorest of the poor, or at least they were. It is true that Calogero was the son of a schoolteacher by profession, bomb-maker by vocation, a man who spent very little but who amassed a fair bit of money. But the people around him are poor, dirt poor, and the memory of poverty is ingrained in them. Not having a proper place to wash; not having a decent place to live; not having the right sort of clothes; not having a job; not having a room of your own; not having enough to eat. Calogero knows this, and he exploits this, their terrible fear of poverty, and the knowledge that though they have escaped it, they could be sucked back in at any moment, if their luck, their fragile good luck, were ever to change. As it is, they are lucky, because of him, but if anything happened to him... that is why they are loyal to him. He is their way out. And it is not about them and them alone; it is about the next generation. This vicious boy, Trajan Antonescu, the prostitute's son; he wants his own children to have a different sort of life; he is very fond of them, I believe, and he wants to engineer their escape from their inheritance. And the same with Calogero. He has married up. He is questionable, but his children will be beyond question. But there will be rivalries, you wait and see. That is where their weakness lies. And there will be differences in ambition. Calogero may want to rise socially; people like Alfio Camilleri will be less concerned with that. There may well come a time when Calogero is embarrassed by his associates. And the associates will fall out. Answer me this: what happened to don Carlo Santucci?'

'You know what happened. He was blown up,' said Silvio. 'Yes, I understand you. What really happened? Well, here it gets a bit murky.' He looked at Chiara, who nodded. 'They blame us, or the Romanians. Anything goes wrong, blame the government or the Romanians. But we think it was an internal job, and the people who did it were the two who ended up in the harbour. Well, they launched the RPG's at the yacht. But who was behind them? Perhaps the brother-in-law and cousin, don Antonio Santucci, the deposed boss of the San Lorenzo crime family, who has been living in his house outside Castelvetrano for the last few months. As I say, it gets murky. The official, but not official, you understand, policy is to shift the blame onto Antonio, in the hope that it may destabilise the family.'

'So, you are encouraging the friends of Carlo to take out Antonio, to start a blood feud?' asked Volta.

'No,' said Chiara. 'We are not involved in a conspiracy to murder.' She smiled. 'We are just sitting back and letting nature, if we can call it that, take its course. Carlo was very well liked in the family. He had the common touch. Antonio is more remote and was not a good man manager. Carlo was hands on, and they loved him. You will have noticed that the Santucci family has now only one active male of adult age, the one called Renzo, and our surmise, our hope, is that he is not up to the job, and, better, dangerously unstable. Apart from him, it is teenagers and lots of women, sisters, aunts, cousins, mothers. The original Santucci brothers had the common dynastic problem, that of not enough suitable heirs, so in fact they have been taken over by Catania, by Calogero di Rienzi. What a fate! My guess is that the Santucci family is finished, and we should not interfere, but let them finish the job themselves. Or do you have a better idea?'

'I think you can ignore the Santucci clan and concentrate on Catania. How is the investigation into the various murders there going?'

Chiara looked down at her food in embarrassment.

'There is no active investigation of any murder at all,' said Silvio bitterly. 'Every premature death has been looked into, sometimes very summarily, and then archived. This boy who hanged himself, the one called Turiddu - case closed and sent to the archives. When that happens, getting the case opened again is very hard because the people who closed the case do not want their judgement questioned; they want it to stay closed so that their original decision looks like the right one and is not questioned. And then there are statistics, damned statistics, and league tables, the curse of modern policing. We all know that Purgatory is the top spot for crime in Italy. Hence the desire to reclassify murders as cases of missing people. Fabrizio Perraino is one of them. Or else the desire to wrap up a case very quickly. So, Rosario was killed by this Maso boy - case closed. Thus, the terrible statistics look better.'

'The Perraino case needs to be looked at again,' said Volta. 'That one is explosive. He was a policeman. He was in league with them. He was the nephew and lover of that woman - how the papers will love that - and he was murdered by that woman's present husband. That will serve to put the cat among the pigeons.'

'We are trying to get that case looked at as a murder,' said Chiara. 'The opposition to having it reclassified is considerable.'

'If people are opposing it, that tells you a great deal about what sort of people they are.'

'It is one person, really,' said Silvio.

'Colonel Marco Andreazza,' said Volta grimly.

The other two nodded.

'And the Rosario case,' said Volta. 'That has the potential to split things apart. People liked Rosario, in fact they loved him, and they do not like fratricide, even if they tolerate murder. Fratricide may be a bridge too far. He was friends with Trajan Antonescu. They were, in a funny way, close. And there are the two girlfriends, who do not know about each other. The lawyer's daughter and the one called Catarina. Neither can be happy with the way he died. But don't send in police for this… that is two heavy handed. Go yourselves. That is my advice. These are your ways in. These two girls, and Andreazza. Were these two girls even interviewed by the police?'

Chiara nodded. Volta, she knew, was right. They had their work cut out for them. The plates were taken away, and as they waited for the main course, the conversation became general. Did he like it here, they asked? After all, he had been in Rome. Was he glad to be back in Sicily? He sighed. His girlfriend was here, and she liked it, and she was having a baby, and they were getting married; his mother was here, and there was a huge discussion over where they would marry. He was Catholic, though not very religious, but his mother was a fanatic who went to Church every Sunday and sometimes in the week too, and wanted him to get married in Church, though he would prefer something quiet, but he realised he would have to give in. And did they like it, he asked? Chiara smiled. The beauty of the place took her by surprise, she said, though this was not her first visit. It was so lovely, and each time one came back, it became even lovelier; the weather too; up north it was either boiling hot or freezing cold, and while in Lombardy and the Veneto everything was very efficient, life was a little bit dull, a bit driven. Of course, she would like to see more of Sicily but they were here incognito, staying in hotels, posing as a married couple, as it was important for people to think that they were not here, that they did not exist. It was so nice to be here, right now, she said, indicating the view of the straits, the sea, the mountain and the Roman theatre. So much beauty, agreed Silvio, so different from the north, from Brescia, from Milan, from Pordenone and places like that. So much beauty, and such great evil.

Some days later, don Renzo Santucci, after a brief absence in Palermo, returned to Catania. This, from a variety of perspectives, was deeply gratifying. It pleased his girlfriend, Elena di Rienzi; it pleased her brother, Calogero, who saw it as proof that Renzo was firmly under his influence; and it pleased Gino Fisichella no end, for the two had taken a shine to each other, and to be noticed by the boss of Palermo was a great honour as far as Gino was concerned. Don Renzo offered opportunities, jobs, tasks, money, as well as the kudos of being in the confidence of the boss and enjoying the luxuries he enjoyed. As for don Renzo, the truth was that he was struggling. Every day he was expected to go into the office of the Santucci group of companies in Palermo and listen to the accountants, look at what they put in front of him, none of which he understood. Figures blinded him. And then people came to him asking for things, and he said yes when he should say no (he saw the surprise on their faces) and no when he should say yes (he saw the displeasure on their faces) and no one told him what he should say, which was disconcerting. They deferred to him, and he sensed the place was drifting, given that the hand on the rudder, his own, was not firm.

He was haunted by the figure of his father. Everyone had liked him. Women had gone crazy for him ever since, he had been told, his father had passed his thirteenth birthday, to the despair of Carlo's mother, Renzo's grandmother. Of course, he had married and settled down, but still found time for numerous affairs. Despite his well-known devotion to his wife and children, there had been, according to legend, other women beyond counting. The stories were numerous: of the times when, at meetings, Carlo had disappeared, only to be found pressed up against a wall with some female employee of the hotel in which they had been staying, or some waitress in the restaurant in which they had been eating. Quite a few of these women had at some point produced children who, after a DNA test, had been suitably provided for. Carlo, generous with his favours, had been generous with his money as well, and had not minded the thought of numerous illegitimate progeny, all of whom would grow up and see him once a year and be grateful for that and the income they received. Some of these half-siblings were now employed in useful jobs, even if they did not have the Santucci name.

As in love as in other things, there had been nothing timid about Carlo; he had committed his first crimes as a teenager and, had it not been for good lawyers and sympathetic judges, would have spent time in Ucciardone. He had killed several men, doing the job himself, which won him respect. In every way, he was different to his cousin Antonio and, his son realised, different to himself. He loathed Antonio, and his loathing was compounded by the fact that he recognised that he and Antonio had something in common. They had inherited a tradition, up to which they did not live.

That was one of the reasons that he liked Gino. Gino had been in prison; Gino was tough; Gino was fearless; Gino knew what life was like, and his life had been very different from Renzo's. Gino knew how to fight, and Renzo was in Catania to fight with Gino as well as to visit Elena and her brother. They were now in the private changing room in the gym, the subterranean space where the special employees met, the place where operations were planned, a grim, oppressive and secret place that only the chosen few could enter. Here, surrounded by the lockers, Gino and Renzo, in their gym clothes, having used the machines in the gym, were now sparring. Gino was immensely strong, his major claim to consideration, and was not hitting Renzo any harder than Renzo could hit him, so they were equally matched. Renzo was getting better at this, or so Renzo thought. He knew he had a lot of catching up to do. He loved Calogero, but was insanely jealous of him, knowing that

Calogero could beat any man he wanted with his fists, and the same was true of Traiano. He wanted to be like that too.

Afterwards, they sat panting, sweating, getting their breath back on the bench. The stink of Gino's sweat filled the place, a smell that, though unpleasant, was strangely reassuring. It meant, in a funny way, he could trust Gino. Renzo reached for the bag he had brought with him, took out his wallet and found a credit card. Then he took out the small packet of cocaine. He saw Gino's eyes light up with curiosity.

'Elena does not know,' explained Renzo. 'I told her I had stopped. Well, I have cut down, but why should I stop completely? As long as she does not know, what is the harm? As long as Calogero does not find out, and you are not going to tell him, are you?'

Gino shook his head, but looked at the door.

'It won't take more than a minute,' said Renzo, 'and it is safer here than anywhere else. Have you got something, a magazine?'

Gino went to his locker, unlocked it, and brought out a large, thick, glossy magazine. Renzo looked at it in curiosity. He had never seen such a thing before now. The pictures made it clear what it was. The words were Hungarian, did he but realise it.

'Stuff I do not want my wife to see,' explained Gino.

Renzo made two lines on the cover of the magazine and snorted the drug.

'Oh Jesus,' he said, flinging his head back, savouring the blessed relief.

He made another two lines for Gino, who did the same, but said nothing. Then Renzo did another two lines and, after a brief pause, offered to do the same for Gino, who declined with a shake of the head. After a moment of silence, Renzo picked up the magazine and flicked through its pages.

'Have you thrown away your phone?' asked Gino.

'Of course,' said Renzo.

'Keep it,' said Gino, of the magazine. 'I have plenty. Alfio and me brought them back from Hungary, when we went to have his teeth fixed. Put it in your locker. But look at the other ones and see if you prefer them.'

'Aren't they all the same, one as good as another?' asked Renzo, who nevertheless went to Gino's locker and saw the pile of magazines in its depths. But there were other things there too, which distracted him. 'Do you have to hide this too?' he asked, taking out a very expensive watch.

'It's stolen. Well, the person who owned it won't be using it any more. I kept it as a souvenir,' said Gino. 'Alfio does not know. He thought I'd got rid of it, along with the body, but it's a nice one, so I kept it.'

'It's a Rolex,' said Renzo admiringly. 'Almost as nice as mine. Listen,' he said, taking off his heavy gold watch. 'Take mine. It won't get you into trouble. This might.'

Gino took the watch with gratitude. This was flattering.

'My father gave it to me for my twenty-first,' said Renzo.

He took the other watch, the one that had belonged to Perraino, and looked at it a moment; then he headed towards the showers, opened the cupboard, and threw it down the shaft of no return. Gino watched in admiration. A man who could throw such a thing away must be very rich indeed.

'They have serial numbers,' said Renzo. 'That one that is now yours cost several thousand. You can deep sea dive in it, and it has diamonds on it; my father was extravagant, I think.' He continued his perusal of the things in the locker.

'Help yourself,' Gino urged, as he watched Renzo look over the pills and small packages.

'What are they?' he asked, unfamiliar with the names on the packets.

'They are pills that are supplied to the American army, under their real names, not brand names. Generic medicines they call them. They are stolen from the Americans and then end up in the hands of various doctors, like our Doctor Moro. Those are painkillers, opiates, very strong. Take them and you feel really great, whatever your bruises. Take two now, you will see. Those are for sore throats, I think; the explanations are in English, which I do not understand, but I think Doctor Moro said they were for sore throats.'

Renzo took two of the pills, swallowing them like sweets, and placed a few more in his bag.

'How is your wife?' he asked.

'OK. Still working. She wants to work, then take maternity leave and then throw in her job. She says she might as well take advantage of the system. She says that being pregnant is not enjoyable. But she insists on going to work. As a result, she is tired all the time, not, you know, interested in sex.'

Renzo made a sympathetic noise.

'What about Elena?' asked Gino.

'She is eager, for everything. But the baby has to wait until we are married. She insists on that.'

When Traiano came in a few moments later, the place was deserted, but he could hear the sound of shower water and merry voices. He settled down to wait on the bench. After a few minutes, the sound of water ceased and the two men entered, wrapped in their towels. He stood and smiled broadly. Any observer would assume that he was very pleased to see the Palermo boss.

'I heard you had arrived and I guessed you would be here,' he said, with warmth in his voice. He shook hands with him. 'Hi, Gino,' he added, shaking hands with him too. 'Listen, I will let you get dressed in peace, and catch up with you later.' He shook hands with Renzo again and, as he left, shot Gino a pointed and unmistakeable look. Gino knew what it meant.

His jaw was still completely numbed by the cocaine when he met up with Traiano, as he knew he was meant to do; they had had some more lines before parting. His head was beginning to ache. They met in the busy bar in the square outside the Church of the Holy Souls in Purgatory. The place was loud with conversation, the sound of the coffee machine, and the scraping of chairs and furniture. If they wanted to bug this place, they could. You would never distinguish a word.

'What were you talking about?' asked Traiano.

'Just the usual things, boss. How Elena is very keen on sex, you know.'

Traiano held up a hand. He didn't want to hear that. He didn't like these male confidences.

'They are getting married?'

'He is here to speak to the boss about it. You know, the money side of things. But yes, they are getting married. And he has to speak to his own mother as well, introduce them, and all that.'

'That is right and proper,' said Traiano. 'She is the boss's sister, he is a boss, though a young one and by default, if his father had not died.... Yes, it is important and it needs planning. Though why he should speak to the boss about money when he is richer by far, I do not know. He is richer than don Calogero. That is for sure. Though I gather the Palermo operation does not make as much as it once did. But with help from us, he should be able to turn things around. With help from you.... But that is not what I wanted you for. You know what I wanted you for. You were going to tell me, weren't you? The excitement of don Renzo arriving drove it from your mind, perhaps. Catarina asked me to come and see her at her place of work. She sent one of the children. I saw her. She said she had spoken to you.'

'Ah, that,' said Gino gravely. 'She told me that some people had come to see her, a man and a woman, not Sicilians, people with northern accents. They were asking about...'

'About what, exactly?'

'About us, our affairs, our business. Of course, she said nothing.'

'Of course, she said nothing,' echoed Traiano. 'She is a good girl. She is your wife. She is from Purgatory. She knows nothing, and she knows that she must never indulge these people's curiosity. Do you know who they are?'

'No,' said Gino. 'Do you?'

'One can hazard a guess,' he said. 'But you must warn her to be like an oyster. Do you understand me?'

'Of course. Boss, what are they after?'

'The murder of Perraino, I should think. What else? They came to speak to your wife, didn't they? This means that perhaps our protection, Colonel Andreazza, is not doing his job. Or it means that he is doing his job, but these are not the police, these are more powerful people. Anyway, they alarmed her. Just tell her that I have spoken, and that we all need to be on our guard.'

They parted. Traiano stepped out into the coolness of the evening. The hot weather had not yet arrived and it was still very pleasant. Of course, Catarina was clever, much cleverer than her husband Gino. Gino would accept what she had said about the conversation, and the mention of Perraino would make him especially cautious. That was no bad thing of itself. He sighed. He had not liked threatening a woman, but sometimes hard things like that had to be done.

They knew. They - whoever they were - they knew. They knew that she had been Rosario's girlfriend in some sense. They had hinted that her now evident pregnancy and her hasty marriage might mean something more than what she pretended it meant. They had done their homework. They knew about Bicocca and Gino's illness there. (There must have been some annoying record of it kept by the prison.) They had tried to use this knowledge as leverage. Of course, she had insisted that they were wrong, that it was impossible, that she had never slept with Rosario; but they knew; Rosario had told Volta, and Volta had told them. She had protested that she had known nothing at all about Rosario's death, had assumed, at first, he had merely gone away, as his messages to her had said. Traiano had told her she needed to stick with this. After all, that child of hers was Rosario's, and should she co-operate with them, the unborn child would not save her.

'He was your friend,' she had said. 'It is his child. You bastard!'

He realised now that he had made a mistake. He should have been softer. By being so hard, he had betrayed something, namely that the murder of Rosario touched him personally, that he, not one of the others, not Maso, had done it. He had revealed too much. It was important Maso took the blame as he was safely dead. If it were to be supposed that he had been the one to kill the boss's brother, to kill his best friend at the boss's request, then there would be many who would never forgive him. For Rosario had been loved. His mother, what would she say? His stepfather, what would he say? But above all, his wife, Ceccina, the mother of his children, who had loved Rosario, what would she say? He realised that while he had leverage over Catarina, she had leverage over him.

The view was magnificent. It was the next evening. Calogero di Rienzi was standing on what would be the roof terrace of his new flat, hundreds of square metres of which would be decorated with pots and greenery and awnings, and which would become a real roof garden, a green spot in the middle of the city. From here, one could see Etna to the north, the domes of the city to the south and the sea to the east. It was perfect. He was glad he was moving up a floor, and glad that all this money he was spending would be put to good use after all.

His hands were on the railing, and he looked down at the square below and the black lava paving.

'The Emperor Tiberius,' he said.

'Yes?' said Renzo.

'When people went to see him on Capri, if the meeting didn't go well, they were thrown off the cliff on their way back to their ships. Well, they lost their footing. Or something. One could do that here. If someone annoyed me, I could easily throw them off, and they would not survive the impact with those lava slabs below us.'

'Have I annoyed you?' asked Renzo. 'I notice you have not said anything…'

Calogero looked at him.

'Annoyed me? How? If you had, you would already know about it. Oh, that. Of course not. You want to marry Elena. I thought something like this might happen, didn't I, Traiano?'

'You did,' said Traiano, standing at a respectful distance.

'Does she want to marry you?' asked Calogero.

'She does.'

'Well then, I am pleased. I suppose you arranged all this last night over dinner, did you? And I suppose by now she has told our mother, your future mother-in-law. Good God. I hope your brother-in-law is more to your taste than your new mother-in-law. But if you live in Palermo, you may not see very much of her. I lost a brother, you know. Now I have gained a brother-in-law. You. I already have one, Assunta's husband, but I try not to think about him. Though I fear that I must from time to time. I am very pleased.'

He enfolded Renzo in an embrace. Renzo beamed. Traiano came and shook his hand, then held him close.

Downstairs, two floors below, Elena was telling her mother the good news. It was now early June. The initial idea was to hold the wedding in October, which did not leave much time. Knowing that the women were in the kitchen and having no wish to see them just yet, Calogero sent Traiano down to fetch a bottle of champagne and three glasses. He was soon back. The women – the signora, her daughter Elena, her elder daughter Assunta – were so busy in conversation, that they hardly noticed his entry into the kitchen, his opening the fridge, his search for glasses.

Traiano did not like champagne, and had not got used to it, as it was a very recent custom of the boss to drink the stuff. Renzo seemed to like it, though. There was nothing to sit on, so they sat or sprawled on the terrace. The sun was going down.

Renzo spoke about the wedding. They planned to live in Palermo. The family house was inhabited by his mother and his sisters, so they would buy somewhere new. They would start looking very soon, indeed had already been giving it some thought. He wanted somewhere within walking distance of the office where, after all, they would both work, somewhere near the Politeama, the best part of the city of Palermo. Quite near where Anna Maria Tancredi lived.

'Good,' said Calogero. 'I am familiar with Anna Maria's place in Palermo. Not to take the shine off your news, Renzo, but Traiano knows this already, and you need to know it now before anyone else. I have married Anna Maria Tancredi. On Easter Monday. The same day Gino got married. It was very quiet. But there has been a further development. She is having another child, due in January, exactly nine months after the wedding.'

There were congratulations. Further drink was poured, at least for Renzo and Calogero.

'Do they know?' asked Renzo, gesturing to the lower floors.

'No, and I would like you to keep it quiet for now. It will come out, but Stefania has not been dead very long. It will come out in due course. One has to think of the children.'

Renzo nodded vigorously at this.

On a lovely evening like this, it would ruin the atmosphere to start haggling over the dowry. Besides, there was something more important that Renzo wanted to talk about. Traiano watched him, guessing what it was. Traiano watched the boss, knowing that he too could imagine what it was, and noting that he was in no mood to help Renzo out by bringing up the subject.

At last Renzo mentioned it.

'The father of Antonio is not at all well. Lorenzo. My late grandfather's cousin. He was always the more fierce of the two brothers.'

'The uncle, Domenico, was more impressive, to my mind,' said Calogero. 'I am sorry to hear the old man is unwell. You mean he may not be able to come to the wedding?'

'I had not thought of that, but I doubt he will be able to come. He might very well be dead by then, or at least incapacitated. But that is to be expected. He is old. Over seventy. He has lived a tough life. Like his brother.'

'They might live several more years,' said Calogero. 'If God is good to them. They might be with us, one or other or both, for a decade or even more. Creaking gates.'

'Do I have to wait that long?' asked Renzo.

There was silence.

'Traiano, get another bottle. This one is empty.'

Traiano leapt up to do what he was bid. When he came back with the fresh bottle, he had the sense that the silence had been unbroken in his absence. He poured more champagne for them both.

'The thing is,' said Renzo, 'that one day Antonio has to go. The only question is when. Whether it would be easier for us sooner or better to leave it for now and do it later, perhaps, as you seem to suggest, years later. It is, I am sure you will both agree, purely a matter of timing. If we do it now, while the two old men are still alive, we have the advantage of surprise. Right now, he thinks he is safe, he is not expecting anything, his guard will be down. I have been to the house in Castelvetrano, many times. It is not a fortress. One could break in at night, and make it look like a robbery.'

'He has got two sons,' said Calogero thoughtfully, sipping his champagne.

'They are teenagers. I have thought of that. Teenagers, as we know, grow up. Antonio made a terrible mistake killing my father, but not killing me.'

Calogero nodded.

'The daughters, the wife...?' he asked.

'They often stay in Palermo. One could choose a night when they are not there. The other thing is that my uncle, damn him, has a boat and he goes fishing with his two sons. It is a small boat. Quite often, people go to sea and never come back. They just disappear.'

'You would do it yourself?' asked Traiano, with the lightest irony.

'Gino would help,' said Renzo.

'Is that what you were discussing yesterday in the showers?' asked Traiano.

'Yes.'

'Good place to talk, no one can overhear you, no one can make a recording,' remarked Traiano easily.

Gino had not mentioned that, thought Traiano.

'The two old men, Lorenzo and Domenico?' Calogero now said. 'I suppose they would not be expecting anything, so Traiano could deal with them, and even I could help. But you do realise all this comes at a price? Gino would want a lot for Antonio, considering his former importance. Fifty thousand, a hundred thousand, maybe more. And the two boys might bump it up even further. As for the old men, they have all the dignity of historic monuments. That would be another hundred thousand at least. You have not thought of getting someone from Palermo to do this? Someone like, what is he called....?'

He looked at Traiano.

'Muniddu?'

'Yes, Muniddu.'

Renzo sighed.

'He might not want to deal with the two boys, let alone the two old men,' said Renzo. 'With Gino, there's no problem. As you say, it will be expensive, but I have got the money.'

'You have spoken to Gino, you say?'

'Yes. But no one else.'

'Good. We have to be very secretive about this. After all, if they found out, we would be the dead ones. What you have said makes perfect sense. It is purely a matter of timing. Whether it is best now, or best left till later, that depends also on what the reaction from your people in Palermo is likely to be. The employees.'

'They hate him.'

'The women of your family?'

'They don't ask questions.'

'The boat is sort of messy,' said Calogero thoughtfully. 'The burglary that goes wrong, the massacre in the lonely house in Castelvetrano, that is more appealing to me. The other thing is that Castelvetrano is not a fortress, as you say. No place with a door that opens ever is. I don't suppose you have seen your uncle since Christmas, but... you can use the women of the family, his wife, your aunt, that is the same person, to engineer a rapprochement. That will make him think nothing is wrong. Then you do not have to break into the house at Castelvetrano. They invite you in. And once you are in, you open the side door and in comes Gino, and the rest, one can imagine. End of story. So that is the first thing to do. Get friendly with your uncle again. The women will all be so pleased. And the fact that you are getting married is the perfect excuse. You are planning to take my sister round to meet all the relations, aren't you? Well, take her to meet them, and for the sake of completion, go to see your uncle as well. The most natural thing in the world. Remember, when planning something of this nature, everything has to go on as normal so no suspicions are aroused.

Seeking a reconciliation with your uncle would, at this stage, be normal; though do not overdo it. That is the first stage, then we can think about the details. It is June now. August is the best time. Holiday time. The police are all asleep in August.'

Once more Renzo beamed. More champagne was poured.

Darkness fell. Leaving his wife and children asleep, Traiano decided to go to the pizzeria. The place was busy as usual and there was a long queue outside. He went in, and there, waiting in the corridor that led to the private room, always kept for the owner and his friends, was Paolo. He was standing on guard.

'Has he arrived?' he asked.

'Ten minutes ago,' said Paolo.

'Make sure no one disturbs them, and call me when they are finished,' he ordered.

He went to the sit at the marble counter, behind which the pizza oven roared. He ordered a coke. He told the waiter to make sure it was brought to him by Amilcare.

'Hi, handsome,' he said, as Amilcare brought him the coke. Never was an epithet less deserved. Amilcare was tall, stringy, nervous.

'Hello, sir,' said Amilcare.

'Don't go just yet. Are you still seeing his mother?'

He looked over to where Paolo was.

Amilcare nodded, but looked a little ashamed.

'Are you living with her?'

'No, sir, I live with my mother and father and two younger brothers. I just go over there from time to time.'

'I saw you at Gino's wedding. Nice of him to invite you.'

'He invited all of us who work here, sir. He is that sort of guy. Nice.'

'Yes, but you and he…. You are the expert on locks, aren't you? What were you in Bicocca for?'

'Breaking and entering, sir.'

'Useful skills,' commented Traiano. 'Pity you got caught! The house at Castelvetrano. Have you thought about that?'

'Yes, sir. I have been there, looked at it. Gino took me over there, and we had a look from a distance. Don Renzo asked us to do so.'

'Of course he did. And the place is easy to break into?'

'I'd say yes, sir.'

'And after you broke in, what would be the next thing?'

'I don't ask questions, sir.'

'Wise man. Forget you ever had this conversation.'

He then told Amilcare to bring four pizzas - he specified which - three cokes and a beer, to the private room. Then he gestured with his hand, telling him to get lost.

A few more moments, and it was clear from Paolo that the private room was now free. He went in. Shortly afterwards the food followed. The Colonel was there, and next to him a small boy, dark haired, black eyed. Traiano poured the coke for himself and the children. The Colonel gratefully received his beer.

'Hi, handsome,' said Traiano to the Colonel and to the small boy, who, he remembered, was called Nino. 'Is your father still in Piazza Lanza?' he asked.

He remembered the father, vaguely. A small time, unsuccessful killer.

'They sent him to Palermo,' said Nino. 'My mother was very upset.'

'Ucciardone? I bet she was, I bet he was too. And you?'

'I don't remember him,' said Nino.

'Well, the police took him away,' said Traiano, examining his pizza, wondering where to start. 'But not all policemen are bad. The Colonel here is good. He is one of us. You like him?'

The boy nodded uncertainly.

'Good,' said Traiano. 'Now you boys eat and drink while we adults talk business. So, what is happening in the Furnaces? I mean I know what is happening, I want the official version, your version, the city hall version.'

'Every street light is broken, so no one will go there at night. They have tried replacing them, but they do not last more than a few hours in some cases. So at night, the place is very dark and people keep away.'

'Little boys with guns shoot the lights out,' said Traiano happily, giving Paolo a poke in the ribs.

'No street lighting, no cars either. Because if you park there, your car will end up scratched or worse. But it gets worse. No public transport, as the buses are attacked. Little boys throwing stones and smashing the windows, and in one case, it seems, shooting at the tyres of a bus. Luckily, it was stationary at the time. So the bus routes are suspended. As people have pointed out, lots of people, it is the one thing the left and the right agree on: the city of Catania has failed to deliver essential public services to one of its most deprived neighbourhoods.'

'The city of Catania, as we all know, is a disgrace,' said Traiano crisply. 'Have they cut off the water and the electricity?'

'Both are experiencing problems,' said the Colonel.

Traiano shrugged.

'So, what are they going to do about it? The police….'

'The police can do nothing,' said the Colonel.

'You mean the police won't do anything, because they refuse to do anything?'

'As you say. We in the police have limited resources, personnel and time. We cannot be everywhere at once. This place, the Furnaces, is not our priority. We have prioritised other areas.'

'Well, done,' observed Traiano. 'And how do the authorities react to that?'

'Funnily enough, the right is pleased and the left is pleased. Sometimes you can please all the people all the time, after all. Apart from the Greens who are furious that all those burned-out cars have been thrown into the canal. But no one cares about them and what they think. This is Sicily, the most beautiful island on earth. We do not need the Greens. But the right is pleased because this is evidence of what they have been saying all along, that Sicily in general, and Catania in particular, is sliding into a vortex of violence and chaotic disorder. They want, you may have heard the phrase, a regime of order, strong government, more spending on the police, harsher punishment for criminals. And an end to immigration, for which they blame the present woes of the Furnaces. And the left reject this: they say that money spent on the police and on prisons is wasted, and that we need more social spending in the Furnaces and places like that, and they say blaming immigrants is xenophobic and racist, and the real fault lies with the mismanagement of the city which goes back decades.'

'And you, what do you think?' asked Traiano.

'I think the whole thing is a mess. Perhaps it is such a mess because the left and the right spend their entire time blaming each other and scoring points off each other, but neither side knows how to administer a city this size.'

'So, what are they going to do?'

'Shout at each other in the council chamber, blame each other, what they have always done. Meanwhile, our dear Archbishop, never slow at putting his best foot forward, has organised help for the poor benighted immigrants living wild in the Furnaces. But....'

'But what?' asked Traiano, sharply.

'Rome has taken notice. The usual breast-beating. Or more accurately, the government wants to know how it can turn this to its advantage, and so does the opposition.'

'So?'

'There was some talk of sending in the army. That is what the far right want. But it has been scotched. The government wants to deny that there is a problem; the police know that there is a problem but think that if the army come, it will be a sign that the police have failed.'

'The police have failed,' said Traiano shortly. 'Don't look like you don't agree with me.'

'Can we have ice cream now?' asked Paolo.

Traiano considered.

'Yes, we can.'

Paolo went to get the ice cream, after asking what everyone wanted. Nino, interested in ice cream, went with him. Traiano watched them go.

'The dogs have been sniffing around,' he said.

'Dogs?' asked Andreazza.

'I don't know who they are. Asking Rosario's girlfriend about his disappearance. And they know about her, as she was a secret girlfriend, through Volta. That bastard Volta.'

'The Rosario case is closed.'

'So you led me to believe.'

'It is closed,' insisted Andreazza.

'Then who are these people, this man and this woman?'

'Not the police. I would know if they were colleagues. They could be from the Ministry in Rome.'

'That does not sound good for me or for you. The one thing we all agree on is that Rome is the enemy. Ask around, find out, be discreet, obviously, but find out what they are up to.'

Andreazza nodded. The children re-entered with the ice cream.

'Are you police interfering with the immigrants?' asked Traiano as they ate their ice cream.

'They are a protected species,' said the Colonel. 'The Church, the left, even the right; they all love the immigrants because they can instrumentalise them. As indeed do you.'

Traiano smiled.

'Yes, and when we have no further need for them, we will get rid of them, and then you will all be grateful.'

At midnight he met with Renzo and they went to the Furnaces together. One of the boys had been out and bought a supply, from different shops, of black and dark blue hooded tops, and black and blue chinos, which were kept in one of the lockers of the gym changing room reserved for Traiano's people. They changed into these hard-to-distinguish clothes there, then took a stolen motorbike from the garage and made the brief journey to the Furnaces. The place had markedly declined since the winter, ever since the squatters had moved in. One of the unsupervised junk yards had become a settlement for the few women and children who dared live in the area. Men, all of them young, had occupied some of the abandoned properties. It was to one of these properties that Traiano and Renzo made their way. It had once been a block of flats, but the last respectable inhabitant had left some weeks previously after the main door to the building had been removed by one of Traiano's men, as it had happened. There were four flats, all doorless inside. In one of these, at the top, in rooms deprived of electricity and water as well, they met the men they had arranged to see.

The decline of the building was evident from the rubbish that choked the darkened stair well and the stink that came from the blocked-up drains in the bathrooms. Renzo wrinkled his nose and coughed. Traiano, who had spent his earliest years in a slum only a little better than this, smiled. The men were waiting for them at the top of the stairs and led them silently into a large room, the floor of which was covered with sleeping bags. The only chairs were boxes. The only light came through a curtainless window, and was the distant dull orange light of the airport runway. The window was open, but the air was hot, fetid and still. Traiano sat down on the box without waiting to be asked, and did not take off his jacket, having both gun and knife concealed beneath it. Renzo did the same.

Traiano said nothing.

Eventually one of them spoke, haltingly, apologetically.

'We are glad you have come,' he said. 'We have wanted to see you for a long time. We have been waiting for this patiently.'

'We got your messages eventually. The Libyans told the people in Palermo, who told us. We saw no hurry, but here we are,' said Traiano. 'Are you the leader?'

The man who spoke, nodded. There were five or six of them in the room, but Traiano looked just at the leader.

'I am the leader. My name is Omar. Are you the Romanian?'

'I am Traiano,' he said with a shrug. 'I am as Sicilian as the rest.'

'We thought you might be a gypsy,' said Omar. 'Or a Muslim. We do not know who to trust.'

'I am neither,' said Traiano. 'And as to whom to trust, there is no one you can trust. Do you trust the Libyans who brought you here? Who left so many of your people to die on the sea? Who put you into leaky boats? Do you trust them, when they told you that Italy was a paradise just waiting to be discovered? Did you trust the people from Palermo who sold you on to us?' With a finger he quietened any objection that Renzo might have made. 'There is no one you can trust,' said Traiano with bitterness. 'You need to realise that. It is a lesson we all have to learn.'

'So we cannot trust you?' asked Omar.

'There will come a time, and soon,' said Traiano, 'when the owners of these properties will want their places back. Or rather the owner. Our boss, a man you will never meet. When that happens, he will move you to the other side of the straits, to somewhere else closer to where you want to go. Where do you want to go?'

'Somewhere with jobs. Germany, UK.'

'My boss will happily send you on your way when the time comes. In a month or two. He will give you in particular, and your friends, Omar, special treatment, provided that you do as we ask in the meantime. Then we put you onto buses and send you north.'

'What do you want us to do?' asked Omar.

'Just work for yourselves and in so doing work for us. The province of Catania is notorious for its crime. Send your friends out and stir up trouble: Rob, steal, terrify. Just do not touch the women. That, we do not allow. If anyone commits a rape, we kill them. No. We won't. You will. You need to keep order here, and you need to spread disorder in every quarter of Catania apart from Purgatory. I presume you are tough enough for this?'

'We have come this far,' said Omar. 'We are not turning back now.'

'Quite right,' said Traiano. 'Others might come up from Pozzallo and other places, trying to join you. It will be your job to get rid of them. This area belongs to us, and you can have it for the meantime. You, but not others. How many are you?'

'Over a hundred men. Some thirty women.'

'All young men, all fighters?'

'Most of us have fought,' said Omar.

'You all have knives?'

The men all nodded.

'Can you use guns? We can supply them.'

Several of the men, including Omar, nodded.

'We will send someone with guns,' said Traiano. 'If you need to see me, I am to be found in the Purgatory quarter. You just need to ask for me there. But better not. We know where to find you. We await your work with interest,' he concluded.

'That place stank,' said Renzo when they were back in the gym changing room. He pulled off his hooded top, and smelt it. The smell of the place had entered the fabric.

'Yes,' said Traiano. 'Those places always do. Throw the clothes down the shaft.'

'How can they live like that?' asked Renzo, not without compassion.

'They are poor. That is how the poor live,' said Traiano. 'It is not just them. There are people in Catania like that too. Who live in filth. Anyway, they will do as we ask simply because it is what they do. They will create trouble. Why did you think they thought I was a gypsy or a Muslim?'

'Aren't you? One or the other?'

'I am a Catholic. So are they, I think. One of those boys was wearing some plastic rosary beads around his neck, didn't you see? Those sorts of people are very clannish. They stick together. They are all Christians. Omar can be a Muslim name but it can be a Christian name too. Of course, what will happen is that another group will turn up, wrong tribe, wrong religion, and all hell will break lose. But that will be good for us too. Once we have got all that land, then we can get rid of them, and people will thank us for it. It was your uncle's bright idea.'

'Him,' said Renzo with contempt.

'He won't annoy you forever,' said Traiano.

Renzo was getting his clothes out of the locker, having thrown what he was wearing previously down the shaft. He looked at Traiano.

'What?' asked Traiano, now pulling his shirt over his head, not having bothered to undo the buttons, a habit that annoyed his wife.

'Shall we do some coke?' said Renzo.

There was a note of anxiety in his voice.

'You are the boss, don Renzo,' said Traiano easily. 'What you say, goes.'

Renzo took out what was needed, the Hungarian magazine, the credit card, the white powder. Four lines were prepared. He consumed two. The other two were offered to Traiano who, considering the kind offer, declined, mentioning that he was going to sleep with his wife later. Why this should make a difference, Renzo did not know, and he was planning to sleep with Elena later too. But why question good fortune? More for him. The other two lines were soon gone.

'Lord, that's good,' said Renzo, with relief and joy.

He savoured the drug for a few moments, while Traiano, bored, looked at the magazine with curious eyes.

Once they had both finished changing clothes, they made their way to the Purgatory bar, where the boss was waiting for them. The place had emptied out somewhat, though the square was full, late as it was, with people enjoying the warmth of early summer. A bottle of whiskey stood before Calogero, and the ever-attentive barman (who was one of Ceccina's more distant relatives, and coincidentally, also related somehow to Stefania) brought over two more glasses and the bottle of Cinzano for Traiano.

They spoke of the Furnaces. The progress in buying up properties in the area had been swift. The boss had recently got his sister Assunta to work in the office, to take Stefania's place, to work alongside the man sent by Tancredi, as well as the lawyer Rossi. The low hanging fruit was long gathered; some of the more difficult fruit had fallen into their hands as well. There were now just a few holdouts. One such was the owner of a scrap yard, which seemed to do no business at all, who was too stubborn to sell, despite inducements. Murdering him was no use, given that he had made a will which left the place to over a dozen nephews and nieces in undivided shares, and getting them all to agree on a sale would be very difficult.

'This will be a job for you, Traiano, but Renzo might like to go as well. Go and call on him and do what you once did to Petrocchi. Hold a gun to his head, and get him to sign. The office will have the papers.'

After a few drinks, Renzo got up to go. They watched him leave.

'He is going to your sister,' said Traiano.

'Well, they are getting married,' said Calogero easily. 'But you want to tell me something. You have been waiting to tell me since you arrived.'

'I didn't realise I was so obvious. Has he told you that he has given up the white powder? He has? Ceccina tells me that he hasn't. And she knows because your sister told her. You know these women, they discuss these things. When they stay in hotel rooms she cannot understand why he is always going into the bathroom. And when they have been in your mother's house, he has taken cocaine in the bedroom itself. Elena says that she does not like it, and he says he is sorry and that he will give it up, but he hasn't so far, and she doubts he ever will. She has the impression he is lying to her about how much he takes. She is not happy. That is Ceccina's tale, anyway. Female gossip, I know. But I know it is true, as he did the same with me just now, in the gym changing room. The man can't live without that white powder.'

'Why should it bother Elena if her future husband takes cocaine, I wonder?' asked the boss, after a pause for thought.

'Because of the consequences. When her brother, our boss – you - discover someone smoking, the punishment is severe. You have already given Renzo one beating, last Christmas. Remember? His balls went purple, like aubergines. What if you discover that he has disobeyed you in something much worse that smoking? You might be tempted to teach him a real lesson. You might be tempted to kill him. But there is more to it than that. Elena wants to be important, more important than her sister, perhaps as important as her new sister-in-law, of whom she knows nothing as yet. Her passport to this success is Renzo. But if he is a dodgy passport....'

'Which he is,' said Calogero. 'Which does not seem to bother you in the least.'

'He is no threat to me,' said Traiano.

'You seriously think I would kill my own brother-in-law-to-be?' he asked with a raised eyebrow.

Traiano was silent. They both knew that family ties were no guarantee. Look what had happened to Traiano's father, stabbed to death with a plastic toothbrush handle in the prison showers in Bucharest. Look what had happened to Rosario.

'Do you want him dead? Why don't you just say so, if you want him dead?' said Calogero.

'I don't want anyone dead,' said Traiano. 'Why should I? If they cause me no problems, why should their continued existence bother me? Besides, it causes mess. No one wants mess. Some people have to go, but that is because they are a threat, even if they do not know it. There is such a thing as self-defence. I don't particularly like Renzo; I like his uncle even less. But the idea of killing the lot of them is, I think, a very bad idea. None of them pose a threat, at least not yet. But Renzo has been obsessing about this. He has taken Gino to see the place in Castelvetrano. Gino did not mention it to me. And they took Amilcare with them… You do not know him. He works in the pizzeria. He's a pitiful fellow, but he is frightened of me, and he told me; well, I tricked him into telling me, pretending I knew. He knows about locks. Renzo has planned all this in his head, getting ahead of himself, getting ahead of you, boss. I don't think he is trustworthy.'

'We will supervise him,' said Calogero. 'You will supervise him. His weakness will be our advantage, you will see. How was tonight?'

'We met up with the immigrants. They can be left to do what they like doing and what we need doing. They need guns. I will arrange that. Their leader asked me if I were the Romanian, even a gypsy, a Muslim. And the people who refer to me like that, who are they?'

'Renzo? Or his uncle?' asked Calogero. 'The ones who mock you now may well come to regret it. They will come to fear you, sooner than they think. One day their mistakes will take them by surprise. As for Gino, this tells us a great deal about Renzo. He is stupid. Gino is the last person to cultivate, as far as I am concerned. He is not bright; he is strong; he comes from

Agrigento. Only one of these is a good thing. That Renzo should conspire with Gino worries me not a bit. And do not worry about Gino. He is useful. And we have a way of controlling him. The wife. She is clever. She will tell him what to do. You are selling them your house, aren't you? And as for the child, I suppose they want Alfio to be godfather? He is her cousin and Gino's best friend. Tell her that she should ask me. It is my nephew, after all, though that is not the reason we shall be giving anyone.'

'They will both be pleased by that, boss.'

'And as for Renzo, we put up with him. You see, the way I see it, if we get rid of Renzo, we might end up having to take Antonio back. And you dislike him even more, don't you? That is the trouble when you start hating people. It clouds your judgement. We should be asking who is the more useful to us, which one can we use. Renzo is young and pliable, and he likes us, and he likes Elena, and the fact that he has this weakness, this drug taking habit, means that he is no threat. I have to confess that I would love to put a bullet through the conceited head of Antonio Santucci. But I must not let that influence me. His father and his uncle were friends of my father but, if they have to go, then they have to go… There is no gratitude in this business. I am sure they know that, and do not expect it. Which, of course, leads to another consideration. The two old men, Antonio himself, they must realise that their situation is precarious. The two old men can reasonably expect to be left in peace, hoping that I will control the more unreasonable impulses of Renzo. But Antonio can have no such illusions. That means two possible things, one or the other, or both. He has made plans to protect himself, or he is waiting for someone to come and take him out and his sons out. Or it means that he knows the danger and plans to take out Renzo first of all in a pre-emptive strike, and perhaps us as well. There are lots of ways of getting rid of Renzo: A car crash; a bad batch of cocaine; some other accident. It would raise a few eyebrows but no more. So, you see, we need to work out where we stand, what we need, and make arrangements. What do we hope for? Our best chance in taking over Palermo permanently rests, I think, with Renzo. Santucci and the old men must realise that. Perhaps the old men do not care anymore. Perhaps Santucci does not either. Perhaps Santucci is just waiting, with resignation, for a bullet in his head, not caring where it comes from.'

'Is Renzo serious? About killing his uncle and his cousins and Domenico and Lorenzo?'

'Yes, I think so. But the question is really, is he clever to want to do so? He will be marked for life as a child-killer. It may be best to try and make peace, or rather keep the peace.'

Traiano nodded. He looked towards the door, and with a pang of something like pity, saw the boy Paolo there. He had seen him, but also seen the boss, and was waiting for permission to enter. Traiano gestured for the boy to approach.

'You know Paolo?' said Traiano. 'His mother is the one who drinks crème de menthe.'

'Hi, handsome,' said the boss. 'Of course, I know Paolo. I have known him since he was born, more or less.'

'He has been helping with the Colonel,' said Traiano. 'You remember? They live in the place where I used to live. I was thinking somewhere nicer….'

Calogero nodded.

'He seems to like you,' he said.

The boy had now sat down next to Traiano and promptly gone to sleep.

'I feel sorry for him. It is a tough life for a kid. He should be in bed. He has been useful with the Colonel and he has been useful in the Furnaces, breaking streetlights, scratching cars. But now we can leave all that to Omar and his merry men. We can think of matters closer to home.'

'My sister's wedding, you mean. In October perhaps. There is a whole summer to plan for that, and it has hardly yet begun.'

'Have you made up your mind?' asked Traiano. He wasn't asking about the wedding.

Calogero considered for a long time.

'No. It is too early to do so. We need to weigh things up carefully. We need a bit of cold-hearted deliberation. How far is it to Castelvetrano?'

'Almost, but now quite as far as Trapani. Three hours by car.'

'A bit less from Donnafugata. We should go over there. Pay them a surprise visit. After all, Renzo has been there and taken Gino with him, and that Amilcare. We need to be in the picture too. And maybe next time I am in Palermo, I should speak to the old men. And maybe you should speak to Muniddu. He is well informed. He wants promotion. So does Gino. So perhaps does Alfio. We need to check out the lie of the land. A murder is just a minute's work. But the planning is immense. As will be the reward.'

They were silent for a moment. Then they were aware of a presence. It was Beata. She had a glass in her hand, and was just finishing off her last crème de menthe of the evening.

'I'll take him,' she said of the sleeping child. 'I hope he does not annoy you, boss.'

'No, he doesn't. I like him,' said Traiano.

They watched Paolo wake up.

'Come on,' said his mother, to the yawning boy. She looked at Traiano. 'We are grateful for the money,' she said.

Traiano nodded. He assumed she meant the money the boy earned running messages, and smashing street lights in the Furnaces, and damaging cars there. Rather than the money he made from the Colonel.

'I have spoken to don Calogero about finding you a better place,' he said.

She smiled and nodded to don Calogero, who had not joined in this conversation at all; then she took the child by the hand and led him away. It was two in the morning. She was finishing her main work for the evening, though not entirely. As she came out of the bar, holding her son by the hand, she saw Amilcare waiting expectantly on the Church steps. He represented a very straightforward proposition. She gave him a distant nod, and the three of them made the short walk to her flat, the single room on the top floor. Once there, the boy

Paolo was put to bed, while she and Amilcare got undressed on the other side of the screen. She adopted a recumbent position, and Amilcare lay down on top of her. Within a few moments his work was done, and after a noise that seemed to suggest a brief but deep pain, he relaxed and fell to nuzzling one of her nipples.

In moments like these, she would think; think of the little boy on the other side of the screen, wonder if he was still awake, and wonder what he thought was happening between her and Amilcare. She would also think of Amilcare. He was a nice enough young man, but rather unprepossessing. He was her boyfriend, not her client. That meant he did not pay. It did not mean very much more from her point of view. Amilcare was rather tongue-tied in her presence, but he claimed that he loved her desperately, as he had never loved anyone else. Indeed, this she could believe. For Amilcare had never known any other woman apart from herself. That did not of itself surprise her: he was shy, he was ugly, he had been in prison, his only expertise, apart from serving pizza, was his ability to get through locks.

It was this that had led to their meeting. Amilcare knew Paolo from the quarter, from the pizzeria, and one day had found him sitting glumly on the church steps, locked out of the flat, having shut the door, leaving the key inside. Amilcare had taken pity on the poor boy and, using his skills, had easily picked the lock and let the boy recover his key. Paolo had told his mother, and she had been suitably grateful, given that the loss of a key would have meant having to apply to the landlord for use of a spare, something that she would much rather not have had to do, for that would have entailed a trip to the glitzy office above the gym, or else an application to Traiano or one of his men, neither of which courses of action appealed.

She had made a point of thanking Amilcare the next time her son pointed him out to her. And then he had surprised her. He had asked her if she would like to join him for a cup of coffee. This invitation was given with a mixture of bold stares, shuffling of the feet and awkward glances to the middle distance. She had sent Paolo away.

'I am a prostitute,' she said, when the boy was out of earshot.

He nodded dumbly.

'If you want to, you can, but it is fifty euros or a hundred, depending on what you want.'

'That is not what I want,' he managed to say.

She was immediately suspicious, but at the same time puzzled and intrigued. What then did he want? She grudgingly consented to meet him the next day in one of the bars in the Cathedral Square. Oddly, she found herself preparing for this meeting with rather more care than it might have warranted. After all, she did not like Amilcare, even if he had saved her the trouble over the key; she did not find him attractive; yet she wanted to know what he wanted.

What he wanted in the end was, she discovered, something very simple. He wanted someone to talk to. He had hated his time in prison, and the only friends he now had were the ones he had made there, though they were not really his friends. He lived with his parents and his two younger brothers in a tiny flat, owned by the commune, in a rundown modern building. He worked at the pizzeria, he spent some time with Gino and Alfio when they needed him – they needed him chiefly to pick locks in the Furnaces quarter, so they could enter, and leave for the vandals all the empty properties there. It was a miserable life. His parents, he felt, did not like him. His younger brothers despised him. Beata felt sorry for him as this recitation of woes emerged over several cups of coffee. She felt the need to comfort him and, because he seemed to be a good listener, she poured out her unhappiness to him in her turn. The great love of her life, whom she had met on her arrival in Italy, namely Paolo's father, had abandoned her on discovering her pregnancy. She had brought up the child herself, alone, without friends, without much help, doing her best, and then taken up prostitution, after the birth. She did not mind her profession, and saw it as a sacrifice she was making for her beloved son. Everything she had done had been for the child, to make sure that he, at least, would have a better life than her own. But then things had begun to unravel. The boy had first of all refused to go to school, though by the time she discovered this, it was too late. He had not been going for at least a year. And then the boy had fallen in with Traiano. Working as she did, at night, and sleeping for most of the day, she had not been able to keep an eye on him, and she had discovered that he had been spending time with Traiano, working for Traiano, when it was far too late. The discovery had come when she had found a huge stash of money, all in five and ten euro notes, under the boy's bed. She had asked him where he had got such a large amount. He had said she could have it. But that was not the question she had asked. Eventually, the truth had come out. The money had come from tips for running messages and doing jobs for don Traiano; nocturnal jobs in the Furnaces. She had pressed her son about the nature of these jobs. The twelve-year-old Paolo had become sulky, then abusive and then violent. But the conclusion she had to draw was a simple one: her son was now a criminal.

Her dearest wish, that her son would escape the life she led, this terrible life, was vain, she saw. She should have been more vigilant. But she had not been told about the jobs the boy was doing for the Colonel; he had kept that from her; and she had not discovered the stash of money, all in fifty-euro notes, that the boy had hidden in a cavity behind the mirror screwed to the wall above the basin.

Nevertheless, she felt that everything she had ever wanted, all the sacrifices she had made, everything was now destroyed, and the person to blame for all this was Trajan Antonescu, the Romanian. She had never liked Traiano, if the truth be told. None of the prostitutes of the quarter did. Traiano made his money through their hard work and, when he had no further use for them, he cast them aside. They lived in the quarter thanks to his permission, and they left the quarter, evicted, when he saw them as past their useful best. Moreover, she had not forgotten the occasion when she had been drinking a mouth-refreshing crème de menthe in the bar when Traiano had called her over to service the young man Maso. She had finished her drink and gone upstairs to one of the rooms set aside for the purpose of commercial sex. Maso had clearly felt the painful humiliation of being sent upstairs with a prostitute. He had resented the compulsion, and he had apologised to her that she had happened to have been passing just at the wrong moment. Then he had undone his trousers and done the business that the boys downstairs had expected of him. When it was over, he had said how sorry he was once more. What had struck her then was something unusual. One of her clients, people with whom she never felt any connection at all, had given her an indication of fellow feeling. They both loathed Traiano. Later, she had seen Maso a few more times in the quarter. He had nodded to her, acknowledged her, established, without words, a shared perspective on the world.

Then Maso had been killed, and Maso's brother had killed the boss's wife in revenge, or so it was said. She felt sorry for Maso, and the man she blamed for his death was not Fabio Volta, who had only acted in self-defence, but the man who must have sent Maso to kill Volta, namely Trajan Antonescu, the Romanian. This gave her another reason to hate Traiano. He had corrupted her son; he had killed Maso; he himself had children, for whom he must feel something; but other people's children? What did he care about them?

All this, she had told Amilcare, who listened with attention. She had told Amilcare, over cups of coffee, because there was no one else to speak to, and because he was a sympathetic listener. She did not expect Amilcare to offer any sensible advice or to provide any help. She knew in her heart that the situation was already too far gone for that. But telling Amilcare these things provided an outlet for her grief.

Amilcare was a timid character, and he feared Traiano. He feared most people, but Traiano more than most. He had heard how he had treated the boy Tonino Grassi at the wedding of Gino and Catarina. He knew Tonino, as he knew most people in the quarter, and he knew, incredibly, that Tonino was now working for Traiano, a man who wielded power through the infliction of pain and the establishment of fear. Traiano seemed to him to be cruel and dangerous. As he listened to Beata, he warned her not to interfere, not to make things worse. Paolo was twelve, which was young, but by the standards of the Purgatory quarter this was old enough to know what you wanted. (Amilcare was a little frightened of Paolo, though he hated to admit this, even to himself.) Besides, he knew what Beata did not know and must not find out. He knew about the Colonel, who came regularly to the pizzeria, and who was now seeing another boy, the one called Nino, whom Paolo had introduced to him. That was bad, he knew, but to make a fuss about all this would only annoy and upset Paolo and drive him away. Besides, Traiano was the man who gave her, and indeed all of them, permission to work in the quarter. What could any of them do about that?

Gradually, they moved on from sharing cups of coffee to her granting him sexual favours, and then allowing him to sleep with her. There were a variety of reasons for this. It was clearly what he wanted, and she did feel sorry for him. She was getting bored with sitting around drinking coffee. It would be a new experience, in a certain sense, for both of them. His total lack of experience meant he was not demanding in the least and, like all prostitutes, she hated men who were demanding, and liked those who were easily satisfied. It was nice too having someone who seemed to like her for herself, as she thought it. And though she did not love him, she did not dislike him either.

The sole awkwardness was the boy. They lived in a single room, and their two beds were separated by a screen. She often heard the boy's breathing at night, but she knew he slept soundly, and she explained to him that Amilcare would be an occasional visitor, and she trusted that the business behind the curtain would be quiet enough not to wake the child if he were asleep; and she trusted that the child was innocent enough not to know the purpose of Amilcare's visits.

Of course, she was wrong about her son's innocence. There was the Colonel and, now that he was twelve, the boy was interested in girls too, and pursuing a girl in the quarter whom he had at least kissed, though no more for now. And she was wrong about Paolo's ability to feign sleep and to listen to what she and Amilcare whispered about as they lay together after sexual intercourse.

Paolo, as he lay awake in the dark, hearing Amilcare's laboured breathing, felt nothing at all. He had no feelings towards Amilcare, either one way or the other. That his mother should want to do this puzzled him, just as much as it puzzled him the way the Colonel behaved. The only good thing about the Colonel was the money. Everything else had been unpleasant. He had had to sit on the Colonel's lap and allow himself to be kissed. Then the Colonel would open his trousers and ask him to touch him. Then the Colonel would do the same to him. He was, luckily, a good actor. He pretended he liked it, but he didn't. But Traiano had said that one day they would kill the Colonel. That pleased him. He could not wait. When the Colonel was no longer useful, then he would die. Serve him right. There were other inducements that Traiano held out to him to which he also looked forward. The girl he was interested in was the chief one. That day would surely come.

Traiano was the source of money, of favours, of wealth and of power. He knew that Traiano was very rich, but that Traiano had started off just like him, the son of a woman from eastern Europe, the son of a prostitute. The boss had raised him up, and made him into a boss as well. Paolo held the boss in awe, and he held Traiano in similar awe. Traiano had men who obeyed him, boys who obeyed him, even policemen who did what he wanted them to. One day, Paolo was determined that he would be in a similar position.

It was thus with alarm that he overheard whispered conversations between his mother and Amilcare, in which he urged her, if she was worried about Paolo, and worried about what don Traiano was doing to the boy, to take herself and her son away from the quarter. Hearing this, Paolo knew it was the very last thing he wanted. They should go away, suggested Amilcare in his throaty whisper, without specifying what he meant by 'they': mother and son, and Amilcare too? He did not want to swap the protection of don Traiano for that of Amilcare.

But where could they go? That was what Beata wondered. Where could one get away from not just don Traiano, but from something infinitely harder - oneself, and the choices one had made? If one took the ferry across the straits, if one left Sicily, would anything in fact change? Would Paolo be any different? Would she? Would the change of geography act as a magic wand? Would the company of Amilcare? Did she like him or trust him enough to want to go away with him? The prospect of living in some dreary place, with Amilcare for company, was not immediately enticing.

And then there was the money. Paolo had made over a thousand euros running errands, doing stuff, for don Traiano. And there was the prospect of don Traiano giving them a better place to live. Perhaps by going, one would be choosing a harder, more lonely and more bitter life.

There were other things that Beata and Amilcare spoke of when they thought they were not being overheard. Amilcare told her about the trip he and Gino Fisichella and the boss Renzo Santucci had taken to a place called Castelvetrano, at the other end of Sicily, and why they had taken this trip. They were planning to kill a man called Antonio Santucci. Paolo sensed that his mother was interested in this, though he was not quite sure why. But she questioned Amilcare about the trip, and later, she asked Paolo, very particularly, whenever he was with Traiano, to listen carefully if Castelvetrano was mentioned and if the name Santucci was mentioned. And whatever he found out, he was to tell her.

Then everything went wrong for Amilcare, for Paolo, and for Beata. The trigger was the most banal thing of all. In the middle of the night, the mirror above the basin fell off and smashed, revealing the cavity behind it which contained the money, all in fifty-euro notes, that Paolo had hidden there. The cavity behind the mirror was the best hiding place in the flat, as far as

Paolo was able to see, but the walls were crumbling and, though the mirror had been screwed to the wall, its fall was inevitable. It woke Beata in the night, and she saw the shards of glass, and the loose notes, that had been slipped one by one behind the mirror into the space and which were now unexpectedly revealed. It woke Paolo too, and it woke Amilcare who, just by the purest bad luck, happened to be sleeping in the flat that night.

There was a moment of silence, succeeded by pandemonium. It ended with Beata picking up the boy's belt (he was clothed only in his underwear) and beating a confession out of him. Amilcare tried his best to intervene, for which pains Paolo stabbed him in the leg with a shard of glass. The boy eventually confessed to his furious mother that the money had come from the Colonel for services rendered or procured, and that Amilcare had been in the pizzeria at the time, and he knew. This drew Beata's wrath onto Amilcare, who was ejected from the flat in his underpants, his clothing thrown after him.

Chastised and terrified that he might bleed to death, Amilcare went limping through the night to find Gino, who in his turn took him to see Doctor Moro who cleaned and stitched the wound. Later, Gino told Traiano, who wondered at what had happened and spoke to the boy Paolo; he assured him that his mother's anger would pass, and that nothing would change, except, he assumed, that she would never speak to Amilcare again. That was a reasonable assumption. Then suddenly, after this terrible storm, everything became calm again, as if nothing had happened.

'Go away, I am married,' he had said, rudely, that first time they had met in a bar in the via dei Crociferi.

'You should learn some manners,' she had answered, watching him realise that he had made a mistake. Yes, she was a prostitute, but she was not approaching him for that.

'You are the lady don Giorgio mentioned?' he asked, in lower, more respectful tones.

'I am,' she had replied.

Fabio Volta looked at her, wondering how useful she would turn out to be.

'Would you like something to drink, signora?' he asked politely.

They were, after all, in a bar. She smiled. Old habits were hard to overcome, but for once she did not need the mouthwash that was crème de menthe. She could drink for pleasure instead. It was a long time since she had done that.

'Fernet Branca,' she said, after a slight consideration, surveying the bottles behind the bar.

'Two,' said Volta to the barman.

Chapter Three

'These people,' said Silvio.

Chiara knew what he meant. They had drawn a blank with the girl Catarina. A blank wall of silence. Yes, she had known Rosario di Rienzi. But she denied she had ever slept with him. It had not been that sort of relationship. They had just been friends. Besides, she was married now. She was sorry that Rosario had been murdered, if he had been murdered, which she was not sure about, very sorry, as he was a nice boy, but it was clear to her that Rosario had been murdered by Maso, if he had been murdered at all, because Maso had tried to steal his computer, and the same computer had been found in Maso's flat later, after Maso had been killed by that man Volta. And why should anyone want to kill someone for a computer, they had asked. But, for this, she had an answer. Maso was a professional thief. And this computer was no ordinary computer, which was why Rosario had defended it with his life. It was full of confidential documents from the lawyer Petrocchi's office. It was not the computer itself, but what it contained.

'Tell us about your husband,' Chiara had said.

'Why? Is he under investigation?' she had asked rudely.

There was nothing to be got out of Catarina Fisichella, that was for sure, they both agreed. And the reason was simple: self-interest. She was married to Gino, and she had the patronage of the boss as well, perhaps. She had much to gain, much to lose, and nothing to gain at all by co-operating with the law.

The next port of call was the lawyer Petrocchi. Here they were more confident. After all, he was a lawyer. With him, one could expect at least the pretence of co-operation. The approach they made was discreet. Posing as a couple of tourists from northern Italy, which essentially was what they often felt like, they lunched at the lawyer Petrocchi's usual place just off the Via Etnea. While he sat at the table, and she got up to pretend to visit the bathroom, she passed his table and, instead of a polite greeting, whispered that they wanted to speak to him about his daughter. He was surprised, but only for a moment. On the way back to her table, Chiara heard him say that he would be in the Villa Bellini at four that afternoon.

At the top of the Villa Bellini was a circle of wrought iron benches surrounding the bandstand, and here they found Petrocchi seated. Chiara sat next to him, and Silvio sat at a little distance. They looked like any other couple and a chance third party. There were others around.

'It was near here that I first met Calogero, don Calogero di Rienzi,' said Petrocchi. 'Who are you? Did he send you? Did Palermo send you?'

'Rome sent us,' said Chiara.

'Rome?' said Petrocchi with a raised eyebrow. 'What would Rome want with me or my daughter? We are small fry.'

'Not Rome, the Rome you are thinking of, but Rome, via Arenula, the Ministry of Grace and Justice.'

'There is a marked shortage of both in this part of the world,' said Petrocchi after a long pause. 'We need both; not one, or the other, but both. So, you are the Italian Republic's latest attempt to save us, are you? I will take your word for it. I assume you are telling the truth. People who speak like you do not work for the other Rome, the shadow Rome. What can I tell you? - Not very much I am afraid.'

'You knew Rosario di Rienzi,' said Silvio.

'That is one way of putting it, I suppose. I knew him from about the age of fifteen. I arranged for his education in Rome. I have no son of my own, and I loved Rosario. Even my wife, who is much more reserved than myself, came to like him a great deal towards the end. As for my daughter, she loved him, and her heart was broken by his death.'

'We have heard from some sources that this boy Maso killed him, in an attempt to steal his computer; and that Rosario defended the computer with his life,' said Chiara.

'Ridiculous theory,' said Petrocchi. 'It was just a cheap computer, one I bought him, if I remember rightly. It would not have cost much. And it would not have contained anything of value.'

Silvio said: 'We know that. The computer's contents were very pedestrian, nothing interesting, nothing embarrassing.'

'What you have got to understand is that when someone close to Calogero is murdered, the cause is not very distant. Occam's razor. The simplest explanation is the easiest. He was the brother of a murderer. Most people are murdered by those closest to them. Again, have you heard of Rillington Place in London. Yes? There is one mass murderer in Purgatory, and you do not have to look further than him. Calogero killed Rosario. There cannot be two such killers in such a small place. Calogero did it himself or got someone to do it for him. And the police, who attributed it to the conveniently dead Maso, are all in the pay of Calogero. I hope you have their names and never trust them again. And I will tell you something else. You will never catch anyone without a confession, without someone turning. And to try and turn people from Purgatory is well-nigh impossible.'

'Why did he kill him?' asked Chiara.

'That is a question I can answer, signora. On the last day of the year, Rosario told me that Calogero's downfall was imminent. I think he meant that he was going to betray him and that he had the sort of proof that would send him to jail. So he was killed to prevent that. But this is Sicily: he was killed because he was a traitor to his brother. He broke the sacred family loyalty. He wasn't like the rest of them, you know. He was a nice boy, a good boy. That is why they killed him. Because he was good.' He turned and looked at Chiara. 'I should be grateful if you did not approach my daughter. She has suffered a great deal. She needs to heal and to forget. Besides, she is in Rome, and may well never come back here, sadly for me and her mother.' He paused and repeated: 'I should be very grateful if you would leave my daughter out of this. She has suffered enough. As it is, she has idealised poor dead Rosario, and I despair of her ever meeting someone else, every marrying, ever having children. She has suffered enough.'

Silvio looked at Chiara.

Chiara spoke: 'We will not interview your daughter.'

'She loved him, he loved her, but if only they had never met. The people from Purgatory, as my wife often observed, were not our type of people. But as my wife does not realise, I have to deal with such people all the time. If one lives here, that is how life is.'

'Do they have any weaknesses?' asked Silvio.

The same question had been put to Volta.

'If they have any moral qualms about what they do, I would be surprised,' said Petrocchi. 'If they did feel uneasy about extortion and murder, they would be unable to sustain careers based on both. No, they have no consciences; and the women, who may have consciences, are careful not to notice anything, anything at all. What they care about is themselves, their families, their children, their wives, their property. You see, these people are the oppressed, at least in their own eyes. They have been oppressed for centuries, ever since the Romans arrived. They see their crimes as self-defence, or a sort of delayed self-defence, revenge for the indignities of the past. And they have an eye for the future, when their children and grandchildren will be accepted in a way that they are not, when they will be able to come out of the shadows. They have no weaknesses, unless you count the overwhelming vanity of Calogero a weakness, or the uxoriousness of Trajan Antonescu a weakness. If Traiano's children were under threat, then he might think again. But it is in his interest and his children's interest to stick with the source of wealth and favour, the boss, Calogero. But, and this is something you must have thought of, so forgive me for telling you what you already know: the Catania operation is recent; it is still growing; it is a strong and vigorous plant. The memory of their origins is still very fresh indeed. They are in no danger of forgetting what it is they want: to rise. But the situation in Palermo is different. The current crop of Santuccis are, what, third, or is it fourth generation criminals. Their dynasty is in decline. They have forgotten what they sprang from. They are very rich, they are spoiled, they live in luxury, they are no longer tough; and, most importantly of all, they have lost sight of the real enemy, because they have started killing each other. I know no more than what I see on television and read in the papers. But that is how it strikes me. You should be looking for weaknesses in Palermo. And now, if you will forgive me, people in my office will wonder where I have gone.'

He stood up and ambled away.

Both Chiara and Silvio sighed, but did not speak. They knew that Petrocchi was right. But as it turned out they had been assigned Catania; Palermo had been assigned to colleagues. They faced the prospect of going back to Rome and carrying a report that contained very little that was new.

A few days later their flights were booked, and the mission seemed to have been a failure. Then Volta got in touch, and everything changed.

Chapter Four

One Friday morning, after Mass, don Giorgio came to call. He knew that don Calogero was going away for the weekend, for the first time since the death of Stefania - for nothing was secret in Purgatory - though he did not know quite where. Even though he came to the door unannounced, he was received handsomely. The two daughters of the house, Isabella and Natalia, who were still too young to be shy, threw themselves at him with joy, and little Renato, following their lead, did the same. Eventually, he was left alone with the man of the house, the one he had come to see, in the study, and his mother came and brought them coffee on a tray and then withdrew.

The study was something of a mess. The shutters were closed, the place was in semi darkness, and the sofa had the look of an abused piece of furniture. There was a thin duvet cast aside next to the sofa. Calogero saw don Giorgio look at it.

'I can't sleep in my bedroom any more,' he said. 'It reminds me of her. This isn't comfortable, but it is only for a time. Besides, my mother has moved into what was my and Stefania's room. Elena is here too most of the time. Anyway, we are moving at the end of the summer, when the upper floor is ready for us, and Traiano will take this place. We had planned this before, but now it seems even more of a good idea.'

Don Giorgio nodded sympathetically.

'How are the children?' he asked.

'The girls want their mother, they need their mother. Renato is too young, thank goodness. I doubt he will be affected. The girls are also asking after Uncle Rosario.'

'And what do you tell them?'

'The truth. That he was killed by Maso. They liked Maso. They knew him from the pizzeria. They knew Enzo too, though he never spoke. It confuses them that people they knew should murder their mother and their uncle.'

'It confuses adults too,' said don Giorgio.

'There is something I have to tell you, Father, which I have been meaning to tell you for some time. But now you are here. I hope you will forgive me for not telling you before this. I have remarried.'

'Oh,' said don Giorgio, in surprise.

'She is Anna Maria Tancredi. We already have a son. She lives in Palermo, but she has a house in Donnafugata. We were married in the Cathedral in Palermo by the Cardinal, very quietly, on Easter Monday. The Cardinal is an old friend of my wife's. We are all going to Donnafugata this weekend. The children are going to meet her and see their new brother. He is called Sebastiano.'

'Congratulations. I do hope the children take it well,' he said.

'I have not told them yet. I want them all to meet, so they get used to her, and then at some point, I will tell them.'

'The welfare of children is paramount,' said don Giorgio.

'Of course,' said Calogero.

'Which is what I have come to talk to you about. I could have gone to Traiano directly, but I hope he will listen to you more than he will to me.'

'I have nothing at all to do with Traiano's activities,' said Calogero, cutting him off. 'If he is doing something you disapprove of, you speak to him, not to me.'

'He is doing something you would disapprove of, and because people see that you are so close, I feel you should know, otherwise people might think you approve of it,' countered the priest. 'It is a matter of safeguarding your reputation.'

'Go on,' said Calogero wearily, admitting defeat.

'Prostitutes,' said don Giorgio. 'They have always lived and worked in this quarter. And Traiano controls them.'

'He does not, but go on.'

'I do not approve of prostitution, though there are certain things than can be tolerated, I suppose. But there is something that is intolerable. And that is the prostitution of children. By other children.'

'What do you mean?'

'You know what I mean.'

'No, I do not.'

'Boys as young as eleven.'

'Which boys?'

Don Giorgio was silent.

'Have you spoken to the police?' asked Calogero.

Again, don Giorgio was silent. The silence endured for what seemed like a long time.

'Can't you just stop it?' he asked at length. 'After all, think of the reputation of this quarter, think of your reputation.'

Calogero raised a hand to stop him.

'I know that this sort of thing is very wrong. It's vile. If Traiano knows anything about it, I will tell him to put a stop to it at once. But not all talk has a basis in fact. There are lots of little boys running around this quarter who are perfectly innocent. And if some of them are saying things about other boys and then running to tell their priest, well, boys make things up. I am sure you know that. And these things are notoriously hard to prove.'

'Oh, I understand that,' said the priest.

'And the reputation of the Catholic Church is not perfect, to say the least, in this regard.'

'There is no need to remind me of that,' said don Giorgio.

'I will speak to Traiano,' he said, closing the subject. 'How is Petrocchi? I have not seen him, or the daughter. In fact, I have not been seeing anyone; I have hardly seen my new wife since I married her. Is Carolina Petrocchi here in Catania now? I feel I cannot bear to see her. How is she?'

'She is sad,' he said. 'She is in Rome. She wants to get away from this place, as it is full of sad reminders for her. My guess is that she will stay in Rome. That is what her parents think too. She won't come back. As for Petrocchi and the Confraternity, they are full of good works. This mobile canteen that goes out to the Furnaces every morning provides breakfast for the immigrants camped out there. That is a very nice charitable endeavour.'

'Is it going well? I must go and see for myself, but, as I say, I have hardly been out since Stefania died, as you may have noticed. I have been a hermit. I suppose Petrocchi takes credit for the mobile canteen. As a matter of fact, it was my idea entirely. But, you know, I am happy to let him take the credit.'

'The Archbishop was on the phone to me only the other day to talk about your mobile canteen. He is thrilled by it. All this taking food and drink to the poorest and most outcast of society. And offering halal meals as well, that is a nice touch. And sending out a doctor and a dentist too. No wonder the poorest of the earth who have wandered into the Furnaces and set up camp there feel so blessed. Other people in Catania, not so much. They say this mobile canteen attracts illegal immigrants. They criticise the Archbishop. He gets into the papers. The Pope notices. Oh well, you know better than I how these things work. I bet the Cardinal, your wife's friend, is furious. He must be desperately thinking of getting a mobile canteen himself. Does it cost a lot?'

'Yes, but the Confraternity is rich. As you know.'

'I do know. I was given a pay rise the other day. Lucky me!' He smiled. 'Carolina Petrocchi is a good girl. I hope one day she will have better luck and make a happy marriage. And I hope she does both far away from here.'

'So do I.'

Having come to say what he had had intended to say, he politely took his leave.

In the kitchen of Traiano's house, Pasqualina, his sister-in-law, was cutting his hair. Because that weekend, he and Ceccina and the children had been invited to Donnafugata, and because his hair had not been cut for months, and because the children kept on pulling it, it was decided that now was the best time for a trim. The only question was how much. He sat on a chair in the middle of the room, while Pasqualina very carefully considered his long curly locks and made well-judged snips. Standing looking at him, and Pasqualina's work, was Alfio Camilleri. His presence added to the jollity of the scene. Ceccina was out with the children, and Alfio was waiting for her to come back so he could tell her the news as well. He had asked Giuseppina to marry him, and she had said yes. This was news that Ceccina would very much want to hear directly, they were all sure.

Pasqualina, without taking her eyes off Traiano's hair, was asking everything she could about the proposal itself, and the forthcoming wedding. Where would it be? In Catania, of course, in the Church of the Holy Souls. They had not yet discussed it with Giuseppina's parents, Giuseppina was there now, telling them the news. He, Alfio, had come on a similar mission to Traiano.

Traiano's congratulations were effusive; and he was flattered that Alfio had come to him first. It showed the right attitude, one of dependence.

'She is such a good girl,' said Pasqualina, appreciatively. 'I am so happy for her after all the sadness of Stefania. And I am so glad she has got you. I mean, we have all grown up together, haven't we? It is nice, it makes sense, and it will be such a lovely wedding! Why don't I cut your hair too, after I have done Traiano's? I have almost finished.'

Alfio assented happily.

'When did you know that you wanted to marry Giuseppina?' asked Pasqualina.

Alfio explained that the realisation had hit him, had become solid, during Gino's wedding. That's when he had known. He saw Traiano smirk. One wedding begot another, he said. It was true after all, that old saying. He asked her if she had enjoyed Gino's wedding.

'Maybe not as much as you,' she answered. 'But it was a very nice occasion.'

The two men exchanged looks. She saw this, but pretended that she had not. She understood what they were driving at.

'I had never met Gino's parents and his brother before now,' said Alfio innocently. 'The brother, Corrado, is rather different from Gino. What did you think, boss?'

'I didn't really speak to him, but you would hardly think they were brothers, would you? Did you talk to him?'

'I did,' said Alfio. 'And he has been back since then, you know, which is unusual, at least Gino thinks it is. He never used to come here before now, but he has been twice since the wedding. I like him. He is a stonemason. He travels around for work. I think he may have been working in the province of Catania.'

Pasqualina said nothing. She had finished with Traiano, and he got up, while Alfio took his place in the chair. She studied his head, adopting a look of the greatest concentration. Traiano went to make coffee in the kitchen; as he left, he gave Alfio a look. Later, when Pasqualina was busy sweeping up the clippings, his discarded curls, and Alfio's straight black cuttings, he was alone with Alfio in the kitchen.

'What do you want to ask?' asked Traiano. 'Though I think I can guess.'

'Thanks, boss. As you know, Giuseppina is the boss's sister-in-law, well, ex-sister-in-law, and she is the boss's children's aunt, and well, the boss is obviously keeping to himself, still, and I just wondered if I could have your support in approaching the boss to ask him, well, not to ask him, but to solicit his approval.'

Traiano was thoughtful for a moment.

'Ex-sister-in-law is right,' he said at last. 'He's remarried.'

Alfio was for a moment uncomprehending. Then it dawned on him.

'That is right. Anna Maria Tancredi. They have a son already as you may know. And she is having another, conceived on the very day of the wedding, the day Gino married Catarina, Easter Monday.'

'Jesus,' said Alfio. 'Giuseppina, her parents, they will be furious and offended.'

'But not for long,' observed Traiano. 'He is the boss after all. People tend not to bite the hand that feeds them.'

'Giuseppina is still his children's aunt,' observed Alfio.

'Of the first three children. Not the other two. That may not make any difference. But…'

'You know her… Anna Maria?'

'Yes.'

'What is she like?'

'Not one of us, shall we say. She is very friendly, very nice.'

'She is twenty years older than him.'

'Quite. The first child was a surprise; the second even more so. But you know how he loves children. She is giving him two children. And other things too. She is a banker, a money woman, one who knows everyone and everybody. He likes her, but not overmuch. He likes what she represents. She is a different world. Look, Alfio, we are friends, aren't we? Giuseppina is a catch for you; she is really nice; a really good person. She has all Stefania's good qualities, and at the same time she is one of us. We all like her. You are a lucky man. And she is the children's aunt. That is important. Family is everything. The children adore her. The children will adore you; in fact, they like you already. This marriage gets you closer to the boss. It is a step up for you professionally. When you ask the boss's blessing, you will get it. And when you congratulate him on his marriage and tell him you understand, he will be grateful for that. Right now, he is sensitive on the topic. He knows he married too soon, but he wanted to legitimise the child, the existing child, Sebastiano. Things could have waited but instead, he decided to marry quietly, and let the news leak out slowly, so people would get used to it gradually.'

'I have got used to it already,' said Alfio. 'It did not take long. I am adaptable, and as you say, he is the boss. It is just Giuseppina I worry about. I don't think she will be happy.'

'Break it to her gently,' counselled Traiano. 'And soon she will have wedding plans to distract her, and then a new house, and then a baby, and all the things that keep Ceccina busy.'

Alfio sighed.

'You are taking the boss's flat, aren't you, and giving this one to Gino, aren't you? At a nice price?'

'Yes,' admitted Traiano. 'I owe Gino a lot of favours, and I owe Catarina some as well.'

'What can you possibly owe her?'

Traiano dismissed this with a wave of the hand.

'But I owe you just as much, if not more. I will speak to the boss and see what nice properties are coming up. Trust me.'

'It is not just getting a bigger flat or a better flat,' sad Alfio sadly. 'I don't much care where I live. As long as it is decent. I certainly do not see things as a competition. But she does. You would not think so, as she is not like her late sister, but she does feel it when other people have what she does not have or cannot have. It is sad for her, and I feel for her. Naturally, I had to tell her before we married. We can't have children.'

'What do you mean?'

'Look, boss, I went to see Doctor Moro.'

'He is a terrible man.'

Alfio checked that Pasqualina was out of earshot.

'He examined me and said what he thought. Then I went to a proper doctor at the hospital for a proper consultation, and they said the same thing. When I was in Bicocca, aged fourteen, there was an outbreak of mumps and that left me infertile.'

'When you were sharing a cell with Gino?'

'Yes.'

'There are no secrets here in Purgatory. We all knew about this. People talk. It may be you cannot have a child, but you never know…'

'Boss, apart from when, you know, I visited the prostitutes, not wanting to catch something, I have never bothered to, you know…. Never. Not once. And nothing ever happened.'

'I have never bothered with that either….' he reflected.

'And now you are expecting your third,' said Alfio. 'Precisely.'

There was silence.

'Gino?'

'That was what I have been thinking, boss,' said Alfio. 'And when you said you owed Catarina favours…'

'You thought, me and Catarina?' said Traiano anxiously looking to the next room, to check Pasqualina could not hear.

'It was the natural thought, boss,' said Alfio apologetically.

'I have only got one woman in my life and would never look at another,' said Traiano.

'So I imagined,' said Alfio. 'It must be Gino's. That is what I keep on telling myself.'

'That is what you need to keep on telling Gino too,' said Traiano.

A moment later, the door of the flat opened. It was Ceccina and the children. They had been shopping for clothes, given that they were spending the weekend at Donnafugata. There were bathing costumes to be bought, and one had to look good. Ceccina was aware that this weekend would be a test, her first meeting with the boss's mistress (she did not know they were married). She was looking forward to it, but anxious at the same time. Her sister Pasqualina, though not going with them, was interested in all these preparations, and it was nice to see Alfio and talk about the forthcoming wedding with him. More clothes, more events, on top of the projected wedding between Elena and Renzo Santucci.

Someone had been talking. That was what weighed upon Calogero. Their whole business and the success of it depended on silence. Now someone had spoken, and it had got to don Giorgio, and he feared it would not stop with don Giorgio. This was the thought that accompanied him to Donnafugata, where Anna Maria was waiting for them; he could not quite think of her yet as his wife. But domestic thoughts, at least for now, made him put business worries aside.

She was waiting for them and came down to the driveway to meet them as they arrived. It was a large house, and they were a large party: himself and his three children, and his sister Elena; Renzo, who came with Elena; Traiano and Ceccina and their two children. His daughters had been instructed that they were going to spend the weekend with a friend of Papa's who had a baby and a very nice house which they would like. Isabella and Natalia, who had greatly enjoyed their trip to the Grand Hotel in Palermo last Christmas, were interested in this mysterious friend, her beautiful house and, above all, her baby. They loved babies. They loved their little brother Renato; they adored the tiny Maria Vittoria; and now they were very keen to see this new arrival, Sebastiano. They had been told about the orange groves, the lemon groves, the swimming pool and the huge house, and all that had excited them too, but the prospect of a baby was in a different category entirely.

On arrival, there was also the unexpected bonus of the beautiful lady who presided over the beautiful house. It was like a fairy tale. There was a maid, called Veronica, there was a nanny who looked after Sebastiano, and there was the most beautiful lady they had ever seen. She asked them to call her Anna Maria, she made sure they had everything they wanted, including lots of lovely things to eat, and she sat with them and Aunt Elena and Aunt Ceccina while they ate it. She wore the most wonderful perfume. And when she looked at them, she smiled so sweetly that after supper they hardly wanted to go to bed, and indeed would not until Anna Maria had promised that she would come and kiss them good night. She did that as they had asked, and received protestations of love and joy from the two girls. Afterwards, their father came to kiss them goodnight, and much to his pleasure, both daughters confessed their delight in being in Donnafugata, in meeting Anna Maria, in staying in such a lovely place, and expressed the desire that they should be allowed to come here again and again.

'Papa,' said Isabella, 'Natalia and I think it would be a good idea for you to marry Anna Maria. She needs a husband and you need a wife. You have been so sad since Mama died.'

He promised them he would think about it.

When the children were in bed, dinner was served. Rather to his surprise, he enjoyed dinner. Ceccina and Elena were determined to shine, not to let the side down, and both had spent some considerable effort on their appearance. Ceccina was beautiful in her new dress, and his sister did not look too bad. Both were deeply attentive to Anna Maria, deferring to her opinions on everything. For once the talk had nothing to do with business, but was about a subject dear to his heart and to Anna Maria's, namely Sicilian culture. They spoke of Monreale and the cathedral at Cefalù, how the Normans had found a home in the warm south, and how people had liked them, unlike the French who had come later, unlike the Savoyards who had come later still. Becket's image was in mosaic in Monreale, created just a few decades after his martyrdom; the south and the north had been joined then, when one considered the wonderful Arabic buildings of Palermo, the way that cultures had fused. The Spanish too, had left their mark, particularly in Catania and Noto and the cities of the south of the island, but now everything suffered under long centuries of neglect. It was as if, having excelled in everything, Sicily had decided to retire from the fray. He understood that. He too, he modestly admitted to himself, had excelled. Everything had worked out for him, everything. He was rich, feared, respected, admired, healthy, and now married to a woman who was even richer, and who owned a priceless, albeit stolen, Caravaggio. He had had little education but was, he hoped, cultured, and she was even more so. She knew everyone, was liked by everyone. Surely now, the struggle could end. Surely now, he had arrived.

The food and the drink reinforced this idea. They started with white wine from France, and smoked salmon. They continued with the most succulent haunch of venison, a meat he had never eaten before, but which was delicious. Afterwards, there were all the Sicilian and Italian cheeses you could hope for, and then they concluded with something called floating island. An adventurous menu, for which he gave her credit. He wondered what they would eat tomorrow, but forbore to ask; no doubt his wonderful new wife had planned it all. He noticed that Ceccina and Elena ate the food as if it were the sort of food they were used to; they did not look around themselves, wishing for bread or pasta or vegetable soup. (He remembered his mother's pasta, her vegetable soup, both, as a matter of fact, in recent times at least, excellent.) He looked at Caravaggio, as Anna Maria called him, and remembered the very first time he had come across him, and remembered him; the night the police had come to the quarter to tell them that his father was dead, and how he had assumed they had come for him, and how he had hidden in Anna's sordid flat, and taken refuge with Traiano, and read his first Holy Communion book with him, until Rosario or maybe it had been Turiddu, had come and told him the coast was clear. He remembered a hot summer afternoon, lying asleep in bed with Anna, both of them naked, and the child Traiano joining them. Too many memories. One needed to keep the present tidy. One needed to tidy up the past as well, one needed to forget the unpleasant memories.

He looked at Renzo, at his bright shining eyes. Was that the cocaine? Renzo had slicked back his hair with some sort of gel which improved his appearance. Ceccina's sister, the hairdresser, had clearly been dispensing advice and perhaps help. She had spent a great deal of time on her brother-in-law, he could tell, whose long dark and curly hair now no longer hung down to his shoulders. As for himself, he had stuck with the same barber for years, and no woman was ever going to get near his head. Look what had happened to Samson! Renzo needed discipline, but Renzo could, he hoped, learn. Renzo was stupid and spoiled but not so much so as to be unable to improve. Renzo had background. The Santucci name counted for so much. And his sister, well, he had underestimated her, he now realised. She had some presence. She was, he had long observed, nicer than Assunta. She was sensible, mature, respectable. She could make something of Renzo. As for Traiano, perhaps he had served his purpose. Perhaps, from now on, life would be like this, not as it had been before.

After dinner, the women rose to go to bed, and it was soon clear that after they had been given a few minutes, the men were only too keen to join them. For once, there would be no sitting around drinking until the small hours.

He went upstairs to find Anna Maria.

'I have something to tell you,' she said.

'And I you,' he replied. 'But this comes first,' he said, undressing.

He was brief but passionate.

She told him that she was sure it would be another boy. In fact, she was going for a scan soon, and early on as it was, perhaps they would be able to see.

'We can call him William or Roger or Tancred, a Norman name,' he said happily. 'It has been so unexpected. But the very best news always is. I have been thinking of nothing else since you told me.'

'What were you going to tell me?'

He told her what Isabella had told him at bed time.

'Everything is going perfectly,' she said.

He agreed, but knew there were some problems to be ironed out.

The children were the first to get up, then the women who looked after them. Calogero stirred at a late hour, and got up, put on his dressing gown, and went in search of Traiano. He found him in bed, asleep alone, and poked him in the ribs.

'Boss,' said Traiano sleepily, turning on his back, watching Calogero look round the room, open the curtains, and even poke his head into the bathroom. From outside came the sound of happy children.

'It takes two hours to Castelvetrano, and I think we should leave soon,' he said.

'Castelvetrano? Today? Is Renzo coming too?'

'Yes, though I have not told him yet. I'll tell him now.'

He was gone a moment, but was soon back. In the meantime, Traiano had got up, and was in the bathroom brushing his teeth.

'We need to get rid of all the prostitutes from our quarter,' said Calogero through the door.

The brushing stopped suddenly.

'They attract the wrong sort of people; they are more trouble than they are worth,' he continued. 'We can make a lot more money using the same properties for other things.'

He heard Traiano spitting.

'What brought this on?' came his voice.

'The nature of the business is changing,' said Calogero.

'If you get rid of the prostitutes, you don't need a pimp any more,' said Traiano, now appearing at the door of the bathroom.

'Your talents are wasted as a pimp,' said Calogero. 'Now get dressed. Someone may come in.'

Someone did. It was Renzo.

'Hi,' he said, with a smile. He was fully dressed. 'Hi, handsome,' he said to Traiano, watching him pull on his trousers.

'Hi, handsome,' replied Traiano. 'So why are we going to Castelvetrano?'

'No particular reason,' said Calogero. 'Tourism. Tell your uncle to expect us, can you, Renzo?'

'Sure, boss,' said Renzo.

'After all, we do not want him to think that we are coming to take him by surprise, do we?' said Calogero.

The idea was that everything should proceed naturally. As they drove towards Castelvetrano, all along the south coast of the island, the road seemed long. They passed the Valley of the Temples at Agrigento, and still the road seemed never ending. In the back seat, Renzo dozed.

'Maybe we should just kill them when we arrive; I have my gun. I could take it out and shoot the lot of them when they least expect it, maybe as lunch is ending, when they are off their guard,' said Traiano.

'Don't be ridiculous,' said Calogero. 'Anyway,' he said, looking at Renzo asleep in the rear-view mirror, 'it may not come to that.'

'I don't like Antonio Santucci,' said Traiano.

'So you keep on saying. Don't let that sway you. I quite like the old men, his father and his uncle. But I would not let that sway me. There is no gratitude in this game. You may feel you owe people some debt, but if it serves your purpose to get rid of them, you have to act and not let your feelings get in the way.'

'True,' admitted Traiano. 'The girls in our quarter....'

'Have got to go,' said Calogero decisively.

'Can you explain why, boss?'

'There are better ways of making money. They do not pay. We can replace them by better things. I want them gone.'

'Just you?'

'Don Giorgio came to see me yesterday morning.'

'To complain about the girls?'

Traiano's voice was incredulous.

'No. To say that the girls are alright and offend no one. To complain about what Colonel Andreazza is getting up to.'

'He mentioned the Colonel by name?'

'No.'

'Someone has been talking,' said Traiano. 'If someone has been talking, I can find out who, and I can deal with it.'

'It depends who has been talking. You cannot deal with don Giorgio. He is a priest. If it is a woman talking, or a child talking, you cannot deal with them either. Well, you could, I suppose… What Andreazza likes is very bad, and people think it is very bad, and we have to accept that. It's not like cocaine or prostitutes - bad things people tolerate. Children – that's different. How old is this boy Andreazza is seeing?'

'The first one was about eleven and a half, but now he is twelve; the other one a bit younger.'

'Holy Mary!' said Calogero. 'Did you not consider what people would think?'

'People were not going to find out.'

'They have. They have found out.'

'These boys know what they are doing. They are old enough to like money.'

'Listen to yourself. You bloody pimp! You have the mind of a pimp.'

'Boss….'

'Didn't you think of the damage you would do my reputation?'

'Your reputation?' retorted Traiano. 'You told me to give Andreazza whatever he liked. So I did.'

'Yes, my reputation.' He said, ignoring the objection. 'We are going to make a fortune in the Furnaces, and if people discover I am in any way connected with supplying eleven-year-olds for prostitution, do you think that will be good publicity?'

'You don't care about the children any more than I do,' said Traiano. 'You just care about yourself.'

'I care about not ruining everything we have achieved,' he said.

'And who did all the dirty work for you?'

They were on a lonely stretch of road. Renzo had woken up.

'Look, I will take care of the kids. There are only two of them. I will take care of Beata, the mother. She is sleeping with Amilcare, and she won't want him to come to any harm. Just leave it to me, as you left all the other nasty things you did not want to deal with to me.'

'Take care of them? You are going to kill a twelve-year-old and a child of, what, eleven? Can't you see what you are saying?'

'I will give them a good beating. But if I have to go further, I will, and please don't be so hypocritical as to object. You were the one who told me, more or less, to give Andreazza what he wanted.'

Calogero shot him a murderous glance. In the back seat, Renzo looked worried. With deliberation, Calogero brought the car to a halt. He got out of the driver's seat, and walked around to the passenger door and pulled Traiano out of the car. Traiano looked at him with stony contempt.

'Hypocritical bastard!' he said.

But he made no move to resist. Calogero pushed him over to the side of the road, and through the oleanders that grew there. On the far side was a patch of waste ground. He pushed Traiano to his knees and then began to kick and beat him with his belt, while Renzo watched.

'Damn you!' said Traiano, repeatedly.

Calogero continued the beating until Traiano fell silent. That took about twenty minutes.

When it was over, he ordered him to get into the back seat. Then, with Renzo next to him, they drove on to Castelvetrano.

Don Antonio Santucci was depressed. He had been depressed since Christmas, when he had effectively lost control of the organisation that was the San Lorenzo crime family. He had been profoundly depressed by the way the entire family had connived at his overthrow and effectively sided with his enemies. Since that unhappy time, his depression had become steadily worse, and his self-imposed exile to Castelvetrano had not helped him in the slightest. He had hoped that the peace and quiet of Castelvetrano, the company of the vines and olive trees, would restore his mind. Instead, the solitude had turned into loneliness, the beauty of his surroundings had reproached him, and the usual delights of the place, such as the boat he kept at Selinunte, had failed to charm him. He had continued to drink more heavily than ever; his wife and children, who had accompanied him, soon made excuses to return to Palermo. The children had to go to school, after all; his wife had her own activities to attend to; besides, a drunken husband was no companion for her.

He might have returned to Palermo himself, but had felt too demoralised to do so, for Palermo was the site of his defeat and humiliation. Palermo was where his father Lorenzo and his uncle Domenico lived, and he could not face seeing them, for he had failed them, failed the family. Moreover, when it was announced that his father was unwell, suffering from cancer, he had been unable even then to do what was expected of him. He simply could not face the visit to the hospital and the sad glance of a disappointed and perhaps dying man. He preferred to sit at home and drink and eat and, in the hot weather, totter round the garden. He felt himself to be a finished man. He imagined that if they did come and kill him, it would be akin to putting a wounded animal out of its misery. He rather hoped they might. He knew that if he had had the guts to fight, he ought to be plotting to kill them, the people who had brought him to this sad and sorry state of defeat. But, that he had not the energy even to contemplate such a thing, underlined just how defeated he was.

His only consolation was his two sons. His two daughters, Marina and Emma, and his wife, Angela, regarded him, he realised, as an embarrassment. They compared him to the late Carlo, now with the angels and the saints, and found him wanting. But the two boys, especially the younger one, fond as they had been of Uncle Carlo, still retained a vestige of affection for their fallen father. Sandro and Beppe still wanted to come and spend time with him in Castelvetrano, in the large house outside the town which had a view of the distant sea, and which was luxuriously appointed. Beppe, the younger one, was just thirteen, and loved the gardens and the olive trees, and had expressed the rather odd desire, in his father's eyes, of wanting to be a horticulturalist. He had a particular interest in lemons, which was unusual in a child of his age, though perhaps not so unusual given that the family had risen to prominence through lemons and their export to the new world. The elder boy, Sandro, was now seventeen, and had a motorcycle which he kept at Castelvetrano, and which he rode around the countryside. Because his father seemed preoccupied with himself, Sandro could come to Castelvetrano and experience a freedom denied to him in Palermo, where his every move, every action, was subjected to intense scrutiny by his mother, his aunts, his grandmother and his sisters. Beppe and Sandro very rarely spoke to each other, given the age gap between them. They had no interests in common, or at least none that were obvious. Of late, this early summer, Beppe had been spending more and more time watering the lemon trees in the company of the elderly gardener and drinking in all his lore with what the old man considered to be gratifying attention. Sandro had been in the house and grounds, but rarely. He had grown his hair long and managed to produce a few wisps of beard. He had even proceeded to dye his hair a peroxide blonde, to his father's consternation. He was rumoured to have a girlfriend.

As it turned out, the arrival of don Calogero di Rienzi and Renzo Santucci, along with the Romanian pimp (as Antonio Santucci thought him), though announced that morning by phone, had happened at the very worst time. Breakfast was late, served by their housekeeper who had been with them for many years. Antonio sat at the table in the garden under the trellis, nursing a cup of coffee and a terrible hangover. Beppe sat at the other end of the table with his yoghurt, regarding his father and feeling sorry for him, and knowing it was best to say nothing, for his father was just at that dangerous point between drunkenness and sobriety where the slightest provocation, however innocent, might have catastrophic consequences.

Then the sound of a motorcycle was heard, and Sandro entered the scene. Without acknowledging father or brother, he helped himself to coffee. He called in the direction of the kitchen window, knowing the housekeeper would hear him, asking for something to eat.

'Don Calogero di Rienzi is coming today with your cousin Renzo,' said his father quietly. 'So, make sure you are both here for lunch and are presentable for once.'

This last barb was aimed at the elder son.

Father and son had had an altercation about Sandro's long and dyed hair once already.

'You are still drunk from last night,' said Sandro.

'Oh, am I?' asked Antonio.

Beppe cringed over his yoghurt. Sandro said nothing.

'Don't you speak to me like that!' said Antonio.

Sandro contemptuously ignored him, and sat down to drink his coffee.

Antonio felt all the pent-up rage of the last six months descend on him like a Bacchanalian fury. Once, everyone had obeyed him. Now he was being cheeked by this seventeen-year-old, his own son. Shaking with fury, he got up from the table, and went into the house.

'You have annoyed him,' said Beppe.

'Fuck off!' said his brother.

Beppe shrugged. He was just trying to help. It never worked.

Their father returned. He placed a pair of scissors on the table. Beppe looked up. He dropped his spoon. There was complete silence.

'Beppe,' said their father, 'I want you to cut your brother's hair.'

'What the fuck?' said Sandro.

He looked up. He saw the gun.

They arrived a little after twelve thirty, and drove into the quiet, shaded and deserted driveway, getting out of the car into the silence. Renzo had been there before, and he led the way round the side of the house to where the swimming pool was, and where the dining table stood under the pergola. The table was set for lunch, and there was a smell of cooking from the kitchen window. Then Beppe appeared.

'Hi,' he said.

He went up to his cousin and hugged him. Then he approached don Calogero more shyly.

'You remember me?' asked Calogero.

'Of course. You gave me such a nice Christmas present when we were all staying in the Grand Hotel in Palermo. I have not forgotten. You have two nice daughters and a little son. I am afraid my father is inside and feeling a little shaken. Sandro is in his bedroom and refuses to come out.'

'Oh?' asked Calogero.

'My father and Sandro had a quarrel.'

'What about?' asked Renzo.

'Well, about Sandro's hair. He has dyed it metallic blond. Peroxide. But it is more than that. Sandro just told papa that he refused to get his hair cut, and papa shot him. Well, tried to shoot him, but his hands were shaking so much that he missed. Which was good.'

'Over a haircut?' asked Renzo in disbelief.

'Yes. But it is more than that. He was out all night, and he told papa to mind his own business when he asked where he was. He says he is seventeen and can do what he likes. I think he has been having sexual intercourse. That's why he was not here last night. Papa was furious, and wanted to kill him. But, as I say, he missed.'

'Jesus,' said Calogero, looking at Renzo. 'We sure picked our day.'

'I think they will be alright in a bit,' said Beppe. 'They just need a bit of time to get over themselves. Then we will be able to have lunch. Our housekeeper was very alarmed when she heard the shot. But she has been with us for years. Even so, it still shocked her. We are having rabbit. I hope you like that?'

'Where is the gun?' asked Calogero.

'I threw it in the pool,' said Beppe. 'It is the only one in the house. I think. Would you like to come and see my lemon trees?'

'I would,' said Calogero. 'I like lemon trees. Let's go and see them, and leave Renzo to your father and to your brother.'

They went towards the citrus groves. Beppe spoke about the lemon trees; about the number they had; which were new; which were old; how much fruit they bore, and what variety they were. Calogero remarked that his wife had a lemon grove. Beppe said that he thought don Calogero's wife was dead. She was, Calogero said: he ought to have said his new wife, Anna Maria Tancredi. Beppe had heard of her and heard, too, of her trees. Calogero invited him to come over and see them one day, and one day soon. His two daughters, a bit younger than Beppe, might like to meet him again. Beppe nodded uncertainly. He remembered seeing them at Christmas, at the Grand Hotel.

'Do you get on well with your brother Sandro?' Calogero asked.

'Not really. He is seventeen. He says I am boring and that whatever I say is boring. We do not talk.'

'Well, he should pay more attention to his brother, in my opinion,' said Calogero. 'Seventeen-year-olds think they know everything, don't they? But they need to learn from their family members. This sort of behaviour, being defiant to your father, might be OK in places like London and New York, but this is Sicily. It won't reflect well on your father either. People used to look up to him.'

'They don't any more,' said Beppe.

'And they won't ever again,' said Calogero. 'Your father should have given Sandro a good whipping. He has left it too late now.'

'Papa was annoyed,' said Beppe. 'But you don't try and shoot your own son just because you are annoyed. Papa is a bit crazy. He is an alcoholic. That is what my sisters, Emma and Marina, say. And this won't make him any better. Poor man. I feel sorry for him. Did he kill my Uncle Carlo?'

'What questions you ask! Of course not. Your uncle was killed by a rocket propelled grenade. Neither your father, nor any other private individual has access to that type of weaponry. Only governments do.'

'Oh,' said Beppe, unconvinced. 'And what about Ciccio?'

'Who?'

'He was found floating in the harbour in Palermo, tied to another man. He was nice. I liked him.'

'I don't know anything about that.'

'They told me about your brother. I was sorry to hear that too. He was nice. We were expecting your friend to come as well, Traiano. Where is he?'

'He is feeling unwell, so he is lying down in the car.'

'I liked him when I saw him in Palermo. I hope he feels better soon. He is nice.'

'You seem to like a lot of people,' observed Calogero. 'When you are older, you can marry one of my daughters. Did you know your cousin Renzo is going to marry my sister? That is why we have come, to tell you the good news.'

Beppe nodded.

'I wonder if Renzo will make a good husband,' he said. 'Do you like your sister? Mine are OK, sometimes quite nice, but not always. As for me, I am too young to think about who I marry just yet.'

'Bullshit! Plan ahead.'

'Don't swear. My mother does not like it.'

'She is not here, is she?'

'No, she isn't.'

'So, don't tell me what to do. Otherwise, I will whip you.'

Beppe giggled, and they walked on in silence.

They came back to the dining table under the pergola. The place was deserted. Everything was ready, the table was set, and there was an aroma of food from the kitchen window, but no people. From the pool, came a slight commotion. They walked over, and there was Renzo, in the water, diving to try and retrieve the gun.

'It's too deep for me, I have not got the breath,' he said, surfacing and hanging onto the side of the pool. 'I cannot reach the bottom. I thought it best to secure the gun, you know, in case of accidents. Though if it is wet, it is useless, I suppose.'

'I can get it,' said Beppe. 'I can reach the bottom easily.'

Renzo hauled himself out of the pool. He muttered a few words of apology, as he had borrowed a pair of shorts and a towel from the nearby pool room, without asking.

Renzo dried himself. Beppe, meanwhile, went to the pool room and came back in his swimming trunks and, after one swift dive, secured the gun. Calogero took it and went to the car. Traiano was there, in the front seat, his eyes closed. He opened them as Calogero approached.

'Still sulking?' he asked.

'Yes,' said Traiano.

'You will miss lunch,' said Calogero easily. 'It smells good. Sometimes I forget what a child you still are. Look after this. Make sure the wrong person does not get hold of it.'

When he returned, the rest of the party had assembled. The signora was standing by with the food, ready to serve the lasagne. Antonio Santucci, wearing dark glasses, was pouring the wine. Sandro shook hands with Calogero in a subdued manner. He too was wearing dark glasses, to shield his red tear-stained eyes. He kissed his cousin Renzo lightly on both cheeks, then sat down without a word. They all sat down, and the lasagne was served. Only Beppe was entirely at his ease. They were half way through the course, the only conversation being how good the food was, when Traiano appeared. He took the only free place which was next to Beppe, and the signora brought him a plate of lasagne.

'Do have some wine, it may help,' Antonio Santucci said grimly. 'I find it helps a great deal, even in the most challenging situations. Nice to see you all. Nice of you to come. You find us in a bit of disarray. But nothing food and drink cannot mend, I hope.'

'It is nice to see you too,' said Calogero. 'Have you heard the news? We wanted to tell you in person, so you could approve it; one marriage retrospectively, to be fair, but one marriage is still to come.'

'Ah weddings,' said Antonio. 'Don't tell me, let me guess. You have married Tancredi?'

'You knew?'

'An educated guess. It is the right move. Congratulations!'

'Thanks. And we are having a second child.'

'More congratulations. How very nice. Four children so far, a fifth on the way,' said Antonio. 'Two sons too, just like me, and two daughters. And the fifth… who knows. May they bring you great joy.'

Sandro preserved a stony silence.

'And Renzo has something to tell you,' said Calogero.

They all looked at Renzo.

'I am marrying Elena, Calogero's sister, this autumn. We have not fixed a date yet.'

There was a murmur of congratulations.

'I am very pleased,' said Antonio. 'Do you plan to have lots of children? She comes from a fertile family. I am glad that my nephew, at least, is settling down and doing the right and proper thing.'

'Uncle, uncle, I am very lucky anyone will have me,' said Renzo modestly. 'And I am particularly lucky to be marrying the sister of a great man like don Calogero.'

'Just as I was lucky to marry the sister of a great man too, namely your father, Carlo,' said Antonio, taking grim pleasure in revelling in all the woes of the family, all of which, he bitterly reflected, were his fault.

Calogero smiled wanly. It was as if he had walked into a bomb site some moments after the detonation. As lunch progressed, Antonio drank more and became more incoherent. Even before the rabbit was finished, he made his excuses and left. His sons, in different ways, visibly relaxed when he left. The visitors were ill at ease. Only the tiramisu gave them something to do. They left shortly afterwards.

'You missed your chance,' said Calogero to Renzo conversationally, when they were safely away. 'When I was up in the lemon trees with the younger boy, you should have taken Traiano's gun, shot Sandro and then shot your uncle, making it look like suicide. Then we could have shot the small boy too. The housekeeper had heard the first shot. She would have been the key witness, and the story would have been that Antonio shot his two sons after a huge quarrel and then shot himself. Bingo! But the opportunity is gone now. You missed it. It would have been perfect.'

'Sorry, boss, I wasn't thinking....'

'You need to think quickly and strategically. You walk into a mess and you realise how that mess can be turned to your advantage. Three little bullets and you have solved the problem; the murder would have been set up by the victims themselves. But it is too late now.'

'Didn't you like the younger boy, Beppe?' asked Traiano from the back seat. 'How old is he, twelve?'

'What has that got to do with it?' asked Calogero angrily.

'Same age as Paolo, more or less, and yet we cannot kill him? What is the difference?'

Calogero did not reply. He turned to Renzo instead.

'It was a missed opportunity, but in the end it does not matter. Your uncle is in no fit state to cause you or us any harm. In fact, the longer he lives, the longer he drinks, the longer he makes a fool of himself – all of that is to our good. People will see that he was not fit to lead. No one could compare you and what you do, to what your uncle might have done, if they can see him there, alive, doing precisely nothing. Kill him, and make him a martyr. Leave him, and make him an example and a reason for why he had to be retired. As for those boys, there is no need to worry about them. That Sandro is someone no one could ever respect. I am sorry for him, but that is the way it is. His father wanted to shoot him, and if his father wanted to do that, could you imagine anyone following him? And the one called Beppe wants to grow lemon trees. That is a harmless avocation, and one to be encouraged. Poor Antonio, he wasn't cut out for this life, and neither are his two boys. No wonder he drinks.'

'He and Sandro are a disgrace,' said Renzo.

'Which suits us all just fine,' said Calogero.

'I'd like to shoot them all, all the same.'

'But you don't need to,' said Calogero. 'That is the difference.'

They came to the same deserted stretch of road where they had stopped that morning.

'Let's stop and have a fight, boss. Let us settle it that way,' said Traiano.

'Settle what?' asked Calogero.

'Everything,' said Traiano. 'Who was right about Andreazza, for a start.'

'Grow up!' said Calogero, driving on.

The children had spent the most wonderful day playing in the garden, enjoying the sunshine of the month of June. They had played hide and seek for hours in the olive groves and the citrus groves, under the eyes of Elena, who kept watch on little Renato, and the nanny who held little Sebastiano. In the kitchen, Veronica, Ceccina and Anna Maria had had long discussions about that evening's menus and wines, and Veronica had demonstrated the way she made gnocchi, which was not quite the way that Ceccina would have done so herself, and the way she made beef olives which, Ceccina was glad to admit, was superior to any way she had seen before now, including her grandmother's. Then they had made their way into the garden and examined the herbs that were growing there, some of which Ceccina had never seen before in the wild. There was also a patch of artichokes which was the object of some study. Thus did the day pass, along with a leisurely lunch, a little sleep after it, and numerous cups of coffee and tea.

The men returned from the long and unsatisfactory trip to Castelvetrano. Renzo went upstairs to have a shower, and told his future wife that he never wanted to go near the place again and that he cared nothing for that side of the family. Perhaps they should not even invite them to the wedding. He was not forthcoming in details. A drunken uncle, a teenage cousin who had dyed his hair peroxide blond, purely to be annoying, these were things he did not want to discuss. As for her brother and Traiano, they had quarrelled. This worried him, but Elena was reassuring. They were always quarrelling and always making up like lovers, she said. There was no need to be worried at all. It was part of the cycle of life.

Calogero lay in the bath, luxuriating in the hot water. His wife looked at him.

'The Cardinal rang,' she said.

'He did? Why?'

'He likes you. But that was not the reason he called. The Archbishop of Catania called him, you see. And the Archbishop called because he had met up with your don Giorgio.'

'That was quick,' said Calogero. 'Tell me the upshot.'

'The upshot is that you need to be whiter than white. That the dirt must be kept as far away from you as possible. The Cardinal says this. I say this too, as your banker. There are certain things that are poison. They can ruin everything.'

He closed his eyes, and enjoyed the warmth of the water.

'So, what are you saying? I was telling Caravaggio that we need to clear out the prostitutes from the quarter. He does not quite see my way of thinking, at least not yet. But I will persuade him.'

'I think it goes further than that,' she said. 'I think you need to cut him loose entirely.'

He was thoughtful.

'The investors in the Furnaces project...?'

'Quite. The project is now coming to a conclusion, at least the first part of it is. Caravaggio was very useful in that, but now, or soon, he may have served his purpose.'

'I wonder if don Giorgio realised what he has unleashed,' said Calogero, more to himself than to her.

'You will know what to do,' she said. 'Remember your children. Remember our children. They need to grow up in a clean world.'

'I thought you liked Caravaggio,' he said.

'I adore him,' she said. 'But business requires a clear head. You know that.'

He knew that.

As for Traiano, all he wanted was her. He lay in bed with his wife, trying not to feel the pain of his bruises, which were now becoming apparent, and which she saw, though did not comment on. Her ability to suspend curiosity, her ability to ignore things, always surprised him.

'How is the baby?' he asked.

'Well, well,' she replied.

'And you?'

'The same.'

'Where are Cristoforo and Maria Vittoria?'

'With Elena and the nanny and the other children. We have some time. Enough time.'

'Good, good,' he said.

Though he felt, as he said it, that time was running out. Perhaps these sweet occasions would not last much longer. The new child was due in the autumn. Would he be alive to see the birth? Would all this be snatched from him? Would the one relationship that had dominated his life, that with Calogero, snap before then, and would that mean the end of everything? It was necessary to think of a strategy, a way out, an escape. There was, as Calogero had said, no gratitude in this game, no personal ties that were beyond discussion, that could not be broken when necessity demanded it. He wanted to get rid of the prostitutes from the quarter, and this was because of Andreazza and the boy Paolo and the boy Nino, and whatever future boys he served up for Andreazza. And yet the co-operation of the police, and Andreazza in particular, had made things so easy for them. How were they to control Andreazza from now on? Was the boy Paolo talking? Was his mother talking? And to whom, if they were? Should he throw them both down the shaft and tell the boss not to worry about them anymore? It could be done. But would the boss ever forgive him for this mistake? For, a mistake, it certainly was. Would the boss, after letting him clean up the mess, then get rid of him, and use Gino and Alfio to do so? He could not quite believe it. They had been so close. But everyone else to whom the boss had been close was dead: Turiddu, Rosario. And he had killed them for the boss. Would the boss now kill him? It was not possible. But there was no gratitude in this game. That was the thought that haunted him.

His wife was speaking of what she had done that day; her adventures in the kitchen and in the herb garden. She took an interest in the pizzeria and in the trattoria in the quarter. Perhaps, she said, one day, she would open a restaurant. She did not ask him about what he had done, what they had got up to in Castelvetrano. They would now be calling off the dogs. Renzo had been told that Antonio and his sons were to be left in peace, that there was no point in killing them. Gino, who had been so hungry for a big job, would be told that this job was off. But would they give Gino another job? Would he be the job? Was he becoming paranoid? When your best friend was also your worst potential enemy, paranoia was the usual state of mind.

His wife was stirring, wondering where the children were, getting dressed, and determined to search for them. He had no such desire to get up just yet.

'If you see the boss, can you ask him to come and see me here?' he asked her, before she left.

About an hour later, he was washed, dressed and ready for the world, ready at least to say goodnight to the children and face the adults, when Calogero came into the room and stood silently before him. He knew what he had to do. Calogero had a weak point: his vanity. He went up to him, put his arms around him, and whispered the magic words in his ear.

'I am sorry,' he said.

'Good,' said Calogero, pushing him away. 'Next time I will make your children orphans. You have come this close to making me do that.'

'I know it is my fault,' he said humbly.

He looked for his jacket. As he did so and put it on, he saw the gun and the knife nearby.

'Come here,' said Calogero.

The next embrace was warmer.

'What do you want me to do with Andreazza?' he asked. 'Are we finished with him?'

'What did you tell that boy about Andreazza?'

'That when he was grown up, he could kill him.'

'Boys grow up fast in our part of the city. If Andreazza dies in circumstances that arouse scandal, then that will gravely damage the reputation of the police. That can only help us. It is just that it should happen some way away from our quarter.'

'Some hotel in Taormina, belonging to the Messina people?'

'Why not? You are clever, you figure it out. Clean up the mess, and use the people who are the mess to do the cleaning. Andreazza being killed by a prostitute will be a huge scandal. One less boy prostitute, one less whore of a mother... no one will notice.'

'Boss, are we OK?'

'We are OK,' said Calogero.

But he did not believe him. He knew that if Andreazza turned into a public scandal, and decided to make trouble for him, the boss would cut him loose.

Dinner, which had been in preparation all day, was spectacular. The first course was pasta with a wild boar sauce; that was followed by roasted quails; and the whole ended with zuppa inglese. The wines were various and all came from the north of Italy. The wild boar sauce had been cooking since that morning, which fully brought out the flavour. All this luxury, all this deliciousness, reminded Traiano of the last meal they were supposed to grant a condemned prisoner on death row in America. He could tell that there had been a subtle change in the way the six adults now related to each other. He could tell in particular that his stock was falling just as that of Renzo was rising. Renzo had seen his humiliation that morning, Renzo, who himself had been humiliated by the boss and, in accepting it, been admitted to intimacy. Now Renzo, though careful to act as if nothing had changed, clearly understood that something had changed. He was being particularly attentive to Elena, his future wife, the woman who would make him the boss's brother-in-law, and marriage to whom would link the two families. The wedding was important, but more important still were the children who would be the living embodiment of the alliance, who would have the blood of both families flowing through their veins. Traiano felt he could read Renzo's mind. He was enjoying dinner but looking forward to what would happen afterwards. The wedding would not be till October, at the earliest. He would want to impregnate her on the wedding night, and perhaps start practising that in a month or two, or even now.

In fact, this was true. He had been pestering her to risk pregnancy. She had been resisting, remembering that both Stefania and Ceccina had married whilst pregnant, and being determined not to follow their example. Elena knew he would bring this up again tonight (she too could read his mind, sense his attitude) and she knew he was ascendant in her brother's opinions, and that this could only be at the expense of Traiano. Renzo's self-confidence told the story. Elena had always liked Traiano, which was to say that she had always liked him more than her sister Assunta or her mother ever had. Her mother in particular could not hide her contempt for him, never referring to him by name, always as 'the Romanian'. She had seen him as an interloper, a foreigner, someone who was not one of them. All of these were things Elena had always been prepared to overlook, especially as she had always found Traiano very attractive, with his tight jeans and his long hair. But now she had to think of Renzo, had to think of her future husband and, if Traiano stood in his way, which seemed likely… if that were the case, she would say goodbye to him and to Ceccina without much regret. It hurt her to be selfish, as they, particularly Ceccina, had always been kind to her, but such was life.

Her brother had always had favourites. Why shouldn't Renzo become the supreme and permanent favourite? There was no stench of criminality about Renzo. He was not from the slums, but from a rich family. He was not the son of a prostitute. Should they even be sitting down to dine with the son of a prostitute?

Neither the boss's sister nor the boss's wife showed much sign of the cooling they felt towards Traiano, but he could read it in the subtle way in which he was no longer the centre of attention. Power was fleeing from him. But if this were a crisis, it was also an opportunity.

He would not stay still and let events move ahead without his participation. One had to create events. One had to act, not just react.

As he ate his quail, he reflected on the money situation. He had quite a bit in cash, some in the bank, indeed in several banks. Then he had the properties that he owned and the shares he had in the various businesses with the boss. If he were suddenly to leave, these funds would be hard to realise, but perhaps some proxy, namely his mother, might be able to do so on his behalf. He had an Italian passport, and he could go anywhere in Europe, even go back to Romania, but would he be safe? Would they send someone after him? Would he end up with a knife between the ribs, a long-distance present from Calogero, to ensure his silence? Or could he negotiate an exit, again perhaps using his mother, the only person, perhaps, whom Calogero feared? But would Calogero ever let him go?

Having asked the question, he knew the answer. Calogero never let anyone go. He never voluntarily relinquished power. You belonged to him or you died. That was all.

There were other prospects as well. He did not have a very high opinion of Renzo. Renzo was a soft boy at heart. Renzo could have killed his uncle and cousins that very day, if he had had the daring to do so. It would have been the perfect crime. The boss was right about that. But Renzo, who wanted to be a boss, did not think like one, did not see opportunities. Instead, he contemplated marriage to Elena, and hitching himself to the boss's family as his guarantee of the soft life, all handed to him on a plate, none of it to be fought for. He could kill Renzo so easily and make it look like an accident; he could ensure he had some poisoned cocaine or that he crashed his car. Or he could just kill him and let people assume that it was some discontented member of the San Lorenzo crime family that did it, even Antonio Santucci himself. He could go to Antonio Santucci, if he could find him sober, and undertake to kill Renzo for him. With Renzo out of the way, the entire group dynamic would rearrange itself.

He looked at the boss, sitting next to his new wife, and wondered whether the best thing might not be to strike there and then. He would not be expecting it. If he spoke to Gino and to Alfio and got them on board. If he undertook to do it, and then to share the proceeds. But the proceeds…. It was all tied up in the new company. One would have to deal with lawyers. He had dealt with lawyers before now. He remembered holding a gun to the lawyer Petrocchi's head to get him to sign some authorisation to buy shares in the Messina bridge company. That had not been subtle, but it had worked. One could get hold of the company with a decent lawyer on board. He owned part of the company as it was. If the boss were dead, the children being so young, who would be there to stop him? Anna Maria? But she was a woman. This was not a game for women. Of course, one could leave the company to her, and concentrate on the other sides of things, the white powder, the prostitutes, the bit of the business he knew really well. Of course, it would mean bigger shares for Alfio and Gino, and correspondingly less for him. But…. He looked at the boss. Of course, he loved him, but there was no gratitude in this game, as the boss himself had said.

As the zuppa inglese was devoured, with almost indecent haste, Elena and Renzo made their excuses, left the table and went upstairs. Anna Maria followed shortly afterwards, claiming tiredness, as did Ceccina, who could sense, he knew, that he and the boss needed to be left alone together. They went into the drawing room, and left the maid Veronica to clear the table. They sat on the sofa; after a few minutes they heard Veronica leave the dining room, and they sensed the quietness of the building.

'Are you going upstairs?' asked Traiano, looking at the whiskey glass.

'I am in no hurry,' he replied. 'What about you?'

'No need. Did my duty earlier, when we got back from Castelvetrano.'

'Both our wives are pregnant,' said Calogero. 'Why bother?'

'Why indeed?' echoed Traiano. 'Ceccina expects it; she likes it. I like it. She was too polite to notice what a battering I had taken earlier.'

'Wise woman. My father beat me…'

'And it did you no harm. You beat me, and it does me no harm,' said Traiano. 'In fact, it is reassuring. It shows you care about me, just as your father cared about you. I would be worried if you didn't. You do love me, don't you, boss?'

'Get lost!'

'That's a yes. Do you want to beat me again?'

'Get lost!'

'Another yes,' noted Traiano, letting his head rest against the boss's shoulder. 'Boss, do you want me to go to Romania and open an Italian restaurant with Ceccina?'

The boss was silent.

'Where did this idea come from?'

'She loves cooking. She would enjoy it. I can speak the language, and she would soon learn. My father is dead, thank God, so there would be no danger of running into him. I have relations there, but... It would be a new start. I am young, she is young, the children are very young. There is more to the world than Catania and prostitutes and white powder.'

'Don't talk like this,' he said at last. 'At least, not yet. Let us see what happens. There is work for you here still.'

'You mean the Colonel and the boys?'

Calogero nodded.

'I'll kill them. I will kill them all,' said Traiano.

It was very late by the time he joined Ceccina in bed, and he did not wake her.

The next day was Sunday, and the morning was all movement as they readied themselves and their children to go to Church. As was always the custom, the women and the children actually went into the Church and took part in the Mass, whereas the men stood at the back, with the exception of Renzo, who though not yet married, was very uxorious. Thus, once more, Calogero and Traiano found themselves alone and side by side. But they did not speak.

Lunch was another enormous meal. This time it was a vast timballo, roast lamb and a very good tiramisu. Anna and Alfonso had been invited and, for once, were not late. He was able to speak to his mother privately, as he had hoped, and when lunch was over, he took his stepfather up to look at the lemon trees. While the rest of them, adults and children, spilled into the various parts of the house, Anna trapped Calogero with a stare.

'He wants to go back to Romania,' she said. 'Some talk about opening an Italian restaurant there. Now his father is dead, and there's no danger meeting him… Why is he talking like this? He has never lived in Romania. He would hate it. I hated it. It's awful. What have you done to him to make him think like this?'

'I have not done anything to him,' said Calogero defensively, resentful that, with Anna, he was always on the defensive.

'We both know that is not true,' she said crisply.

'You seem to think I am a monster,' he said.

'I know you are a monster,' she replied. 'You killed your own brother. Don't try and deny it. I know you did.'

'I am surprised you don't worry I might kill you.'

She considered this.

'I don't worry about that,' she replied.

'Or your husband,' he added.

'Why should you even threaten that?' she asked. 'You know my silence is assured. I have taken the money and I have shut up. But Trajan. If something should happen to him. Then I might talk. But you know that. If you do not want him anymore, send him back to Romania. He would not bother you there. Give him what he is owed and send him on his way.'

He looked very, very cross. She saw that she had made her point.

'If you are going down the legal path, you will not need him anymore,' she reasoned. 'I have no illusions about my son. He is a criminal and a thug. Just like the others you employ. Well, if he wants to go, let him go.'

'He told you he wants to go?'

'Yes, this morning.'

Calogero was thoughtful.

They were standing by a lemon tree.

'How's the baby? My new brother or sister?' asked Traiano.

'All is well,' said Alfonso.

'I need your help,' said Traiano. 'We are blood relations now, so I trust you.'

'What do you want?' asked Alfonso.

'Your help handling Anna Maria,' said Traiano. 'Not now, but later. You have known her for how long?'

'A long time, but not well.'

'Get to know her well. Start today. Think of it as an investment in the future, the futures of us all.'

Alfonso nodded, and they walked back towards the house.

Chapter Five

It was on the Sunday night that they came for him. He was sitting at home with his wife, with his child, watching television after supper, when the doorbell sounded. She answered it. Yes, the Colonel was at home; she found him slumped in front of the television and told him that some colleagues were here to see him. He was surprised and asked her if she knew which colleagues. They were coming up in the lift, she said. They had northern accents, that was all she had caught. Anyway, she was not interested - not interested in his work anyway - though she constantly bemoaned the way work took him away at unsociable hours, especially at night; Sunday night too.

He opened the door to them, and the man and woman facing him had a grave air, which immediately alerted him to the seriousness of the moment. They had chosen Sunday night, when everything was shut, when everyone was tired, when defences were low. They presented their identity cards. He understood that they were investigating magistrates, and investigating him, perhaps. He did his best to play it cool, asking them to come in, asking them to step into the dining room. They settled into chairs. The man and the woman looked at each other. The man was the first to speak.

'Colonel Andreazza,' he said. 'We are working for a secret unit, which is secret for the very simple reason that we do not want it to be compromised by the forces that we are working to eradicate. We have reason to believe that your life is in danger. Or rather, that it will very soon be in danger. You see,' continued Silvio, watching as Chiara opened her attaché case and placed some photographs in front of him, 'We have these two people. They are already with us in a secure place. Others, perhaps, may follow. I think you recognise them?'

The photographs were of the boy Paolo and his mother Beata. Each bore a date: the day before yesterday.

'I have never seen this woman before in my life,' said Andreazza evenly.

It just happened to be true.

'Who is she?'

'She is the mother of the boy,' said Silvio. 'Do you deny knowing him?'

'He looks a bit rough to me,' said Andreazza. 'Catania is full of boys who look like that. How on earth should I recognise him? He could be anyone.'

'Sir,' said Silvio. 'This boy can give evidence that he has met you, that he was introduced to you by Trajan Antonescu, without his mother's knowledge and consent, and that certain illegal activities took place between you and him.'

'That is impossible,' said Andreazza. 'I have never met Trajan Antonescu. I have certainly never met the woman who you say is the boy's mother. Antonescu is a well-known criminal. He has never been arrested or charged with anything, but... I have never met him. I have never communicated with him. The idea that I might meet such people is just crazy. If you look through my phone records, look through my emails, you will find that I have never ever had anything to do with Antonescu.'

'Antonescu has no phone and has no email, so that is hardly surprising,' said Chiara quietly. 'But the boy has a phone, and it is full of calls to a number which has called him regularly, and which we can trace to near your house and near your place of work. Of course, we know that that is not watertight. It could have been someone else in this block. It could have been someone else in the vicinity of your work. But we could look for that phone, which has only ever called the boy's number, and if we found it in your possession, Colonel, the game would be up. Of course, we would need a search warrant, and we would have to call in a forensic team to search this flat high and low until we found it. We can do that quite easily and with little delay; turning this place upside down would not look good in your wife's eyes.'

'She has nothing to do with this,' said Andreazza quickly.

'Nothing, nothing at all,' agreed Chiara. 'Let us hope she never is involved. We could also arrest you, or have you arrested by your colleagues, for the obstruction of the course of justice. That too would not look good.'

'What?' said Andreazza.

'The Perraino case. A missing person, who is certainly dead, and certainly murdered, but whom you insist on treating as a missing person. Yes, we know there are no hard facts, no solid evidence that Perraino was murdered or is even dead, and these things have to be proved in court, which is hard. But that is not what we are talking about here. We are talking about the failure to investigate. You have let the case gather dust. Every time someone has tried to restart the investigation, it has been stalled; and each time, the person involved has been you. Yes, there have been others, but you were at each and every meeting; you are the common denominator; you are the roadblock. Oh yes, we know it is hard to prove, and it could look like a simple administrative error, of which there are many, but this was the favour you granted Antonescu. And in return for blocking the investigation, he gave you what you wanted. And now, given that the boy is talking, and given that you represent a threat to Antonescu, given that you can send him to jail, your life is in danger.'

'What has this boy said? What has he alleged?' asked Andreazza, feigning a calm he did not feel.

Silvio looked at Chiara, and she rose to leave. The door clicked behind her.

'Look,' said Silvio. 'We know what you have been up to. Men are all different. We do things that we would very much rather that our mothers, our wives, did not know. We are not wanting to spill this all over the press, the television. This boy, I have met him; he is very grown up for his age. I mean, this is Catania. A boy of twelve, as he is - though he was younger when he met you - a boy like that, the son of a prostitute, knows more than a boy of sixteen from Milan, shall we say, or a young man of twenty from London. People grow up quickly in the slums. The trouble is, not everyone will recognise that; they will see this boy as a victim. And they will see you as a monster. Moreover, once it is out, lots of other complainants will come forward; that is how it works. One shakes the tree and sees what fruit will drop. Not pleasant for you. And the truth is we do not want the whole of Italy to think you are a monster. We simply do not. What we want is Antonescu and then we want Calogero di Rienzi. You know how it works. Use a little fish to catch a bigger fish. We are offering you a deal. We are using you to catch Antonescu. And after that, we do not bother you again. This is the ministry of Grace and Justice, do not forget. Justice for Antonescu. Grace for you.'

'Grace and Justice, Sicilian style?' asked Andreazza contemptuously. 'You are as bad as them. This is blackmail. May I remind you, you have no evidence. If you did, you would have arrested me already, and I would be in a cell. This is a fishing expedition.'

'We do not want to arrest you. You are not the accused. You are a witness.'

Chiara came back into the room. They waited for her to sit down.

'You think you know a great deal about boys from the slums and their prostitute mothers. Well, so do I,' said Andreazza. 'I have been a policeman in Catania for long enough to know what these people are like. Trajan Antonescu is a boy from the slums with a prostitute mother, don't forget. These people have one characteristic they all share: They never speak. They certainly never speak to outsiders or to the police, who are outsiders. They never speak to people like you from Lombardy and from the Veneto. You are foreigners, people from another planet. They hold the ministry of Grace and Justice in contempt, if indeed they ever think about it. If you were to arrest Antonescu, he would not speak. He would prefer to go to jail than to co-operate with you. He would certainly never betray his boss, his alleged boss. And you want me to believe that this boy, whose name I do not know, has spoken to you, co-operated with you? That he trusts you? That is impossible for me to believe. Do you honestly think that these people would ever believe that you, the ministry of Grace and Justice, could offer them something that their own people cannot? Do you believe that they are more frightened of you than they are of Calogero di Rienzi? Do you think that they imagine, even for a moment, that you can protect them from Calogero if he wants to silence them? That boy will remain silent because he knows that, by remaining silent, he remains alive.'

'And what applies to them, applies to you?' asked Silvio. 'You serve them, not the Italian Republic?'

His tone expressed disbelief.

'Don't give me that hypocritical nonsense. You work in the dunghill that is Rome: no grace, no justice, no honour, nothing. You have nothing on me, nothing at all. My professional behaviour has been exemplary. My record is a good one. The Perraino case is the way it is for a variety of reasons. Shortage of manpower. The fact that no one, apart from his aunt and mother, ever liked Perraino. The fact that if we were to investigate Perraino, lots of embarrassing things might come up. The fact that we have to massage our figures. And above all, because we have better things to do. The chance of a result with the Perraino case is minimal. As you know. As for this boy, I have never met him. As for Antonescu, I have never met him.'

'You have been too discreet to let yourself be seen with him,' said Chiara mildly. 'You have met him.'

'And this boy that you have got hold of, he has not spoken. His mother may have done, but she is not a witness to anything. If she tells you some man was interfering with her son, that could mean any man. Not me. Certainly not me.'

'We have offered you a lifeline,' said Chiara.

'No. You have offered me a rope with which to hang myself.'

'Would you like to accompany us to then station to make a statement?' asked Silvio.

'No. I would not,' said Andreazza. 'It is Sunday night. If you want a statement from me, you can come to my office tomorrow morning.'

There was silence for some time. Andreazza waited. No silence had ever felt so long. If they were going to arrest him, now was when they would do so. But the seconds, which felt like minutes, ticked by. He saw them exchange glances. It was clear that they had failed, that they were not going to arrest him. But he did not let his guard slip. The boy, as he had bet - and what a bet it was - had not spoken. The mother had. But not the boy. Because they had mentioned the boy Paolo, but not the other boy, the younger one, Nino. That meant Paolo had not spoken, not told the whole story, he was sure. It meant he was safe, for the moment, though there were definite perils ahead. He had no illusions that these people from the Ministry of Grace and Justice would now do their utmost to have their revenge, and that they would never forgive him for his lack of co-operation. But he had Traiano to protect him. He had called their bluff.

After a moment, the visitors got up to leave.

'We shall meet again,' said Chiara.

'No doubt,' he replied easily, as he showed them to the door.

When they were gone, feeling pleased with himself, he went and locked himself in the bathroom. Just in case they returned with a search warrant, he took the small mobile he used to call the boy Paolo, and removed the SIM card, which he chopped up with nail clippers and then threw down the lavatory, pulling the chain, checking that the fragments had disappeared. Then he went to rejoin his wife, who was in the sitting room, watching the television.

'I thought they would never leave,' she said.

'Me neither,' he replied.

'What on earth did they want?' she asked. 'On a Sunday night too?'

'Some case they think can't wait until Monday morning. I told them it could. Nothing important.'

She then began to recount the bits of the film that he had missed.

On their return from the weekend at Donnafugata, Traiano decided that it might be nice to go for a pizza and invite Alfio and Giuseppina and Gino and Catarina to join himself and Ceccina. After spending the weekend in exalted company, it would be a good idea to remind these close associates that they had not been forgotten, and that despite the invitation to Donnafugata, he and Ceccina were faithful to their origins. As with all these trips to the pizzeria, they had the private room to themselves, and the long table took up its usual arrangement: the three men sat at one end, the three women at the other, and the children either sat in the middle or gravitated to some parental lap.

Catarina and Giuseppina were very keen to hear everything about Donnafugata, the house, the food, and above all, what she was like, and when she would be coming to Catania. She was, after all, now his wife, something that Giuseppina found hard to accept; but one assumed she would not, on grounds of taste, step into what had been Stefania's house, and would wait until the summer was over and the new flat ready. Indeed, was she going to come to Catania, or would she stay where she was, and the boss go to her? It was all very unclear. And the children, the children, they seemed to like her a great deal, Ceccina reported, conscious that this might upset Giuseppina. But Giuseppina said she was glad: if they were to have a stepmother, it was best they have an affectionate one. And if they were to have a stepmother, it was best they have one who was both rich and well-connected too. She knew what this meant. Her sister's children were destined to rise through this connection. Catarina was more down to earth. The boss would not dare bring his new wife to Catania, simply because he was frightened of his mother. Nor would the new wife want to come, for, if she had any sense, she would be frightened of her too. Giuseppina laughed. It was true the signora and Stefania had never got on, but she found her surprisingly kind, and she was a very good cook. Ah, the food. Ceccina then gave an account of exactly what they had eaten at Donnafugata. This was of immense interest.

At the other end of the table, talk was of business, and conducted in low, subdued voices. They had known each other for many years; they had worked together; they knew each other; they were supposed by all to be close friends, though Traiano did not particularly like or trust Alfio. Alfio had always done what he was told, and had always accepted the authority of the boss and of Traiano, by several years the younger man. It was true that Alfio and Gino had both quailed before Traiano's belt, and both had the scars to prove it. But Traiano now suspected Alfio of being greedy and ambitious. If he married Giuseppina, as he surely would, this would make him the boss's children's uncle, make him a member of the family. And if he never had children, which was surely likely, all his energies would be channelled into getting closer to the boss. As for Gino, a man whose only recommendation was his brute strength and his seeming willingness to do whatever was asked of him without question, he had never liked him either. It occurred to him now that perhaps Gino did not like him either; he had never really considered what or whom Gino might or might not like. But it was now necessary to reinforce relations, he felt; one had to cultivate people, lest they feel neglected. He was aware, for example, that he was richer than they were, and that their women might sharpen their consciousness of this. One had to smooth things over, flatter egos, make sure that one was not later to encounter trouble in either quarter. One day he might need Alfio or Gino, or both.

Oddly the conversation between the men was on domestic matters at first. Gino was curious about the new wife. Alfio wanted to know whether the new wife was pleased with her conquest. Traiano said that there was no indication of that, and the marriage, the clandestine marriage, was not spoken of. The children still did not know.

Alfio nodded and looked sulky.

'Giuseppina is not happy,' he said. 'As you can imagine.'

Gino looked guarded.

Traiano sighed with sympathy.

'I am not surprised that Giuseppina is not happy about it,' he said.

Alfio nodded.

'The boss can marry whom he wants, and it is rather soon, I know, but this signora Tancredi had had his child, truly I understand. But Giuseppina, and the rest of her family, they feel that it is too soon after the death of Stefania. Not even three months. And they feel too that they should have been told, that he should have asked them, that he should have explained himself. But in fact, they found out from you, not even from the boss himself.'

'You know what he is like,' said Traiano. 'He doesn't feel he owes anyone an explanation. He is the boss. He does not consult anyone; he does what he likes.'

'Well, he does owe some people an explanation: his wife's family and his own children,' said Alfio decisively. 'Giuseppina is really offended. It is as if it were all my fault. I have heard of nothing else. And then this trip to Donnafugata. Why wasn't she invited? Why was Elena? OK, she is his sister, but he never cared much about her before now.'

'Well, she is marrying Renzo….' said Traiano.

'And we are now going to take orders from him? He is a kid, for God's sake. Yes, I know, you are younger than any of us, but you know what is what, you have done stuff. What does Renzo know?'

Traiano looked at Gino.

'You were teaching him to fight, weren't you?'

'Yeah, but,' said Gino. 'If you need lessons in how to fight, it is a sign that, well, you are never going to learn. Did you have lessons? Neither did I, neither did Alfio.' He paused. 'Is the boss pleased with him?'

'Oh yes. He is the way in to the world of Palermo, you see. Like the wife.'

'What is wrong with Catania?' asked Alfio.

'Quite a bit, it seems,' said Traiano. 'At least the boss seems to think so.'

'Catarina tells me that Ceccina told her that you went to Castelvetrano,' said Gino.

'We did,' said Traiano. 'Not a good trip. If only we had acted swiftly. But I was in the car outside for the first part of the visit, and the boss and Renzo went in. I regret it now, very much, not being there. You see, Antonio Santucci had just fired a gun at his elder son, and missed. He was dead drunk. The housekeeper was most alarmed, poor woman. Antonio is off his head. If I had been there, walking into that situation, I would have done the job there and then: shot Antonio and the two boys and made it look as if he had killed them and then himself. The perfect murder. But by the time I turned up, the moment was lost. One has to seize the moment. But the boss thinks it is not worth killing Antonio or his sons as none of them are a threat, nor are they likely to be in the future. He has a point. But I am tidy. I would have liked to have taken all three out. But the boss says no, and has persuaded Renzo as well.'

'I was looking forward to that,' said Gino. 'I needed the money. I still do.'

'I need the money too,' said Alfio.

'I have bad news, I am afraid,' said Traiano. 'The boss will tell you himself, soon, perhaps. He wants to shut down the prostitutes. He wants to clean the place up. He wants to make it a little more respectable. So that means a lot less money for all of us. But the thing that affects you two the most is this: He is now married to the aunt of the man you killed, that policeman, Fabrizio Perraino. Right now, Perraino is not officially dead, as you know. That is because of Colonel Andreazza dragging his feet and making sure that Perraino is treated as a missing person - not a dead one. Andreazza does that because he comes to the pizzeria and is introduced to a little bit of what he likes. He is a pervert of the very worst sort, but it suits us. The boss wants me to get rid of the kids who service Andreazza, and get rid of Andreazza. He says that sort of thing will ruin our reputation, and have a negative impact on the Furnaces, the first stage of which, as you know, is coming to completion.'

'Thanks to us,' said Alfio.

'Thanks to us,' said Gino.

'Thanks to us,' echoed Traiano.

'You told him….' said Alfio.

'Of course I did. I said the girls are the lifeblood of this place. And that we never allowed ourselves to get cold feet about certain things we might not have approved of. If they want it, and they pay, we do not make judgements. He was not happy. Indeed, he was very angry. He whacked me with his belt.'

'Badly?'

He showed them, lifting his shirt a little. The bruises were now at their worst.

'Jesus!' said Gino.

'Holy Mary!' said Alfio.

There was a long silence.

'He needs to see reason,' said Alfio.

'Any idea how?' asked Traiano.

'We can always make money somehow or another,' said Alfio. 'But if the police designate Perraino as a murder victim and start asking questions, at best, we will never have a moment's peace, at worst, we will both go down for a very long time. He was a policeman. They don't like that. My God, I can't even remember why we killed him.'

'We did not like him. That had something to do with it,' said Traiano.

'We need Andreazza,' said Alfio, 'and if he needs little boys, then we must do whatever it takes. What has made the boss think like this?'

'Don Giorgio received a complaint and passed it on to the boss. The Archbishop of Catania was told, who told the Cardinal, who told the boss's new wife.'

'Who has been talking?' said Gino. 'Because they do not like that sort of thing, and it could turn nasty for you.'

'It must be the boy's mother. The one who drinks crème de menthe. Beata.'

'I know her,' said Gino. 'We all know her.'

There was silence.

'She would not be a problem,' said Alfio. 'Me and Gino could sort her out. We go up there and we dangle the boy out of the window by his ankles. That would work. We would not threaten her; we would threaten him. And Beata has started sleeping with Amilcare. We threaten him if she misbehaves.'

'Getting them to shut up would not be difficult. Other people have been shut up before now. They know, generally, where their interest lies,' said Traiano. 'But the boss wants a radical solution. Kill the lot. The child, the mother, the other child, Andreazza. That way, no one speaks. And clear out all the prostitutes. He wants to be respectable.'

'And once you get rid of the prostitutes, you get rid of the pimps, the enforcers, and shortly after that you get rid of the cocaine too, I bet. And we are left without a job,' said Alfio. 'It could not come at a worse time. The wedding is costing me a fortune. I have said to Giuseppina that we don't have to spend that much, but she will not listen. She remembers what her sister had; she remembers what you had, Traiano, and what you had, Gino. She wants to outspend the lot. Very soon, I am going to end up in debt. The boss has always been generous, but…'

'If we had a few major jobs,' said Gino. 'That would bring in the cash. But here we are, ready and willing to do what is necessary, and there is no one to work on.'

'What we need is to speak to the boss, or for you to speak to the boss. Try and get him to be more reasonable,' said Alfio to Traiano.

'I have tried and I will try again,' said Traiano. 'But the truth is that he is taking his new path, with the new wife, into these business ventures, and he is not going to have much more use for me. I have been speaking to my mother, and I have mentioned it to the boss, just so you know…. I am thinking of leaving, going back to Romania, with Ceccina and the children, starting afresh there.'

There was silence.

'Ceccina wants to go?' asked Gino.

'If I want to go, she will go too,' said Traiano. 'But we are only talking about it at present. The boss needs to consent. He is not happy with the idea. But….'

'If you want to go….' said Alfio.

'He may not let me,' said Traiano. 'I know too much. He may feel I would be a worry to him far away in Romania.'

'Does he still trust you?' asked Gino.

'I don't know,' said Traiano.

The waiter came with the first pizzas. It wasn't Amilcare. Traiano called the boy over and asked him to fetch Amilcare. As the next tranche of pizzas arrived, Amilcare arrived with them, looking uncertain, looking, it seemed to them, not merely nervous, but frightened.

'Boss, there is something I have to tell you,' he said, before Traiano could speak to him, anxious lest he be accused of holding something back. 'Beata and her son have gone.'

'Gone where?' he asked calmly.

'I don't know,' he replied. 'They said nothing. They just disappeared. She did not tell me she was planning on going away. She just went.'

Traiano was silent.

'She won't get far, worry not,' he said, cutting into his pizza and taking a swig of coke. 'Make sure you hang around and are free when I want to speak to you, OK? Don't get lost, you hear me? You can go.' He caught the eye of the other waiter, who came over. 'Send someone to find Tonino Grassi, and get him to wait for me when I have finished here. I will need him later.'

The conversation continued. They spoke of the Furnaces, in which the criminal part of the enterprise was nearing completion. Everyone had either sold or was selling. The whole area was now in the boss's hands, or more accurately, in the hands of the company that the boss had set up; now it awaited development, which would be slow. First of all, the toxic wasteland would have to be cleared and the area landscaped. The canal would have to be dredged and restored; the huge amount of building rubble and rusting metal and general detritus would have to be cleared. Luckily, the boss had bought a disused quarry which was licensed to be used as landfill, and a company that did earthworks of the kind needed. As for the stuff that needed brute force, the immigrants were there for that. The boss had run up huge debts with all this outlay, all underpinned with various loans, but the good news was that much of the expenditure could be paid in cash, particularly to the immigrants, and cash was something of which they had plenty. The Furnaces was one vast money laundering scheme. The quarry and its landfill opened up new possibilities for making people disappear. Landfill swallowed corpses almost as well as the sea.

Traiano sighed. He loved his wife, he said, looking at her down the table, and he loved his children, and that meant one had to love the relations as well: her parents, her uncles, her aunts, her grandparents, and all the cousins. The children adored their relations. If only they could find someone for her sister Pasqualina. She was such a good girl.

Gino and Alfio smiled at this. Corrado, Gino's brother, had spoken of coming to visit soon. He had never shown such interest in Catania, but since the wedding, where he had met Pasqualina.... He asked Gino about his brother. Gino shrugged and admitted that his brother was OK.

They finished the pizzas, and then the ice-cream and other delights arrived, and there was a general shifting around of seats. Traiano, by design, found himself between Catarina and Giuseppina. He liked Giuseppina. She was a nice girl, quite unlike her sister Stefania who had been rather too ambitious for his liking. But there was no doubt that Giuseppina was one of them; she was marrying Alfio, after all. Unless he was wrong about that, it was not such an ambitious choice, at least not on her part. As for Catarina, she was ambitious and clever, and he rather feared her.

'How is the boss's godchild?' he asked.

'You are arranging that?' she asked.

'Absolutely. And your new house. Though I doubt it will be in time for the birth. Either your birth or Ceccina's. The people doing up the new place for the boss are so slow.'

'How is the boss?' she asked.

'Doesn't your husband tell you?'

'He does not; besides, I doubt that he is as observant as you.'

'The boss… He is hard to read. He is happy. But things like happiness do not really apply to him. He has married her, but it is hard to see how that will work out. She is twenty years his senior. Of course, they have a child, and another on the way, and he has three with Stefania, but he will want more. He wants lots of children, just like me.'

'Your wife may get bored of it,' said Catarina.

'She wants as many as I do,' said Traiano. 'I know her.'

'This new wife, what does she want?' asked Catarina.

'Oh him, of course. She is very keen on him. She has had lots of lovers before this, I have heard. Now she has him. But whether she keeps his interest is another thing. Or whether she maintains hers. She likes younger men.'

'Well, our boss is certainly that. How much younger can she go?' asked Catarina.

Traiano smiled.

Outside, in the early summer night, he saw Amilcare watch them depart, and he spotted Tonino waiting in the square. He walked the family home and helped Ceccina put the children to bed. Then, some twenty minutes later, he returned to the pizzeria. Crossing the square of the Church of the Holy Souls in Purgatory, he gestured Tonino to approach.

'You did some good work,' he said cheerily to the fourteen-year-old. 'In the Furnaces, I mean. You will do some more here tonight, I hope. But for now, I just want you to watch and pay attention.'

They walked to the pizzeria, and waited outside, in full view of the place. Inside, Amilcare saw them, spoke to the manager, and was dismissed for the night without question. He stepped out into the street, feeling the eyes of everyone upon him. It was clear he was frightened, but not of what. The other pizzeria employees, seeing that it was Amilcare that was summoned, not them, looked relieved, and instinctively looked away from the condemned man. It was as if he were already a dead man, consigned to oblivion.

Amilcare stepped into the street and approached.

'You are sure they have gone?' asked Traiano.

'Yes, boss. I went to the flat, and I was able to get in easily enough, and everything was gone. Not that there was much to take. But they have left. That is clear. And in a hurry, I would say, because the place was not tidy.'

Traiano nodded.

'Just wait around in the bar, and I will see you later,' he said. He turned to Tonino. 'Come with me,' he said.

They left the square and went along one of the narrow rubbish-strewn streets. They came at length to a street door, where he rang the bell. At length, because it was late, it was answered. They went up. At the door of the flat they sought stood a worried looking woman in her night clothes.

'I am sorry to be here so late, signora,' said Traiano, apologetically. 'But it can't wait until the morning. Is Nino in bed? You had better wake him. Ah, there he is,' he said, seeing the child behind her, standing there in his underwear, roused from bed.

They went into the flat, and sat at the table. The signora said nothing, but was attentive.

'Your husband,' began Traiano. 'You know we have been looking out for him. By the way, this is Tonino, whose father is in the same place. Not a nice place, Ucciardone. We have heard that your husband may have upset some of the wrong people. This won't hurt him, of course, as he has friends in Ucciardone, we have made sure of that. But sometimes these nasty people come calling on the family of the man inside. But don't worry, I don't want you to worry. This is a precaution. I want you to go away.'

'Where?' asked the signora.

'You have relations on the continent?'

'I have a brother in Milan, and a sister in Pordenone.'

'Then you need to go and stay with them, and tell no one you are going there. When it is safe, you can come back. It may be you can come back in a couple of weeks. I will let you know when. Write down the number of your brother and your sister and give them to Tonino here. Now there is a train to Rome at eleven and, if you hurry, you can catch it. Tonino will walk with you to the station. Nino,' he said to the boy, 'You are big now, aren't you? You can help your mother, and you can make sure she does not worry, can't you?'

Nino nodded. Then he asked a question.

'Where is Paolo?' he asked.

'Somewhere safe, but don't worry about him. Now, your mother has plenty to do, so I am going to give you something to do.' He was wearing his jacket, and out of it he took a wad of notes that he had taken from his own house, with just this in mind. 'Now let's count it,' he said, watching the boy's widening eyes, and noting too the mother's interest. 'These are fifties, OK?' He counted them out. 'How much does that make? Correct. Five thousand. Now put them in a safe place, because you will need it for the train fare and for the presents you will buy in Pordenone and Milan.' He looked at the mother. 'Is he a good boy, signora?'

'Very,' she said. 'He always does what he is told, and he does not ask questions. Not like some boys.'

'Good,' said Traiano. 'Tonino will walk with you to the station and help you onto the train. Don't miss it. Have you been on a train?' he asked Nino. 'You have? But not at night, I bet. Now, goodbye, for now at least, and remember to obey your mother. Remember what happens to bad boys.'

'What happens to bad boys?' asked Nino.

'Tell him, Tonino.'

'They get the belt,' said Tonino.

He kissed the child, he shook hands with the signora, he told Tonino he would see him later, and then he disappeared.

He walked back to the square. There, as he expected, was Amilcare, waiting for him, worried. He looked at him for a moment in silence. Then he spoke.

'Amilcare, you know I am a fair person, and that provided that people are grateful for what I do for them, then I have no problem with them. You have not had a taste of my belt, have you?'

'No, boss,' he said, barely able to speak.

'Look, I know that you were sleeping with this woman, and that you had some sort of altercation. People were talking about it. She threw you out into the street, and you were in the street with your clothes around you, wearing just your underpants. What the hell happened there? And why did I find out about it indirectly, not from you?'

'It was private, boss,' Amilcare managed to say.

Traiano slapped him hard on the cheek. Amilcare whimpered.

'Nothing is private,' said Traiano. 'You had better tell me what happened, and tell me now.'

'The mirror fell off the wall in the middle of the night. We all woke up. Behind the mirror, that was where the boy was putting the money she did not know about. She forced it out of the boy, and then she asked me if I knew, and she threw me out.'

'Ah,' said Traiano. 'So you told her about what Paolo got up to in the pizzeria and what he was paid for? Perhaps you mentioned the name of Colonel Andreazza. And perhaps other things you overheard or saw?'

Amilcare nodded in mute fear. He tried to enunciate some sort of apology.

'Shut up,' commanded Traiano. 'Give me your phone.'

He was unfamiliar with phones, though he had seen his wife use one often enough. He scrolled through the messages and the phone calls. It was as he suspected. Dating from a couple of days back, endless messages to Beata asking where she was, what had become of her; the record of more than sixty phone calls, none of which had been answered. The messages grew in desperation.

'It says here that you want to die because Beata has left you,' said Traiano with a sigh. 'But you know, Amilcare, she is not worth it, and that boy of hers is a nasty creature. There are lots of other women like her, so do not despair. Or are you in love with her?'

Amilcare was mute in his misery.

'Look, Amilcare, I am trying to be kind here,' explained Traiano with patience. 'You need to think about what is in your interest and the interest of your family, your two brothers and your parents. Your brothers are good boys, aren't they? Well then, think of them, and think of yourself and realise this: Your interests coincide with mine. We are all better off without Beata. Do try and grasp that. Look, I am not going to hurt you. But you need to do what I say. If Beata gets in touch with you, I want to hear about it immediately. Now think. Where could she have gone?'

'I don't know,' was the desperate answer.

'Who does she know? Has she gone back to Poland? Has she any friends?'

Traiano listened patiently for any information that might emerge. It did, little by little. She had family in Gdansk, but she hated them. The boy's father, she had had no contact with for a very long time; she cannot have gone to any of her relations. She had some friends in Palermo, but they were not close friends. The boy's only friends were in the quarter. The boy was friendly with other boys and with the girl called Lydia.

Traiano had heard of the girl Lydia, he had heard Paolo speak about her. That was a possible lead.

'If the woman gets in touch, I want to hear about it. If the boy gets in touch, I want to hear about it. Let us hope they do, for your sake. Let us hope you are able to find them before I lose patience. Understood?'

A noise from Amilcare seemed to signify that he did.

'And if you tell anyone that I am looking for the woman or the boy, I will not be pleased. Remember your parents and your two brothers. You need to protect them, to keep them safe.

And don't tell anyone that I have even spoken to you about this. And remember another thing: you cannot run away, there is nowhere to run to. Understood?'

'I understand,' he said. 'Boss,' he added.

He dismissed him and watched him go. He wished he could breathe a sigh of relief, but knew this would be premature. Indeed, the conversation might bear fruit, but it was unlikely. The woman might get in touch with Amilcare; the boy might do so; but this was a slim chance, a very slim chance. They had fled, and were under police protection; unless they were complete fools, a possibility which he did not discount, they would make sure they were never heard of again. But sometimes people could never bring themselves to leave a place without saying goodbye; without giving some reason; without making some excuse. It was just possible that they might get in touch with Amilcare, though this felt like clutching at straws. In addition, he was not quite sure that Amilcare understood the threat he was under. There was something not quite right about Amilcare. As for the boy Nino, that did not worry him so much. If he could take care of Paolo and his mother, in fact just Paolo, Nino would never dare say anything. Paolo was the key to ensuring silence. The same would work for Andreazza. Once Paolo was gone, there would be no case against Andreazza, who could deny everything. It all hinged on the boy.

Wherever Paolo and Beata were, it was somewhere designed to make it impossible for them to be reached. Of that he was absolutely sure. But equally, he knew that they could not be kept in a high security fortress for the rest of their lives. One day, they had to emerge. Then they would make a mistake, and he would get them. That had to happen. He was counting on it. But when would it happen? As it was, for the first time in his life, he was worried. Would the boy talk? Would the woman? Would Andreazza? Were they coming to arrest him? Were they getting a case ready?

Perhaps one day the police would arrive and take him away. But not just yet. The police case was not quite watertight, he thought, whatever it might be, if it depended on the word of Paolo. The boy Paolo would be the strong part of the case, he thought, because he had real evidence, if he spoke. But the weak part was Andreazza who, he was sure, would squirm and squirm before they extracted anything useful out of him. Had they spoken to Andreazza? He knew that he had to find out.

Tonino came into the square. Judging by the time, he had put Nino and his mother on the train and watched them leave. That was one relief. Nino and his mother knew what was what; and Paolo had not told the police about Nino, that was clear, otherwise the police would have seized the younger boy too.

He heard what Tonino had to say. They had left; the train was heading north. The tickets had been bought with cash. He nodded.

'I have more work for you. First of all, I want you to think very carefully. You knew Paolo, didn't you? Was there anyone he was close to? Anyone he might contact now he has gone away?'

Tonino thought. He mentioned the names of several boys Paolo played football with. But none of these were particular friends.

'There was a girl,' he said. 'Her name is Lydia.'

'I know her,' said Traiano. 'You may do too. You may know her mother, I think. She goes with men. The daughter, Lydia, she goes with boys, if they pay the mother.'

He spoke with disapproval of this.

'Do you know her?' he asked.

'A bit, boss,' admitted Tonino.

'She liked Paolo?'

'He said so. He liked her, I think. I am sure he went with her. He boasted that he had.'

'Then he may try to get in touch with her. Meanwhile, you get friendly and ask her if he does so. But be subtle. Can you be subtle?'

'I can try, boss.'

He took some money out of his pocket without looking at it and passed it on to the boy. Tonino looked at it briefly, before putting it in his pocket. Two fifty-euro notes. His mother would be pleased.

'Meanwhile, keep an eye on Amilcare, and let him know you are keeping an eye on him. Don't let him relax. And another thing. In the morning, first thing, you need to go to an address in the city, and wait outside the door for Colonel Andreazza. You will recognise him. He will come out to go to work, and you need to speak to him, discreetly, and tell him I need to see him; then come back and tell me where he wants to see me. If he seems doubtful, tell him he *does* want to see me. I am going to bed soon, but come up to my flat and wake me up when you have seen him and when you have a time and place. Let me sleep, but give me good notice. OK?'

'Yes, boss,' said Tonino.

He was as good as his word. He came to the flat at five that afternoon, to announce that the Colonel, who had been surprised to see him, would be in the Collegiate Church on Via Etnea at 6pm, attending the evening Mass. And so it turned out. There was Andreazza sitting at the back of the Church, while the business of the Mass went on at the altar. Coming in, Traiano saw him at once, genuflected and then knelt at a bench behind him, slightly to his left.

'Good evening,' he began, politely.

Andreazza did not turn, recognising the voice.

'You have almost ruined everything,' he said in a fierce whisper. 'If I had not kept my head, everything would be over by now.'

An old lady, intent on the Mass, looked round with a severe look on her face. Seeing Andreazza, she meditated a rebuke for talking in Church, but thought better of it, getting up and moving a few benches forward.

'The magistrates came. They were bluffing. They have Paolo, but he has not talked. If he had, I would be in jail, and so would you.'

'So that is where he has gone, him and his dear mother. I thought so,' said Traiano. 'Do you know where they are holding him?'

'Of course not! I cannot even ask, as that would make me look very suspicious.'

'But you must hear people whisper about these places.'

'The Castle of the Women, that is what they call it. That is the term they use for the safe place they have for these people, the protected witnesses. What the hell that means, I have no idea.'

'Interesting,' said Traiano. 'It means Caltanisetta, of course. But this is a big island and Caltanisetta is a big province. Could be anywhere. But I will find out. Do not worry. Do not panic. Besides, the boy knows very little of importance. The woman, the same. And that boy will not speak. He hates them as much as I do. He is a proper Sicilian, like me. And you know the one person he loves more than any other? No, not you. Me. And his mother has intervened. He will not forgive her. He must be repenting his repentance already. As for the magistrates, they will regret it. They have the most useless witnesses on their hands and the expense and trouble of keeping them safe. And let me tell you this, Andreazza. When it turns out those witnesses were not so safe, that the Italian Republic could not protect them after all, that will be the biggest triumph. The state thinks it has power, does it? That power is an illusion. There are no safe places where we are concerned. Understood? Castle of the Women or not, however high the walls are, we will get them. They have set us a challenge, and it is a matter of honour for me to meet this challenge.'

'You sound very confident, but I doubt you will succeed,' said Andreazza.

'Who are these magistrates?'

'Silvio Pierangeli and Chiara di Donato. I know nothing about them. They are simply names. That is, I suppose, the point. Northerners. Those may not even be their real names.'

'And you did not think of giving them what they wanted?' asked Traiano. 'Your co-operation?'

'You bastard,' said Andreazza. 'How could I? I have too much to lose.'

He did not turn, but he could sense Traiano smirking. A moment later, he felt that he had left the Church, and a slight breeze, as the door closed, confirmed it.

It was the month of June, and one day, suddenly, as it often did, the stifling heat of full summer arrived. Having enjoyed beautiful warm weather, the city of Catania was now transformed into an oven which, after a few days, became intolerable. The school holidays were already in sight, and those who could, fled the city for the weekend, and those who could not. stayed where they were, suffering under the haze of heat and pollution. During the day, the immigrant men and the immigrant women worked under the boiling sun at the Furnaces, clearing debris, which was loaded into trucks and taken away to landfill, to the sound of huge earth movers which were levelling the land and restoring the canal to its pristine and original condition. Traiano was there at dawn, when work started, when the day was at its coolest, and don Calogero was often with him, and they watched the former wasteland take shape. The first signs that the place was developing was the sight of a beautiful young woman, wearing tight jeans and wellington boots, who came to oversee the planting of the trees that would eventually stand between the houses and the blocks of flats. A lot of rubble from the demolished buildings was being used for the foundations of the planned tree-lined roads. The young woman complemented her wellington boots with a totally unnecessary hard hat, something which brought about an inexplicable desire in several men to adopt the same headgear. If it looked good on her - and by God and Saint Agatha, it did look good on her - perhaps it would look good on them too. Even Alfio and Gino came out to the Furnaces very early in the morning to see what the fuss was about, and duly stood at a distance and appreciated her beauty, her long dark hair, her perfect figure, her wide apart eyes, her long eye lashes. They opined that she knew she was being watched and appreciated.

'Oh Jesus!' said Alfio, 'Look at her. How beautiful!'

'Oh Mary!' said Gino. 'Look at her. I can tell that she wants it!'

But the young lady continued her work, oblivious to the admiration and looks she aroused. She concentrated serenely on the planting of oleanders, pines, ficus and bougainvilleas. She gave efficient and clear instructions to the men, who dug the holes, placed the mature plants in them, and tamped them down. When the sun rose higher, and she retreated from the field, she stopped for a cup of coffee at the mobile canteen and took her refreshment with the calm of one who loved landscaping and nature above all things. By this time, Alfio and Gino were long gone, and only Traiano was there, contemplating the brown land that was to be transformed and win their fortune. They conversed, politely. Her name was Gabriella Bonelli.

When night fell, some truce was granted by the unrelenting heat. At midday, the streets were deserted; at midnight, they were full. Calogero di Rienzi alone perhaps was not bothered by the heat as his flat, the only one in the quarter to be so, was air conditioned, one of the luxuries installed by his late wife. His children, accompanied by his sister Elena or his former sister-in-law Giuseppina, and occasionally his mother, would come out for exercise when the sun was down, either to walk to the Villa Bellini, or to walk up and down the Etnea, or to perambulate in their own square, outside the Church of the Holy Souls, in order to take the air. When the holidays came, then they would go to Donnafugata, they were promised, to be guests of Anna Maria Tancredi and to see dear little Sebastiano. They were longing to go to Donnafugata, which was so nice; but at the same time, they enjoyed these hot early summer nights, walking with one of their aunts or their grandmother, meeting so many people in the quarter, all of whom either knew them, or were their friends, or were related to them and their friends. They all asked the same question: how was their father, how was don Calogero? A question asked with sympathy, after all the poor man had lost his wife in horrific circumstances only in February, and it was now June, and concern, as he had hardly been seen since. It struck Isabella, and it struck Natalia (Renato was too young to be aware) that all these people cared about their beloved father, which was very nice indeed. And their aunts and their grandmother, they thought the same thing, though in different ways.

In addition, for Isabella and Natalia, there were all the other youngsters to be seen, of whom they had not seen enough. Isabella looked in vain for the boy Paolo, hoping to see him, remembering seeing him at the wedding of Gino and Catarina; she wondered where he had got to; but she saw Tonino Grassi whom she did not know at all, and noticed the very respectful way he spoke to her aunts and in particular to her grandmother, all of whom knew his mother. Tonino was interesting to both Aunt Elena and Aunt Giuseppina, both of whom seemed pleased to see him. Indeed, even their grandmother seemed pleased to see Tonino. A nice boy, she called him. And he was. Big for his age, though not tall, but well built in Isabella's eyes, one of their own, as her grandmother put it, a boy from the quarter, though it was a pity, she added, that he spent so much time with that Romanian, which was how she referred to the man the girls called Uncle Traiano, even though he was not a relation. But he felt like one. It was nice to have an uncle. They missed Uncle Rosario; and they missed their mother but, and this was the thing, there were other distractions now, now that summer and the good weather were here. There was Anna Maria; there was the house in Donnafugata; there was Sebastiano; there was the prospect of long school holidays; and there were boys to meet as well. Isabella remembered Beppe Santucci, seen just once in Palermo. She wondered when she would see him again; perhaps at the wedding when Aunt Elena married Uncle Renzo, his cousin. But that was far ahead.

As Elena walked through the quarter, meeting various friends, with her nieces in tow, and carrying her small nephew or pushing him in his chair, this was the other topic, apart from her brother, that people wanted to discuss. The wedding. The truth was, they could not be sure of a date, even now. Her brother's recent bereavement, she explained, trying not to be ironical about it, as she knew that he was already remarried, even if few others did; that was one cause of delay. The other factor causing uncertainty was the fact that the cousin of Renzo, don Lorenzo Santucci, was unwell. Yes, it was cancer, and he was old, but he was being treated, and the latest news was that they expected him to recover and be well enough to come for the wedding, so that meant the wedding would take place when don Lorenzo was up to it. And then, and then, there were her own misgivings, of which she did not speak. She was not blind to her prospective husband's faults. She knew about his cocaine use, and she was coming to accept that it could not be cured, but had to be tolerated. She was realistic about that. But it was not a good thing to take into a marriage. The way he made love to her had, at first, flattered and pleased her, but now left her rather unmoved. But these things, one could accept. They were his limitations. It was her own limitations that troubled her. She had wanted to marry a man she could love passionately; and here she was settling for Renzo instead. It was rather demoralising to be faced with this revelation of one's own calculating nature. She wanted a husband; she wanted a rich husband; she wanted an influential husband who would increase her standing in the family, with her brother, with her mother (who liked Renzo for some reason) and her sister Assunta; and a husband who would bring with him some standing in the world of men. She knew what was what. She had seen her sister-in-law Anna Maria, and she knew that men needed women who could, like Assunta, run offices, be accountants and bankers, deal with all the legal things that people like the Romanian and Gino and Alfio could not. In the end. these people, people like herself, would be infinitely more powerful that people like Traiano. If it came to a choice between romance and power, then she chose power.

Like her brother, she was attuned to the idea of power and all its delicate shifts and balances, and she knew that these questions about his welfare conveyed an undercurrent of concern. The people of the quarter knew that he had not shown his face for some time, and this worried them. They liked Calogero much more than they liked Traiano, or Gino and Alfio, or any other of his associates. They liked the boss and seeing him, dealing with him directly and not through intermediates. Like all people everywhere, they wanted everything to continue as before, to be normal. Calogero was their normality. It was a pity about Stefania, and it was worrying about Anna Maria, for they all knew about Donnafugata, though they did not know about the marriage, only the child, and then only the first one, for the rumours that circulated were incomplete. But there was a feeling that the boss needed to reassert control; the king needed to emerge from isolation; that all was not well.

Indeed, all was not well. Elena could sense it, though perhaps Giuseppina did not notice, perhaps her mother did not either. And what was not well was somehow summed up by the news of the disappearance of the boy Paolo and his mother Beata. The disappearance of a prostitute and her son would not normally have come to Elena's attention, for she did not associate with that sort of person, not at all. But the disappearance was a fact that could not be hidden, that had created waves, made a disturbance in the quarter. One day Beata had been there, drinking crème de menthe; and the boy had been there, playing football in the square; then suddenly no more. Moreover, their flat, their single squalid room, had been abandoned, clearly in a hurry. Most of their possessions, meagre as they might have been, had been left behind, it was said; their clothes, their toothbrushes, everything. Neither of them were answering their phones. Beata's clients had rung, had messaged, and had received no reply. The boy too had had a phone, and from this too there had been no reply. So, what had happened? Their sudden and complete disappearance created space for fertile rumour. Had they been murdered? Had they fled from some terrible threat, some debt collector, leaving no forwarding address? Had one of the associates of don Calogero, their landlord, got rid of them? But evictions were public events. This had been clandestine. Had they discovered something? The men who had known Beata wondered what knowledge she had gained which had caused her to flee. They wondered if they who had known her were in some sort of unsuspected trouble too.

This came to Elena through her niece Natalia, who had said that Isabella was soft on Paolo. Elena herself remembered the child, a small but sturdy lad with blue eyes and an abundance of blond hair, unusual in Catania. She remembered Beata, and the crème de menthe. She mentioned the fact to her brother, asking what had happened to the woman and her son. Calogero answered that he had no idea. People came, people went; no doubt she had left a lot of unpaid bills behind. But he brought the matter up with Traiano, who had been going to tell him anyway. The pair had fled. The pair might be co-operating with the forces of law and order, but it was unlikely. Because if they were, Andreazza would have been arrested by now. But he would find them. Rest assured, he would. He had people looking. Boys like that could not be trusted. The boy and the woman would be homesick. They would get in touch. They would give themselves away. Oddly, the boss accepted these assurances.

Meanwhile, on those hot summer nights, Tonino was doing his bidding. He spoke regularly to Amilcare, drumming into him the necessity of telling him as soon as he heard from Beata which, Tonino assured Amilcare, was certain, given that Amilcare was her only real friend in the quarter. He also impressed on Amilcare the futility of running away; if he did try and disappear himself, his parents were in the quarter, and two younger brothers, and they would suffer for it.

And then there was the girl, Lydia. He knew her slightly, and he cultivated her. This was not hard. After laying a fifty-euro note on the table in the tiny flat she shared with her mother, he was allowed to go into the girl's bedroom, with the understanding that the mother would not disturb them. The room was tiny, there was a fan and an open window, through which came the sounds of the quarter, but the atmosphere was stifling. The room was overwhelmed by soft, fluffy and predominantly pink toys. The bedspread too was pink. Clearly, thought and effort had gone into the decoration of this room. There were posters on the walls, which he stared at with curiosity. He had no sisters, he was an only child, and he had never been in a girl's bedroom before now. He was a little shocked that she had invited him to come up, and that she had specified that he had to make a payment of fifty euros to her mother for the privilege.

She made him take off his shoes, and he lay next to her on the narrow bed. She was wearing a very short skirt and a very tiny top. One was lowered, the other lifted, not by him, but by her. She urged him to take of his tee shirt, which he pretended he was keen to do, given the heat and closeness of the room.

'Look,' he said, hesitating.

'You don't want to?' she asked.

'It is just that....'

'You don't like me?' she asked.

'No. For God's sake. Of course I like you. Who could not like you? It is just that Paolo told me you were his girl, and Paolo is my friend.'

'Paolo is gone,' she said. 'He does not reply to phone calls or messages.'

'Did he say where he was going?'

'No. He did not even say that he was going. He just went. I think I am finished with Paolo. If he wanted me, he would have told me where he was going, why he was going.'

'He told me nothing either, and we were friends,' said Tonino. 'Did he ever mention me to you?'

'No.'

'We both did work for don Traiano.'

'What sort of work?' she asked.

'He may have gone because his mother made him go with her. Or he may have gone because don Traiano asked him to. I do not know. But the thing is, he may come back, and then if he discovers that you and I… He would be very angry.'

'Are you frightened of him?' she asked.

'No.'

'Well then.'

'It is just that if a girl belongs to one man, it is wrong for her to go with another man, and it is wrong for that man to go with her, if the first man is still her man, if you see what I mean. Paolo and I are brothers and we must not quarrel.'

Lydia looked at him.

'Have you come to talk about Paolo?' she asked.

'No, of course not….'

'Can't you ask don Traiano where he has gone?'

'He wouldn't tell me. You liked Paolo, didn't you?'

She admitted she did.

'You and he…'

She admitted they had. And not only with Paolo, though that seemed not the sort of thing one should admit. And in truth, she was only here with Tonino because of the fifty euro note on the table in the living room. She tweaked his earlobe, and he laughed.

'If he calls, you'll tell me, won't you?' he asked.

'He won't, but I will,' she replied. 'But maybe he will.'

Chiara di Donato, at her desk in a large barely furnished room, sighed and looked at the ceiling. She had spent the last thirty minutes shouting at her husband in Brescia, over Skype. She now savoured the silence. These conversations were so debilitating. And they always started well and ended badly. There was a gentle knock at the door. It was Silvio, who had perhaps been waiting for her to finish, and now came in with a cafetiere of coffee on a tray, accompanied by those really excellent biscuits the Sicilians made and which, even here, were not in short supply. He said nothing, but put the tray down on the desk and then drew up the only other chair in the room. She liked this way her colleague had: when there was nothing to say, or nothing useful to say, he said nothing. If only her husband and her son and daughter could learn that lesson. He poured her some coffee, without waiting to be asked, and handed her the cup. From the courtyard outside, they could both hear the regular thud of a football hitting the wall.

'Thank God for ball games,' said Chiara.

'It is his sole occupation, along with eating and sleeping. He does not read, he does not like television, he does not talk…'

'He does not talk,' said Chiara.

She sighed.

'You never told me why you got divorced,' she said, by way of conversation.

This was an admission that after working together for so long, after being together in so confined a space, and not just here, in the Castle of the Women, but beforehand, they had become friends.

'Why does anyone become divorced?' said Silvio, pouring himself some coffee. 'I was away a lot. In those days I was often working on cases in Sardinia, another cursed island, though not in the same league as this place. She felt neglected. She felt that I did not pay her the attention she deserved; that I was married to my work; that the children were missing me. So, after seeing so little of me, she decided it would be best to see a lot less.'

'She didn't meet anyone?'

'No. Still hasn't. I think she became resentful, and when you become resentful it is very hard to let go of the resentment. She talked herself into it. She couldn't forgive me. She was very unreasonable. Of course, there is one group of people who never get divorced, never, ever. They get resentful, and the husbands are so rich and powerful, they pacify them with whatever they want. And they have a code of behaviour that sets limits on human irrationality, it seems to me.'

'You mean like saying adultery is OK, at least for men?' asked Chiara.

'And for women too, as long as no one knows. And of course, with this lot, no one knows anything, ever. Their ability to ignore what is in front of them is extraordinary. And useful. If they did not, then they would probably go mad.'

'This boy…..' began Chiara, feeling the dreadful subject could be no longer avoided.

'I wish I could say he was a nice child,' said Silvio with a hardness in his voice, 'But he isn't. Far from it. I wish I could say that he has just had a bad upbringing, but that does not quite cover it either. The poor mother. I feel sorry for her. The boy – it's very unpleasant.'

She knew what he meant. He had done the same to her. He had refused to speak sense, been abusive, dropped his shorts, exposed himself, made obscene gestures. She herself had been a little shocked. She wondered if it were worse for a man.

'We have to face the fact that we are not getting anywhere,' she said. 'The woman is co-operative, but everything she knows is at second hand, which is not useful. The boy would have been at his most communicative when we first brought them in, but he didn't speak then, and I do not know if he will speak now. I was telling my husband just now that I was here on important business, vital business, not that I could tell him, and all he could say was that our daughter was not doing her homework as she ought, and I ought to be at home to make her do so, because he could not. Now, I know my daughter's homework is only relatively important, but it becomes more so the more we contemplate the dead end we are in here. This place, this huge operation, what is it all for, if a woman speaks, who has nothing to say, and a twelve-year-old who might have something to say. refuses to speak? I am beginning to think that I perhaps ought to be at home helping with the homework, that perhaps we should throw in the towel and admit defeat.'

'I sort of agree,' said Silvio, 'But there is a huge problem with all this. We have potential witnesses who will not speak, or rather, one who won't. If we just let them go…'

'Antonescu kills them?'

'Almost certainly. And that would be a catastrophe. We would never get even a sniff of a witness again. No one would ever trust us. No one would ever dare approach us again. And the state would fail and be seen to fail, unable to protect its witnesses; people would register that the witnesses were useless. And we personally would suffer, and suffer badly. Our careers would never recover. You would have the rest of your life for thinking about your daughter's homework. So, we are stuck with Beata and Paolo for ever, as far as I can see. We have invested too much in them to be able to cut them loose. Besides which, cutting them loose would be immoral. If they returned to Catania… No, we have to resettle them somewhere under new names. It is not hard. It can be done. Though the boy seems to have no real appreciation of the danger he is in from Antonescu. Does it occur to you that we have been tricked?'

'It has occurred to me,' she said. 'Do you mean tricked by Antonescu? Or Andreazza?'

'How did these witnesses come to us?'

'Ah, yes, by Volta.'

Silvio was silent. He said, after a pause: 'Perhaps Volta gave us these two to throw us off the scent, to send us up a blind alley, because he thinks the person who must catch Calogero di Rienzi is him. He does not care about justice, he cares about glory, his own glory. It is also possible that Volta, who supposedly hates them, and was an object of an assassination attempt, hates us more. He is a Sicilian. Perhaps he has thrown us these morsels, on which we will choke, as a way of sending a message to Antonescu and Calogero di Rienzi. To tell them that he is ready to change sides.'

'That seems Machiavellian in the extreme,' said Chiara. 'But possible. Volta recruited the woman. Perhaps we could call him up here, get him to speak to her and the child. It might just work. And if you are worried that he might betray the hiding place, then we can transfer them the very next day. Or something. Perhaps we should have Andreazza arrested. Though by now he will have surrounded himself with lawyers. And he is just the sort of man to slap a defamation suit on us, which would blow everything out of the water. No. Let's call Volta.'

The boss had emerged from isolation. One morning, very early, he went to the Furnaces and saw how work was going there. He even met the young woman who was planting the trees and the oleander bushes. He spoke to the foremen who were using the mechanical diggers, and then he went to the mobile canteen and had a cup of coffee and spoke to the volunteers who were staffing it, and who were all aware that it was the Confraternity, namely don Calogero, who was financing this charitable endeavour. The women in the canteen were charmed by him. They had heard of his recent double loss and were sympathetic. Traiano watched this and felt a bit of cynicism at the way the act was so perfectly brought off. The young woman who was in charge of the planting, Gabriella Bonelli, came in and joined them for coffee. It turned out that not only was she beautiful, she was also clever and knew her job, which was reassuring. She spoke of the toxicity of the soil and how certain plants might cure this; she spoke of the state of the canal and the stream which fed it, and how its waters could be brought back to life; and she spoke of the perfect trees that she had chosen for the site, and that, though expensive, these would be a good investment, because people loved trees and wanted trees to look at from their windows. She was expecting a consignment of 200 or so lemon trees, which were the perfect Sicilian tree. Calogero, who had been brought up in the close confines of Purgatory, but who now was looking forward to a summer in Donnafugata, where his new wife commanded a spectacular garden, asked about olive trees and vines. Gabriella listened attentively, nodding as he spoke. It was as if, in her passion for nature, that she had discovered a kindred soul. They spoke of plants that attracted the right sorts of insects, and how, if there were fish in the canal, these would eat any mosquitoes, and how the fish and the insects and the water would attract birds, whose guano would fertilise the soil. She spoke of a suburban ecosystem, the sort of thing that people who were trapped in Catania longed for. Then suddenly they were joined by someone else: it was the Archbishop of Catania himself, coming to visit the canteen, coming round to shake hands, though most people bent over and kissed the proffered hand. The Archbishop beamed; the photographer snapped away. The Archbishop accepted a cup of coffee, as did his secretary and the photographer. Then, when things were quieter, he looked around him and saw, as if for the first time, who he was with. He had come there to publicise the work of the Confraternity and the Church with the immigrants; as a way of pulling a fast one on the Cardinal of Palermo, who was always in the papers posing with some worthy cause, trying to get himself noticed by the national papers and the people in the Vatican. Well, two could play that game, he knew. But here he was facing someone he recognised, though had never met before now. And there were photos to prove it. He wondered if this photo opportunity had been a good thing after all.

Don Calogero di Rienzi saw the Archbishop's sudden discomfort, and felt a thrill of enjoyment. Traiano noticed this and thought it unwise. He felt it incumbent on himself to engage the Archbishop in conversation, knowing that the Archbishop had no idea who he was. The Archbishop, who had not risen to such heights without knowing how to talk to people, spoke to what he assumed was a pleasant young man. Traiano asked him to pray for the safe delivery of his child, which was soon, well, in three months.

'Your first?' enquired His Grace, surprised that someone so young should be a father already.

'Our third, Your Grace,' said Traiano. 'We married young. Don Giorgio, our priest, had to get special permission from you, not that you will remember, as I am sure you have to do a lot of such permissions.'

'Not as many as I would like,' said His Grace with a friendly smile.

He enquired after the names of the children, the name of his wife, and the name of the new child, if they had thought of one already. It was a pleasant conversation. Eventually, though, Calogero approached, knowing he had been spotted.

'I heard about your poor wife and your poor brother,' said the Archbishop with a degree of sympathy.

Indeed, he had. But it pained him to have to express such sympathy. Yes, he felt sorry for the man, but he felt more sorry for himself. Here he was, past the age of seventy, having devoted his life to God and ecclesiastical climbing, having arrived at this heady height of being the Archbishop of Catania, the guardian of the shrine of beloved Saint Agatha, and what in the end did it mean? One found oneself having to be polite to a man like this. Somewhere, somehow, he did not know when or where, his life had taken a wrong turn. God was laughing at him.

Calogero was speaking: 'Your Grace, I have remarried. The wedding was very quiet, given the circumstances. My new wife is expecting a child. My fifth in total. She is much older than me. But I think you know her. Her name is Anna Maria Tancredi.'

'Of course, I know of her,' said the Archbishop. 'A great friend of the Cardinal, isn't she?'

'It was His Eminence who married us,' said Calogero.

'Congratulations,' said the Archbishop, his eyes narrowing. 'Anna Maria is certainly very well connected.'

'I was thinking, Your Grace,' continued Calogero, 'when this project gets going, when we start building, I would like to consult you about building a church here. A small one but a nice one, in the centre of the houses, it would add so much to the place, make it a real place, a real focus. Naturally, the land would be donated and the expenses covered; it won't be so much, given all the builders and people who will soon be here, but of course the whole thing needs your approval.'

The Archbishop inclined his head, acknowledging the compliment. God Almighty, these people were clever.

'Make an appointment with my secretary,' he felt forced to say. 'And bring the lawyer Petrocchi with you when you come. He is a useful man. We need churches in our suburbs.'

That evening, don Calogero joined his children and his sister and sister-in-law in their walk around the quarter. He was greeted obsequiously by everyone. He shook hands with many, and all the children who came up to him were kissed, had their hair ruffled and were given presents in accord with their age, one euro coins, two euro coins for the tiny ones, five, ten and fifty euro notes for the others. One youngster was marked out for special favour: this was Tonino, who was given fifty euros and a kiss on the cheek, and allowed to walk with the boss and his family for a few paces, given the fact that his mother was an old friend of don Calogero's mother. The boss remarked on how tall and big he was getting, and Tonino was pleased.

Later, in the middle of the night, don Calogero went to meet the others in the basement of the gym, a place he had until now never visited since the reconstruction of the entire building. Traiano brought him in, and Gino and Alfio were waiting for him. To show a spirit of camaraderie, he brought with him a bottle of whiskey, the peculiar Scottish brand that he liked, and a bottle of grappa if that were not acceptable. Traiano hated both, indeed he loathed most alcoholic drinks. The boss brought a glass for himself, but was content to let the others drink from the bottles, which they did, leaving the whiskey to him.

He didn't like camaraderie; Traiano knew this; the death of his wife had allowed him to retreat into himself and drop the pretence that he did. But now he knew he had to come out of hiding, and these trusted lieutenants needed to see him and needed to be reassured that he liked them.

'Nice place down here,' he remarked. 'Nice and cool in this weather. Of course, I have never been here before now. I gather you and Renzo use it for training, Gino?'

'Yes, boss,' said Gino happily.

'Can my future brother-in-law fight?' asked Calogero.

'He's not bad for a rich kid from Palermo,' said Gino. 'He is getting better. But I let him win. Most of the time.'

'A rich kid from Palermo, eh?' said Calogero. 'Well, I am glad you have not knocked his teeth out, because he has to look his best when he marries my sister, whenever that is. Though nowadays, when your teeth get knocked out, you can have new ones put in, I believe. Costs a fortune, eh, Alfio?'

'And hurts like hell, boss,' said Alfio.

'But worth the trouble,' said Calogero. 'Let's just hope the new teeth stay in. It would be a terrible waste of money if they all got knocked out.'

'No one would dare, boss. They know I am your friend.'

Calogero smiled.

'Not just friend, brother-in-law as well; your will be the children's aunt's husband, their uncle and the father of their cousins. And you will be the husband of the cousin of their cousins, Gino, if that makes sense. One family. We stick together.'

There was great satisfaction at the way he acknowledged these relationships.

Calogero looked at Gino, and put down his glass.

'Come on,' he said, 'Show me how good you are. And do your best not to let me win.'

Needless to say, Gino was delighted. This was a rare privilege, sparring with the boss. Calogero knew this, and knew too that he was effectively trumping the special favour shown by Renzo. Gino was immensely strong, but so was Calogero, and they were evenly matched. If Calogero had an advantage, it was that he was lighter on his feet, and was eventually able to wear his opponent down. Finally, repeated blows to the shoulders and the stomach led to the collapse of Gino's resistance, and after half an hour, he surrendered. By that time his shirt was drenched with sweat and blood flowing from a cut lip. Calogero was unscathed. He offered Alfio a chance to avenge his friend, which he happily took up. Alfio was lighter, but less strong, and a few punches to the ribs were enough to convince him that surrender was best. Calogero laughed with delight, while Gino bathed his lip, took some painkillers of the type prescribed by Doctor Moro, and tried his best to clean up with a damp towel.

Then it was time for more drink, and the real reason for the meeting, the talk of business. Calogero was assured that there was no chance that the place could be bugged, that their conversation could be monitored.

'We are all going to make a huge amount of money,' said Calogero. 'I mean really huge. The white powder is at the basis of all; and that money is being ploughed into the Furnaces development and the refurbishment of a lot of the flats in this quarter. We pay many of our workers cash in hand. Just this morning, we got a new opportunity to launder drug money. I promised the Archbishop I would build a Church in the Furnaces. It will swallow a huge amount of money, paid by ourselves to, yes, you have guessed it, to ourselves. It will give us a wonderful opportunity to recycle a lot of dirty money, which we are already doing in the pizzeria, the trattoria, the bars, and of course the apartments we rent out. You have done well so far, but you are going to be doing so much better from now on. And we are going to get rid of the women who live here, and replace them with better tenants who pay more. They bring down the tone of Purgatory. We need to make it more respectable, more fashionable, less criminal. But above all, more profitable. Now, you have heard about this woman, Beata, and her son?'

They all nodded.

'Beata is in witness protection. But she knows nothing. The magistrates have her in this safe place they call the Castle of the Women. What could she know? What has she seen? Nothing, at least nothing first hand. Did either of you know her?'

'I did, boss,' said Gino.

'You screwed her?'

'Boss....' said Gino with a shrug.

'What about you?' he asked Alfio.

'Same here, boss,' said Alfio. 'She was, you know, nice…'

'And did either of you ever tell her anything important?'

Both shook their heads vigorously.

'As I thought. So, what does she know, what could she know? And the boy may know something that his mother has squeezed out of him, but which he will never admit to the magistrates or the police. The boy was being screwed, or whatever it was, by Andreazza, and he was not the only one. But they have not got the other boy, have they? And they have not arrested Andreazza. They have got an uncooperative witness. Andreazza is safe, and that means you are safe from any worry about the Perraino murder. And so am I, given that I am now married to his aunt. Perraino stays a missing person. All is well. And when the magistrates let these witnesses go, we will get them, and that will be an excellent advertisement for what happens to those who speak to our enemies. And it will destroy the magistrates' credibility.'

'What about Volta?' asked Alfio. 'I guess he was behind this?'

'It must have been his idea. Don Giorgio would have put the woman in touch with Volta. All I can say is that Volta is not as clever as he thinks he is. He should have left the woman and her son in place to find out more. He pulled them too early.'

'Are we really going to find them, Beata and the boy?'

'Yes,' said Traiano. 'No worries at all. I have leads.'

'We won't kill Volta,' said Calogero. 'We will do something better with him. We will win him over. We will get him to work for us. You watch. When Volta realises he cannot beat us, he will have no choice but to join us.'

Chapter Six

Theirs was a large island, Volta reflected. When one grew up in Catania, often it was only Catania that one knew. He himself had lived in Rome, but was constantly surprised by the friends and acquaintances who had never left the island; those from Catania who had never been to Palermo, and those from Palermo who had never been to Catania. And there were so many who had never visited the interior of the island, for the simple reason that they had no motive to do so. People often travelled to such places to visit the tombs of parents and grandparents; but if you lived in Catania, would you ever go to Caltanisetta, Caltagirone or Piazza Armerina, unless you had to? Perhaps if family members were buried there, perhaps if you had a strong interest in Roman mosaics, or ceramics or… But he was not sure why anyone would go to Caltanisetta, the Castle of the Women. He had been to see the Roman villa at Piazza Armerina; he had been to the ceramic shops of Caltagirone, but Caltanisetta was new to him, though he did not stop, but drove on into the wild country beyond, country that was scorched brown by the July heat.

Clearly, something had gone wrong. They obviously needed him, otherwise they would not have called him. It had been made clear to him originally that this was their case, and that they could do without him, would do without him, and were expecting to do without him – in fact that any involvement on his part would be a nuisance and potentially damaging. But they had changed their minds, or circumstances had changed their minds, and, credit where credit was due, they had decided to call him in, rather than deny that they had a problem or refuse to make use of him. That was a sign of humility, he supposed. He was grateful for that. He knew that the great task of the last decade was nearing completion, and they, the police, would have to complete it; he trusted them to complete it. But he knew too that these sorts of investigations rarely ended with convictions, and that quite often they failed at the very last hurdle. Some clever lawyer, some arcane rule, some witness losing their nerve….

According to the guide book that he had consulted before leaving, the castle was not open to the public and contained little of interest. Constructed in the Norman period, allowed to fall into partial ruin in subsequent centuries, severely damaged by earthquakes and, to cap it all, bombed by the allies in the Second World War, when it had been, it was rumoured, headquarters to German intelligence, it had been rebuilt and repurposed as a government run centre for research into infectious diseases. Its remote location was the reason for this purpose, though this meant that those who worked here had this same long and tedious drive up the mountainside, a good forty minutes from the motorway, on the wrong side of Caltanisetta.

On arrival, he was checked thoroughly by the Carabinieri on duty at the gatehouse who, even though he was expected, looked at his identity card with careful interest and scanned his face with grave attention. He drove though into the first courtyard, where he was told to leave his car. This was a narrow dark space, even on a sweltering summer's day, trapped between two high walls. Along the outer wall, were a series of modern constructions, which were, he supposed, the research centre for infectious diseases. There were a few men and women lounging in the only part of the courtyard that got any sunshine, smoking cigarettes and drinking coffee, no doubt on their mid-morning break. He directed his steps to the second gate, and was once more surveyed carefully. Then one of the Carabinieri unlocked the gate and let him through. On the other side was a smaller, less lugubrious courtyard, dominated on one side by an arched and elegant range of buildings, and on the other by a high walled keep of medieval date. Standing in the courtyard, waiting for him, was the member of the magistracy who had called him here.

'I am Silvio, you may remember,' said the man, advancing, smiling, with a hand held out. 'Come to my office, and we shall have some coffee. It is a long journey.'

At the far end of the courtyard, where there was sunshine, the boy was playing with a football, shooting it against the bare wall. He ignored them. This, Volta knew, must be Paolo, whom he had not seen before.

'Thank God for ball games,' said Silvio, leading him inside. 'Boys would go mad without them, and so would we.'

The office was a large vaulted chamber, cool in the heat, comfortably furnished compared to a lot of official spaces which Volta had entered. There was an adjoining room where the one he recognised as Chiara sat, and she entered with the coffee.

'This is Chiara, you will remember,' said Silvio. 'She is, among other things, our psychologist. Thanks, Chiara. It is all first name terms here and no uniforms. So it is not like a fortress or a jail. The idea is that they relax, are happy, and, well, as you know, tell all.'

He smiled.

'But….' said Volta.

'But indeed,' said Silvio. 'We have run into problems. The mother has been co-operative, in some ways too co-operative. She has been hysterical. We have got a doctor to see her, to see if they can give her anything to calm her down, but the sheer level of anger she has in her… It's understandable. She feels that men exploited her; and now they have exploited her son, and all the sacrifices she made for him have been in vain. She is angry with herself for not noticing something was wrong before this; she is angry with Antonescu; but above all, she is angry with Paolo. The result of all this maternal anger is that the boy has clammed up. He refuses to speak, at least to speak to any purpose. He did not do anything; he does not know the Colonel. Don Traiano is a good person, that is all he will say. He thinks if he denies everything for long enough, we will give up, let him go home; and if he denies everything to her, she will somehow act as if none of this happened. That is his attitude. That you can repair the past. That you can go back to how things were. Of course, one cannot.'

'Indeed, one cannot,' agreed Volta. 'And Andreazza is at large?'

'Another reason why the mother is furious. Furious with us, that is: She can't understand why we have not arrested him. I believe you told her that we would?' asked Chiara.

Volta was not sure if this question was barbed or not.

'Naturally, when one wants a witness to come over to our side,' said Volta, stressing the 'our', 'one wants to induce them and at the same time not arouse unrealistic expectations. But yes, I told her that as long as the boy spoke, then Andreazza was finished. As it is, you know that Andreazza is on their side; you just can't prove it; but you know; so Andreazza is finished, isn't he, in the sense that no one can ever trust him again.'

'They trust him,' said Chiara. 'He is their asset. If he gets promoted, if he goes further, that will be a sign of their influence.'

'But you cannot arrest him?' asked Volta.

'He called our bluff,' said Chiara. 'No, we can't arrest him. He knows that we know, but there are things we do not know, which prove to him that the boy has not told us anything at all. We assume that it is something to do with other boys, that there was not just one. There is a lot more to come out, and the fact that it hasn't means that Andreazza is safe to defy us. We know nothing, or so he thinks. At least we do not know enough.'

'There was no attempt to gather electronic evidence?' asked Volta.

'Naturally we thought of doing so, but there was not time. The woman panicked. As soon as she made contact with us, she wanted to be extracted. She wanted to get the boy away. The boy, of course, is furious at being taken away,' said Silvio. 'Frankly these two represent a dead end, or so I am beginning to think. Tomorrow, we get them out of here. If you can speak to them, get some sense out of them…. The one thing is that we have got them, and that certain people, Antonescu I mean, will be worried about that. Moreover, other potential witnesses will see their successful escape and wonder, and may in time come forward.'

'There's that,' conceded Volta. 'Beata had a lover…'

'The police have spoken to him. Not a word out of him. They have got to him, and got to him well. He is not saying a word. Amilcare he is called. A bit of a mental defective, if you ask me. Not the only one on this island,' said Silvio carelessly.

Volta's face did not change as he heard this. He remembered his years in Rome, when people would forget he was Sicilian for a moment and make some disparaging comment. Or else people would say: 'Of course, you, Fabio, you are one of us, you are not like them…' But he was one of them, he was Catania born and bred, and it angered him to hear his own people insulted, for the insult directed at them so carelessly was an insult directed at himself. But he pretended, once more, not to notice.

'You interviewed the boy with his mother?' he now asked.

'She insisted,' said Chiara. 'We had no choice. Suitable adult and all that.'

'If I could persuade her not to,' said Volta. 'She has listened to me in the past… I suppose you had tape recorders and all that? It may be better to try a more informal approach. And it may be best to have one firm objective: namely the arrest of Andreazza.'

Silvio, he noticed, looked displeased. For the truth was these two magistrates had mucked the whole thing up. They had had one job, to put intolerable pressure on Andreazza, and they had failed. Moreover, they had alienated the boy and his mother. Heavy handed, thought Volta. Typical northerners, no understanding, no finesse, no idea how things worked. He realised he could do better, and would do better, simply because he spoke their language.

'Could I?' he asked.

'The place is yours,' said Chiara.

Silvio said nothing, but his expression conveyed the belief that Volta would have no more success than he had had.

Volta stepped out into the courtyard. He was immediately aware of the boy playing with the football at the far end in the sunshine, and aware that he, without giving any outward sign, was aware of him. There were two men in the courtyard as well, in plain clothes, either police or carabinieri, seconded to this special operation. They, perhaps as bored as the boy himself, looked up as he came out into the open air. He went and spoke to them, offering a hand to each, introducing himself.

'We have heard of you,' said the first man, whose accent placed him from somewhere in Calabria.

'He means, chief,' said the second one, 'that we were told you were coming, you know, that they' – he nodded towards the room Volta had just come from - 'they needed your help, given that we are all at a dead end here.'

The second man had an unmistakeably Campanian accent.

'Ignore him, chief,' said the first. 'We heard of you yesterday, but we heard of you before this, because of, you know, what happened in Catania. That guy trying to kill you.'

There was silence. That guy had tried to kill him, been foiled by the stab proof vest, and ended up being stabbed himself and bleeding to death in an ambulance in the middle of the Catania traffic.

'These bastards kill us,' said the first man. 'But when one of us kills them, oh my goodness, the law really gets going. The outlaws have the law on their side, and we fight with one hand tied behind our backs. But chief, when you dealt with that piece of lowlife scum, there were cheers the length and breadth of the peninsula, and nowhere louder than in our barracks. We know what is what; not everyone does.'

They all knew who the 'everyone' meant. They all nodded.

'How has it been here for you boys?' asked Volta.

'Fucking awful!' said the Campanian. 'I have a girlfriend waiting for me in Caserta, and I cannot tell her where I am, I cannot phone her, I am stuck here in the middle of nowhere. But thank God it is over tomorrow. It has not been so long, but it feels like months. We have you to thank for that too.'

'What do you mean?' asked Volta with effortless curiosity.

'They told us you were coming,' said the Calabrian, 'and that means the place would no longer be hermetically sealed, as they put it. So the kid and his mother are being moved on tomorrow, and this place closed up.'

'Because I might go back to Catania and tell everyone they are here?' enquired Volta.

'Something like that,' said the man from Caserta. 'The further down the peninsula you are, the less they trust you. You are from Catania, so... hermetically sealed, that is what they said.'

'How is the boy, how is his mother?' he asked, ignoring this.

'He is a nasty kid. The moment you are alone, he pesters you for use of a phone. Of course we do not have them. Nothing. Hermetically sealed. But he wants to call up his friends. Desperately,' said the Calabrian. 'I mean he is very persistent, and embarrassing....'

'Madonna!' said the Calabrian in agreement.

'You mean?'

'Yes,' said the Campanian shortly. 'The mother may have been a prostitute, but she is his mother, and he offered her, and he offered.... I don't like to think about it. It is vile.'

'If you like a twelve-year-old, or if you like a prostitute past her best, then it's heaven on earth, but, as he says, it is vile. I cannot wait till tomorrow, when I am back to normal duties,' said the Calabrian.

'You have someone waiting for you?' asked Volta.

'More than one,' said the young man, with a broad wink.

They shook hands, and Volta turned to the boy who, though hanging back, was clearly waiting for him.

The boy looked at him with curiosity as he crossed the courtyard.

'Hi,' said Volta. 'I am Fabio.'

'I know who you are. They told me you were coming. You are the one who got us into this mess. Are you getting us out?' said Paolo, without smiling.

'Aren't they sending you somewhere tomorrow?' asked Volta. 'Away from here?'

'Where?' asked the boy.

'They won't say until you get there,' said Volta. 'It will be a surprise. A nice place, I am sure. Maybe Milan, or Turin, or Verona, or Florence. Somewhere like that. A big city. Far away. Where you will be safe from those who want to harm you.'

'Who wants to harm me?' asked the boy, aggressively.

'Andreazza. To shut you up. To stop you talking. Don Traiano Antonescu. Just as they shut up Turiddu, if you remember him. Just as they shut up Rosario, if you remember him. But you are a brave man, you are not frightened of them, are you?'

'Fuck you!' said the boy. 'I don't know Andreazza, and if I did, I am not like that.'

'Like what?'

'You know what. I don't like that. I am normal. I like girls.'

Volta nodded, understanding. He gestured and they both sat down next to each other on the step beneath the arcade, out of the sun. Volta took out some cigarettes, and saw the way Paolo looked at them.

'Want one?' he asked.

The boy shrugged, and took the proffered cigarette, because, in the end, there was nothing else to do. Volta lit it for him. He lit one for himself.

'They told me you wanted to make a phone call,' said Volta evenly. 'Anyone special you want to speak to?'

'Yes. Do you have a phone?'

'It is in my car. They told me to leave it there. Is it Amilcare you want to speak to?'

Paolo looked at him pityingly.

'No. Amilcare is soft in the head.'

'Wasn't he close to your mother?'

'No. He used to come round. He stayed the night sometimes. I used to hear them. I knew what they were doing. Amilcare is pathetic. I am not sorry about never seeing him again. I want to speak to Lydia. Do you know her? Can you give her a message?'

Volta considered. It seemed unkind to lead the boy on, but it was the only way to do it, the only way to gain some leverage.

'If you write something, I can take it to her,' he said. 'Just make sure you do not let them see you writing anything. Then give it to me before I go. I doubt they will search me as I leave. But listen. I want Andreazza to go to jail. Do you understand? Why did he come to the quarter?'

Paolo made a gesture with his hand, the meaning of which was unmistakeable.

'Ask the Colonel what he did with Nino,' he said.

'And who is Nino?'

'A boy in the quarter. He is ten or eleven. He used to… you know.'

'Do you know his surname?'

'No. His father is in prison, that I know.'

'OK,' said Volta. 'Look, you go and write to Lydia, and I will go and talk to your mother.'

The boy scampered away. Volta sat down and then lit another cigarette. After a moment, he went back to the office he had come from. Silvio and Chiara looked up, as he entered. He shut the door carefully behind him.

'I have got something for you,' he said. 'Something important.'

'They have said that we are never going back to Catania,' said Beata. 'But they will find us somewhere nicer to go to. Perhaps Bologna, somewhere like that. I do not like cold, though. I do not want to go back to Poland.'

'They will find you a place, a nice place, don't worry.'

'Does don Traiano want to kill me?'

'Yes. Without a doubt. You have broken the most important rule. He fears what you will do.'

'Because I will talk?'

'Yes. But not only that. You will inspire others to talk. There can be no escape from the octopus. If you escape, you get away, you prove they are not all-powerful. That would be fatal.'

'But I won't talk. I have nothing to say.'

'They probably think you won't. But they like to be quite sure. Dead women tell no tales. They want to make an example of you.'

'He always seemed so nice. Well, not to me. To his wife, his children.'

'He isn't nice. He has killed lots of people. Killing people is wrong.'

'You killed that poor boy Maso,' said Beata accusingly. 'I liked him. The police kill people all the time. Why is it right when people like you do it, and wrong when people like him do it?'

'One can kill in self-defence,' said Volta. 'But we have to keep things legal. Calogero di Rienzi and Trajan Antonescu act outside the law. But we need the law. The law is keeping you and your son alive.'

'You won't catch them; they are too clever for you. You will never catch them,' said Beata. 'They do what they like. How long are we going to be here? All summer? They say we are being moved tomorrow, but I am not sure I believe them. It is like being in prison. We are the ones in prison. Andreazza should be in prison, not us. And Traiano.'

He said nothing, for he sensed that whatever he said, she would not believe him.

'I fear for him,' she said, referring to her son. There was no need to mention his name, for who else did she care about? Not herself, that was clear. 'If this all goes wrong, and we are cast defenceless on the world, Traiano will kill him. And kill me. Me, it does not matter so much. But him… And maybe it is too late. I came out here onto the loggia because I could no longer hear the sound of the ball. I always look to see who he is talking to. After what that man has done to him, I wonder if he will fall prey to others. The guys on guard duty, they are guards, even if they do not wear uniforms, they are all young and very nice, and it is kind of them to play football with Paolo - after all, they don't have to, unless that is all part of the plan. But when I see people, men, being kind to my son, I worry if they are really being kind, or if they have something else in mind. I wonder what the boy thinks. They interviewed him. The lady psychiatrist. They said it was best for me not to be there. But I was there, I insisted. I have to be there to protect my son, to make up for all the times I wasn't there, when my back was turned. I wonder at the damage those men have done. They have children, it's unforgivable. I blame myself. I am not angry. I am heartbroken. I wanted my son to have a future. Instead, they made him into a prostitute. Perhaps I did too. The last thing I wanted for him, was him to become like me. Jesus, Mary and Joseph!'

'It is not too late,' said Volta. 'He can have a future. Just one far away from Purgatory, far away from Catania. The important thing is his evidence, your evidence. They need just enough to reel in Andreazza; then they can reel in Traiano.'

'That is just it, I don't have any evidence. My son was used by these men, and I never even noticed until it was too late. It was very hard getting him to tell me where he got the money from. If I had not noticed the money, I might never have found out. So it all hinges on Paolo. It happened.'

'But it all hinges on Paolo convincing people it happened,' said Volta. 'The strategy is to get Andreazza to confess, and for that we need him to panic, and then we won't need Paolo's evidence at all. And then when Andreazza comes onside, we get Antonescu.'

'As long as Antonescu goes to jail forever, I do not care. I want him separated from his wife and children. I believe he is fond of them. Let him suffer as I have suffered. He took my child away from me. Let his children be taken away from him. Tell me. Can they find us here? And how long will we be here?'

'They can't find you here. It's hermetically sealed. You have no mobile phones and you told no one where you were going because you did not know yourself. The people here are all trustworthy. I mean they are specially picked. I don't know if you noticed what I noticed. Neither Silvio or Chiara is Sicilian, and neither were the men on either gate. I could tell from the way they looked and the way they spoke. They all come from far away, and that is deliberate. They do not have friends and relations here with whom they gossip. And even if they find out that you are here, they cannot get to you. The walls are too high, and these boys who play football with your son, they may look like average guys, but they are all very well trained. You are in the middle of an armed camp. You have nothing to fear. As for when you leave, I do not know when, but if they say tomorrow, maybe it is tomorrow, though I do not know where, except somewhere new but equally safe, unless they decide to put you in a place of your own under supervision. That means somewhere far from Sicily, where you will be safe. They say these criminals have a long arm, but very soon they are going to be worrying about a lot of other things. Will you miss Sicily? Will you miss Catania?'

'No, I will not miss Catania. Do they know I have gone?'

'Yes, of course they do. The magistrates have been to see Andreazza; Andreazza will have told Traiano by now, as is to be expected. The longer it is they hear nothing, the more worried they become. Then they may start to make mistakes. Was there anyone special you left behind?' he asked as delicately as he could.

'There was Amilcare,' she said. 'He used to come and see me once a week. He was a sort of boyfriend. He is very nice, a bit soft in the head, I think, and he worked in that pizzeria. He had been in Bicocca, that is how he got the job. And he could pick locks. I can't say I liked him so very much, it was more I tolerated him. The boy liked him, or so I thought. I always wanted to have someone around whom the boy would like, whom Paolo would look up to. It's my fault he has no father figure, I feel. But Amilcare was the only volunteer for that role, and perhaps not the ideal one. I should have said goodbye to him. I feel a bit guilty about that.'

'If they suspect that you might be in touch with Amilcare in the future, it would probably cost him his life,' said Volta carefully. 'Traiano and his gang will be on the lookout for anyone who may have contact with you, and who may be able to lead them to you. If they found out that he had heard from you, they would not believe that he did not know where you were. They would torture him to death. It is best, for his own good, to forget about him.'

'Easily done,' said Beata.

The boy then came in and pressed a piece of paper into his hand, which he immediately put into his pocket. When the time came to say goodbye, Beata kissed his cheek, and the boy, silently and shyly put out a hand.

His last conversation with the magistrates was in the outer courtyard, where in a shady spot, as the afternoon reached its hottest point, they spoke before he drove away.

'Were you followed?' asked Silvio. 'Did they track you? If they did, it does not matter, as we are moving them tomorrow, and we may not use this place again for some time.'

'We have explained it to them,' said Chiara. 'We have told him that if he gives away his location, he is a dead boy, Traiano will kill him. And Traiano will kill his mother. But this does not seem to register completely. He does not trust us. I know you are a Sicilian, but you must understand what I say when I say that this is the problem with this island. They do not trust us, they do not trust the rule of law, or law enforcement, or any authority of the Republic. We are the enemy, just as the Savoyards were, the Neapolitans were, the Spanish were, the French were, the Arabs were, perhaps even the ancient Romans were. The rulers are the enemy. They prefer people like Calogero di Rienzi and Antonescu because they are their own people, and we are not.'

'You are right, of course, at least to some extent, but not all of us are like that,' said Volta. 'I am Sicilian and Italian and happy to be both. I do not think I have betrayed my island and my city by being loyal to the Italian Republic, even if the Republic leaves a lot to be desired. It is after all the only Republic we have got. And really, if we are to be ruled by someone, as we must be, better the politicians in the city hall of Catania than Calogero di Rienzi.'

'You know him, don't you?' she said, with interest. 'And don't like him.'

'I try to form impartial judgments,' he said.

'And what is your impartial judgement?'

'He is clever, dangerous, and he must be stopped. He has been extremely lucky. First the Santucci family saw him and used him; then he started to use them, and has taken them over. He married his wife, and then Anna Maria Tancredi took him up. She is twenty years older, but my goodness, he will use her. He uses people like ladders, and when he does not need them anymore, he kicks them away. Using that method, there is no limit to how high he will rise. And because he has no feelings for anyone, he is very dangerous.'

'No feelings for anyone?' she asked, with interest.

'His family,' conceded Volta. 'Or at least his children. His sons. But they are tiny children. His daughters, maybe. His sisters are useful to him. His mother, he is not overly fond of. These are things I found out from his brother. Antonescu, he uses, and perhaps likes. Antonescu himself has strong feelings for his wife and family, but for no one else. Of that, I am sure.'

'Then the family is his weak spot,' said Silvio. 'The wife, the children. If he was threatened with losing them…'

'And of course Antonescu is young,' said Volta. 'That is the key to nailing him. He is very young. He claims to be in his twenties, but I am sure he is not out of his teens. His major crimes were committed when he was a minor. At least that is my impression. Like a lot of these people, the official data are murky. He only got an identity card when he married. His birth was registered in Romania. I reckon they got a doctored certificate. He was considerably younger than Rosario di Rienzi; of that, I am positive. When you put it to him that he can get off on grounds of age, that opens a lot of doors.'

The magistrates nodded.

'If we take in Andreazza, will you come back?' asked Chiara, before he drove off.

'Sure,' he said.

On his way back to Catania, he stopped at a service station and examined the piece of paper the boy had given him, addressed to the girl called Lydia. He read it with difficulty. As he assumed, the boy was barely literate, the letters had the unformed quality of the writing of a five-year-old. The content was obscene, leaving no room for doubt as to the nature of their relationship. He destroyed it in disgust.

Summer advanced; and hot weather came; even hotter weather. In the interior of Sicily, fires raged in the forests and in the scrubland, ignited by no one knew who, given force by the tinder dry conditions and the wind. The television and the newspapers spoke of an ecological disaster. The boss, who had left with his children for Donnafugata, smelt the smoke of burning scrub even there; they smelled it too in Castelvetrano, where Antonio Santucci continued his descent into alcoholism, where his elder son Sandro continued keeping irregular hours with some local girl, and where his younger son Beppe continued to devote himself to the lemon trees; they even smelled it in Palermo, where they wrinkled their noses and decided to go away to cooler, northern climes. Catania itself hung under a haze of smoke and pollution. Smoke was familiar to the people of the city, the smoke from Etna, along with the thin layer of ash that it brought.

The boiling heat, and the unresolved question of what had happened to the boy Paolo and his mother, caused Traiano to be irritable. He had taken pity on his wife, in her pregnant state, and sent her to a house he had rented for the summer near Acireale, where she could stay with her mother and father, with her sister, with the children, and with whatever other relatives she chose to invite. Because most of these people did not need more than a hint of an invitation, the house was very soon full to overflowing. Aci was several degrees cooler than Catania; it was less polluted and there was a stronger sea breeze. There was a garden too, with trees, a veritable paradise. To this place, whenever he could, Traiano came, on his motorcycle, for short visits, as he had to be in the quarter or at the Furnaces. But he came, often just before dawn, and climbed into bed with his wife when she was often not expecting him, and sometimes left as dusk fell, to get back to the city.

One night there was bad news. He went down into the subterranean room in the gym, and there he met Alfio and Gino gloomily sitting on the bench in the middle of the room. He could tell from their demeanour that something was wrong, very wrong.

'Andreazza has disappeared,' said Alfio.

'Who says?' he asked.

'The police told us; at least one of the police who comes to the quarter. We found out just a couple of hours ago. He has not been seen all day. No one knows where he has got to, whether he has been sent away, or arrested, or what.'

'OK,' he said calmly. 'Do not worry. You are not about to be arrested for the murder of Perraino. There is paperwork involved, and it is July as well. I will handle this. I need to speak to Tonino. Has Amilcare heard anything? Has that girl, Lydia, heard anything?'

They both shook their heads glumly.

In early August, over a month later, Volta was recalled to the Castle of the Women. He made the same drive, went through the same gates, and into the same courtyard. The only thing different was that the countryside was now burned even more than before, and the heat was blistering. The fires had ceased. Everything there was to burn had burned, or so it seemed. This time he was admitted into the medieval keep and walked up a narrow spiral staircase. The first floor was a large well-furnished room with a door that led out onto a terrace; the only warning sign that this was not a normal place was that the terrace, commanding a fine view, was wired in with a fence of metal mesh, to stop anyone who might have an idea of flinging themselves off to their death. There were two men with Andreazza, both youngsters, one reading a book, the other playing patience. They looked up when he was brought in, and quietly left, so that he was alone with Andreazza.

Volta had wondered how Andreazza would greet him, how he would deal with this situation and in particular the knowledge that he now stood exposed before Volta, and that Volta knew his shameful secret. Would he try to brazen it out? Would he humbly ask for forgiveness and help? He looked at Andreazza, and saw Andreazza looking at him, wondering, perhaps, how to play it. He said nothing, took a chair and waited for Andreazza to speak.

'I am glad they have allowed me a visitor at last. I was hoping to see my lawyers, but you are welcome too. I cannot afford to be picky. When you are thrown down an oubliette, any company is most welcome. I presume you are a visitor, not a resident? Thought so. I had heard about this place,' said Andreazza. 'I did not know it was here exactly, but I knew it existed. Of course they have several such places. They say that they kept the most important informants here, the grasses, the supergrasses, the people who, well, you know the role they played. I never expected to see it from the inside.'

Volta nodded, giving a hint of sympathy at this sudden change of fortune that had overtaken Andreazza, his fall from high estate. His sympathy was not entirely false. Andreazza was a man of high social standing, he knew, or had been until now. A Knight of Malta, a father and a husband, promoted young in the police, well connected thanks to his wife. He wondered how she was taking this.

'My wife has left me,' said Andreazza, as if reading his thoughts.

'Really?' he asked, surprised.

'When they came to see me the first time, I assumed she thought nothing of it, but it turns out that she did. When they came the second time to take me away, they said the usual thing, that they had credible reason to believe that I was the subject of an assassination plot and I needed to go into hiding at once. I am not sure she believed them. She was given the choice of coming with me. She decided to go to her mother instead.'

'That does not mean....'

'It's disappointing,' said Andreazza.

'I imagine it is,' said Volta.

'I am on suicide watch,' he said. 'I am sure you noticed. They are leaving me here to stew. I have lost count of how many weeks I have been here. What a way to spend the summer. Honestly, if I had known this was what it was like, I think I would have blamed my wife less. Perhaps she did the right thing. We would have got on each other's nerves imprisoned here.'

'True, they are leaving you here to stew. But there will be someone else stewing too. Antonescu. Don't forget that. He knows you are gone, and he must be worried that you will crack, and then they will come for him.'

'I have thought of that,' said Andreazza. 'If Antonescu thought I would crack, then my life really would be in danger. But I am not going to crack, as you put it. Have you been sent here to help me crack? I have never met Antonescu and I have no interest in framing him. I have never met either of these two children they say that I knew. I have never been to the Purgatory quarter except as part of my duties and then only rarely. I am not guilty of anything they allege. I am not going to admit anything or cut a deal. Eventually, they will be the ones to crack. They will realise that it is useless and they will let me go, and I will be back at my desk as if nothing had happened. I very much doubt that their holding me here against my will is legal. All these special laws they have passed… against people supposedly involved in organised crime. Where is the evidence that I have anything to do with organised crime? There is none. Emails, phone calls, nothing.'

'So, your strategy is to be patient?' asked Volta.

'Yes. To enjoy the free holiday. To read books, to look at the view,' said Andreazza. 'Until they realise they have nothing against me. Nothing at all.'

'Well, it may come as a surprise to you, but I can see you being returned to duty. Are they treating you well here?'

Andreazza shrugged.

'If burial alive is treating people well, I suppose so. I have read the whole of Dante; most people pretend they have done so, but now I actually have. I have started *War and Peace*. Perhaps by the time I finish it, someone will walk in and tell me I am free to leave.'

'They have these boys, two of them,' said Volta.

'They can have as many boys as they like,' said Andreazza. 'But what they need is evidence. That is what they do not have. They have the boys and the boys are not speaking. Or so I suppose. And they are not speaking because there is nothing to say.'

'But you have lots to say,' said Volta. 'You know what is what. You know about these people. You loathe them, surely. So then, co-operate. Give them what they want.'

'Have I said I would not?' he asked. 'I want to leave this cursed island. Perhaps go somewhere like, oh, I don't know, Bari, or Brindisi, or Ancona. Somewhere completely different. Somewhere I can persuade my wife to join me.'

'Well, ours is a big country, and I am sure they will find you something. Venice, for example. Lots of ceremonial posts there, with very little to do, apart from the odd tourist losing their passport. They will put you out to grass. You are young, but…. And they will keep an eye on you. I mean, no one cares about your private affairs, but, if it comes to persons under a certain age…. That is where you are looking at a jail sentence. You see, the people downstairs are actually acting on your behalf, and trying to calm down the parents and talk them out of exercising their legal right to have you prosecuted. At this point you need to realise who your friends really are.'

Andreazza was silent.

'You all want me to admit to something I cannot admit to,' he said quietly.

Volta realised that this was the truth. Pride was the sticking point. To admit to that, to admit to the fact that Antonescu had found his weak point and exploited it; to admit there was a weak point in the first place, and that it was a weak point of this nature, to admit anything but that… One could admit to a lust for power, or money, or women, a lust for anything, but not that. We all have our weaknesses, they both knew, but this one weakness was intolerable, not just to society, but to oneself. It could never be admitted.

'You do not have to give yourself away,' said Volta, with a touch of sympathy in his voice. 'Just give them Antonescu, and then they will leave you alone.'

Andreazza laughed.

'Do you really think, Volta, that you can beat Traiano Antonescu? Maybe you can. And Calogero di Rienzi? Perhaps you can beat him too. The people in Palermo, the people in Rome? This goes all the way up, you know. The people in the Vatican, the people in Brussels? In the end you cannot win. They are too powerful. And if I give you Traiano, about which I seem to have little choice, and then go to Venice or somewhere, one day you will find me dead in a canal. I will be a dead man, even if I survive for ten or fifteen years. They will get me in the end. This place is a watertight cocoon, but outside of being locked in here, there is no safe place. So, when you imply I should know who my real friends are, these so-called real friends are inviting me to commit suicide. In the end the criminals always win. You know this, you are Sicilian, not like those idiots downstairs.'

'Don't you have any faith in the Republic and its ability to protect its citizens?'

'Not much,' confessed Andreazza.

'That is a sad confession from one who has spent a career in law enforcement. Is the law really so weak?'

'Against the power of sinful human nature, yes. I know I have done wrong. But I could not help it. They do wrong, and they do so compulsively. How can law or concepts like the Republic stand against that?'

There, he had admitted it. But he had also admitted something even more important, the almighty justifying excuse. Yes, he had done wrong, but in the face of evil they were all powerless. It depressed Volta. He wondered if he were right. If they brought in Antonescu, if they brought in Calogero di Rienzi, would it make the slightest difference in the end? His own life, his own career, where was that heading? Was virtue really its own reward?

He sighed. If Andreazza, a man who was in the police, knew the law was so weak, how could any citizen trust in the forces of law and order? And he knew too at that moment what Andreazza was waiting for. He was waiting for the state's case to collapse. In other words, he was waiting for Antonescu to kill the witnesses. Of course, he knew, and surely Andreazza knew too, that one of the witnesses could not be found, and even if found would probably remain silent, the boy Nino, who had been spirited away. Clearly, Antonescu had got to him. It was unforgivable incompetence on the part of the forces of law and order not to get to the boy Nino first. What had held them back? And the other witness, the boy Paolo, who was also saying nothing, would Antonescu get to him as well? If he did, that would mean the end, not just of this case, but of the state's credibility. He sighed again.

'What about the Perraino case?' he asked. 'Could you not give them that? That Antonescu and you conspired to cover up a murder?'

Andreazza rolled his eyes.

'I am amused, yes, amused - that is the very word - by the sudden interest in Fabrizio Perraino. When he was alive, people loathed him: he was arrogant, loud, greedy, on the take, and worthless, a completely worthless character. Then he disappeared. Did I say when he was alive? I will get to that. He disappeared and no one was sorry. Well, maybe his mother was, and his aunt, the aunt he used to screw, I need hardly remind you. What a scandal. He disappeared from view, and no one paid any attention. The case became just that, a case, subject to regular review. Now, you and I know that Perraino had ample cause to disappear and hide himself somewhere, perhaps the Balkans, isn't that where they all go when they want to hide? Serbia, Kosovo… And the reason? He had been involved with the drug dealer Carmine del Monaco, who was later killed. His protector dead, he felt perhaps he was next on the list. Whichever way, his disappearance, as a disappearance, was entirely credible. But now someone has remembered his disgraceful episode with the aunt; and that aunt is now married to Calogero di Rienzi. If we can pin his murder on Calogero, then we seriously muck up his domestic life. I understand that perfectly. But why on earth would Calogero have him killed?'

'Perraino had Antonescu, Camilleri and the other one, Fisichella, arrested. They would have done it. And Calogero would have let them,' said Volta. 'Look, admit this at least: Antonescu asked you to put the Perraino case on the back burner, and you complied.'

'And why would I comply?'

'Because he was blackmailing you, or providing you with what you like,' said Volta bitterly.

'I am not blackmailable,' said Andreazza. 'And how could I have consorted with, or done favours for, a man I have never met?'

Volta groaned and held his head in his hands.

'Look,' said Andreazza, 'Think what you like. But you are married, aren't you, and our wives are friends. You surely would not want your wife to know everything you have ever done in your life, would you? Or your parents-in-law? And the other thing is, my dearest Volta, in the end, when one has to choose, one chooses whom one trusts more. I trust certain people more than others.'

Volta looked at him.

'Antonescu?' he asked.

Andreazza nodded.

Soon after, he left the tower and went down to the weary magistrates below. He advised them that they were wasting their time, something that they surely knew. And he expressed a hope that the boy Paolo and his mother were somewhere safe, very safe, because he was sure that Andreazza was counting on their murder as the prelude to his release. Then he drove back to Catania under the burning August sun, full of despair.

All the evidence pointed to Andreazza, now being held in the Castle of the Women; of that Traiano was sure. He had put out feelers trying to find out what exactly had happened to Andreazza. This was done in the most obvious way possible at first, by getting various third parties to phone up the police asking to speak to the Colonel. These were variously told that the Colonel was away for the summer; and later, as summer advanced, that the Colonel would not be coming back, but had been transferred. But they did not say where to, and were vague when asked for a forwarding address. It was as if the Colonel had disappeared, or died, or both. A more sophisticated approach was made though the various contacts that Traiano had with the police, in other words with policemen who came to the quarter for various reasons. One always knew these types and it was useful to surprise them as they bought cocaine in the pizzeria, or came for their presents of a free meal, or were caught literally with their trousers down in the rooms above the bar. They were, unlike Andreazza, all from the lower ranks, and though willing to help, knew nothing of the man's whereabouts. They provided a wealth of unhelpful speculation about where the Colonel had got to. The only interesting fact to emerge was that his wife and child had gone as well. It was assumed by all that either Andreazza had been arrested for some unspecified corruption, or was involved in some undercover operation.

None of this was very helpful, and it merely increased his nervousness. The boy Paolo was an unexploded bomb waiting to blow them all sky high. About Nino, he had no worries; he trusted the mother, he trusted the boy. Even if they found them, which he was sure they would not, neither would say a word. As for Paolo, he would be the detonator who would make Andreazza explode. Once they had Andreazza singing to their tune, he would be finished. But once the boy was out of the way, Andreazza would be useless to them. He had to find the boy. The alternative, the other thing, the not finding the boy, was the end.

He now found he was contemplating the end more than ever. He was not quite eighteen, and death stared him in the face; it entered his head at every quiet moment; the thought of death was present, in the background, every moment of the day. The feeling he had was not fear, for why should he be afraid? He had seen death up close, seen the blood spurt, seen the eyes become sightless, and seen how easy it was to die. Death was something he could live with, paradoxically. What was hard to live with was not the end of life, which would surely come, but the long shadow it threw over the business of living. Death was not so very terrifying. Far worse than death would be arrest by the police, being locked up, being placed in a cage in the bunker-like courtroom, being made a spectacle of, being told that he and his kind were responsible for all the woes of Sicily, that they were an unspeakable evil, and then being locked away in Piazza Lanza for thirty years. That, the humiliation, the loss of control, the living death of imprisonment, that was far worse than dying, which was why, if ever he was taken, he was determined not to be taken alive.

But the thought of it ending now, the thought that that wretched boy, schooled by his mother, could bring him down, along with the odious Andreazza, that angered him and numbed him. As he made love to his wife, he felt the dreadful sensation that there would come a time when he did this for the last time; there would come a time when he would be shut out of paradise. As he bathed his children in the evening, or sat at table with them, he was chilled by the thought that one day, perhaps soon, they would have no father to feed them, and that the youngest, yet to be born, would never see him. Of course, if he did what he had to do, and died rather than let the boss be betrayed, then the boss would certainly look after them. Perhaps they would be better off without him. Ceccina would manage, the children would manage. All would carry on. The only difference was that it would carry on in his absence.

While these worries were real, he was not yet utterly despairing. He was pretty certain that Andreazza would be well hidden. He was also sure that Andreazza would admit nothing, unless he were forced to by the boy speaking. And the boy had not spoken, at least not yet. It was a waiting game, and it needed lots of patience. Paolo might be well hidden but, being a child, would not be as careful as an adult might be. They would tell the boy what to do and what not to do, speak to him seriously about the danger he was in, but would he listen, would he understand? Boys of that age were very bad at following instructions. You told them one thing and they went off and did the complete opposite. He remembered his own twelve-year-old self. Indeed - and he clung desperately to this - somehow or another, Paolo would not be able to help giving himself away. He was sure of it in his more confident moments, and not entirely despairing of it at other times.

The terrible heat had turned Purgatory into a broiling cityscape, a place of revolting smells, as the rubbish in the streets festered in the sun and the drains dried out. Thank God for the house he had rented for Ceccina, the children and whichever of her relatives wanted to join her, on the outskirts of Acireale. It was a pleasant spot overlooking the sea. There were orange and lemon groves and there was a zigzag road that led down to a beach of smooth lava rocks, in the midst of which an icy stream, all the way from Etna, debouched into the warm Mediterranean Sea. As often as he could, he had gone there in the small hours, let himself in quietly and joined her in bed, then had breakfast with her and the children and the various relatives. But these simple pleasures were being vitiated by the thought of what was to come. What would they do to his reputation once he was dead, he wondered? How would they speak of him? What would his children hear about him?

One very hot night, he stood in the bar looking out on the square, with a glass of Cinzano full of ice. It was here that Tonino found him, but had nothing to report. Amilcare had been messaging and phoning Beata, but there was no reply. The girl Lydia had given up texting and phoning Paolo. She too had heard nothing. But if he heard anything at all.... Traiano dismissed him with a wave of his hand.

Meanwhile, in the midst of all these worries, there was some amusement to be had. It was work of the simplest and most satisfying kind, the sort of work that made fools of the people he most despised. The boss had organised some people from the quarter, all tenants of his, to join the Green Party and stir up concern about the state of the canal that ran through the territory of the Furnaces. This created a glorious side show, as radio phone ins became jammed with people complaining about the filth choking not just the canal that ran through the Furnaces, but which choked every street and every alley in the city. Given that the state of the environment was a subject on which both Left and Right and Greens felt vulnerable, this sort of discontent worried all who worked in city hall. Moreover, the state of the canal and the general degradation of the suburbs gave all a chance to complain about what really annoyed them, namely the arrival of clandestine immigrants from Africa. One could not complain about them as such, but one could moan about the mess as a proxy for the new arrivals. And one could complain about crime as well, as another proxy, as well as the way all the roads were falling apart, none of the street lights working, and so on. In the midst of all these horrors, the prospect of Catania Developments Ltd, the owners of almost the entire territory, developing it somehow, rescuing it from being an urban wasteland, seemed like manna from heaven.

The first thing that Catania Developments would do, its spokesperson declared, was clean up the canal, clear it of filth, reeds and weeds, let its waters become clean again, and develop a linear park through the district. This, the spokesperson declared, would be done for the benefit of the people, as an act of public munificence. The spokesperson for the company was none other than Assunta di Rienzi, who was interviewed on the local television news, and whose strong persona defied any hard questioning. Questions, of course, remained. When would this be done? What guarantee was there that it would be for the public benefit? Naturally the television station found someone else who raised just these questions. That person was Volta. He pointed out that Catania Developments Ltd was partially owned by Calogero di Rienzi, a notorious slum landlord, who had no concern other than personal profit. The studio host scented an opportunity here, and soon there was an on-air row on one of the late-night television shows between Volta and Assunta, who had never met face to face until now.

Assunta was, even her brother, who had never really liked her, had to admit, magnificent. She pointed out that her brother, for whom she worked, was, like herself, a person of the people, born and brought up in one of the poorest quarters not just of Catania, but one of the most socially deprived areas in the whole of Italy, where he still lived. To paint him as some corporate developer who knew nothing of Catania was simply wrong. It was true he had become well off, but he was still very attached to his roots. Moreover, as a leading member of the Confraternity of the Holy Souls in Purgatory, and as a leading contributor to it, he had donated thousands of euros to people in need, all done (until now) on the quiet. Despite being personally acquainted with tragedy, as viewers might remember, he was always prepared to help others, and this current development was trying to bring a solution to an area where everyone else had failed to act, or failed to bring about results. Her brother, moreover, loved the environment, and was a keen proponent of Sicilian products such as citrus fruit and olive oil, as anyone who ever visited the pizzeria he owned, or the trattoria, which he also owned, and where he often ate, would know. Volta, she concluded, born into the middle class, perhaps found that sneering came to him too easily. Her brother would have liked to have answered these charges himself, but he was a shy man, and currently in the countryside, enjoying the environment created by olive trees, oranges, lemons and prickly pears.

In fact, the shy environmentalist, the man of the people, was back in Catania just briefly, partly to see Traiano and partly because he had grown bored of the fruit trees and prickly pears, and his own new wife. He was seated on the sofa with Traiano, in his office. They laughed and laughed at Assunta's words, and they enjoyed the way Volta was put on the defensive. The boss had his usual whiskey, Traiano had coke. The air conditioning was a blessing. Afterwards, they leaned against the high window, looking out over the square, seeing the floodlit dome and façade of the Church of the Holy Souls in Purgatory. Calogero had his third or fourth glass of his usual whiskey in his hand. As he had on previous occasions, Traiano was now attempting to drink whiskey as well. He had never really drunk it before now in all of his eighteen years. It was interesting the way the blessed spirit coursed through the veins, deadening the limbs. It was like an anaesthetic. No wonder so many people liked it. No wonder so many people were addicted to it. How curious that this drink from far away Scotland, a country of which he had no real clear picture, except as a place of mist, rain and cold, should be so popular here in Sicily on a warm, indeed stifling summer's night. There was a whole bottle to be got through. There would be other bottles in the house. On his first night of serious whiskey drinking, he might very well drink himself into oblivion.

They spoke of the women and children at Donnafugata, how Anna Maria's pregnancy was now advanced, but how well she was. How Isabella and Natalia loved being at Donnafugata, enjoying the pool, the gardens, the fresh air, the spacious house. Renato too was happy, as was Sebastiano, a very happy baby; and the four children got on so well and were looking forward to the fifth. The girls had worked out that the new baby was their father's, and were pleased. They were also happy to be told that he and Anna Maria were getting married, had got married, the details were left vague. Children craved stability, and now they had it. They seemed to have forgotten poor Stefania.

Indeed, how forgotten was poor Stefania. Her own children had forgotten her; her own sister Giuseppina, now preparing to marry Alfio, never mentioned her. Her own husband had never, they both now realised, ever really loved her. Of course, he had loved the children and valued her for that. He had valued her for the way that, unlike his own mother, she had been able to adapt herself, become fashionable, look rich but not look newly rich. He had liked the fact that she was clever, outgoing, sharp. But he had not loved her. He had married her because he had needed a wife, needed a family, needed children, needed status; but he had not needed her. And was it not the same with Anna Maria? He had acquired her as one acquired a company; it had been a business move, a takeover bid. She had taken him over, or so she thought, but in the end had been taken over herself. There she was, in Donnafugata, looking after his financial interests, looking after his children, three of them not hers, one hers and his, another on the way. She was happy with this arrangement, thought Traiano. She loved him. He did not love her. He liked her; no more.

Some women, then, he had liked but not loved. Those were the women he had married. Then there were the women who knew him well, whom he had not liked at all, only tolerated: his sisters and his mother.

'Did you see what my mother did? The black widow spider?' he now said. 'She came round and picked up all the dirty clothes you left lying around and washed and ironed them, and left them in a neat pile.'

'It is very nice of the signora to do that,' he said. 'I should have left things more tidy. I feel rebuked.'

He had been sleeping in the airconditioned office while the boss was away. It was so hot, especially during the day, that he could sleep nowhere else.

He spoke now of Acireale, where Ceccina and the children and all relatives were staying, how one could walk down to the rocky lava beach and, if one had the guts, swim in the cold outflow of the stream. It was very refreshing. He took another slug of whiskey. He loved Ceccina. They both knew that. He was looking forward to the third child, not long now, after the summer was over, when things would be cooler, which was nicer for all parties involved. The horror of giving birth in August! And then his mother would give birth too, to Alfonso's son or daughter. Perhaps that would be her last child; Anna Maria would certainly not give birth again. But Ceccina would go on having children. They would have six or seven. He smiled at the thought. Those children would grow up and inherit the earth.

He turned and looked at the boss, who was looking at him.

'What news of Andreazza?' asked the boss, calmly, as he knew he would.

'They have got him,' said Traiano. 'They must have him. He has disappeared without trace, which means he is being held somewhere very safe, very secluded, hermetically sealed, this place they call the Castle of the Women. But he has said nothing. Neither has the boy, wherever he is. Andreazza will not speak, will not admit anything. He is too proud. So is the boy, despite the fact that he is only twelve. They are both true Sicilians. They can't admit their weaknesses to strangers. Andreazza is silent, sitting there, waiting; if he had spoken, we would have heard. Eventually they will let him go, give up the case, when they see it is hopeless.'

'And when will that be?'

'That will be when we find Paolo and his mother and silence them both. Sends a message.'

The boss held up a hand to silence him. He did not want to hear details, or plans, or anything that might connect himself with a future crime. There had to be several clean breaks between himself and any criminality, so that when the time came for denial, the denial would be plausible. Traiano knew this too; when the time came, he too would be beyond suspicion.

'Boss,' he said suddenly. 'Why did you kill Turiddu?'

'You killed him, not me,' he said with a smile.

'Only because you told me to,' he said. 'Why? He was my half-brother's father.'

'And we are better off without him,' said Calogero.

'Oh, true. But you liked him once.'

'I liked him very much indeed. But I associated him with bad memories.'

'So you had him killed.'

'Yes. I am a tidy person.'

'And Rosario?'

The boss was silent.

'Are you sure you want to raise that subject?' he asked.

'I loved him,' said Traiano.

'He was talking to Volta. I loved him too, but he did not love me, and he did not love you at all. He was planning to send us both to jail.'

'Volta is a bastard,' said Traiano with decision. 'We should kill him.'

'We will do something better. We will buy him. You shall see.'

'I will never go to jail. They will never capture me. I will never be put in a cage and mocked. I will kill myself first. They will not take me alive,' said Traiano.

'Good,' said the boss. 'That is what I like to hear.'

Then he said: 'Let us open another bottle. I need some more whiskey.'

Chapter Seven

Mid-August was the empty season. Trade in all the places in the quarter was sluggish. Even the boys playing football outside the church seemed to be affected by the heat. Only at midnight did the place become alive as people emerged into the night air in search of some coolness. There was desperation in the air, the thought of never-ending summer; the hope, slight, faint, that one day, cooler weather would come. In the middle of August, everyone longed for gracious October.

The boss's family was at Donnafugata still, but there were several trips to be made to Catania. He had some time previously instructed the people in the office (which meant his sisters, the people provided by his wife, and the lawyer Rossi) to buy a disused quarry, some distance away, along with a fleet of trucks. The idea was that as the Furnaces were cleared, the disused quarry would become landfill. But this meant a change of purpose for the quarry, along with the necessary paperwork and, after various delays, a visit to the city hall. He was now a respectable businessman, and so he was not shy about going in person, accompanied by his bag carrier, the lawyer Rossi. He was pleased by this show of legality. He delighted as well in this new persona that clever Assunta had invented for him, a do-gooder, an environmentalist, a lover of his native city, a man of the people. In the city hall, he had his chance to explain what he planned to do with the Furnaces, an area his company now owned. The first and most important thing, already under way for several weeks, was the clearing of the rubbish that choked the site; the reeds and the weeds; the rusting metal; as this progressed, they were now able to dredge the canal and start to landscape the area. The application was already in for planning permission for units of housing, which the officials at the city hall heard with raised eyebrows; but the conversation moved on swiftly to the matter of the various types of waste that were to be removed and buried in the former quarry: organic waste, toxic waste, all of which were terms that the lawyer Rossi seemed to have mastered. The matter was settled. The company that was to do the clearance was his own company, recently formed. He was not going to contract it out.

They left the meeting room and arrived in the courtyard of the city hall where the various bored employees would gather, especially in the slack month of August, to smoke idle cigarettes and to converse. As he was saying goodbye to Rossi, he saw Volta looking hot, bothered and, he thought, rather angry. He smiled at him. Volta turned his look of hatred and annoyance into a mild frown. It was irresistible. He went up to him, holding out a hand.

'This heat,' he said, conversationally. 'They have air conditioning in the bar opposite. Can I tempt you to join me? I have half an hour before my next meeting, which is nearby.'

Volta could not think of an excuse, so they left the city hall and crossed the road. They stood at the bar and enjoyed the air conditioning. Two glasses of vermouth arrived. Calogero was wearing a pale linen suit, highly polished brown shoes and a white shirt, unbuttoned at the top, showing off just a hint of smooth brown chest and the tan gained by the pool at Donnafugata.

'You have not been away?' asked Calogero, surveying the pale and sweaty Volta.

'My wife has given birth just recently. So, no.'

'Ah, sleepless nights. I understand. But congratulations. At long last. You are a father. You must be very pleased. My wife is having her second at the start of next year. That will be five in all for me.'

'Congratulations! I had heard you had remarried.' He added: 'I was sorry to hear about your first wife.'

'Stefania, yes. That was a tragedy. That boy Enzo who killed her was, as we all knew, not right in the head. Autistic. But, we did not think, violent. The death of his brother traumatised him. I don't blame him. As for the death of Maso, that was clearly self-defence. I do not blame you for that; I would have done the same. It was lucky that you were wearing the stab proof vest. Do you still wear it? Terrible in this heat, I imagine. But perhaps you think it a sensible precaution. Though I note you don't have a police escort. Surely they offered you one?'

'I declined.'

'Yes, if they are going to get you, they are going to get you,' said Calogero cheerfully. 'That is what I think. We all have enemies, don't we? Well, poor Stefania didn't, or at least so I assumed. Not that that helped her in the end. But you and me, that is different. In every successful career, a man makes enemies.'

'If they are going to get you, they are going to get you,' echoed Volta. 'And who are they? That boy Maso could have told me. Pity he died.'

'They are a figment of the national imagination,' said Calogero fiercely.

'I killed an imaginary boy?'

'No, of course not. That boy was doing what he was doing for his own reasons. No one sent him. He was just a chancer, an idiot.' He looked at his watch. 'I am seeing the Archbishop shortly. With the lawyer Petrocchi. Can't keep him waiting. We are going to discuss the building of a new church in the Furnaces. Of course, we are paying, but we want come to an agreement as to just what sort of church it is going to be. Modern, not modern, you know the sort of thing. And, this is the real sticking point, the dedication. I never knew that so small a thing could generate so much fuss. But there is time before we meet. What do you think we should call the church?'

'You should dedicate it to that priest who was murdered some years ago. Now the Blessed whatever he is called…'

Calogero ignored the irony.

'That is a good idea, but I doubt the people who are going to live in the Furnaces want to be reminded of such a sad story. Why not Saint Francis, the patron of the environment? Or Saint Benedict the Moor? That is the one the Archbishop wants. It's fashionable, don't you think? Why don't you come and work for me?'

'Doing what?' asked Volta, aghast.

'Well, as I imagine you may know, I am divesting myself of the pizzeria, the bars and the trattoria that I owned. I am selling them to Gino and Alfio. They are like brothers; one is married to the other's cousin. You may remember her, a girl called Catarina. I believe she and my brother were once close. They are a pair of knuckle draggers, both of them. Well, Alfio less than Gino. They will be great business partners. But I am glad to have got out of that side of the business. You know, Volta, I am a very forgiving man. You did your best to turn my lovely late brother against me. That hurt me so much. But he is dead, and that is over, and all is forgotten, and what is forgotten is forgiven. Anyway, from now on it is all property, this new development, and I have my eye perhaps on some hotels next. Not in Taormina which is full of them, but here and in Syracuse. My wife has a keen eye for a good investment. We need someone who will oversee the public relations side of things. That could be you.'

'And you are seeing the Archbishop…?'

'Aha, clever of you to realise how that is connected. I am not as religious as my brother was, but I do go to Mass. Do you go to Mass?'

'Never.'

'Tut tut! It is a very important thing to do. Now you have a child, you should go again. The Church does a huge amount of good. The Church is the only voice in society that we can trust because it is not standing for election, it does not make false promises. It does what is right because it is right. Look at the current mess we are in. The right wants to criminalise immigrants, and the left wants open borders. And we Sicilians have gone all over the world and have been let in, and now we want to stop others doing what we once did. Only the Church sees sense on this matter. I am seeing the Archbishop, not just to discuss the new church, but because the Confraternity has been working with the immigrants, trying to give them some dignity; and I am already employing many of them in clearing up the mess in the Furnaces. They want work after all, and they are all big strong young men…'

'Your hypocrisy is breath-taking,' said Volta.

Calogero smiled.

'So is yours. And you are just the person to point out to the world just how much good I am doing in the world. Just wait and see what we are going to do. Now, I must not keep His Grace waiting. By the way, that job offer was sincere. You know where to find me. I am reasonably confident that I shall hear from you, sooner or later.'

And Volta hoped he never would. And yet, and yet…. The state's plan which involved the child Pavel Bednarowski and the disgraced Colonel Andreazza had run into the ground, as far as he could see, thanks to the stubbornness of the potential witnesses. The hope that very soon, Calogero di Rienzi would be behind bars, was proving to be ephemeral.

The Castle of the Women, as they called it, was now empty, and would not be used again, unless for some future case, if ever. The whole shop had been shut up, the men who had staffed it returned to their normal duties in various parts of continental Italy. The boy and his mother had already been flown north, and so had Andreazza, who had been taken to a secure airbase - so the magistrates had told him in their last meeting – and been confronted there, as a desperate last gamble, with the mother of the child, Beata herself. The two had never met before now, and it was thought that such a meeting might bring about a result, namely, the collapse of the Colonel's silence.

It had been hoped that the Colonel's brazen self-defensiveness would crumble before the accusations of an outraged mother. But the opposite happened. Andreazza smelled blood. He knew what her profession was, what her son's profession was, and he was adamant that they were both liars. They had both been put up to this by Trajan Antonescu. It was an attempt to entrap him. Let the woman storm however much she liked, but he was not moving from this position. He was the victim of a plot by Antonescu, a man he had innocently met, he now admitted, in the house of Anna Maria Tancredi, the aunt of a colleague, missing, presumed dead. All these accusations were lies, and he wanted to see his lawyers.

Those handling Andreazza felt that he was one of the hardest men they had ever had to deal with. He did not seem to realise who his real friends were. They offered to let him return to Catania at once. This threat, he saw as a sign of weakness. If they were guilty of false imprisonment, of holding him here against his will, they could hardly expect him to assent to be let go and forget about the whole thing. He had to see his lawyers. At last, in despair, they let the lawyers come.

The lawyers, when they came, turned out to be a mixed blessing. They spoke realistically about his chances, and seemed to suggest that throwing himself on the mercy of the state was probably his best course of action. Paedophilia was a serious crime – they used that terrible word – and carried a very heavy jail sentence. The state would overlook what he had done, provided he co-operated and brought down Antonescu. If he continued with his stance of non-co-operation, the state might lose patience. They might start searching for evidence in other quarters, put out feelers, ask around… Such a fishing expedition would be highly embarrassing.

Andreazza was furious and offended. There was nothing for such a fishing expedition to find. Moreover, he wanted to sue the boy and his mother for defamation of character. The lawyers looked at him aghast. He did not seem to understand the gravity of his situation. He countered that the state seemed to be acting under instruction from Antonescu. He was an innocent man and there was no evidence against him. He would only co-operate once the state promised him a promotion to Venice. He was adamant on this point. He wanted to go to Venice, a city where there was very little crime and very little to do, but a city he knew his wife would consent to live in. She had often, in the course of their relationship, said she would love to live in Venice. If he were to be transferred there, she would come, and her love of Venice would overcome her disdain for himself, he felt sure. But if he told her that he was being transferred to some terrible place in the middle of Sardinia, then his fate would be sealed. She would leave him, and his reputation would collapse. He was determined to preserve that reputation.

The magistrates lost patience. Andreazza was removed from the air base, under arrest, the next day, and he got his wish. He was transferred to a former madhouse, now used as an occasional prison, in the middle of the Venetian lagoon. From his far from comfortable cell, he discovered that he could just make out the bell tower of Saint Mark's if he stood on his desk and craned his neck through the bars of the window. As he did so, he realised that someone, somewhere, who was pulling the strings, had a sense of humour, but the joke was at his expense. In the summer heat, the lagoon stank.

If his fate was being decided far away, this was more true that he realised. His future depended on his wife, on someone sitting at a desk in Rome, who was probably, now August was here, not sitting at his desk at all, but on holiday; in the mountains, on the beach, enjoying himself, leaving the decision that mattered to cooler weather, while he languished on the lagoon. And perhaps his fate depended on the boy Paolo, and what he would say, what his mother would get him to say, and what the police, his own people, would coach him to say. His fate was being decided by a bored child in a hot city.

On the 10th August, the feast of Saint Lawrence, the meeting of the San Lorenzo crime family took place in a small but luxurious hotel in the hills outside Palermo. Traiano was there, and so was Renzo, soon to be the brother-in-law of Calogero. So were the representatives of the various enterprises in Trapani, Messina and Agrigento. It was at this meeting that Renzo and Traiano were admitted into the honoured society, as they had been promised; and there was a business meeting which dragged on for hours in an air-conditioned room which, despite the coolness, became quite stuffy. This was the first time that don Antonio Santucci had not been present; and the place was haunted by the ghost of the late murdered don Carlo, the presence of whose son could not make up for that of the absent father; also absent were the two retired leaders, don Lorenzo and don Domenico Santucci. There was, with the realisation that the management had changed, a sense of uncertainty, even fear. And there was talk of profits being down, thanks to people growing slack, thanks to a lack of discipline. They looked to don Calogero to restore discipline. This, he assured him, he would do.

In the evening, for they had booked the hotel for forty-eight hours and had it to themselves, there would be a gathering for all the senior employees, about a hundred people in all; all men, no women, apart from those supplied by don Carmelo, the boss from Messina, a busload of whom were expected at sundown.

Before that, the three of them, Calogero, Renzo and Traiano drove down to the hospital in Palermo where, in the heat of August, one of the old men, Antonio's father, Lorenzo, was taking a long time to die. They came into the room, and don Lorenzo's wife, who was sitting with the old man, discreetly withdrew to go and have coffee and make phone calls.

It was a long and emotional meeting between Renzo and his cousin; there were tears and there were kisses. The old man stroked Renzo's hand and told him to follow Calogero's advice in all things. Then he kissed the young man and told him that he would be a great man one day, as long as he followed Calogero's advice. He told him too that he had long known that Renzo's uncle, his own son Antonio, was not up to the job, and he knew from observation that his two grandsons, Sandro and Beppe, were likewise unsuited to the life. His own son, his own grandsons! It was too sad. Let them live off the money that was theirs by right, but let them not have any direct influence on the business. He would be dead soon, and would not come to the wedding, but he was glad it was happening, and he was supremely glad that the two families would so soon be united in this way. As he said this, he looked at Calogero and said: 'Moderation in all things.'

He then spoke of Calogero's father, Renato di Rienzi, the infamous, in some circles, Chemist of Catania; the clever bomb maker whose luck had so spectacularly and sadly run out. He sighed as he recalled Renato's skill, his discretion, his usefulness, for he had been the man Rome had asked for whenever there was a political problem to be solved. And how well he had done that job. Of course, Renato had come from their own town originally, Montelepre, the place to which he himself would soon return. He was silent a moment as he contemplated his own funeral, how they would all be there, how there would be a Mass in the parish church in Palermo (he had given exact instructions), and then the long slow drive into the hills to the cemetery of Montelepre, where the rest of the family who had gone before him already lay. And he would be inexplicably absent. Well, it was what it was, and who knew what lay beyond death, though he was sure that his wife and his daughters knew, and the other female members of the family, and they would perhaps spend much time, energy and money paid out to the clergy, for the salvation of his soul. He was not frightened by the prospect of a journey to the next world; after all, he had sent plenty of men to the next world himself; and now, if he were constrained to follow, so be it.

He congratulated Calogero on his new marriage and on the new child. A miracle, Anna Maria producing two children at her age. He hoped it would be another son. He turned to Traiano, and congratulated him on his imminent third child; a son and a daughter already, and perhaps another son. If it were another daughter, Traiano said, he would not mind. They were both young and they had plenty of children to come, he was sure. The old man turned to Renzo, urging him to get married soon, not to wait (though aware that one of the things making him wait was his own long illness) and have a son quickly.

Afterwards, on the drive back to the hotel, Renzo asked Calogero what he had understood by the words "Moderation in all things."

'Lorenzo meant to recommend what was his own path to success. Be moderate. Always use the least force to achieve your aims. Now, we have just bought this former quarry which is going to be used to dump all the rubble from the Furnaces. The guys at the meeting know this; think of all the corpses you can hide in landfill. It makes a better private cemetery than the sea, or Mount Etna. Put a body in there, dump a ton of broken bricks on top, and it will never be found again. Useful. But did any of the guys start drawing up mental lists of whom they wanted to see in our quarry? Perhaps they did, but they were careful to hide it. Perhaps they did, but they were noting the possibility of some day in the future, if it ever became necessary. When you have someone erased, you solve a problem, naturally. But it is a radical solution, and it can't be carried out too often. Feuds, the search for revenge, that would lead to lots of deaths. I myself think indulging in revenge is silly, and ultimately self-defeating. That boy, that stupid boy who killed my wife Stefania - may she rest in peace, my first wife - he is now locked away in some mental hospital, but if they ever let him out, I would never dream of seeking revenge. Why?'

Renzo nodded.

'So, tell us why you killed Vitale,' said Traiano.

'I was sixteen, and I had to prove myself, of course. Besides, Vitale had mucked things up for my father. He was his supplier. One wanted to send a message. The message was received by the very person we have just seen in hospital. You know, they say that a good king is a merciful king. Actually, a good king is one who will take hard decisions and not let himself be swayed by pity or other emotions. Lorenzo is Antonio's father, but still, he knows... I had nothing against Vitale, but... I was indifferent one way or another. It was a strategic decision. But traitors, they have to die, and die at once, without any hesitation. Those are necessary deaths. You respect me because you know I can make hard decisions. Because I am completely in control of my emotions.'

Renzo nodded again. But Traiano wondered.

'Wives, friends, they all need to be held at a distance. Children are slightly different. You can love them as much as you want. But wives need to be kept in check. When you are married to Elena, make sure she knows who is in command: you, not her. But she will know that. She had the example of my parents to learn from. You might think that I gave Stefania too much freedom, particularly in the matter of spending money. How she spent it! But that was deliberate. I wanted to create the impression we were rich, I wanted us to look rich, to think like rich people. It was a question of building up prestige. She liked shoes, it kept her happy, but she turned me into the sort of man that Anna Maria found attractive.'

'I was there when you met,' said Traiano. 'But I cannot remember what you were wearing. Perhaps that heavy overcoat you liked so much. But I don't think it was the clothes that attracted her, really….'

Calogero looked at Traiano in the rearview mirror.

'She likes something a little rough,' he agreed. 'She liked you, Caravaggio. But if you are going to commit adultery, Renzo, for goodness' sake do it for the right reason. Do it for money, for power, for advancement. That was what I did. I did not expect to get a wife through it, or two more children. Adultery does not count for much, but if it does count, make sure it really counts. I fell in with the most important woman in Sicily. You have my sister. And you, Traiano, you have done well too. She is a nice girl. Anna Maria likes her; my children adore her. They are all at Aci?'

'The whole lot,' said Traiano. 'And it gets bigger all the time. I mean, Ceccina is getting bigger all the time, but the family gathering seems to get bigger too: the cousins, the sister who does my hair, the mother, the father, the grandparents. The children all adore it, of course. And I do not mind at all. It is in fact very nice. When I was growing up, it was just me and Anna. Now I have lots of relatives. Several are working at the gym. Several more are going to be working at the Furnaces. They all treat me very nicely, very well.'

'Of course they do,' said Calogero. 'They know who you are.'

Traiano laughed.

'My children don't. Cristoforo now wants a puppy. The people next door have a dog that has just produced puppies, and Cristoforo is taken there every day to see them, and I have to go too when I am there. I get there at six in the morning and slip into bed, and at eight I am pulled out by my son who wants to take me next door to see these puppies. I think I shall have to give in. They are mongrels, but I like mongrels, and they are very cute and, if we do not take one, there is the possibility that the people will drown it, which would upset me and would upset Cristoforo if ever he were to find out. And we will have a new house, lots more room, and Cristoforo will soon be able to look after the dog himself. Or so Ceccina says. She thinks it will be good for him. After all, he is nearly three. I think that is far too young, but she does not agree. She claims to interpret his wishes in a way that I find extraordinary. A mother's privileged position, I suppose.'

'I wonder if Anna Maria would like a dog for Donnafugata?' said Calogero. 'I will ask her. How many are there? Six? And they drown the ones no one wants? That is very cruel. Drowning perfectly healthy dogs. I too like mongrels. I will speak to Anna Maria. My children would be delighted. Stefania never liked pets. But Anna Maria.... When you marry a second time you have to forget so much and learn so much that is new.'

'I hope to be married only once,' said Traiano.

'And so do I,' echoed Renzo.

'The dog had six, but I shall only have five,' said Calogero. 'This one will be the last. We rely on you, Renzo, to provide me with many nephews and nieces. I am sure Elena will understand.'

'Of course, boss,' said Renzo. 'We will both do our duty. When the time comes.'

'When is the wedding?' asked Calogero casually.

'It is still not decided. Next spring now seems the earliest. It seems that Elena needs to take account of when Giuseppina marries Alfio. She does not want the two weddings to be too close together. Giuseppina neither. You know, people are sensitive… My wedding will be the bigger one, because it is your sister, and it is my family, well, all the females of the family really, and one does not want to put Giuseppina in the shade by making hers look less important by comparison. So we have to wait for them to get their wedding out of the way, and then allow us all a breathing space, a suitable interval.'

'With Gino Fisichella and Catarina, it was much simpler: she was pregnant, so it had to be as soon as possible,' said Traiano.

'Just like my wives, both of them, both times,' said Calogero. He looked into the mirror once more. 'You know that the boss from Messina, don Carmelo, is bringing a busload of girls to entertain us all? Are you going to be entertained?'

'No, boss, that is not for me,' said Traiano.

'Your wife is pregnant,' said Calogero.

'So is yours,' he replied.

'What about you?' asked Calogero, turning to Renzo.

'Your sister would not like it,' said Renzo evenly.

'No one would tell her,' said Calogero.

Renzo sniggered.

Presently they arrived back at the hotel and they parked the car outside, noting that a large bus had arrived earlier, no doubt bringing the treats from don Carmelo. There was no one in the carpark, and they went in to the hotel to go up to their rooms and get ready for dinner which was due to begin in an hour. Passing the dining room, which looked over an olive grove, which in turn hid a swimming pool, it was clear that a magnificent antipasto was being assembled. Traiano went up to his room and, on entering, began to loosen his tie, then paused. Someone was there, waiting for him. It was Tonino.

'How did you get here?' he asked quietly.

'I persuaded Alfio and Gino to bring me,' said Tonino.

'Did they take some convincing?'

'A little, boss.'

'Well, you must have decided to come, uninvited, because something important had happened. Tell me what.'

He cast his jacket aside.

'Amilcare,' said Tonino. 'He came to see me, just today. The boy rang him up on his mobile phone, Amilcare's phone. The boy rang this morning.'

Traiano held up a hand to cut him off.

'He called? From where?'

'A public telephone. They won't let him have a phone of his own. But there is a bar near the flat where they live now, which has a public phone, and he called from there.'

'He had Amilcare's number?'

'Beata did, written down. He found it in her handbag. At least he assumed it was Amilcare's number, and he found it and gave it a try. Paolo would not say where they were, and Amilcare did not want to ask as it might seem too suspicious. Paolo was only ringing Amilcare, who he does not even like, because he wants Amilcare to get him the girl's number. He said he was not able to say goodbye to the girl. He wants to speak to her. He said he would phone back when he had a chance, and that Amilcare should get the girl's number for him.'

'So then what happened?'

'The next part was easy, boss. I used my brain. I went to the girl's house, and I took her phone. I then gave the number of the phone to Amilcare.'

'Did the girl object?'

'I gave her a hundred euros, boss. She didn't ask any questions. I just said I needed it and that was that.'

'Good. Good work. Do you have the number of the bar he was phoning from?'

'It's on the girl's phone,' said Tonino. 'It is a number starting with 02.'

They both understood what that meant. It was a Roman number, that was clear, from the opening digits.

'You have tried it?'

'Not yet.'

'Try it now. Use the girl's phone. Ask to speak to Mr Rossi, if need be.'

That was the commonest surname in Italy.

Tonino, who did not have a mobile of his own, carefully called the number that had called earlier. Eventually the number rang. The rings were interminable.

'Yes,' said a voice, in an unmistakeable Roman accent. 'Bar La Vendetta.'

Traiano signalled for him to cut the line, which he did. He was thoughtful. He then went to his jacket, took out his wallet and removed two fifty-euro notes. He gave them to Tonino.

'Go downstairs. There is someone at the reception desk, and they have a computer. Ask them to look up for you Bar la Vendetta, Rome. There can't be too many bars with that name, even in a big city like Rome. When you have found out where it is, come back here.'

Tonino nodded, and disappeared. He was back within minutes. The bar was in the Via Tiburtina and was the only bar of that name in the city. He had the street number too.

'When he phones again, when he phones the girl, he will phone from somewhere else, I am sure. Some other bar, not too far away from where he is living. He thinks he is clever, but he is not that clever. If we get several calls, then we will be able to work out roughly where he is. The thing is, do not answer the phone. By this time tomorrow, you might have several missed calls, all from Roman numbers. Good work. You're clever.'

'Thanks, boss.'

He told him to wait, and left the room. He rapidly found the room he was looking for. He knocked, and there, lying on the bed asleep, or just waking up, was Muniddu. His eyes expressed surprise at the sight of Traiano.

'Boss,' he said, scrambling to get up, holding out a hand a little uncertainly. 'I gather it is congratulations…'

'You are very kind,' said Traiano modestly. 'It is thanks to all the lessons I learned from talking to you. And, well, old friend,' he held his hand tight when he said this, 'I am in a position to put something nice your way. The other guys, Gino and Alfio, they are people I trust too, but you, you are very special. And I know I can rely on you to do this job well. It is important. They are not important people, but the whole thing, if done well, will be very important for all of us.'

Muniddu was all attention.

'My room is down the corridor. Come and see me there when you are ready, before dinner begins. There is someone there I want you to meet. The job has a price tag attached: eighty thousand.'

He disappeared.

A few minutes later, Muniddu entered the room he knew to be Traiano's. The boss was not there, but there was a teenager sitting in the one armchair the room had: a thickset boy with wiry hair, who looked up with wary surprise. He saw a sturdy man with dark short hair, a strong chin, about thirty-six years of age. From the bathroom came a voice.

'Talk to each other,' commanded Traiano.

He joined them a few minutes later. He had changed his shirt and brushed his teeth.

'After this party is over, tomorrow night, you are both going to go to Rome. Your quarry is in the Tiburtina quarter somewhere. You will hunt them both down and deal with them. Muniddu, you know how. Tonino, you know them both and you will find them and point them out to Muniddu. For that service I will give you twenty thousand euros. You will do this without leaving a trace. You will buy tickets for the night train with cash. You will travel as father and son; get used to calling each other the appropriate names. You are going to visit relations in the Tiburtina quarter. When you track the quarries down – Tonino will fill you in – you deal with them and leave no clues behind. Then you come back to Sicily as soon as possible. When the train divides at Messina, Tonino, you take the carriages that go to Catania, while you, Muniddu, carry on to Palermo. When you get to Catania, Tonino, you find me and you tell me that everything is OK. We never talk about this again, and we do not mention it to anyone. Tonino, listen to what Muniddu says, and obey him without question. He has got lots of experience. I hope you make me proud and yourself proud. You will be able to discuss this further between yourselves tonight, but do not give the impression you are plotting anything, even here, where we are all friends. Oh, Tonino, does your mother know where you are?'

'No, boss.'

'Better that way. Will she ask?'

'No, boss.'

'Even if you are away for some days?'

'Not even then, boss.'

'Excellent. She understands. Never ask questions. Never raise matters, leave everything be.' He turned from Tonino to Muniddu. 'Does it sound difficult to you, this job?'

'Not really,' said Muniddu. 'It may take a bit of time, but the quarry has already broken cover. We will find them.'

His tone was easy. He wanted to give the impression that this was a routine job. He knew it was not. But the boss was pretending it was, and he wanted to go along with the boss's pretence. There was to be no panic, that was clear. And why should there be? But at the same time, he noted that the job was crucial; and he, like the boy's mother, would ask no questions.

Tonino had never left Sicily before now. It was strange, taking the local slow train to Messina the next afternoon, then taking the ferry from Messina to Villa San Giovanni across the narrow strait that separated Sicily from the continent. He and his supposed father (and they did in some ways look alike; alike enough at any rate to pose as father and son) were dressed in jeans and tee shirts and jackets, with backpacks which contained, he knew, a change of clothes, a gun with a silencer, and in his case, a sharp retractable blade. The girl's phone was in his pocket, switched off. There was little conversation between them, for questions were not to be asked; Tonino amused himself by looking out of the window, at the scenic coastline between Palermo and Messina; Muniddu dozed; sometimes Tonino looked at his fellow passengers, the vast majority people of his grandparents' age group; there were few teenagers or children, few youngsters.

On the deck of the ferry, midway across the straits, they spoke. Muniddu asked if he had enjoyed the party. Tonino considered. The food, he replied, had been magnificent. He did like wine, and all the wines he had tasted been of top quality as well. But the food, he had never seen food like it. Muniddu nodded. The food had been there to satisfy hunger, to some extent, but much more than that: it had been a feast to remind them all of the poverty from which they had sprung, of the time when there had simply not been enough food on the table, of the time, long ago now, when they had been sent to bed as children, hungry. This time was more mythical than actual, but no less real for all that. The last time of starvation had been the war years and immediately after, particular the harsh winter of 1948, long before their births. But the spectre of poverty was always there; and this banquet, this luxurious excess, was a way of banishing that memory. They discussed the food for some time. The antipasto; the lobster with linguine; the beef; the chicken; the various puddings; the coffee; the biscuits; the pastries; everything you could imagine wanting to eat had been there. And all served by statuesque blondes wearing towering high heels, strings of fake pearls, and nothing else, provided by don Carmelo, the boss of Messina.

'Did you…?' asked Muniddu.

The question was left hanging. It was clear that many had. The girls had been available, and when the eating stopped and the party spilled out into the garden, it was clear that several people had retired to their rooms with the girl of their choice, and one or two had frolicked under the olive trees and by the pool, and in some cases in it.

Tonino nodded his head thoughtfully. He had been a little shocked by what he had seen, and strongly disapproving, at least at first. He had disapproved in particular of don Carmelo, the boss of Messina, a man in his fifties, rumoured to have thirteen children, not all by his wife, either. Of course, the girls were all very beautiful, taller, blonder, and more beautiful than any girl he had ever seen before, but they had been prostitutes, paid to walk around like that, paid to behave like that; this was immodest behaviour that no normal girl should ever undertake. Of course, they were foreigners, from Eastern Europe, and they needed the money - and that was some excuse - but God forbid that any Sicilian girl should ever behave like that. Of course, Sicilian girls did not, on the whole, not even Lydia, and that was the entire point, he could see that. Because Sicilian girls behaved, and men sometimes felt the need to misbehave, well, someone had to help them, and this quasi-orgy was a sign that the men involved had money and power and were not like the rest of male humanity, condemned to unwanted chastity. But if the women had behaved badly, some of the men had behaved worse. In the garden it was clear what some of them were doing behind the trees, and what was worst of all, he had seen don Renzo climbing out of the pool, accompanied by two girls, in a state of nudity and arousal. He had been completely, utterly shocked and disgusted. And at the same time, he had understood what was going on. Don Carmelo wanted to show off his power, his wealth; men wanted this, and he was happy to provide it; moreover, with him the usual laws of decency and behaviour did not apply. But it was also clear to Tonino that don Calogero disapproved of this sort of thing, and so did don Traiano. He mentioned this to Muniddu. He said he had not dreamed of touching one of those girls where others could see it, but he had taken one to his room, as that seemed to be too good an opportunity to miss, and besides, people would expect it of him. And the truth was, he despised don Renzo for appearing like that. It was not dignified. And the other men. It was shocking. They had no self-respect, no sense of proper behaviour. How could one respect don Renzo? How could one? He was spoiled and selfish and supposed to be marrying don Calogero's sister. And he knew that this was precisely the point too. Don Renzo acted like that, and people despised him; they were meant to despise him; that was what don Calogero wanted.

But he himself had been careful, he told Muniddu. He reflected for a moment on the encounter behind closed doors, how the girl had satisfied him, which had not taken long; she had asked him how old he was, and he had said he was eighteen, and she had laughed. He had drunk a glass of champagne, or tried, but the bubbles got up his nose; then, when she had asked him if he wanted anything else, he had slapped her on the buttocks, not hard, for some time with his hand, which he had enjoyed, and then she had satisfied him again. He wondered what Muniddu had done, but dared not ask.

At Villa San Giovanni, they had a sandwich each and boarded the train, the long slow train that traversed the peninsula in the night, slowly; they did not have couchettes; that involved handing in identity cards, and they were travelling without trace. Only the very poor travelled in this way, slumbering in upright comfortable seats without the comfort of lying down; sleep was snatched at irregular intervals; at the various stations, places one had never heard of, like Tropea, one was woken up and frustrated by the intermittent noise and the long wait. In whispers, when there was no one with them, they discussed things, mainly the people they worked for, the bosses, a subject on about which Muniddu was curious. Tonino knew don Calogero, had known him all his life, and he had exchanged words with him on many occasions, and he was touched by the great man's kindness. Don Calogero was rich, but he knew that he shared his origins with the rest of the Purgatory quarter. Don Calogero was kind, and his mother, who was all alone in the world, was looked after well; so was his father, who was in prison. He was there because of mistakes he had made, chiefly getting caught; but because of Tonino's work, don Calogero, he was assured, would ensure that his father came to no harm. Don Traiano, he knew well; he spoke carefully of him; he was kind, he was generous, he was exceptionally strong and brave, he was brilliantly intelligent. He did not lose his calm; he thought things out, and when he needed to act, he acted. You did not mess with him; you saw he was a serious person. Of course, he could be strict. If you displeased him, he punished you. The sting of his belt was not easily forgotten, and he had experienced it several times. But that was what it was. People who betrayed him or failed him paid a much worse price. But if you worked well, the reward was excellent; and it was not just the reward of money; it was something else, his approval, that was so precious. Both the bosses were proper men; both had wives and children; both were expecting new children; not like those who fooled around with prostitutes.

Muniddu was thoughtful. He too disapproved of don Renzo's behaviour, but he had known Renzo as a child and he had known and liked don Carlo. Of course, Renzo took all the drugs he could lay his hands on and slept with every girl who crossed his path; and the drugs and the drink and the girls came to him because he was very generous, or rather very extravagant, as he had always had so much money. He was not haunted by poverty. He remembered his own very abstemious youth. He had met his wife when they were both teenagers, living close to each other in the same quarter of Palermo, near the Ballarò market, but my goodness, he had had to prove himself worthy of the privilege of even talking to her before he was allowed anywhere near her by his father-in-law, a man who was in the same line of work as himself. The old man protected his daughter, and he had to earn the old man's trust. It was rather like the story in the Bible, where Jacob had had to work for seven years before gaining a wife, then another seven to gain the wife he actually wanted. But at last, after seven years, the Biblical span, they had been allowed to get engaged, and after another couple of years, married. Then the children had come, a boy and a girl, both a little younger than Tonino, both still at school. He had done well; after this job, he would do even better, and his son would be in a different line of business provided he stayed at school. Maybe after this job the money situation would be so good they could have another child. That was what he wanted. After all, why else get married, why work, why save, unless you had someone to leave it to? He loved his children. He liked and respected don Traiano and was envious of his two children and another on the way. That was what he wanted. But it was different for the bosses: they had unlimited money and thus could have unlimited children, as many as they wanted. With the rest of them, money was always tight.

He asked if Tonino had met someone yet. 'No', said Tonino. He thought of the girl Lydia, but that had been work, and after this, he realised, he did not want to see her again, or did not want to see her more than was necessary. She was OK, but he had been seeing her in order to try and find out where Paolo had gone, and in addition he knew she had slept with Paolo, and that annoyed him, and he had been pleased that she had wanted to sleep with him, and seemed not to care about Paolo any more. (This, he knew, would hurt Paolo, not that Paolo would ever know.) But he knew that she wanted to sleep with him for the money he gave her and her mother; she was greedy; but it was money the boss gave him, so that meant he did not care; the sleeping with the girl was a byproduct of his work. He did not like the girl. He was not sure what sort of girl he would like. Perhaps Lydia was too young for him, being Paolo's age, and like Paolo, full of childish things. For her it was all a game. The same was true for Paolo. But he knew it was serious, very serious. His ambition was to meet someone serious. Muniddu nodded as he told him this.

He saw that Traiano trusted the boy because Tonino was serious, trustworthy. This mission carried risks but, properly managed, the risks were minimal. The biggest risk of failure was if the police decided to move the woman and her son, which they would do either because they got wind that their cover was blown, or because they routinely moved people. The other risks were real: getting caught, or worse, getting killed in the attempt. What if the woman and her son were aware of the danger they were in, and determined to defend themselves? How big was the son, he asked Tonino, with interest. Tonino considered. Not small, he conceded. Big for his age. But nothing that he could not handle. The implication was clear: he was looking forward to handling him.

Dawn was coming up on the right-hand side of the train as they moved northwards, stopping at Pomezia; the carriage was empty. Muniddu outlined his plan. They had to do it quickly, to strike and then withdraw in the minimum time. The police would know who had sent them, so there was no need to make it look like anything other than what it was, a straightforward assassination. Indeed, it was important the police should realise that it was what it was, that the very people they were protecting them from had struck, so that they realised that there were no hiding places which were safe, that no one could be protected from them. Sometimes with these jobs, it was right to create the maximum horror, make the victims suffer, but in this case perhaps death would be sufficient, that would dismay the forces of order enough. There was no need to add anything, at least he did not think there was, at least not at present. Perhaps when he saw them and judged, then he might change his mind. He asked Tonino to describe the woman's appearance to him. He listened with interest. Sometimes it was necessary to be heartless.

'What does the boy like doing?' he asked.

'Playing football,' said Tonino, after a moment's consideration.

It was not quite what he had expected Rome to be. It was a big, ugly city, just like Catania, as far as he could see. Because they had to keep out of sight, as his mother constantly told him, they had not been to the centre of the city, the parts that the tourists visited. Instead, they had remained, for what seemed like a long time now, in the area of Casal Bruciato; the furthest he had been to the real Rome was when he had gone to the bar in the via Tiburtina to use the telephone, which he was not supposed to do, and which he had done when his mother was at work.

His mother had a job, working in a supermarket on the via Tiburtina; when she was at work, he was supposed to stay at home and watch television, or, if he absolutely had to, he was allowed to go out into the via Sebastiano Satta, where they lived, and play, as she put it, on the patch of scrubby grass opposite their apartment block.

His mother had changed since leaving Catania; she had become tense and moody; she frequently lost her temper with him, or burst into tears for no reason. She had put on weight, and she had altered her appearance. The policewoman who visited them once a week had advised this. It was easy to do; Beata had simply stopped dyeing her hair, and reverted to her natural mousey brown colour, instead of her blonde look. As for Paolo, they had discussed dyeing his hair from its natural colour to something darker, but the police lady and his mother reckoned that as he grew up (he bristled at this – he *was* grown up) his hair would darken naturally, and they had merely taken the precaution of cutting it very short. Just as his mother looked different, so did he; he hardly recognised himself, he said, with the very short fuzz on his scalp in place of his long blonde curls. That, they both said, was the point; that he should not recognise himself, and no one else should recognise him either.

The police lady was adamant that no one would find them, that no one could find them, that Italy was a large country, and Rome a large city, and even if they guessed they were in Rome, why, even then, how could they find a woman and a boy in a population of three million? He overheard her saying this, reassuring his mother, but at the same time aware that his mother was not reassured. He himself was not worried. Let them find him; they did not scare him. One day he would go back to Catania and show them. He resented the way they had been forced to leave Catania, and then been imprisoned at the Castle of the Women, and now come to Rome, which was far from the promised land they had told him it would be. And he resented the implication that somehow all this was his fault.

There was nothing to do in Rome but stay indoors except, every evening, as the heat decreased, at about 5pm, to go with his mother to the park opposite the house where the other boys of the quarter would let him play football with them. A new player was always welcome, that was clear, though they did not like his accent, and they wondered what a Sicilian was doing in Rome though, if truth be told, there were plenty of them around; but his accent was raw, and he had, he realised, to undergo the compulsory ritual of abuse before he could be accepted. They called him potato-head as well, thanks to his new haircut and to the somehow or other preternatural ability Italians had to spot the foreigner in their midst. They assumed he was Polish, he could see that, even though he was now supposed to go by the name of Paolo Rossi. That, he reflected ruefully, fooled no one. After playing the game for some hours, with his mother watching, always watching, it was time to go home, have a shower, then eat, watch television and go to bed.

There were no girls in the quarter, as far as he could see. There were, of course, there had to be, but it was clear that they did not come to the park; they did not hang out with the boys. What he missed most of all about Catania, apart from the friendship of don Traiano, was one girl in particular, Lydia. Who was enjoying her company now? Had she forgotten him? How could she have done so, if she had? Had her passion for him not been equal to his for her?

More than anything else, he wanted to see Lydia again, but he was not sure how this was going to be possible. He could take the train - he did not see why not - and meet her half way, perhaps in Reggio or Naples or Messina (his geography was vague). To this end he had made the two phone calls when he had left the house while his mother had been at work. He knew calls could be traced, but he was pretty sure that he was being careful. He had found a bar in the via Tiburtina and phoned Amilcare from there. He did this because he had found Amilcare's number written on a piece of paper in his mother's handbag. Then he had phoned Amilcare a second time, to get the girl's number. The number secured, he went to the market and bought a small pay-as-you-go phone which, he thought, was untraceable. It did messages and it did calls, nothing else. Then, at the very first opportunity, he had phoned the girl, only to find there was no reply.

It was early morning. Traiano stood in the middle of what had been the Furnaces. Next to him was Omar, the leader of the gang of workers. Everything had been arranged. There were about fifty men getting ready to work: for weeks now, they had been busy clearing the ground; getting rid of the reeds choking the canal; digging out the sludge where the machines could not; removing piles of rusty old metal. A short distance away were trucks, ready to transport the spoil to the disused quarry. The men were equipped with overalls, boots, gloves and spades, but the main thing they brought to their work was their brute strength. It was still early in the morning, and not yet searingly hot; indeed, it was hardly light. But Traiano knew that when the sun rose, when the heat began, they would probably discard the overalls and work in their shorts, with little regard to health and safety. The van that provided refreshments, courtesy of the Confraternity, was there, he noticed, at a little distance.

Everything was arranged. Omar had just been given the agreed amount, five thousand per week, which he could share out as he saw fit when the week's end came. Traiano wondered how much of the five thousand would reach the workers, not that he cared. Even if they got a mere fifty for a week's work, and many might get far less, that was much more than they would get begging. And if anyone was killed during the work, provided no one saw what was happening, the body could be disposed of in one of the trucks heading towards the quarry. Omar and his closest associates had guns, which Traiano had given them; all the men had knives, one supposed, but guns would give Omar and the other leaders a competitive edge. He knew he did not have to urge Omar to kill anyone who caused trouble, for he sensed that this advice was more or less redundant. There would be no trouble. Omar would see to that.

The truck drivers were all friends and relations of his wife, or of Alfio's, or of Caterina's, Alfio's cousin, Gino's wife. They could be trusted too. All this activity, all this noise, all the uprooting of invasive plants and bamboos and rushes, all the exposure of black stinking earth, all this looked like hell itself; and the infernal quality was enhanced by the twilight before dawn, the swarming workers, and the shriek and whine of aeroplanes going over their heads, the morning rush hour into Catania Airport. But they were here for a particular reason, a site meeting; they were here in the very centre of the Furnaces at the place where the most important building would stand: the church. For Calogero had decreed that there would be a church and that, with exemplary piety, or perhaps hypocrisy, the church would be the very first place to be built. Moreover, after much thought, he had decided on the dedication for the church, which he would reveal this morning, when those summoned to the site meeting were assembled.

The site meeting, as far as Traiano was concerned, was a pain in the neck, a terrific bore. He had hardly slept the night before, as most of his activities were nocturnal. Moreover, he knew that Tonino and Muniddu were in Rome right now, solving that little problem, and until he saw Tonino again, he would not know whether the problem were laid to rest or not. It would be, he was sure. Wherever they were hiding, they would be found; Paolo would be careless, the Italian state also would be careless; and Muniddu knew what to do, and the boy Tonino was clever. But he did not like having to wait. It was two days since they had gone.

The architect was talking of the church to be built, passing round photocopied pictures of what it would look like: a double cube, the perfect proportions, a pitched roof, a tower for the bell, an apse at the back, a parvis at the front. This was where the one called Gabriella came in. The Church was on a slight eminence, as was fitting, and the soil would be hospitable to olive trees and oleanders, placing it in a little *rus in urbe*, a green space. Everyone nodded. The engineers alone were not happy; the soil was marshy and the building heavy. It might be necessary to create a huge concrete plinth on which the building would rest. The architect wondered if they needed a crypt. Others wondered whether the concrete plinth might not create more difficulties than it would solve; all this technical talk was silenced and shelved by the arrival of the Archbishop, accompanied by his secretary, both in cassocks and, Traiano noted, shiny black shoes that would not stay clean for long. The Archbishop was introduced to everyone, and his hand was kissed. It was then that Calogero, with a degree of humility that he showed to no one else, suggested the name of the Church, Our Lady of Loreto. The Archbishop nodded. Traiano felt the temptation to giggle, for at that moment a plane passed overhead drowning out all speech, and everyone knew that Our Lady of Loreto was patroness of aviators. When conversation was possible again, Calogero explained his suggestion: he was thinking of the Holy House of Loreto, as depicted by Caravaggio in his greatest painting, the one hanging in Saint Augustine's in Rome. The Archbishop smiled. The name met with his approval. His benediction of the project given, the great man left.

His Grace departed, it was back to the technical difficulties, as the chief engineer of the project called them. It was all very well having a heavy church and a tower, but both would be swallowed up by the soil; they would subside, because the ground was unstable. He was insistent on this point. He had done tests, he had looked into it, the place was a former marsh, there was no rocky subsoil, just metres and metres of back mud. He looked at Gabriella as he said this, and the gardener, the expert, nodded.

'Well, if there is a problem, there is also a solution,' said Calogero evenly. 'We have promised the Archbishop a church, and a church there is going to be.'

The engineer adopted an apologetic look and began to explain the solution. The reason for his look was soon obvious. The solution he was thinking of would cost millions: It was the construction of a floating and buried platform, like a waffle, of steel and concrete, on which the Church and the tower would rest, though the tower might require some concrete piles, which would be another expense. The waffle, as he called it, would spread the weight of the building, and allow trees to be planted as well, above the perforations in the platform. And of course, it would allow for a car park, essential for every church. And though the waffle would be a hideous thing, it would all be covered up; no one would see it.

'How much would this thing we would not even see cost?' asked Traiano suspiciously.

Calogero looked at him blandly. Yes, he was shareholder. But this question was unexpected.

'Several million,' said the engineer. 'And I need hardly remind you that these sorts of things tend to spiral out of control. The cost of materials is rising every day.'

They always said that.

'If the soil is unstable here, is it not going to be unstable everywhere?' asked Traiano. 'Are we going to have these waffles under each building?'

'Let us stick to the church, shall we?' said Calogero. 'You may have heard the famous story about the Republic of Venice voting to finance the Church of the Salute, and how the budget was supposed to be unanimous, and one man always voted it down. They asked him why. He said that there should be no fixed sum, no upper limit, for a building that honoured the Madonna. Likewise here. There is no upper limit. Do whatever it takes. And the rest of you. I know some of you are shareholders, but this is my decision, and you will accept it. This church will be built and that is that, whatever it takes. And so far, we are just talking about the exterior, never mind the interior, which will be magnificent. Ok, we need a waffle; make sure we get one.'

'Boss,' said Traiano.

The meeting broke up. Hands were shaken. Alfio and Gino, neither of whom had much reason to hang around, wished they could hang around longer to enjoy the presence of the beautiful Gabriella, but drifted away. Traiano was left for a moment with the boss.

'Clever,' he said.

'Of course,' said Calogero.

'Your wife's idea?'

'Mine,' he retorted.

He smirked and left, and Traiano got ready to leave too. But now, drifting towards him, was Gabriella, the beautiful gardener, who had clearly been waiting to get him on his own. He was immediately suspicious. Of course, Gino wanted her; of course, Alfio wanted her; they would. One could see why. She was beautiful, and Alfio and Gino were the sort of men who collected trophies and who wanted beautiful women, though in that matter their success rate was rather patchy. As for this girl, the beautiful Gabriella, he was sure that she would never look at either of them; she was not ambitious, he was sure, but rather one who had good taste, exquisite taste. She was beautiful and she liked the beautiful things in life, he could tell instinctively. She had come to this awful place, this horrible sea of mud and wreckage, with the mission of making it beautiful and, most importantly of all, she knew how to make it beautiful, if her confidence in her mission was real, which he thought it was.

He found her a little intimidating, he realised. There was nothing beautiful about himself, he thought and, like the boss, he had been born in a place where taste was in short supply. He had grown up wearing the wrong sort of clothes, the wrong sort of shoes, the wrong underwear even; and then, when trying to wear the right sort of stuff, he had perhaps overcompensated. Of course, that had changed now, as he wore suits, had cut his hair properly and, to some extent, learned how to speak, and begun to recognise the shapes of right and wrong behaviour. But all this was learned behaviour, and with this girl it was effortless; she had been born with the right instincts. She knew how to dress, how to speak, how to hold a fork. She had not had to learn. This girl, this Gabriella, was so slim and beautiful, it almost made him annoyed, for even her beauty was effortless, and she must be approaching thirty. He realised then that he did not like women or indeed men of this kind; he was happy only among his own, the people of Purgatory.

'I wanted to ask you something,' she said with a smile.

'You did?' he said, in a perfectly friendly manner.

What on earth could they have to discuss he wondered. Was she a police spy? That was not beyond the realms of possibility. If so, he needed to be on his guard.

'Your wife is having a baby,' she said pleasantly. 'When is the happy day?'

'Middle of next month. More or less that same time as Gino's wife, by purest coincidence. And the boss's wife, sometime after that. She is forty-five, so it was something of a surprise. You like babies?' he asked.

'Very much,' she said. 'Not that I have got one of my own.'

He smiled. It was not his place to tell her what he thought, namely that at her age, she ought not to leave it too long, indeed she had left it too long perhaps already. It gave him a little satisfaction to think that he had beaten her there.

'I gather your mother is also in a happy condition,' said Gabriella. 'You see, I realise I have met your stepfather. I have just put the two together, if you see what I mean. I don't know him well, but he knows my brother, and my brother and he had a great friend in common, a certain Professor Leopardi. My brother was talking about Alfonso Agostini and then he mentioned that Alfonso - Fofò - had got married and was expecting a child and his wife, well, was your mother.'

'You know Fofò?' said Traiano, feeling the ice melt.

'Well, he and my brother were close, are close, you know, he is more Ruggero's friend than mine, but yes I know him and I like him.'

Traiano smiled. He loved his stepfather passionately. He regretted not seeing more of him.

'I would like to meet your brother,' he said, before he could stop himself.

'Funnily enough, he said he would like to meet you,' she replied. 'He has heard about you, and, well, he would like to meet you.'

He wondered what she wanted. It would not do to ask. But it would come out eventually. It always did. What she wanted might be advantageous to him, he realised.

'What does your brother do?' he asked.

'He is an art dealer,' she said.

He noted this, and realised it was important, but he thought it best not to betray any interest. Instead, he switched the conversation to plants. There followed a long disquisition about oleanders, hibiscus and bougainvillea, and the right sort of trees: mimosas and pines, and Mediterranean oaks. Gabriella was against the indiscriminate planting of pines, which ruined the chances of anything growing under them and were, in her estimation, bald and boring trees. She preferred the ficus and the palm. But a few pines would have to be planted, that was for sure, but as they grew slowly, they would be enjoyed by the children yet to be born. And maybe the same was true for a few plane trees. None of this was particularly interesting to him, but Traiano listened very carefully. He was after all a shareholder, so should take an interest. The gardens of the new development would be a major selling point. In that direction lay profit. But he himself had lived in a place where there were no gardens, where the nearest green spaces were the little park outside the city gate, or the Villa Bellini, places to which he realised he had scarcely paid due attention. On gardening matters, he was completely ignorant, but he realised that Gabriella was an expert, an artist, like Fofò; like Velasquez; like Stefano Ittar; like Caravaggio. These various men had passed through a place, looked at it, improved it, and left beauty in their wake. So much beauty where there had been ugliness before. Having listened to Gabriella talk about trees for what seemed at least twenty minutes, he mentioned the gardens at Donnafugata, and how he had spent time there.

'I imagine they are lovely,' said Gabriella with a touch of envy. 'They say Anna Maria Tancredi has great taste. That is very well known. And I hear she has some wonderful pictures as well.'

Once more he was suspicious, but hid it. He was so good at hiding things.

'An Immaculate Conception by Murillo,' he said. 'School of. She relies on it to help her get through her pregnancy. It worked last time. It goes with her wherever she goes. She is very religious. It is a nice picture, but nothing compared to the Spanish Madonna in our church in Purgatory.'

'The famous one that was stolen and then recovered?'

'Yes, that one.'

They walked over, through the working men clearing the ground, past the vast earth-moving machine and its noise which momentarily stifled conversation, until they came to the mobile canteen, which had finished its work of providing breakfast for the workers and others.

'Have you been married long?' Gabriella asked Traiano.

'It feels like forever,' replied Traiano. 'We got married in the early summer of last year. But this isn't our first child, or even our second. It's our third.'

'Congratulations,' said Gabriella. 'You are very lucky.'

It was as if, thought Traiano, she was apologising for her failure to reproduce. Or lamenting it.

'Is your brother married?' he asked.

'Ruggero? No. He's… He had a partner, but they are not together any more. Ruggero, well, Fofò will tell you, he has not always been lucky in his choices. Perhaps he was a bit wild and unpredictable when younger, even now. Not made for the stability of married life.'

Traiano shook his head as he heard this. He himself valued the stability of married life above all other things, and the stability of family life as well. He thought of his wife and all the relations waiting for him in Acireale. The children, his children, his sister-in-law Pasqualina, his parents-in-law, and the uncles and the aunts. These were all, in their various ways, important to him. Indeed, as he thought of this, something happened. One of the truck drivers waved to him from a distance, and he recognised the man, a second cousin of Ceccina. These ties counted. These ties were everything. But people like this Gabriella and her brother, they were rootless. He wondered what she thought of him, what she thought of the boss, what she thought of all this. But what was it she wanted? What did her brother want?

'All the people I know are very uxorious,' he said. 'You know that word? We stick with our wives and we do not get divorced. I have never heard of anyone in Purgatory getting divorced. And we are polyphiloprogenitive. The boss taught me that word. We like having children. You know Gino? He is devoted to his wife. And Alfio is devoted to his fiancée, who is the sister of the boss's first wife, which makes him the future uncle of the boss's elder children. These things are important.'

'I know Gino and Alfio,' she said, a little tartly. 'I have seen them looking at me. What a pair of beauties they are. I am surprised they are so devoted to their wives and girlfriends as you say they are.'

Traiano laughed.

'They like looking at a beautiful woman, it is true,' he said. 'It is very bad of them. I would never do that. I never look at anyone, at least not in that way.'

'And is don Calogero so very uxorious? His present wife was his mistress when he was still married to his first wife.'

'True. People made a bit of a fuss about that, particularly his mother and his sisters; and Giuseppina, Stefania's sister, and Alfio felt he had to support her; and indeed the other wives felt it was an affront; not him having a mistress, but him marrying his mistress so soon after his first wife had died. But he had to do that, as they had a child, to legitimise the child, and then the other child came along. But that will be the last child, as Anna Maria is now surely past the age. Tell me, if I can ask, what do you think of our boss? This project is all his idea. And marrying Anna Maria has been something of a big thing for him.'

'And for her too, surely. Calogero is certainly clever and forceful. We saw that today,' she admitted after a pause. 'He has a commanding presence. He gives off a dangerous air. I have noticed him. He is the sort of man you notice.'

'I suppose that is what Anna Maria did. She noticed him. I was there when they met. Being a banker, she has an eye for projects with a great future. So does he. This place will make our fortunes. We have sunk a fortune into it already. But please do not think that we just think of money. Or that we are selfish brutes who just want to get on. We don't do this for ourselves, but for the next generation. My children are very young, one not even born, but they will have the good things of life, I am determined they will. They will be educated and cultured and, I hope, intelligent. But not spoiled. Good, ordinary people. That is what I want for them.'

'A noble ambition,' she said. 'My brother is very interested in everything to do with Calogero. He has asked me lots of questions about him.'

'I assumed as much. What does he want?'

'To offer a business opportunity. A chance to invest. For you personally.'

'Why does he not speak to Anna Maria Tancredi?' he asked. 'If it is business proposition, if it is a matter of investment? What do I know about anything like that?'

'He does not know Tancredi. He does not know you, either, but I do, and you know how things work. He needs a personal introduction. At least that is what I assume. The other thing is, the sort of investment he is looking for might be more attractive to you than your boss.'

'I don't know what you mean by that. I don't do anything without the boss knowing all about it. The boss is very interested in art, as it turns out. So am I, but he even more so. So is Tancredi. Look, I need to get back to the family. I have not slept all night and I have a bed waiting for me in Acireale. But…. Well, I would like to meet your brother, and indeed you too. It may well be very interesting.'

She handed him a card, on which was her name and her mobile number. He took it. He had no card to give, but that was to be expected. He half-smiled at her, and then left, walking swiftly to the place where he had left his motorcycle.

Chapter Eight

It was still very early in the morning, and he calculated that he would be in Acireale just as the family was waking, in time to see them all for breakfast and then leave them and sleep. With his last remaining dregs of energy, he made it onto the motorway under the shadow of Etna and then, shortly afterwards, as his motorcycle cruised through the traffic, he saw the blue lights and heard the sirens sounding. Nothing was coincidence, he knew, and he felt a numbness as he heard the sound approach. He slowed down and, as the cars - two of them - approached, he drew onto the hard shoulder and stopped. Two pairs of police came out of the cars, and approached him. His face was impassive. So, this was it. His first thought was that the boy had spoken, after all, the woman had spoken, Andreazza had spoken. He was going to be arrested. His wife, his children, the relatives, all of them waiting for him, his comfortable bed, all seemed so far away. He might never see them again.

The police were polite. That in itself was threatening.

'You are not wearing a helmet, sir,' one said. 'That is illegal.'

He shrugged, waiting for the next thing.

'You will have to come with us to the station,' another one said.

'I am tired and I am going home,' he said. 'I can give you my identity card and come to the station later today.'

The policemen all looked at each other. They clearly had not expected this.

'It is better that you come to the station right now,' they said. 'It is better that way.'

Again, he shrugged. He got off his bike, prepared to leave it by the side of the road. Perhaps it would stay there forever. He prepared to get into one of the cars, through an open door. As he stood by the car, one of the police lightly frisked him. No gun; they seemed relieved by this.

'I am not dangerous,' he said, to no one in particular.

He assumed they were going to take him back to Catania, but to his surprise they turned off in the direction of Nicolosi, the place where the gun club was, half way up the mountain. But they were not going to the gun club, but to a secluded house outside the town. This was no police station. He saw that now. He was not going to be arrested or charged, he thought. Then what? They had been watching him, that was clear, and they had got him right now when he was sleep-deprived, at his very lowest ebb.

They stopped, and he got out of the car. He was taken into the house and led into a room where a man and a woman were waiting for him. They were sitting behind a table. Then the escort that had brought him withdrew, leaving them alone. Then someone came in with coffee, which struck him as very civilised.

'Thank you for coming,' said the man, who had an accent that he immediately placed as Lombard. 'My name is Silvio. This is Chiara.'

'Hi,' said Chiara, gesturing towards the coffee. He nodded. She poured him a cup and passed it to him.

'I will not introduce myself as you know who I am,' said Traiano. 'But who are you? Who are you really?'

'That will soon be clear,' said the Lombard. 'Indeed, we do know who you are. We know very well indeed.'

On the table were various pieces of paper and photographs. Silvio pushed two photographs over towards Traiano. He looked at them without much interest.

'The woman and the boy, you know. That is Beata Bednarowska and her son Pawel, known as Paolo. Until recently, they were both resident in your quarter of Catania. They were your neighbours, in a manner of speaking. Right now, they are with us. You can see, if you care to look carefully, that there is a newspaper in the picture with the date clearly visible. Just in case you think that this is not a recent photograph. And this other picture is Marco Andreazza, whom you also know. The woman and boy are now safely hidden, as is Andreazza.'

'And what are they hiding from?'

'You,' said Silvio.

'Why on earth should they need to hide from me?' asked Traiano. 'Are you the police? May I see your identification? May I call a lawyer? Are you arresting me? Is this a police station? Isn't this illegal?'

'I am glad you are so concerned about legality,' said Silvio without any sarcasm in his voice. 'We are indeed representatives of the Italian Republic and the forces of law and order, though not the police as such. Tell us how you met Andreazza.'

'It was at lunch last December, I think, yes, two days before the feast of the Immaculate Conception, so 6th December. He came to see Anna Maria Tancredi, and I was there with Rosario di Rienzi, and we all had lunch together. I presume you know who all these people are.'

'We do. Why was Andreazza there?'

'He came to tell Anna Maria about the progress, or lack of it, in the case of her nephew, a policeman called Fabrizio Perraino, who had disappeared. But I imagine you know all about that, don't you? He was a bad man and a corrupt policeman.'

'When did you see Andreazza again?' asked Chiara.

He noted her accent, from somewhere in the Veneto.

'I didn't see him again,' he said, with decision.

'We know you did,' said Chiara. 'We have the testimony of the boy Paolo. He told us that you introduced him to Andreazza, and that Andreazza paid Paolo for sex, and you encouraged this, and you even encouraged, indeed, ordered Paolo to procure another boy for Andreazza, a boy called Nino. All this happened in the pizzeria in Purgatory.'

'And you have multiple witnesses to back all this up, have you? Listen to me, young lady, as I am sure you know very little about Sicily in general and about Catania in particular. Calogero di Rienzi, with whom I work, has been trying to evict the prostitutes from the Purgatory quarter for years, for a very simple reason. They bring down the value of the properties. Everyone knows, or used to know, that if you want to meet a cheap whore, you go to Purgatory. They have always known that. The expensive ones are in Taormina. And everyone knows, of those who are interested in these things, that male prostitutes are also not impossible to find there either. Have you heard of the Baron von Gloeden? Yes? And John Maynard Keynes? Why did they come to Sicily? For twelve-year-old boys. Well, it is disgusting, and it is wrong. But what I am saying is that if Andreazza likes twelve-year-olds, then he can come to Purgatory and find one quite easily without any help from me. In fact, quite the opposite. Acting on the wishes of Calogero, it was my job to make sure that this sort of thing does not happen in Purgatory.'

'You tempted Andreazza, knowing his weakness, and you were blackmailing him. We can guess why. Fabrizio Perraino. The one you murdered.'

'Fantasy,' said Traiano dismissively. 'How would I know what Andreazza's weaknesses were? He is a married man with a child, isn't he? We discussed that over lunch. Am I some sort of psychologist who can tell that someone is a paedophile just by looking at him? And if you know anything about our quarter, you will know that boys of twelve, or whatever this Paolo is, can quite easily make decisions for themselves. I know. I was twelve once. And let me tell you, the idea of prostituting someone is the very last thing I would ever do. I am the son of a prostitute, as you know, I am sure, and I have a young son and daughter. The idea… Children need to be protected. And you have got hold of this Paolo and filled his head with lies. Has Andreazza admitted to being a paedophile? Did you seize his computer and find evidence?'

'We have got lots of evidence,' said Silvio.

'I am delighted to hear it,' said Traiano.

Another photograph was pushed towards him. He looked at it without interest. It was not a good photograph, but a blurred image, clearly part of an original photograph now blown up, the subject having originally been in the background. He knew what it was immediately. It was the only image they could find of the late Turiddu.

'Who on earth is that?' he asked.

'Your mother's former boyfriend, the father of your half-brother Salvatore,' he was told.

'Turiddu? I had forgotten him.'

'He has not been dead too long. Three years or so. You were how old when he died?'

'Why do you ask me questions when you are so sure of the answers? I was fourteen or so. And I did not like Turiddu. I want to forget him. I want my little brother Salvatore to forget him, not that he can remember him at all. He was not a good person.'

'You killed him,' said Chiara quietly.

'Signora, as a servant of the Italian state you must know that such an accusation has to be backed up by evidence. And there is no evidence for that at all. I was fourteen. The fact that I did not like him does not mean I killed him. And besides, you know, as an educated person, which I assume you are, that the simplest explanation is usually the right one. He was depressed. He hanged himself. That is the simple and accurate explanation for the facts as they appear. There is no need for further theorising. And at the time, that was the conclusion the police reached.'

'What do you say about *him*?' asked Silvio, pushing another picture towards him.

He recognised Ino.

'A boy from our quarter. Older than me. I did not know him well. Is he dead too?'

'Of course he is dead. Calogero di Rienzi wanted him dead, and you killed him. You stabbed him in the street outside the hospital.'

'You have witnesses? If so, arrest me now. But before you do, why not accuse me of every other unexplained murder? Why not undo years of police ineptitude by solving everything at once? Why not pin it all on me? Let me give you a hint. Tell me about the time I murdered my best friend, Rosario di Rienzi. Come on.'

'Did you?' asked Chiara.

'Well, most people who are murdered, or so I have read, are murdered by someone close to them. We were very close. Tell me why I would want to kill him. Please, I am waiting. I want to know why I would do something so very stupid.'

There was silence.

'You killed him because he was talking to Volta, and because he was going to betray you,' said Silvio.

Traiano paused and considered. Then he said, in a low, reasonable voice.

'You do not understand the first thing about Sicily, do you? You don't come from here. You are foreigners. Oh yes, I was not born here, but I came to be conscious here, I grew up here. You think I am the close friend of Calogero. So I am. But long before I knew Calogero at all, I knew Rosario, and he was my friend. My mother always took me to Church, and that was where we met. He was older, of course, and he taught the catechism classes for my First Holy Communion; and then I was an altar boy and so was he. There was never a time I did not love him, or he did not love me. We were closer than brothers. The idea that I would harm him is simply untrue. And we know who did harm him. That miserable creature Maso, the one Fabio Volta killed, he had Rosario's computer. He was caught trying to steal it and he got into a fight with Rosario and killed him, disposing of the body I do not know where. A computer is unimportant, I know, but it was what was on the computer that Rosario felt was worth defending. It was lots of personal stuff. He was silly. He should have let him take it. But that would have been humiliating. Maso should have given up, but that would have humiliating too; besides it would have won him the disfavour of Calogero, if Rosario had told him. As for Volta, he is a liar. A liar. A man who wants to make himself important. Rosario knew him, and so did Calogero. He investigated their father's death. But that was all. The rest is empty boasting. The idea that he had someone on the inside, an informant in this secret society of criminals... Volta wants power. He is sick of being a backroom boy. Oh, how he lapped up the glory of killing Maso. Maso was a computer thief, no more. Where is the glory in that? Volta thinks he is some sort of crusader. He isn't. He is just another ambitious politician.'

'But the boy and his mother have spoken. Andreazza has spoken,' said Chiara. 'And that puts you in the frame for procuring the boy for prostitution. A very serious crime. It means that you would, when you get out, meet your latest child as an adult.'

'What she says,' said the one called Silvio. 'And there is more.' He looked at Traiano. Chiara got up and quietly left the room. 'Look,' he continued. 'You know what we are doing here. We know what you are doing here too. You are here because you want to see what we have got on you. Otherwise, you would have walked out by now. After all, we have no reason to hold you, at least no reason to hold you that we have told you about. Maybe you think we have no reason at all. But perhaps it is just that we are keeping that card till later. Maybe we do not want to arrest you and charge you and see you convicted. We have got a great deal on you, as you might realise, or might fear; enough to get you sent down for a very nasty crime, that of prostituting the boy to Andreazza. If they both give evidence against you, that should be enough to see you get several years. Years in which your children will grow up without you. But in a way I agree with what you said, or what you implied: That boy must have known what he was doing. He was a boy from Purgatory, after all. Just like you were once. But here is the thing, the courts always believe that children have no autonomy. The courts do not understand Sicily, how children live, what children are like. He had sex with Andreazza because you told him to, and it must all therefore be your fault. That is what they will think. That is a fatal consideration as far as you are concerned. But that very consideration is also your salvation. You are only just eighteen. All the crimes you committed for Calogero happened when you were a child. Well, most of them. And even the ones which did not – and I mean your murder of Rosario di Rienzi – happened because you did your master's bidding, because Calogero had a hold over you, because he manipulated and abused you. He is the guilty one.'

'Why are you telling me all this?' asked Traiano, feigning a lack of interest.

'I am offering you a way out,' said Silvio. 'I know you have had a hard life. Your mother… you knew about her from an early age. Even before you fully understood what sex was, you knew your mother had sex for a living. The other boys must have teased you and made your life a misery. You saw your mother prostituting herself. You heard her doing so. Then, aged fourteen, you committed your first murder, and people stopped teasing you; they feared you; they respected you. You saw some terrible things; you did some terrible things. But you must realise, we represent the Ministry of Grace and Justice. We can execute justice, have you arrested and sent down for the crime of procurement. Or we can exercise grace, have you absolved, have you forgiven. I am offering you what you want. I know you want it. We know you want to escape from Sicily and from Calogero, and above all from your mother.'

'Is that it?' he asked. 'Grace and justice? But grace that is not free is not grace.'

'That is true. Give us Calogero, and you go free,' said Silvio.

'You are friends of Volta?' asked Traiano. 'I bet you are.'

Silvio laughed.

'Yes, we know Fabio Volta, but he is not one of us anymore. He is a politician, as you say. And a fool, I think. I do not trust him, and more importantly I do not like him. You are right about Volta. And you know I am right about Calogero.'

'How are you right about Calogero?' asked Traiano curiously. Conversationally, almost politely, as if he wondered what insight the magistrate might have.

'He is a hard man to break with. He commands loyalty. Abusers always do. The abused child clings to his abuser like a limpet and thinks that the abuser is his friend, when the opposite is true.'

Traiano immediately realised what he meant. He was talking of the boy Paolo, who still regarded him as his friend. That told him what he needed to know. It told him that Paolo had not spoken yet, that the dam had not broken, the flood of evidence had not come out. That he was not going to be arrested. He felt a stab of relief, but he affected not to show it.

'But Volta can get hold of you and pass on messages?' asked Traiano.

'Yes.'

'If I want to get hold of you. But if you are watching me, you can get hold of me whenever you like, can't you? What exactly do you want?'

'The head of John the Baptist, here and now, on a dish,' said Silvio, and then laughed.

Chiara had come back into the room.

'We want someone on the inside,' he said. 'It is not what you think. We know about the import of drugs into Sicily. We could stop that tomorrow, well, we could not stop it, but we could disrupt it, but that is not the main point at all. What goes on in Palermo, what goes on in Catania, none of that really matters. It is what goes on in Rome. It is the subversion of democracy. That is the real problem. It is the people who are elected so that everything looks as if it is changing, while everything is staying the same. That is the real problem. The manipulation of elections.'

'You are mad,' said Traiano, with a laugh. 'You think everything bad is caused by this non-existent organisation, this secret society in the state. That they say who will be mayor, and hey presto, that man is mayor. How can that possibly be the case? And national elections? You think we tell people how to vote and they do as we say?'

'No one thinks that,' said Chiara crisply. 'But whoever wins in Sicily usually forms the government in Rome. If you do not win in Sicily, if you win elsewhere, it may not help you too much. The people vote because they look to people like your don Calogero, or don Lorenzo or don Carmelo or don whoever it is, and they see who he likes and they tell themselves that that is the person to like. They are led like sheep. It is subtle.'

'Too subtle for me,' said Traiano. 'In case you have not noticed, I am not subtle. I am someone with very simple tastes. Myself, my family, my friends. In that order. The state? It commands no loyalty, because I look around me and see how useless it is. Now, I think I have to go. If you will excuse me.' Traiano stood. 'I want to go. I have a wife and children waiting for me. You cannot stop me. Perhaps your men can drop me off at the place on the motorway where my motorbike is?'

Silvio, seeing there was no more to be said for the moment, nodded. There were no hands shaken, no goodbyes; they all knew they would meet again.

In Rome, something had happened. The phone had buzzed; the girl Lydia's phone that is. In a stiflingly hot room near Termini station, which he was sharing with Muniddu, Tonino looked at the screen. And studied the message.

'Can you speak?' Paolo was asking.

'No, my mother is in the room. She is angry. She does not want me to speak to you. Text only.'

'I need to see you.'

'Are you in Sicily? She is always keeping an eye on me, but I can give her the slip.'

'Fuck her! Give her the slip. Take the train. Come north.'

'Where?'

'I will meet you at Termini Station.'

'But where will we go from there?'

'Don't you want to be with me?'

'Of course I do. But if I come all the way to Rome, where will we be able to be alone?'

'My mother goes out to work. I am alone in the flat. She won't know. If she finds out, so what. She knows I am grown up. She knows we have been to bed. Or if she does not know, she is stupid.'

'My mother knows which is why she is trying to stop me coming. She wants me to stop thinking of you and start thinking of others.'

'I hope something nasty happens to her.'

'Maybe it will. Termini is big. What if I cannot find you?'

'Phone me or message me.'

'If I lose my phone? Or if it gets stolen? I am worried my mother is going to take the phone off me. Especially if she thinks I have been talking to you.'

'Get the night train. Get to Termini and then come here for 10am, when she is out.'

'Where is here?'

'I am not supposed to tell you.'

'I am a prisoner here. But I will escape. She may take the phone off me if she notices me talking to you. As it is I have to hide it.'

'Via Sebastiano Satta, number 20, internal 17.'

'OK. I won't write it down. I will memorise it. I will cancel the message at once. She is coming. I may not be able to speak again. I will come soon. Expect me every day from tomorrow at 10am.'

Tonino switched off the phone. He laid it on the ground next to his bed, and looked across the room to where Muniddu was snoring. He sat up, and leant over to Muniddu and poked him apologetically in the ribs. Muniddu stopped snoring.

'What?' he asked.

He could see the boy's face was eager, and he heaved himself into sitting position.

'I have an address,' he said. 'He texted Lydia, and thought I was her. Via Sebastiano Satta, number 20, internal 17.'

Muniddu nodded.

'Tomorrow morning, we will be back home,' he said, with grim satisfaction.

He had come into the house when the others, not rising early, as they were all on holiday, were having breakfast. He announced his immediate desire to go to bed and left them, once he had kissed his wife and his children, shaken the hands of his father-in-law and grandfather-in-law, and kissed his mother-in-law and grandmother-in-law, and planted a kiss on the cheek of the younger cousins. Then he left them, and woke some hours later, aware of the hot sun coming through the shutters. Heaving himself out of bed, he walked to the kitchen to make some coffee and, checking the clock, was interested to see that it was past two in the afternoon. He had slept soundly and well. The older men were in the sitting room, one dozing, one looking at a magazine, and informed him the others would be back soon. He was pleased that he had slept so well, as this showed he was not worried, but confident. The magistrates did not frighten him, or even worry him in the slightest. He would string them along. And very soon, he was sure, he would have the assurance that the Paolo problem was solved. He knew he could trust Muniddu. He had full confidence in Tonino. It was almost on the tip of his tongue to ask the others if anyone had come by; but he forbore; one must not do anything unusual. He never asked useless questions, and neither did they.

Having dispatched his coffee and felt the healing effects course through his veins, he went back into the bedroom he shared with his wife and found what he was looking for. It was Gabriella's card. He wondered whether her brother was very keen to see him. He thought that perhaps he would find out. He went to the landline in the kitchen, and dialled the number. But before he pressed the last digit, he stopped. An immediate invitation would look as if he were keen, too keen to meet. But that was perhaps worth risking. He pressed the last digit.

The conversation with Gabriella was brief. She would be delighted. She paused the phone to ring to Ruggero. He would be delighted. Traiano gave them the address. He said he would expect them at eight that evening. The house was easy to find; he described the road, and the track down which they had to drive; opposite the track there was a permanent police patrol parked in the oleander bushes. Look out for that, then turn right. That permanent police patrol was a joke, but it did have some use when giving people directions.

And then suddenly, they were all back from the sea: his heavily pregnant wife, her mother, her sister, her grandmother, the children, the various cousins. Ceccina was grateful to relinquish care of the children and let the children kiss their father, while she went into their bedroom to lie down. It was here he found her a few minutes later. He lay next to her and was enfolded in her warm embrace.

'We have two more guests tonight, Gabriella and her brother Ruggero,' he said, almost apologetically.

'The others are cooking,' she said placidly. 'There is always plenty. Granny always produces so much; and you know what a good cook she is; and Alfio and Gino and don Renzo are coming, aren't they? Or had you forgotten? And Giuseppina and Catarina and Elena. But not don Calogero. You said he was going back to Donnafugata. We will have great fun. I wonder if Catarina is as huge as me? What is this Gabriella like?'

'Alfio and Gino like her… for me, she is just normal. The brother may be interesting.'

'I hope our food is good enough for them,' said Ceccina dreamily. They kissed. 'Be careful,' she said.

'Aren't I always?' he replied.

They were just in time for their train. It was one of those old-fashioned trains with couchettes, six to a compartment, and a long narrow corridor connecting them. They had perhaps bought the tickets for the last two couchettes on the entire train, and they were just in time to board, each with a small knapsack. They shook hands on the platform, and parted without words. Muniddu went into one of the carriages that was bound for Palermo, and Tonino went into one of the carriages bound for Catania and Syracuse.

Because they were later than the other passengers, Tonino found his compartment just as the train was drawing out of Termini. There were four people in it, ideal for his purposes, four Americans, none of whom could speak the language, for which he was grateful. The two girls were clad in shorts and their legs were the most beautiful legs imaginable; one was dark, the other blonde. They were talking in their own language, pouring over guide books and maps, and swigging water from bottles. The air was unbearably hot, and after wishing them a polite good evening, which they managed to reciprocate, he went out and stood in the slightly cooler corridor. After a time, as the train gathered speed, he went to the lavatory, and there disposed of, bit by bit, the clothes he was wearing: a pair of shoes, a pair of socks, a pair of jeans, and a tee shirt, throwing them out of the window one by one, knowing that they would lie by the track side for a long time before anyone found them, and that no one would ever, perhaps, connected them with a crime. There had been no blood. But it was best to be sure. Muniddu had told him to do this. From the knapsack, he extracted the clean clothes which he had bought in Rome, and put them on in the confined and narrow space. They were more or less identical to the clothes he had thrown away. The last thing he threw away, bit by bit, after breaking it up, was the girl Lydia's phone. His gun was in the waistband of his jeans and covered by the baggy tee shirt. The knife was in a holster attached to his calf, covered by his jeans.

In the corridor, there was someone else outside his compartment, a fellow Sicilian by the look of things, a boy older than himself, smoking a cigarette, despite the sign that said one could not.

'Hi,' he said, nodding to Tonino, making a gesture of the head to signify that they were sharing their compartment with the Americans who, one could see through the glass, were still examining the maps.

'Hi,' said Tonino.

'Americans, eh?' said the other one, offering him a cigarette.

He took the cigarette, understanding what he meant. The Americans, they were from a different world. They came here to Italy, they had so much money, they talked in loud voices, they wore shorts, they were burned by the sun, the girls seemed to be allowed to do whatever they wanted, and they were all so unfairly beautiful. They made love the length and breadth of the peninsula, they treated it as their playground, and then they went home, leaving the beautiful country to those who lived there every day of the year, and who struggled in chaos, filth, squalor and poverty. He thought for a moment of his mother, whom he loved, and the place where they lived, and how she put up with having so little, and how her dignified resignation was a reproach to him. He thought of his father in Ucciardone, and on this hot night, he felt cold at the thought of him there for years, and the thought that one day something similar might happen to him. He thought of the girl Lydia and their encounters in that hot pink room, the way he had lain with her in the narrow bed, with the knowledge that there had to be more to love than this. And he thought of the life that Paolo and his mother had led, and how it had ended, in the shabbiness of the periphery of Rome. But he had proved himself, he had not lost his nerve, and the money would be waiting for him in Sicily. And it wasn't just the money, it was the prestige, the thought that he had done a man's job, and that they would now take more notice of him. He drew on his cigarette, and how delicious the tobacco tasted!

He thought back to the events of the day that had passed. The long, long wait; the way they had put on the sort of overalls that workmen wore; dressed as such, wearing rubber gloves, they had made their way to the via Tiburtina. There they had spied Paolo playing football, his mother seated on a bench looking on. They had gone into the block of flats, Muniddu and Tonino both knowing how to pick locks, and, when inside, were challenged by no one, just two workmen with their case of tools. They had entered the empty flat and lain in wait. After about an hour the mother and son had come.

Muniddu had been calm, emotionless, as he had held them at gunpoint and tied them to chairs, taping their arms and their legs, and, most importantly of all, their mouths. They could not speak, but the eyes, the eyes had said so much. Muniddu had explained it to them. They had betrayed the boss. The boy tried to look away as the mother was made to suffer, first by Muniddu, then by Tonino. He had not expected this, and it had not been explained to him, but it was plain that he had to do what was expected of him. The boy tried to look away, but was forced to watch, and when he tried to shut his eyes, a gun was placed next to his temple. Then it was his turn. He too was violated, while the mother howled, howled in that terrible way one did when gagged, a deep unhappy bellow of horror. They killed the boy first, then her, stuffing cloths down their throats till they choked. It had not taken long. Then it was back to Termini, to abandon the overalls and the tool kit, and wait for the train south. Well, he was glad they were dead. They deserved it. And the manner of their death underlined that all who placed their trust in the state to protect them miscalculated badly.

He finished his cigarette and threw the stub out of the window. His new friend offered him another. Then, looking through the glass to the compartment, they fell to discussing the two beautiful American girls.

The most beautiful breeze had blown up and the sun had declined, and now the garden of the house outside Acireale was delightful. In its centre, on two chairs, sat the two heavily pregnant wives, Ceccina and Catarina. Around them sat the mother, sister and grandmother of Ceccina, and Elena, whose wedding date was still not yet fixed, and Giuseppina, who was to marry in the autumn. The talk was of babies and pregnancy.

In the distance, Traiano observed the women; but he was listening to don Renzo, while Alfio and Gino stood dolefully by at a slight distance. The garden was large and their part was in deep shade. He listened intently to don Renzo, but said nothing. He paused. Then he looked at Alfio and Gino and waited for them to withdraw.

'If don Calogero heard about this, what do you think he would say?' he asked.

'He would not be pleased,' said Renzo gloomily.

'He would have cancelled your wedding. You know how? By putting a bullet through your head. Easy, so easy.'

'It's not that bad, is it?' asked Renzo anxiously.

Traiano noted his submission.

'Yes, it is that bad. Of course, Alfio and Gino brought it to me, because they respect you, as a Santucci. You can thank your luck of being born a Santucci. Anyone else, they would not have come to me. They would have sorted it out themselves. But you should have sorted it out. You are the boss, not them. In the absence of Calogero, they looked to you. And you showed a lack of leadership.'

'What was I supposed to do?' asked Renzo.

'What your grandfather would have done, what your father would have done, what even your pathetic uncle would do. When there is a threat, you take action, swift and decisive action. This man, this soft in the head idiot....'

'Amilcare.'

'Soft in the head, as I say. He actually came to you, asking about the woman and her son, some sob story; he had spoken to the boy on the phone, and then given the boy the number of his girlfriend, and now he wondered if he had put him in danger. Don't you see how people like that have to be dealt with? Idiots like that have to be dealt with very firmly. This Amilcare thinks we want to harm the boy and his mother. God knows what he has been saying, and to whom. He will put ideas into people's heads. What protects us, do you think? Not the gun, not the knife, but the power of silence. I warned Amilcare. I made it clear to him that he had to keep silent. But he has got some sort of passion for this prostitute woman, and he can't keep his mouth shut. OK, go. Get me Gino and Alfio.'

Renzo left. Gino and Alfio approached.

Traiano was precise in his instructions.

'This party is going to go on all night. You are going to stay the night here. There are plenty of bedrooms. At about one or two in the morning, make sure Catarina goes to sleep and Giuseppina as well. They will not ask questions. You two, take my motorbike and go back to Catania and fix Amilcare. Shut his mouth forever. I imagine he has been talking round the quarter. Make an example of them, all of them, the parents, the two younger brothers. I cannot believe you have not fixed him already! How long has this been going on?'

'I think some time,' said Alfio.

Gino nodded.

'Fix it,' said Traiano. There was a pause. He knew what they were waiting for.

'Fifty for both of you,' said Traiano.

'I am getting married and I am in debt,' said Alfio.

'I have a baby born soon, and the cost of everything is huge,' said Gino.

'You think I have a hundred thousand just lying about? I have to borrow from the boss, and he has to borrow from the bank. OK, the bank is his wife, but even so. Make it sixty apiece.'

There was silence; then they shook hands.

'When you leave, don't even let me notice,' said Traiano.

He walked back to the guests, the other guests. Gabriella had been speaking to the two heavily pregnant wives, and she looked up and smiled at him as he approached. She was wearing a cool summer dress, and her long dark hair was tied back in a simple ponytail. She had guessed correctly. This was not a smart party, they were en famille, and she was pleased to be there. There was so much domesticity to be discussed. They had been talking in depth about little Cristoforo and Maria Vittoria and how they had been born, how they had developed, and both Ceccina and Catarina had spoken of the coming births, one as an experienced mother, the other as a first-timer. Ceccina spoke with ease about these matters, for she was knowledgeable; Catarina spoke with confidence too, as she wished to impress the beautiful stranger who, as a childless and unmarried woman, was at something of a disadvantage, in her eyes at least. Then the conversation had turned to baby names, and what they were going to call the two new children and, of course, whether they would be girls or boys. Catarina had already decided that hers was a boy and would be called Agostino, after the great doctor of the Church; Gino did not like the name very much, but she had made up her mind, and Gino, she was sure, would come round. She spoke of her husband as someone who thought he was in charge, but who was always flexible to her will. Then there was the question of the name that Anna Maria Tancredi would give to her baby, and a discussion of the absent Anna Maria, to which Gabriella listened carefully.

Ruggero, her brother, was on the edge of this conversation, a glass in hand; he was, he realised, the oldest person present, being in his mid-thirties and greying, though, he told himself with some satisfaction, still good looking. He was enjoying himself. The smell of food coming from the house was astonishingly enticing, the drink was nice, and there was certainly the prospect of cocaine to come, as he had identified Renzo as a user, which was not hard. He had been struck from the first by the immense beauty of Ceccina, this goddess in the midst of the garden, heavy with child. He had never seen such a beautiful sight. Not even his own sister or his own mother could compare to her. The men too enthralled him. Gino and Alfio were simply ugly, brutish and thuggish, and it was amusing to see such monsters here, with their womenfolk, surrounded by children, good family men, uxorious too, and yet men, he was sure, who had killed without pity or compunction.

'I think my sister told you I know your stepfather,' he was saying to Traiano. 'We are friends, though I do not see him often. We are both in the same line of business, more or less, you know, artistic things. Did Alfonso ever mention a Professor Leopardi to you?'

'Never, no,' said Traiano. 'Who is he?'

Professor Leopardi had in fact died some ten or twelve years ago, and had been a friend of Ruggero when Ruggero had been a student at Catania University; the Professor had, years previously, taught art history, been an art critic, but more importantly a collector of artworks. He had lived in a large flat on the main floor of a building very close to the house where the composer Vincenzo Bellini had been born, just behind the monument to Cardinal Dusmet. The Professor had died, leaving no children, never having married, and leaving his entire estate to Ruggero. His relatives - and there were always relatives in Sicily, were there not? - had averred that this testamentary disposition was a sign of the old man's senility, and had tried to have the will overturned in favour of a previous will which favoured them, not the interloper. The whole thing had gone to court, as neither party, Ruggero or the family, had wanted to settle; the case had lasted nearly a decade, which was not unusual, as the family had fought it all the way to the Court of Cassation, getting each verdict overturned by a higher court, and then having that overturned in turn, until the Court of Cassation had ruled in Ruggero's favour, and all legal challenges had been exhausted. But there was more to come. In the long years of litigation, the flat and the collection and the entire inheritance had been sealed, and he had sued the family for denying him his legal rights to what was his own, and the loss of income that accrued from that. They had lost that case, and he had been awarded costs, so now he was well off enough not to work, and in possession of this huge flat and a huge collection of artworks.

Traiano nodded.

'And you have made a huge number of enemies in the Professor's family,' he observed.

'There is that,' said Ruggero. 'Maybe I need some friends to counter my enemies.'

Traiano nodded.

'What are you going to do with the inheritance?'

'I already have a business, dealing in artworks,' he said. 'I am now going to deal some more. The Professor's stuff is good. I will sell it off, bit by bit. I have a shop, well, gallery, behind the post office. You may have seen it. It's been quiet for a long time, but now… Most sales are done, not in galleries these days, but on the internet. I will be busy, I think. I will use the flat as a showroom for the nicer pieces. I would like to show you the flat. It is enormous.'

'I'd like that. But tell me, you are already rich. Why do you want to be richer? Why bother? Why not just relax and enjoy yourself?'

'I couldn't do that,' he said. 'It's not in my nature. Nor is it in yours. I mean, you are rich too….'

'Only in debts. We have borrowed a fortune of late, all of us, to invest. And investments are risky. I may lose everything. And end up with nothing. Well, I started with nothing, so I would be used to that, though it would pain me to see my children reduced to what I once had. I suppose that is what drives me: the thought that my children should have a very different life from mine. And, well, after a time, you become addicted to risk; you start to enjoy walking the tightrope. But you, you have everything you want, don't you? Why bother wanting more?'

'All of us have our ambitions,' said Ruggero.

'And our ambitions can lead us astray,' said Traiano with a smile.

'The thing is this. My sister met this man. They were together for a bit, but not for long. I met him though her. He is originally from down here but he works in Rome. He is one of the Carabinieri who work in Saint Ignatius Square in Rome. You know them? The art police. The ones charged with recovering stolen works of art. He is a nice guy, and we got talking. We are friends. He no longer sees Gabriella, but he is in touch with me, and she knows and does not mind. He is a Carabiniere, but his is an office job really, and he has access to the database of stolen works of art. He is a computer man. He curates the list of stolen items that they are looking for. Like me, he has a degree in art history from the University of Catania. So, he fills in all the details, he knows what is what; if something is a Correggio, he knows what to look for; he knows who Correggio is, and if something is a copy, he knows that too.'

'I suppose the star of the database is the missing Caravaggio: *The Holy Family with Saint Lawrence and Saint Dominic.*'

'Yes. You know about that?' asked Ruggero, surprised.

He had actually seen it.

'Everyone knows about that,' he said. 'Everyone. But go on.'

'This guy, the one working in the Saint Ignatius Square, he can remove things from the database.'

'You trust this man?'

'Yes.'

'Are some of the things you have inherited on the database?'

'Maybe. At least I can check if they are,' he said.

'So that is what you are offering me?' said Traiano.

'Yes. That is what I am offering you. He is very clever. He can interfere with the database and make it look as though no one has touched it. All without leaving his desk.'

Traiano, who knew nothing of computers, looked indifferent. Ruggero felt a stab of anxiety. He had never failed to charm people before now, to get what he wanted, to impress, to press himself forward. But he saw that this young thug was rather harder to bring aboard. He was sniffing, but he was not biting. Or perhaps he was interested, but just determined not to show it.

The train had left Naples, and when it was safely out of the station, after the confusion of people getting on and off, the bunks had been put down. The Americans were now decidedly less friendly, both the Sicilians noticed. The reason for this was because they had disapproved, all four of them, of the way the two Sicilians had been smoking in the corridor in blatant disregard for the rules. But the two Sicilians did not understand this, though they did notice the unfriendly demeanour, which they immediately put down to the girls; the American boys were protective of the American girls, who perhaps felt the dangerously attractive presence of the Sicilian boys. As it turned out, the other guy, who was called Roberto, could speak some of their language, and they negotiated who should take which bunk: the girls wanted the top two, the American boys the next two, leaving the bottom two, the best two, for Tonino and Roberto. The latter waited outside while the girls got under the harsh railway sheets, and then went in while the two Americans lay down underneath the girls. Then there was silence, darkness and stifling heat.

As he lay there in the darkness, fully dressed, unable to sleep, hearing the snores and the breathing of the others, Tonino's mind went back to the early evening of the previous day. (It was now past midnight.) He remembered the way they had both treated the boy Paolo and his mother Beata, and how he had followed the lead of Muniddu. But it was not the violence of the action that he remembered or the sheer strangeness of witnessing a man do that to a woman. It was rather the indifference that Muniddu projected as he set about the task. It was simply something that had to be done, and Paolo and Beata, they were just meat, they had ceased to be human. It was very strange: he liked Muniddu; and Muniddu, he was sure, liked him. He would, he hoped, see more of Muniddu in future.

The food was magnificent. Even Ruggero, who was used to soft living, even Gabriella, who lived a comfortable life, were impressed. There was a whole roasted suckling pig which had been cooking all day, and which was now devoured in slices eaten with bread rolls. There were numerous salads and cold vegetables. There were fruits of every description, and at the end there was cassata. And the drink, the drink... There was wine and beer and limoncello. Traiano, never one for alcohol, found this last, if served straight from the freezer, quite palatable. As he sipped it, he listed to Ruggero talk about Correggio, about Boldini, and about Caravaggio, without giving away any interest at all.

For Traiano the night passed slowly. These parties were work as far as he was concerned. There were so many people to be polite to, to be respectful towards, such as his father-in-law and grandfather-in-law and their wives, people who were much older than he was and much less successful, people who depended on him for money, and who should not be reminded of that fact; the ancestors, as he thought of them, of his own children. Then there were the people who had to be soothed, and that meant mainly the women. They had to be flattered, cajoled, made to feel important, simply because, and he was honest about this, they were important. Chief of these was his wife, his beloved Ceccina. This was indeed a joyous task, spending time with her, listening to her, kissing her, making love to her, being with her, telling her and showing her that in the end, she was the only one that mattered to him, and that all the others, apart from his children, were people he had to court for what he termed political reasons. They had been together from the beginning, and she had been a virgin when they had first slept together; their mutual devotion was unshakeable, and this was something he was very proud of. He did not believe in the sort of immorality practiced by Alfio and Gino, for example. Or indeed the boss himself; but she, knowing how important he was in the quarter, could never quite believe that he was all hers. And as he talked to Gabriella, for example, he could feel her eyes upon him, worried that he was talking to someone he might find attractive. He had to turn and look at her from time to time and convey, via the telepathy of marriage, that he was hers and hers alone.

He also had to pacify the boss's sisters. Luckily, he saw very little of Assunta, and he had not thought it necessary to invite her and her husband tonight. Assunta ran the Catania office, the top floor of the building in whose basement was the gym. He often had to ask Assunta for things, and she made him feel her furious disapproval of him; Elena less so, Elena had always been the nicer one; and Elena, going to marry Renzo Santucci, could perhaps pretend that he was beneath her notice, and that to show her disapproval was somehow undignified. Besides which, there was the simple matter that Traiano could handle her future husband in a way she could not. So, she was beginning to rely on him, even though she did not like to admit it. Both girls had got this dislike of Traiano from their mother, and out of a natural jealousy given the way that both their brothers had shown an evident preference for him. Then there was Catarina, Gino's wife, soon to give birth, a clever woman and a threat who had to be kept in check. Then there was Giuseppina who, as the boss's former sister-in-law could, with some justification, feel slighted. And finally, his sister-in-law Pasqualina, who must not be overlooked. He was mystified why she was not married or at least on the way to getting married. He hardly dared discuss this with Ceccina; he knew the women resented male interference in their romantic lives.

It was late, very late, when the excited children finally got sleepy and were put to bed; then the men were left momentarily on their own, and this was the moment that don Renzo Santucci saw fit to go into the house and come out again, glassy eyed, taking Ruggero with him. No one was tired. The weather was so hot, they had spent most of the daylight hours in a somnolent state, and now it was cooler, and one had to make the best of what coolness God sent. Renzo was now drunk, or drugged, or both, and he staggered to the end of the garden to open his trousers and urinate against the wall. Traiano watched him go. He looked at Ruggero and Gabriella and raised an eyebrow slightly. The women returned from putting the children to bed. Alfio and Gino had disappeared, he noticed; maybe others noticed as well, but no one commented.

It was simple, the simplest thing imaginable, as far as Alfio was concerned. He had always been the cleverer of the two, and Gino took his word for it. They came into the city on the motorbike that Traiano had lent them, leaving it at some distance, and then walked into the quarter. The building that Amilcare and his two brothers and his parents lived in was familiar to both of them. Amilcare had long been an associate, though not an important one, after all. It was old, run down, poorly maintained, and, this was the key point, owned by the commune of Catania, who were notorious for their mismanagement of the properties under their care and their failure to look after them. The sort of accident they had in mind was very common. Both he and Gino knew how to pick locks, especially simple ones like these. They entered the building and found what they were looking for by a process of deduction, by looking at the post boxes just inside the front door. One was overflowing, the sure sign of an empty flat or a family on holiday. By lucky chance it was the flat on the top floor, and they made their way quietly up the stairs, past the penultimate floor which was where the family of Amilcare lived. The front door was not hard to overcome, and once in the place they headed for the kitchen. As expected, the gas was switched off, but luckily, they had brought a torch and were able to find the place where the gas supply could be switched on. They switched it on. Then they checked that all the windows were closed, and switched on the gas cooker, being careful to switch off the torch first. The soft hiss of the gas was reassuring. Then they left, leaving the front door open, and knowing that the gas was heavier than air and would travel downwards, to be ignited by someone doing something as simple as switching on a light. A few moments later they were on their way back to Acireale.

In the coolness of the night, the city of Catania was alive with people, enjoying a respite from terrible August. Even at this very late hour, the pizzeria was full. Those employed there knew that don Traiano would not be in that night, as he was in Acireale, holding a party for all his relatives, or more accurately, his wife's relatives, which was a large number of people, and that Alfio and Gino would be there too, and probably other hangers-on such as the young Tonino Grassi. As for don Calogero, the boss of the quarter, he was with his new wife at their house in Donnafugata, with his children. All the important people were not in the quarter, and this produced a frisson of unease. Of course, they were all innocently enjoying themselves away from the heat and noise of the city, but even so, what if they were plotting something? But overlying this sense of fear, was another type of dread. With all the bosses away, who was there to protect them from the evils that lurked? The bosses were the evil, but at the same time they were the protection from other evils, unspoken evils, the grave misfortunes that fate might throw at them, and which fate, historically, had thrown at the island of Sicily.

Amilcare was still on duty in the pizzeria, but eager to go home and rest. The other men in the pizzeria, all much younger than himself, teenagers really, did not like him. He knew that. They thought he was soft in the head. Well, he knew he was not the brightest of sparks. His father had told him that often enough as he had been growing up. And when he had landed up in Bicocca, that had, as far as his father was concerned, proved it. Well, he was the only one in the family who made any money, and he dutifully handed most of it over to his mother, and they were still not grateful. Even his younger brothers had picked up this idea that he was stupid and worthless. It depressed him. And it reminded him of the one person who had been kind to him, Beata. And now too, she was gone, and perhaps he had not helped. He wanted to be back with Beata. He knew she was in Rome; he knew that she had betrayed the boss, or Paolo had, and that she was in danger. For that reason, he had approached Alfio and Gino, asking them to spare Beata, pleading her cause. It now struck him that he might well have made things worse.

As the pizzeria wound down for the night, Amilcare cleaned up, mopped the floor, and waited to be paid. He went out to the square outside the Church of the Holy Souls in Purgatory and sat on the steps, watching the boys play football, watching their passionate involvement in the game. He was aware that the boys playing football had noticed him and were conscious of him watching, and resented it. One of them made an obscene gesture at him. It was only the dregs of the quarter that were out so late, as it was now way past midnight; though on a summer's night, when sleep was impossible, being out was the only thing to be. And there was no school tomorrow, as it was the summer holidays. But even if there had been school, most of these boys never or hardly ever went. They were the dregs, he knew, because these were the ones whose families never went away, like his own; these were the ones who did not have friends or relations in the mountains, in cool places like Enna or Erice; or by the beach in Giardini Naxos or Lido di Noto; or Donnafugata or Acireale. These were the families who were condemned to a summer in the inferno of Catania, who never went anywhere, who had no escape. He knew what they lived through, as he lived through it himself. His own family had nowhere to go. He had nowhere to go, except to the flat in which they lived, where one could hardly breathe in such weather; even the people upstairs had gone away. But not them. He dreaded going home, even though he knew, eventually, he must.

With leaden feet, he crossed the square and wandered over to the bar. The respectable clientele had departed. A pair of traffic police were having a drink at the bar, and one or two of the girls, perhaps desperate for someone, were still there, hoping against hope that someone would come in. He looked towards them, but they avoided his glance.

The traffic cops liked the place, so did the police, who valued the free drinks and who, realising that nothing was free, but all had to be paid for, would often impart nuggets of useful information. The traffic cops knew whose car was parked outside whose house all night; the police knew who was on duty, where the attention of the police was directed. Funnily enough, never towards Purgatory, the most notorious quarter of the city, the only place where bag snatching and pick-pocketing never happened. Sometimes the police would come and the traffic cops too, and the people of the quarter would, with Traiano's permission, make representations, which ended, often with a parking ticket lost, or a good word put in for a local boy. This was the place where favours were done.

The two girls still there had perhaps been there all night without much luck, and one of them would, sooner or later, look up, look at him, and think such an assignment better than nothing, certainly better than going home after an utterly fruitless evening. And one of them did look up, saw him still there, and relented. She slid off her bar stool, and approached him.

'Don't ask me about Beata,' the girl said with evident weariness. 'You already did, last week. Or if you did not ask me, you asked someone. No one is talking of Beata, no one at all. We are not stupid.'

'What do you know?' he asked.

'Nothing, nothing at all. I don't know any Beata. I never knew her. I never heard her name.' The girl angrily lit a cigarette. 'Look,' she said, relenting. 'This place is not as nice as it once was. But if you go round stirring things up, you will get us all into trouble. And you have been stirring things up. You are stupid. Beata's gone. Forget about her. Don't think about her. And don't talk about her. Look, I am sure you are a nice guy, but Beata did not care about you at all. Forget her. Before it is too late.'

'What have they been saying?'

'Don't ask stupid questions. Go home.'

She turned away. He prepared to go home. Home was only a five-minute walk away. The street was narrow and full of rubbish and parked cars. He put his key in the front door, and pushed it open. At first, he thought someone had urinated in the stairwell, or worse, again. The smell was horrid. Then he groped for the light switch, and pressed it.

A few hundred metres away, in the bar, where the barmen were washing up the glasses, the windows shook, and they looked at each other uncertainly. The traffic cops, just about to move on, looked alarmed, thinking it must have been a bomb, but where?

Always a light sleeper, don Calogero's mother, the Black Widow Spider, woke, wondering what it was that had awoken her.

In various beds around the quarter, some slept on, others not. Some of the girls from Eastern Europe knew what that sound and the shock wave meant. They had heard and felt bombs before, back home, but had never expected to hear such a thing in peaceful Catania. The men they slept with slept on. After a considerable delay, one could hear the sound of sirens and police cars and ambulances.

Over the straits of Messina, the glorious August sun rose. The journey was short, a mere twenty minutes, and below deck, on the train carriages, the passengers for the most part slept. Only a few had come up to look at the view. Tonino was one of them. And in his hand was a cup of coffee, the best coffee he had ever tasted, and a rice ball, which was delicious. The night passed below in the train compartment had been most uncomfortable, and the cool air was a refreshing delight. He was glad to leave Italy behind him.

Next to him stood Roberto. He had got up as quietly as he could do so, and he had left the compartment without wanting to wake anyone up, and he had certainly not sought the company of Roberto; but on reaching the ferry deck, after a few moments, there was Roberto, come to join him. He had not invited him, and Roberto knew he had not been invited, but Roberto had chosen to come. This was interesting, worrying, and a little flattering. It was clear that Roberto wanted something. It was also possible that Roberto had some leverage over him, which would make his wanting something more likely to have a good outcome, but which surely carried risks.

He could guess what it was. On getting into their couchettes, Roberto had followed the example of the American boys and stripped to his underwear, piling his clothes up to bolster the thin pillow. The two girls were on the uppermost bunks, no doubt with their faces turned to the walls, so this level of male immodesty was just about acceptable. But Tonino had not undressed and had, when he thought everyone was asleep, when the lights were out, transferred the gun to his knapsack and placed that under his pillow. Had Roberto noticed the gun? The gun was now safely back in its usual place, in the waistband of his trousers, under his tee shirt. But had Roberto seen him put it there?

They regarded each other in silence, and Tonino, noticing Roberto's hesitancy, made no attempt to help him speak. They were half way between Sicily and Italy; it seemed to Roberto, half way between two lives. He had been with some relatives in Rome, and things had not quite gone the way he had hoped; there was no help to be had there; now he was coming home, to Catania. Things in Catania were difficult. But where to begin?

'You speak good English,' said Tonino at last, taking pity on him. 'Where did you learn?'

'Only a few words, really,' he replied modestly. 'At school, at the university, they run a course; I am doing law, but it is a course you can do on the side, so to speak. Very useful. Well, useful last night.'

'What year of university?'

'About to start the second. What about you?'

Tonino shrugged. Roberto did not pursue it. He had, of course, noticed the gun; and he knew the most basic rule. No questions.

'Are you getting off in Catania?' asked Tonino.

'Yes. My family live near the Via Plebiscito, near the Castle, if you know it.'

'I do,' said Tonino. 'I live in Catania too. In the Purgatory quarter.'

That was an admission, as was living near the Castle, near the via Plebiscito. People who lived in that quarter could not look down on anyone, apart from people who lived in Purgatory which was the only quarter with a less savoury reputation. And yet Roberto was going to University, he could speak a foreign language, he was tall (something Tonino was always sensitive to), he had a beard, and he was very handsome. What could he want? He ought to ward him off, but he hesitated. Instead, he spoke, perhaps without caution.

'Do you know the gym in Purgatory? No? It is the only one. You can ask for me there, and someone will always come and find me for you.'

'This evening?' asked Roberto.

Tonino looked at him. Roberto immediately saw he had made a mistake by showing too much eagerness. But perhaps not. He felt a stab of fear, for he knew this boy was dangerous.

'I have to see a few people when I get back,' conceded Tonino. 'But we will meet, we will meet. You will see me at the gym. Just tell them when you arrive there that I have given you free membership. They will let you in. What is your name?'

'Roberto Costacurta.'

'I will tell them to expect you.'

He felt a new and strange sensation, the pleasure that comes from feeling flattered. This Costacurta seemed keen to be his friend; this Costacurta was someone from a similar background to himself, but educated, someone who could perhaps get on in life; he was taller, he was older, in his twenties, and he was clearly impressed by Tonino. He had seen the gun, he had recognised something in Tonino, that made him want to know him better. This might be advantageous to both of them.

The ferry had almost reached the Sicilian side. It was time to go below.

He came downstairs at about eight in the morning, while the entire house slept, leaving his sleeping wife upstairs, aware as he came down of all the sleeping bodies around him. He had pulled on a pair of crumpled jeans and an even more crumpled shirt, and when he arrived in the kitchen the first thing he did was switch on the television very low and listen to the local news very carefully. It was as he supposed. A terrible accident, an explosion in the Purgatory quarter of Catania, probably caused by a gas leak which, in turn, the man on the television was saying, had been caused by poor maintenance by those responsible for the building, the commune of Catania. Five dead, an entire family. Several injured. He switched off the television. He would hear all about it later, he was sure. That was enough for now. In fact, he had the feeling he might hear little else for the next few days.

More interesting for the moment, as he made the coffee, was the thought of what he had learned last night from Ruggero Bonelli. The Carabiniere who worked in the Safeguarding of the Artistic Heritage, or whatever they called it, was called Pasquale Greco. He and Ruggero saw each other a great deal. Pasquale Greco was about thirty and his birthday was the 8th September, because Ruggero had mentioned he would be seeing him then. That meant that Pasquale Greco would be easy to track down, to check out, to see whether he was to be trusted, whether he was the sort of person with whom one might find leverage. Clearly, it was this relationship with Greco that he was being offered; Greco's help would give them a competitive edge in the art market. Gabriella too had been helpful. She had told him that her brother's art dealing made little money, but he had the inheritance, and now he wanted opportunities to expand. He could see it all, how it would work out. He knew why he was being approached. There were lots of art works that couldn't be sold, but perhaps could be marketed, and to these art works, Ruggero clearly thought he, Traiano, had a way in.

As he waited for the coffee to heat up, he looked out of the window. There was someone at the gate. A boy. It was Tonino Grassi. He had almost forgotten about Tonino. He went out to the garden, towards the gate, feeling the stones underneath his bare feet. Tonino approached.

'There is trouble in Catania,' said Traiano. 'I was just watching the television. Have you heard? No? Have you come from there?'

'No, boss, I just came on the train from Messina.'

'All well?' he asked.

'All well,' said Tonino. 'Could not ask for better.'

'I have got something for you,' said Traiano, meaning the money.

'Thanks, boss.'

'Do you want cash?'

'I would like a nicer place to live for me and my mother,' said Tonino.

'That can be arranged,' said Traiano. 'I can always speak to Assunta; she organises these things, and you can have a better place. As a matter of fact, I have already thought about it; there was someone here last night who has an empty property which needs looking after. There's something else too that needs dealing with… but I have to speak to Gino about that. It will be a nice little income stream for you. You stink by the way. When did you last have a shower? Days ago, I bet. And you stink of smoke. Have you been smoking? What did I tell you about that?'

'That I wasn't to do it and that you would beat me if I did.'

'Well remembered; not that I have forgotten either. Have you been smoking?'

'No, boss. There were people smoking on the train, and I suppose the smoke sort of drifted over and made me smell of it too.'

'You find us in a bit of a state. We have the family here, and we had friends last night. In fact, several of them are still here. We did not go to sleep until a few hours ago. Alfio is here, Gino is here; they have been here all night. When they get up, they can drive you back to Catania. Mind you, Catania being the mess it is, perhaps you had better spend the day here and go to the beach. I can lend you some swimming trunks. I rather fancy going to the beach myself.'

He pulled Tonino towards him and kissed him. Tonino went scarlet, not with embarrassment but with pleasure. This was a rare sign of the boss's favour. He led the way into the house, and to the much-needed coffee. He left him in the kitchen, and taking Tonino's backpack, went upstairs. His wife was still asleep in bed. Sitting on the floor, he reached under the bed and took out a suitcase. He placed four neat packages, each containing 5,000 euro, and consisting of one hundred fifty-euro notes, into Tonino's backpack.

Traiano returned. He handed the backpack to Tonino.

'Thanks, boss,' said Tonino, gratefully receiving the backpack.

'How's the signora?' he asked, meaning Tonino's mother who, as everyone knew, was an old friend of signora di Rienzi, don Calogero's mother.

'She is well, boss, I hope. She was last time I saw her, which was only a few hours ago.'

'Doesn't she wonder where you get to?'

'She knows I am grown up, boss,' said Tonino.

'We all like the signora,' said Traiano. 'Ah,' he said, for Gino had now entered the room. 'Ruggero Bonelli was here, and so was his sister last night. He has inherited a property near the monument to Cardinal Dusmet, and he wants a caretaker. He is not going to live in it himself, but use it as a picture gallery. He needs someone to clean, to keep an eye out, to guarantee security. It's a huge place and it has a set of rooms where you and your mother could live. What do you think, Gino?'

'If Ruggero wants it, and Gabriella wants it, then I am all in favour,' said Gino. 'You know Gabriella?' he asked, looking at Tonino.

'She is the beautiful one who is in charge of the planting of the trees?'

'Correct. She is an angel who has come down straight from heaven. Alfio, me and don Renzo are having a competition to see who can have her first.'

'Luckily, she can look after herself,' said Traiano. 'I saw on the television that there has been some trouble in Catania, in our quarter.'

'Has there?' said Gino.

'Are you going back soon?'

Gino nodded.

'I think you should stay her and enjoy the beach,' he said. 'Can you give Tonino a lift, if you go back tonight?'

'Yes, boss,' said Gino.

The boss nodded.

Chapter Nine

As it was getting dark, he entered the building and walked up the stairs to the floor where he lived with his mother. He put his key in the lock and entered. The first thing he sensed was the aroma of soup. Was she expecting him? He was not sure. Perhaps she hoped for him to walk in, just like this, at any moment. She looked up at him as he entered the tiny kitchen and smiled. He kissed her cheek, and she kissed his forehead, but did not ask where he had been, or what he had been doing, or why he had been absent so long.

He sat at the table, and she put the soup before him. He tasted it. It was delicious.

'Don Traiano said he would give us a new place to live,' said Tonino at last. 'Would you like that? He has to speak to a few people first, but it is all arranged. Or so I think. If he says so, it happens.'

'I'd like that more than anything,' said signora Grassi.

'I discussed it with don Traiano this morning. I was in Acireale, where he is staying. We went swimming in the sea. It was very nice, especially in this hot weather.'

Signora Grassi nodded. She was used to deferring to her son. The same son now put his soup aside and turned to the knapsack he had placed by his feet on the floor. Out of it, he took two thousand euros in fifty-euro notes. He laid the forty notes on the table. The signora took them and placed them in a jar by the cooker, while her son returned to his soup.

'You saw Ceccina?' she asked, when she returned to the table. 'Is she staying there in Aci until the birth?'

'Yes, I saw her. I think so. I think they are staying there until the end of August, though he comes back when he has to.'

'I just hope that when the time comes, they do not get stuck in traffic. It can only be a matter of weeks now. Well, I am glad you were in Aci. You have missed all this. Last night. The explosion. The whole building shook. I thought it was going to fall down.'

She told him what had happened. He paid attention to the exact building that had been destroyed.

'That is where Amilcare lives,' he remarked. 'You say there were some killed? Amilcare, God have mercy on him, is soft in the head. If there was an accident with the gas, I bet he caused it.'

'They say a whole family has been wiped out,' said his mother sadly. 'But they have not said who. What a terrible accident.'

Tonino knew there were no such things as accidents; and he also knew that one should act as if this was what they were saying it was: an accident, nothing more. When he had finished eating, he picked up his backpack, kissed his mother and prepared to leave.

The first thing he did was walk to the Via Etnea, to a second-hand phone shop, where he was known, and where he bought a mobile phone for a few hundred euros. Then he walked towards the Church of the Holy Souls in Purgatory. Taking one of the alleys off the main square, he went up to where Lydia lived with her mother, to give her the new phone and to thank her for lending him the old one which, he said, apologetically, he had lost. She did not question this; and why should she, when she immediately saw that the new phone was much nicer than the old one? Nor did she ask him to stay; she was, he realised, and was pleased to realise, much more interested in the new phone than him. A few minutes later, after this duty was done, he was crossing the square, and absent-mindedly crossing himself as he went past the door of the Church of the Holy Souls in Purgatory.

Outside the Church, he met don Giorgio. They shook hands. He was always very respectful with don Giorgio, whom his mother revered.

'You have heard about this accident?' the priest asked.

'I was away in Acireale,' he replied. 'But my mother told me, and from what she said, it was Amilcare's house.'

'It was. Five bodies, three children, two parents. The other people in the building were away, thankfully. Nearby buildings damaged. Still…. It is upsetting. You were in Acireale?'

'Yes, don Traiano is staying there, and there was a big party there last night, lots of people there, and they all got drunk and stayed the night rather than drive back.'

Don Giorgio took this in.

'Have you heard anything about Beata and her son Paolo?' he asked.

'Nothing, don Giorgio, nothing. I know that they left and told no one where they were going, and that Amilcare was terribly upset not to hear from them. Poor Amilcare. Is it certain he is dead?'

'Yes, but it has not been announced yet. I went there, and the police let me through the barriers and I said a prayer. They were recovering the bodies, or what was left of them. They were frightened of further explosions.'

'That was kind of you to go and say a prayer,' said Tonino. 'May they all rest in peace. I think one of the brothers was a bit older than me, and one a bit younger?'

'Yes, the youngest was thirteen.'

They fell silent for a few moments, then they parted. It was now dark but not late, and he walked towards the gym, which was under the office block where Assunta, the boss's sister, worked. It was a narrow street, choked by parked cars and overflowing rubbish bins, like so many in the quarter, picturesque and squalid. The gym entrance was next to the entrance to the offices, and standing next to the door was don Calogero in conference with his sister Assunta. He had clearly just arrived from Donnafugata, for he was wearing jeans and a crumpled tee shirt, not his usual sharp suit and highly polished shoes. He and Assunta were in deep conversation, and while don Calogero noticed him, he clearly did not want him to stop. He carried on and went into the gym.

The guy on the desk looked up as he entered.

'Hi,' he said, with a trace of anxiety in his voice.

'Hi,' replied Tonino. The guy was a very distant relation of Ceccina. 'Look, there is a guy coming, I am not sure when, but some time soon. He is called Roberto Costacurta. I told him he can have free membership. Can you fix him up with a locker in the changing room and a card and the rest of it?'

'Sure,' said the guy on the desk.

'Don Calogero is here, outside. Has he come in?'

The guy shook his head.

'Are you expecting your cousin, don Traiano? It is just that I saw him today in Acireale, and he told me that he and don Renzo, Gino and Alfio were all going this very evening to Agrigento to visit Gino's parents. If anyone asks…'

'Really?' said the guy behind the desk, not surprised at all, as if this sort of thing were most usual. 'Did you get the impression they would be away for some time?'

'Two or three days. Because Catarina is having the baby soon, as is Ceccina, Gino wanted to go away while it was still possible, and the others decided to go with him. That is what don Traiano said. They wanted a bit of a holiday while they could still have one.'

'There have been a lot of guys looking for you,' said the guy behind the desk.

Tonino nodded and went down the corridor and into the part of the gym reserved for people like himself. In the changing room, where he was alone, he opened his locker and transferred the cash into it, noting that the amount of money was now becoming almost unmanageable. He took his knapsack and filled it with various small packages from the locker, emptying the entire stock into the bag. Then, equipped with this illegal pharmacy of generic medicines, he went upstairs to the men's changing rooms. His entry was immediately noted, and one by one, they approached him, each asking for his particular needs, each handing over the money, until all the things he had to sell were gone, and he knew that he would have to go that night, or tomorrow, to Doctor Moro, to restock.

Stepping back out onto the street, there was something far more important for him to consider, which put the thought of Doctor Moro out of his mind for the moment. Don Calogero was still there, but now evidently finishing his conversation with his sister, who he pecked on the cheek and whom he watched leave. Tonino paused. His instinct was correct. The boss, the real boss, wanted to speak to him.

'Hi, Tonino,' he said, with a broad smile. 'You have grown. You will never be tall, but you are taller.' He pulled Tonino towards him, and kissed his forehead. Tonino beamed. 'Is Traiano here?' he asked.

'He told me, boss, that he was going tonight to Agrigento with Alfio and Gino and don Renzo. I was with him in Acireale this afternoon, and he mentioned that they are staying for a few days. A holiday before Catarina's baby is born.'

'Well,' said Calogero. 'Perhaps they need a little holiday, though he has been in Aci long enough. How is Ceccina? Fit to burst? And Catarina? The same I imagine? My wife, whom you have never met, is a few months behind them. Anyone else pregnant that we know of?'

'Not that I know of, boss.'

'Things are going to get a little difficult around here in the next few days, so I have got a job for you,' he said to Tonino, with great casualness. 'Now listen. There is going to be trouble, and you are going to help create it. All the boys you can get hold of, tomorrow, I want them outside the city hall, calling insults at the people who work there as they go in and out. Throw coins at them too. These people murdered Amilcare and his family. The flat they lived in belonged to the commune, and the commune did nothing to maintain it, or check the gas; the commune takes our money, from us the poor, and then leaves us to die. That is the message. Take this' – he pressed a roll of banknotes into Tonino's hands – 'and spread it around. The more successful you are, the more you will earn. Now there is a man called Volta who works in the city hall. You know him?'

'The one Maso tried and failed to kill. You want me to kill him?'

'No. Don't get carried away. I want you to tell him to come and see me. He will tell you to get lost at first, but, when he sees the way things are going, he will change his mind, I think.'

'Understood, boss,' said Tonino, trousering the money, feeling its weight.

It had been a hard day in the city hall, and one could sense that the situation was spinning out of control. No one knew what to do. The television reports were not good for the junta. All television stations were leading with the story that there had been an accidental gas explosion, but that this was an accident that could have been, should have been, prevented.

'Are they saying that we neglected to do what we ought to have done, and that this was our fault?' asked the Mayor, time and again.

That was precisely what they were saying. And there did not seem to be any way of getting round it. It was an accident, but it was not an accident, it could have been foreseen. The Mayor, seeing his authority under attack, decided on sacrifices. Several people in the housing department were sacked. There were a few calls to Rome, to party headquarters, asking for help and advice. But in party headquarters in faraway Rome, they were beginning to think, or so it seemed by their tone on the line, their delay in answering emails, and then not answering them in depth - or was this simple paranoia? - in Rome they were thinking, perhaps, that the Catania party was not worth defending, and should be cut loose.

Exhausted, the people who worked at the city hall all went home. That night, the names of the dead were announced on the television. In bars, in restaurants, and in private homes, in the Purgatory quarter in particular, people were glued to their screens. There were photographs, not of Amilcare, who was not very photogenic, but of his two teenage brothers and his parents. There were vox pops at the pizzeria where he had worked and in the square outside the pizzeria. Once or twice, Tonino came into the pizzeria, and spoke to various young men, handing out ten euro notes surreptitiously, explaining what needed to be done; he visited the trattoria and the bars as well. At quiet moments, the waiters stood around with nothing to do, discussing it. Poor Amilcare. No one had liked him very much when he was alive, but they liked the commune of Catania even less. These were the people who sucked the blood of the poor (in other words made them pay tax) and gave them nothing in return. These were the lords of misrule who had presided over a millennium of Sicilian decline. When these things were said, everyone nodded vigorously. During the course of the evening, don Calogero came in, still wearing his jeans and his crumpled tee shirt, to show that he had come back from Donnafugata in a hurry. He shook a lot of hands. At about one in the morning, the pizzeria was silent, and the floor was mopped, and the men waited around for their pay. That done, they all departed.

The next day, Catania, after the tension of the previous day, awoke into a nightmare. It really did seem, and not for the first time in the city's long history, that the rulers had lost control. In the middle of the road that crossed Terpsichore Square, the very heart of the city, at its nodal point, hooligans had blocked the traffic with rubbish bins which they had set on fire, and the traffic police had done nothing as yet to remove the obstruction. The calls from city hall to the traffic police became more and more heated until, with the city gridlocked and the horns of frustrated motorists blaring in the air everywhere, the Mayor lost his temper and threatened the head of the traffic police, when he finally deigned to come to the phone, with the sack. Ten minutes later, it was announced that the traffic police were on strike.

The blaring of the horns was what woke Tonino, who had been so tired that he had hoped to spend at least part of the morning in bed. Dressed still in his underwear, he went to the window and opened it. He leaned out. One could sense the anger in the air. Something was very wrong. Less than half a mile away, the Mayor felt the same, perhaps.

He got dressed and went to the kitchen.

'There's coffee,' his mother said. 'I am going out, to the square, because this is a terrible business, as don Calogero has said, and we must tell them how angry and sad we are, and that we won't put up with it any longer.'

'Which square?' he asked. 'Ours?'

'No,' she said. 'To the square with the Elephant.'

She withdrew. He heard the door close after her. Tonino was pleased. He had not told his mother what to do, but someone had; not that she needed much prompting, he imagined.

Meanwhile, in the corridors and the palatial rooms of the city hall, in the usual quiet and grave courtyard, all was depression, paralysis and chaos. If the traffic police were on strike, damn them, then someone had to clear the roads; but the police were strangely uncooperative, as were the Carabinieri, as were the real army. Orders were shouted down the phone to each in turn, and only excuses came back. The junta and the Mayor had the distinct feeling that people were desperately rowing away from the sinking ship. But they had been through worse and survived. They would survive this – another strike, another day of chaos. This was Sicily after all, this was Catania. Chaos was, if not normal, at least not unusual.

A call was put through to the Ministry of the Interior, on the Viminal Hill in Rome. It was important to get one's complaint in first. They were in charge of policing at a national level, and it was important that they realised just how useless the forces of law and order were proving to be in Catania. But it proved to be hard to get through to either the minister, or the minister's various assistants. They were not taking calls. When one was finally put through, it was to be told that the Viminal Hill had more important things to worry about than what was happening down in Catania. Once more, Sicily was made to feel like an unloved, distant and useless colony. The Mayor swore and shouted even more than before. And at the same time, he was disturbed. He had always been able to count on the Viminal.

It was Volta, by no means the highest-ranking person in the junta, indeed, an unelected special adviser, who picked this up. An ex-policeman, who had worked in Rome, he still had contacts there, and he made a few phone calls. These were friendly in tone, and sympathetic. There was trouble in Catania? The Mayor was losing his grip? There were people shouting in the streets? The police and the carabinieri refused to do anything about it? These were the usual sort of problems one faced from time to time, but that they should all occur at once, that was unfortunate. 'And what was happening in Rome?' he asked, for he had heard not all was well on the Viminal.

The story that came out was incomplete. No one quite knew. Something had gone wrong. The Viminal was blaming the Ministry of Grace and Justice. The Ministry of Grace and Justice was blaming the Viminal. But over what, no one knew, but whatever it was, it had to be serious.

Volta put down the phone and thought for a few moments. He understood. At least he thought he did. Then phoned his wife on her mobile.

He got straight to the point.

'Andreazza's wife. Your great friend. Phone her. Tell her that he will soon be home and smelling of roses. They have nothing on him and will release him, and soon. Tell her.'

He cut short his wife's desire to speak. He dialled again, the number that the magistrates had given him. The one called Silvio picked up.

'You have fucked up,' he informed Silvio.

'You have heard?' asked Silvio gloomily. 'It was supposed to be a secret, for obvious reasons. I have only just heard myself.'

'I guessed. This was always going to happen. They are dead, the boy and his mother?'

'Yes, they are dead.'

He put the phone down on Silvio. The man seemed not to realise what this meant. Everything was now changed. The Italian Republic had proved that it could not protect the people it had guaranteed to protect. If that was the case, what could it do? It had failed.

Outside, in the via Etnea, a crowd had gathered since early morning and not dispersed, chanting 'Murderers! Murderers!' all day long. It consisted almost entirely of women and children. (That had been Tonino's idea, his stroke of genius: a crowd of angry young men would be one thing, but this was a crowd of the friends and neighbours of dead Amilcare, whose grief and anger looked much more convincing, much less open to misinterpretation.) The women were banging cooking pots together.

When the people who worked in the city hall, secretaries, clerks and officials - their nerves on edge thanks to the constant if distant sound of metal on metal - had ventured out to take their usual coffee breaks, they had been pelted with coins, jostled and, in a few cases, spat upon. There were cries of 'Traitors!' and 'Murderers!'

Meanwhile, in other parts of the city, in broad daylight, gangs of little boys were turning over cars and setting light to them. In one part of the city, a boy with a gun had hijacked a bus and set that alight. The forces of law and order were nowhere to be seen.

In the main meeting room of the city hall, those who had not seen the writing on the wall, and had decided to go home, were gathered in a conference that had begun in the morning and dragged on most of the afternoon. As evening came, no resolution was in sight. It struck Volta, looking round the table at the thirty or forty worried faces that filled the room, that the atmosphere must have been similar in Versailles on the fateful day the mob had marched on the château demanding bread; or the terrible day a couple of years later, when the tocsin had sounded and the rabble of Paris had attacked the Tuileries and killed the Swiss Guards, and caused the Royal family to flee for safety with the Legislative Assembly. On both occasions, Louis XVI had been unable to take a decision, unable to act. And it was the same now. No one knew what to do.

Volta had made notes as the afternoon wore on. Everything done so far to calm the situation had failed. None of the press briefings had worked. They had thrown the man in charge of housing to the dogs, but that had not quelled popular discontent. Now the question was: should they shut the door of the city hall, in case the people outside came in and made trouble? Was this not a wise precaution? But would it be seen as provocative? Or would it be seen as inviting an attack; would it mean that by shutting the door, they were frightened of their own citizens? If that were the case, that would be fatal. They were supposed to be representing the citizens, not trying to shut them out: open government, and all that. So, no decision could be made about shutting the door.

Given that the crowd outside were a nuisance and behaving in a threatening manner, should they order the police to disperse them? But would this make things worse? And would the police co-operate? If the police did disperse them, what if they merely came back the next day? And if the police failed to disperse them, what if there were a riot, what if they burned cars, threw stones, or worst of all, fired guns? What if someone were killed? Of course, elsewhere there were rumours of riot, so perhaps it was too late. And the police, damn them, were not taking their calls. So, no decision could me made about the use of force, and all discussion of it was pointless anyway.

Given that this family had died in a property owned by the commune, should the Mayor go out and speak to the crowd, say that the authorities were sorry, and that the people had a grievance which was to some extent justified? But if they did that, were they opening themselves up to being sued, as some clever, or not so clever lawyer would see this as an admission of guilt? And would that pacify the crowd? Would it not be possible that the Mayor would be humiliated by the people, which would certainly kill the prospect of re-election? But if the Mayor went out with the entire junta and showed how sorry they all were? But the entire junta was not to blame, only certain members. Why should they take collective responsibility? So it was decided, because no one could decide who was to blame, that there would be no taking of responsibility by anyone.

One of the more sensible suggestions was to call the police forensic department and get them to give a press conference explaining just what had happened. In other words, to resolve who was to blame by reference to scientific facts. But even this idea gained no consensus and no traction. First of all, the forensic scientists would not co-operate. They had five bodies to look at, and this took time; they were still investigating the scene of the accident, and that too could not be done in a hurry. Besides which, they failed to see why they should hurry along their investigations in order to help out the politicians, the very people who had cut their funding so many times. Moreover, they made it clear that even when their investigation was complete, it was quite possible that they would be unable to say what exactly had caused the explosion that had killed the five people. This lack of co-operation caused deep alarm. It was pointed out by the politicians that the false narrative was out there – namely that they had caused the explosion by failure to maintain the property correctly, and that every commune owned house and flat in the city was a death trap. This was surely false and desperately needed to be corrected as soon as possible. But Forensics were adamant. They were scientists and they could not prostitute science by using it to dig the lords of misrule out of a political hole.

The forensics department was roundly cursed. The people outside chanting 'Bastards!' and 'Murderers!' were roundly cursed as well. It was August. Only the scum of the earth was in the city at such a time, so it was not surprising that things like this happened. (All the people in the room had come back from holiday, some more quickly and more willingly than others, when the crisis broke, when it was clear that the crisis was a crisis. They had been taken unawares, which did not help. They were the sort of people who went on holiday, which did not help either.) The dead family were scum, from the worst part of the city, as were the protestors, from the Purgatory quarter. One rumour going round was that the eldest son had been deserted by his lover, a prostitute, and had in despair killed himself and taken his brothers and his parents with him. More surprising things had happened. Of course, it was an accident, and would perhaps eventually be proved to be an accident. But in the meantime, let people think it was the one called Amilcare, and let him take the blame. This seemed like a suitable expedient to take the heat off them; but it was shot down by several moral types who pointed out that accusing an innocent man of a crime was a crime itself, even if he were dead, and could well backfire, and there was no reason to assume that the family had been murdered by anyone, let alone by one of its own members.

By now it was getting late, and in complete despair they began to discuss how they would leave the building to go home. Should they go out the back? Was that safe? Would that be an admission of cowardice, or of guilt? Or should they leave by the main door, and face the anger of the mob? Or would the television pictures - for the cameras had now arrived - signal the end of their authority?

For it was clear from the television pictures that things were getting worse by the minute. For this, the media was to blame; you began to film a protest and it at once got bigger; you interviewed people on the street, as if their opinion mattered, and at once opinions became inflamed. And now, worst thing of all, the Archbishop, who lived in a palace, for goodness' sake, had walked over from the Cathedral, and was giving an interview to the television cameras. Oh, he could never resist a camera! Nor could he resist putting the boot in. His Grace faced the cameras and looked sad, knowing these pictures would be watched all over Italy and above all in Rome. He mourned the loss of an ordinary working-class family in the city, who had struggled for a decent living against the odds for years, as so many people in Catania had to. He was shocked that the commune had not expressed any regret at all. He sympathised with the anger of the people. He felt that today ought to be a day that marked a change for Catania: the beginning of responsible government, a government that listened. He felt at this point it would not be right to take any questions, and after this masterclass in public displays of hypocrisy, he withdrew to the Cathedral to pray, he said, for the souls of the dead.

Most people in the meeting held their heads in their hands and swore softly to themselves. Perhaps, someone said, they should invite the cameras in, where it would be safe, where someone could put their case. Protracted negotiations followed. The media were not interested in deflating this wonderful story. Moreover, in the city hall itself, there was no agreement of just whom to put in front of the camera.

Then, suddenly, all became irrelevant. The television cameras began to broadcast from outside the hospital, where the release of the bodies for burial was rumoured to be imminent. It was at this point that Volta felt real despair. He could picture it, all of it: five coffins emerging from the hospital to be received by a hysterical crowd. And then he could see exactly how this was going to end. Exactly. City Hall had, he realised, lost control of the narrative. And someone else was going to pick it up. Inside his chest, his heart felt like lead.

It had been his sister Assunta who had alerted him to the news. Not for the first time, he had realised how clever she was, how observant. He had looked at the television news, seen the report, and understood that things had the potential to get out of control. He had kissed his wife and children, taken the car, and driven back to Catania. He had spoken to Assunta, he had spoken to the boy Tonino and to others like him, he had unleashed the dogs of war. This was now the second day the story had dominated the news, and now was the decisive moment, now was the time to act. The circumstances were right. He had arrived at the hospital mortuary just as he was, still not having changed, wearing his jeans and a by now very crumpled and somewhat dirty tee shirt. There were lots of people he knew milling around, discussing the tragedy, asking themselves how such a thing could have happened. There was a sense of hopelessness, a lack of direction; but with the arrival of don Calogero di Rienzi, a sense of purpose entered the room. All the people were from the quarter, and he knew them. He listened to their accounts of events. The entire block had been evacuated, and was declared unsafe. It might be years before those who lived there would be allowed to go back, even to get their things. They were, some of them, lucky to have relations and friends they could stay with; others were effectively homeless and did not know what they were going to do. They had been sleeping in their cars for the last night, or on the streets. Calogero heard this with concern. Borrowing a phone, he called up an undertaker; he called up don Giorgio; and he called up the lawyer Petrocchi. When finally it seemed the bodies were to be released, he spoke to the man in charge, out of earshot of everyone else.

'I want you to release the bodies to the Confraternity of the Holy Souls in Purgatory,' he said. 'I don't want to hear this crap about the Confraternity not being the next of kin. There is no next of kin. The entire family are dead, and whoever is next of kin is not to be found. Besides which there is no one to pay for the funerals, apart from me, that is. So, be grateful that someone wants to take the bodies, and release them to the Confraternity. And do it now. If you have any doubts about the legality of this, the lawyer Petrocchi over there will reassure you. Or don Giorgio, the parish priest of the deceased, will assure you that this is the right thing to do. If you are still in doubt, consider this: if you do not do what I say, I shall have you stabbed in the guts; but if you do what I say I will give you five hundred euros. Make your mind up. Just do it quickly.'

The man considered for just a moment, and made his mind up. The papers were signed.

Calogero went into the morgue with the black suited undertaker and his assistants. He had never been into a morgue before this, and looked around him with interest. The dead occupied five trolleys. The air was blissfully cold for August, thanks to powerful air conditioning. The corpses had been swathed in body bags that completely covered them. The undertakers' men began to bring in five coffins, and the undertaker examined the labels attached to each body bag to check who was who, who had been who. He unzipped the bags to uncover the faces of the corpses: a mother, a father, Amilcare, two younger teenage sons. Before the undertaker covered them up again, Calogero ordered him and his men (they all had camera phones) to photograph the corpses. The place had a nasty smell. The style of coffin had already been approved by Calogero. Once they were in their coffins and placed on trolleys, he called in don Giorgio and then stepped out into the crowded corridor.

'What now?' asked Petrocchi, who had arrived a few minutes previously, and was waiting in the corridor.

'This now,' said Calogero, seeing the arrival of new people. 'Who sent you? The city hall? You are too late. The bodies have been signed over to us for burial. Please speak to the lawyer Petrocchi. There is nothing you can do. And given that you are the ones who killed them, you must allow us, the Confraternity and their parish, to bury them. Go away.'

The men from city hall were indeed too late. Volta had suggested they come, to prevent just this, a provocative funeral.

'You killed them, now leave us to bury them,' said Calogero.

The men from city hall, even though they had been given specific orders to stop just what was happening, did not dare protest. The crowded corridor was hostile. They withdrew.

The coffins came through the door, pushed on trollies, accompanied by don Giorgio. Two minibuses were waiting outside to drive them to the Church of the Holy Souls in Purgatory. As the coffins emerged into the open air, where the vehicles were waiting, there was, after the Italian custom, a smattering of applause.

In the palace, the Archbishop was having supper. Before him lay a plate of cold ham and salami, a basket of bread (none too fresh) and some tomatoes and a green salad. There was a modest decanter of his favourite white wine and a bottle of mineral water, with gas. The secretary, who usually ate with him (so much business was done over the quiet supper table) was absent, called away. The secretary re-entered, just as His Grace was pouring himself his first, well merited, glass of wine. He looked up.

'Was it Palermo?' he asked. 'Or was it Rome?' he added, with a note of hope in his voice.

'Neither, Your Grace,' said the secretary apologetically. 'It is someone from next door. They have sent someone over.'

'Next door' was the phrase they used for the city hall.

'Have they?' said the Archbishop with great interest. 'They must be getting desperate. Send whoever it is in, and let me speak to him, while you listen and remember what is said.'

The secretary departed, returning a few moments later with Volta. He introduced him. Volta managed a respectful bow.

'To what do I owe this pleasure?' asked the Archbishop. Then he softened. 'You need a drink,' he said. 'And something to eat. Don Pinuccio, a glass, another plate. Do sit down.'

Volta gratefully sat down. A plate and a glass appeared before him. He ate and drank while the Archbishop and the secretary waited. He had forgotten how hungry he was. Eventually he spoke.

'Thank you for seeing me, Your Grace. I haven't had anything to eat or drink all day. We sent out for something a few hours ago, and all the places we phoned refused to take our order. We are under siege in there. Things are not just bad; they are finished. It is worse than anyone seems to realise. They are coming to realise it, but slowly. The game is up. The people in Rome are now shouting down the phone every minute. Not the Viminal, they have kept quiet, but the Chigi Palace, the Prime Minister's office. They have seen the television pictures. They fear contamination. Right now, they are trying to persuade the Mayor and entire junta to resign en masse; that seems to be the only thing that will defuse the situation. But they are all arguing even about that. Some claim they ought not to resign, others that they will but only if the others all do so too; and the Mayor, unbelievably, is talking to his lawyer, and arguing about his pension and his severance pay. At least he realises his career is over, but he does not seem to realise that in the present circumstances, thinking about himself does not look good. And, because the place is in such chaos, and has the feel of a sinking ship, some people have been texting the media, and the Mayor's arguing about his going has become a story.'

'Well, he ought to resign. They all ought to resign. The whole thing is disgraceful. Someone needs to take responsibility. His career is over, he must see that. The state of public housing in this city has been a disgrace for years. The neglect, the theft of funds… Do you want me to come over and tell him to go?'

Volta marvelled at the old man's cunning. He saw that he had walked into this.

'You have sat here too long! In the name of God, go!' he said. 'It has a certain ring to it. Your Grace could well go there and, well, cleanse the temple.'

'Then I will do that,' said the Archbishop. 'You think they would? Would go, I mean?'

'Give them a couple of hours, and they will be grateful to anyone who comes and delivers the coup de grace,' said Volta. 'Although any intervention by Your Grace would be a bit of gesture politics, as all the same people would be back at their desks the very next day in a caretaker capacity. But gesture apart, it might help defuse the situation. It would be a great opportunity for the Church to assert the values it stands for, values that the current administration has sorely neglected.'

'An administration with which, Volta, you are closely involved,' said the Archbishop.

'For which may God forgive me. This family, this family of innocents, we do not know how they died as yet. I mean an explosion… But Forensics won't say what caused the explosion. By the time they come to a conclusion, it will be too late. No one will believe what they say, even if it is the truth. No one will believe that this was sheer bad luck. They want someone to blame and they have found someone to blame. That in itself is bad, but understandable, and manageable. After all, people have always blamed their governments. This is Sicily. We have been blaming our rulers for things that go wrong for almost a thousand years. But what has just happened now makes things far worse.'

'Namely?' asked His Grace.

'I have spoken to some people…. The whole thing is very bad news for the government itself, Rome, I mean, not Catania. A woman from the Purgatory quarter and her son… Let me just say that the state had a strong case against a very powerful and influential criminal in our midst, and yesterday that case collapsed. The two witnesses were found dead in the place where the state had placed them. I do not know how they were found, who found them; it is just clear that they are dead. I had a distressing conversation with this man who goes by the name of Silvio; he and his assistant, a criminal psychologist, had spent months building the case. Now it is all gone in a puff of smoke.'

'Who killed the witnesses?'

'It is too early to tell. Maybe they will find some forensic evidence which may help. That may lead them to the perpetrator. If indeed the perpetrator is known to the police. But the thing is these people often use what they call a 'clean skin', someone with no record, for these sorts of crimes. The person or persons behind this crime were all sitting in their holiday houses while it was being committed, laughing at us. It was my hope that the state was going to make some very significant arrests and perhaps pull at the thread which would lead to an unravelling of the entire organisation. But I now see that they are untouchable. And it gets worse. These victims of the explosion – their bodies are on their way to the Church of the Holy Souls in Purgatory. I was trying to get hold of don Giorgio, but he has his phone switched off. We tried to stop the bodies being taken away. But we were too late once more. The whole thing is going to get a lot worse. That is why I have come to you.'

'You want me to stop the funerals?'

'It is too late for that. But I want you to moderate the funerals,' said Volta.

There was silence in the archepiscopal dining room.

'You mean….?'

'Calogero di Rienzi has effectively hijacked these funerals. I know that the Confraternity has in its constitutions something about burying the indigent dead. It will be seen as an act of charity and kindness, but Calogero di Rienzi will be doing this not because he cares about these poor dead people, but because it will make him look good, and the city government look bad. He is not a stupid man, by any means, and he will use this opportunity to gain great power, unless someone stops him. And the only person that can stop him, Your Grace, is you.'

The Archbishop nodded and said he would finish his supper and come over; and then he would go to the Church of the Holy Souls in Purgatory.

Out in the street, by the Cathedral, someone came up to Volta. It was a sturdy teenage boy. He recognised him. He knew what was coming. Something worse than a bullet.

'Don Calogero wants to see you,' said Tonino.

Without waiting for a reply, he disappeared.

Meanwhile, in the peace of Acireale, the women, now having the house more or less to themselves, as the men had gone off to Agrigento, were discussing the things closest to their hearts. Ceccina and Catarina had both been talking about how the heat made pregnancy more difficult than it might otherwise have been. But this was a dull subject, and what they fell to discussing with great relish was the forthcoming wedding. It had been decided, at long last, that Elena would marrying Renzo in Palermo; she had explained why Assunta had married in Catania, in their parish Church, and she did not want her marriage to be a rerun of her sister's. Besides, Renzo's family were in Palermo, which was full of beautiful churches, and there was the Grand Hotel for the reception afterwards. Her brother had married, albeit quietly, in the Cathedral, so they would choose somewhere else. But it would be Palermo and probably in the middle of winter, when, thank God, this terrible heat would just be a distant memory. But no date had been fixed as yet. Renzo was, Elena had said, hard to tie down.

Elena was now back in Catania with her mother, but this is what she had confided. Catarina, Giuseppina, Ceccina and Pasqualina had been thoughtful when she had spoken of Renzo not wanting to be tied down. Perhaps don Calogero should have a word, in order to bring the young man to heel. It was a glittering prospect, this marriage to Renzo, but, as they all saw, it would have its challenges. He was very rich, and they would have everything, but he was not what one would call a steady character, like dear Alfio.

Alfio had been quite content to be tied down, and his marrying Giuseppina was fixed for the cool month of October. Giuseppina was more or less related to Elena, being her deceased sister-in-law's sister, so things had not been quite straightforward. They had agreed, given the overlap in the guest list, that Giuseppina should go first, and Elena second, so there would be no clash of dates. Indeed, keeping the two dates as far apart as possible had seemed best. Then there had been the question of the possible clash of venues. Giuseppina wanted to marry in the Church of the Holy Souls in Purgatory, where her sister had married (she had been bridesmaid) and had been relieved that Elena had decided to marry in Palermo. So that was good news. Then there was the question of wedding presents. Elena and Giuseppina had decided they would not exchange presents. This had been Elena's idea, and Giuseppina had accepted it grudgingly. For the truth was that Renzo was one of the richest men in Sicily, and could easily have afforded to give them something extravagant, whereas she and Alfio were, in comparison, quite poor, and would have got away with something more modest. Whichever way, they were going to each other's weddings, and Giuseppina was glad theirs was first, so it would not be in the shadow of the grander Palermo wedding. It would be very nice, down to earth and not cost a fortune. She and Alfio had nothing to prove.

She was, on this topic, a little bit defensive. She and Elena had grown up together in the Purgatory quarter, though they had not known each other well until the time, now a decade ago, when Calogero had married Stefania. In those far off days there had been no social difference between them, but now of course, Elena had pulled ahead by marrying one of the richest men in Sicily. Well, one could not grudge her that. After all, if Renzo was from a very rich family, Elena was the sister of one of the richest men in Sicily too. So the honours were equal on both sides, really. And Renzo, despite his wealth, was not such a catch. Not even his mother would describe him as handsome. On this, all of the women agreed. Poor Renzo. He was a little awkward to look at, and his clothes never seemed to fit him properly. And he was a little rackety. No doubt Elena would civilise him, but there was the cocaine use hanging over him, the previous very unsuitable girlfriends, the spoilt rich kid character, the whole, how could one put it, unsavoury reputation of the younger generation of the Santucci family. It was a question of inherited wealth rather than money come by the hard way. Elena was not spoiled but she would be living with a spoiled man, and that would be hard. As for Alfio, a boy from the quarter, one of themselves, who could not love Alfio? He was so sweet and so kind. That was what they all thought. And, ever since he had had his teeth sorted out, not bad looking at all. And not spoilt: in fact, very eager to please. Not a catch like Renzo, but in every other way to be preferred.

Catarina was pleased to hear this praise of her cousin, and she hoped her cousin and Giuseppina would be very happy together. Now that she herself was married, and about to be delivered safely of a child in a month or less, she had a certain perspective on matters. She had always liked her cousin Alfio, and if he hadn't been her first cousin, might have considered marrying him. Well, she had married his best friend, and here they all were, together, all except Elena who had risen, or who would rise, through marriage, and leave their city, and leave their little circle. So be it. Elena was escaping from this world, into another world, but a world which would prove, she felt, to be much the same. She too had dreamed of escape once.

They were now talking of the accident in the quarter, that had killed the family of five. None of them had known Amilcare, except very vaguely. They must have seen him at the pizzeria. But still, it was horrible. Each of them needed to get their gas checked out, if indeed it had been a gas leak. And one of the boys killed had been just thirteen. What a shame!

Later, after such a lazy day, they all settled down to eat, and to watch the evening news. It was then that they saw the pictures of the coffins being brough into the Church of the Holy Souls in Purgatory. But Ceccina insisted it be switched off, though the others insisted that

Cristoforo was far too young to understand. Ceccina said that he understood more than they realised.

He stood on the steps of the Church of the Holy Souls in Purgatory, still wearing his jeans and his crumpled shirt, with his sister Assunta next to him. They were very alike, and not just in age; he spoke, she looked at him, and the camera concentrated on him; he had done these pieces to camera before. He was glad Assunta was there; overweight and not particularly attractive, she cut a particularly Sicilian figure, and seemed what she was, a woman of the quarter; he looked younger, slimmer, handsomer, with the wide set apart eyes that marked him out and her out, but which in him were an advantage, though not in her case. Through the open neck of his tee-shirt, one could see the gold chain from which hung the cross that he had been given for his First Holy Communion, and which he had never taken off, despite his atheism, which was expressed only in private. Now, in front of the camera, he was explaining to the reporter that the mission of the Most Noble and Ancient Confraternity of the Holy Souls was charity, and a part of this mission was the burial of those who could not afford funerals. Given that this poor family were ordinary working people, and given that they had to be buried soon, the Confraternity would place them not in the municipal cemetery, which was in a shocking state of disrepair, but in the crypt under the church. The Confraternity had provided the coffins, the services of an undertaker and the other necessities. The dead family had not only lost their lives but also all their property. This blow, in other words, had fallen on a family that had had very little to start with and had now lost even their lives.

He spoke emphasising his Sicilian vowels; the word he used for coffin was the same words that was used in Arab lands. When asked a question about the membership of the Confraternity, he said that its members ranged from princes, dukes, counts and lawyers all the way down to working men of little education, such as himself, who had grown up in the Purgatory quarter. He was asked too about the protests and disturbances that had rocked the city of Catania. These, he said, out of respect for the deceased family, should stop at once. Had he any comment on the mass resignation of the junta, just announced?

'Good riddance,' said Calogero. 'I am not political, but the junta has failed, and we need a fresh start. Left, right, Green, I do not care. Competence should be the requirement. We need energetic people who can prevent accidents like this happening, who can clean up the municipal cemetery, who can keep the traffic moving, and who can grant planning permissions in a way that is transparent and swift. Things need to change, and I hope they do. The poor of Catania have waited too long.'

'Shameless,' the editor of the piece thought, knowing who Calogero was married to, and how rich he was. His revenge was to make sure that when this went out on the national news – for the story had become a big one – that Calogero's words had subtitles in standard Italian.

The city of Catania, the island of Sicily, the whole Italian Republic boiled with rage. Everything conspired to make this rage worse; the only question that exercised intelligent people was how this rage was to be managed and used to advantage.

The coffins came to the Church of the Holy Souls in Purgatory, where they were to rest all night. They had been sealed, naturally enough, but photographs of the charred and scarred remains of two parents, their eldest son and two teenage boys had circulated widely on the internet, along with the accusation of murder aimed at the junta of Catania. The photographs were so horrible that this reaction was quite understandable. All the crimes of the junta, all their omissions, were now remembered, and all the decades of stored up anger came forth. As the evening wore on, as night fell, crowds gathered, to file pass the coffins, to pray, to visit the Church, to light candles, to implore the help of the Spanish Madonna who had so singularly failed to help this poor family. And don Calogero stood on the Church steps, greeting those who came out and those who went in. The Church did not shut that night, and he did not sleep.

It was expected that members of the junta would come to the Church, to file past the coffins themselves, but there was no sign of them, and it became clear that they were too ashamed to show themselves. Indeed, the junta had gone home, dissolved into the night, having realised that their continuing to sit was completely useless, futile, pointless. This realisation had come to them as a result of the despair they felt, and the coup de grâce had been dealt by the Archbishop, who had come to their meeting, and told them to go home. The injunction to go home, which really meant to resign, rang in their ears, and no protest was made. Amongst those to go home in despair was Volta. Power had fled from the men and women in city hall. The city of Catania was ungovernable. The junta, whose members had all been on holiday before the crisis, returned to their families, scattering to the four winds.

That night, after some considerable negotiation, Anna Maria Tancredi was able to get through to the person who counted more than any other in Rome.

'My dear,' came the dry, saurian voice down the line from the modest flat he occupied with his blameless elderly wife overlooking the Tiber, 'It has been many years since we spoke.'

'I am very pleased to have this opportunity to speak to you,' she said.

'I should congratulate you on your recent marriage,' said the old man. 'It raises you in my estimation, were that possible. And it raises your husband. You are a very clever woman to spot his talent, and he, a clever man to recognise yours. This latest news that I have been following from Catania just confirms my suspicion that he is a genius of the highest order. You will not have heard it, but the government here in Rome has, with remarkable swiftness - you know how hard any decision is to make, and how long it takes – decided to suspend the administration in Catania. This latest piece of incompetence is the last straw. People want action, and we are sacking the lot. In a few months there will be fresh elections. This represents a great opportunity for us, and for you, and for your clever husband.'

'I understand,' she said.

'Your husband needs to pick the next Mayor of Catania.'

'I believe,' she said, 'he already has. That was why he rushed back when this story broke. He saw the opportunity and he is not a man to lose an opportunity. The man he has in mind has impeccable credentials, and he will have little trouble persuading him, I think, once he has got over his initial surprise.'

'The people in Rome have despaired, as have the people in Catania,' said her interlocutor. 'A couple of days ago, two people who were under police protection were found assassinated; they had been living under assumed names somewhere in the via Tiburtina quarter of this city. No one knew they were there. No one was supposed to at any rate. But they were picked off. The assumption is that the witness protection programme has been infiltrated. What was assumed watertight has leaked. The whole apparatus of the state has been called into question. For the foreseeable future, the only investigation that will matter and that will take up everyone's time is this one into who leaked, how it was leaked. Everything has been compromised. So you see, they are prepared to let the debacle in Catania go. They cannot keep their eye on that and the fact that the anti-organised crime initiative is useless. For us this is a historic opportunity. Your husband has my blessing.'

Afterwards she sat in the house of sleeping children and marvelled. She wondered at her luck. She had always felt a strong attraction to younger men, and when she had acquired Calogero at Noto she had been following her animal instincts. But it was true: the man was a genius. She felt the heaviness of the child within her, his child. She sensed the other four children asleep in the house, her house, now his house, his children. She wished she could phone him now, but knew that he had no mobile phone. He was out of reach. How she longed to speak to him. When would he return? In the silence of the night, she felt a terrible longing for her husband.

Chapter Ten

Peace had been restored. Standing on the roof terrace of his new flat, Calogero surveyed the city. It was hard to believe that only a few days ago something as innocent as a gas explosion had caused the downfall of the junta; and that events in Rome had led to, according to the most recent news, the sacking, or at least sudden retirement, of the Minister of the Interior. The government was tottering, but would perhaps regain its balance. In Catania there would be fresh elections. And then things would start again.

In Agrigento, all was peace too. It was Sunday morning. Traiano had got up early, very early, for today was the day they were supposed to return to Catania, and he had decided that he wished to go to see the Valley of the Temples. It seemed a shame to come all this way to Agrigento and not see the Greek ruins, one of the wonders of Sicily. He had seen so little of the beauties of his own country; and he had never been to the continent, which was a shame. He had cultural interests, after all. They were the sort of interests that reproached him, for they reminded him of the great truth that he spent most of his energy and time dealing with the sordid part of life.

He had got to the Valley of the Temples before it opened, so eager had he been to leave the villa in which they were staying. Of course, he had been here for work, and had learned everything he needed to learn about the man he was interested in, Pasquale Greco, who had been born in Agrigento, as he had noted from his conversation with Ruggero Bonelli. He had spoken to the right people, and the information had come tumbling out. Pasquale Greco was eager to use his inside information for an illegal purpose, because Pasquale clearly needed the money. His family were poor, his tastes were not those of a poor or frugal man. He liked women a great deal, and he liked cocaine, and he liked having lots of money to spend. He was extravagant. He was in debt. The same sort of character as his friend Ruggero, Gabriella's brother, in fact. Most useful. The prospect of using these two to make lots of legal clean money was enticing.

He had checked out the family of Pasquale and actually seen them, without talking to them, of course. Two parents, two sisters; the sort of vulnerable people Pasquale would want to protect. Where they lived, how they lived, it was clear from both that they were not getting much support from Pasquale, the selfish creature. He himself prided himself on the fact that none of Ceccina's relatives went hungry. He provided for them all, generously too. But Pasquale seemed incapable of doing the same.

He wondered, as he sat under the shade of an olive tree outside the gates of the archaeological area, about another family he had seen, spoken to, got to know. This was the family of Gino, his parents, his brother. They had gone round to see them. Their poverty too was tangible. He had taken it up with Gino. Why hadn't he helped them? Gino had protested that he had tried, but they had refused. Or more accurately, the brother, Corrado, had refused. His initial reaction was that someone should teach Corrado a lesson. After all, Corrado was refusing to let Gino help his own parents. If Corrado wanted to be poor, that was his choice. But it was not his place to condemn the parents to poverty. Corrado, it had been, who had suggested he visit the valley of the Temples, and he had asked Corrado to accompany him, and he was waiting for him now.

He was glad he was early, because on getting up early to leave the house, he had found an envelope pushed under the door of the villa, with his name on it. Who had delivered it, and who had known that he was there, at that particular address? The people who had rented them the villa, obviously. The various prostitutes who had visited, not him, but the others, sent all the way from Taormina, the very best Russians that don Carmelo, the boss of Messina, could supply; Gino's family, which included Corrado. He had told people he was coming to Agrigento, because he had wanted people to know. But he had told no one where he was staying. Had it been don Carmelo? But whatever way, the magistrates had found out, because this envelope was from them, he saw at once. There was no sign that it was, but from who else could it be?

It contained two forensic reports. The first was heavily redacted. A woman in her thirties, a boy aged twelve; no names, but he knew who they were. The cause of death in both cases was asphyxiation, thanks to bits of cloth rammed down their throats. The woman had been raped, as there were traces of seminal fluid in her vagina and in her anus, as well as trauma to both areas. The boy had been violated as well, probably with some instrument like a broomstick. None of these injuries were post mortem, and he pictured what this meant. Beata had been raped in front of her son, who had been forced to watch; and then the son had been violated while his mother had been forced to watch.

The other forensic report was that from Catania. There were photographs of Amilcare, his parents and his brothers, the victims of the gas explosion. He did not want to look at them for long.

Who had sent these gruesome documents? Was it the magistrates? Was this their way of showing him that they knew, even if they could not prove it, that this was what he had ordered? Did they want to make him feel shame for the empire of cruelty over which he presided? But it cannot have been the magistrates, he realised. These documents sealed their fate, these documents proved what everyone with any sense had always known: that there was one power in the land, and it was not the Italian Republic, it was something else, it was the power that could strike down its enemies wherever they hid.

He thought of Muniddu, that happily married man, with children. Had he raped Beata? Had he violated Paolo? Had Tonino? Had Muniddu urged Tonino to do so? Had they enjoyed it? And why? Well, he knew the answer. Anyone who tried to harm them would end up like this; this was a death sentence, not a quick death, but the worst sort of death. Had they killed the boy first, and made his mother watch? Or done it the other way round? Who had sent the forensic reports? Did it matter? It might have been the magistrates trying to shame him, or someone in Rome, who knew he would pass them on and thus destroy the last shreds of credibility that the state might cling to. Somebody in Rome, somebody in Catania, someone who had been given the nod. Perhaps the delivery had been made by one of his contacts here in Agrigento, who knew where he was. Perhaps they had delivered it without knowing what it was; the envelope had been sealed, naturally enough.

He put the reports back in the envelope, and placed the envelope under the car seat. Should he show it to the others? Should he show it to the boss? Or should he just pass it on to someone who would publish it, some blogger, someone who worked at a television station, some journalist? Another thought occurred to him. Had someone passed this onto him wanting to discredit Muniddu or Tonino? No, they were too unimportant to discredit. But he was aware that this was something of great importance.

He had no sooner put the papers away than the man he was to meet appeared on the scene. He came in a car that was old, barely roadworthy; Traiano's car was expensive but modest, not designed to attract attention; this car attracted attention because it was so very run-down looking. Out of it got Corrado, Gino's brother. He extended a hand, but did not smile. They had met before, very briefly, hardly acknowledging each other, at Gino and Catarina's wedding; they had met again the previous day, when he had accompanied Gino to visit his parents and his brother. Corrado had been reserved on both occasions, but when Traiano had said he wanted to visit the Valley of the Temples, he had said he would accompany him. He could, he knew, have happily gone on his own; what Corrado was really saying was that he wanted to speak to Traiano alone.

The gate to the archaeological area was now opening, and they both went in and bought their tickets. It was still early, the sun was bright but the heat was bearable. The ruins were beautiful, and as long as you did not look towards the town and the hideous elevated motorway nearby, the whole was peaceful, idyllic and charming. And it was nice to have the place to themselves.

'How is work?' asked Traiano, by way of conversation.

Corrado looked at him suspiciously. He looked like his brother, but less heavy. He had a beard (something no one who worked for don Calogero had) and longish but neat hair; his eyes were bright blue. Traiano saw he had struck a nerve.

'I have been working in Noto. There is nothing for me here. I used to get jobs on building sites, but they dried up. So I travel around; there is someone in Noto who likes my work, and he is doing up some houses there and needs a stone mason, so for the moment, I am good. I live there in the week, sleep on site - it costs nothing - and come back here for weekends. It is a struggle. My father is unemployed, my mother depressed.'

'So I heard, so I saw,' said Traiano. There was no sympathy in his voice. 'Gino offered to help....'

Corrado said nothing to this.

'How is your work?' he asked, changing the subject.

Traiano detected the irony. He was not used to people asking him questions; nor was he used to this tone; but he decided to do his best to be polite, to be normal, to pretend things were normal.

'My work is fine. We have this huge project which, when it comes to completion, will make us all rich. The thing is that we have borrowed very heavily to finance it, and we are up to our necks in debt. I have sunk in everything I have, mortgaged my future, so a lot hangs on it. But hopefully our ship will come into port. As I am sure you know, so much can go wrong with construction.'

'Let's hope they change the flight path for you, otherwise you will have a white elephant on your hands,' said Corrado.

'Don't you want me, and don Calogero and your brother to succeed?' asked Traiano coolly, forcing himself not to be provoked.

'Gino and I are not close. We were once, very close, but not anymore. It is Gino's fault that I cannot get work, that my father cannot get work. Maybe we should have moved. Well, it is not Gino's fault. He was young, he was stupid, they put him in Bicocca. He was fourteen. He was in a fight with one of the people here. They blamed him; they blamed us; later, when we made it clear that we did not want anything to do with them or with Gino, well, they found that unforgiveable.'

'Well, if you are going to take the poor but honest pose, you will pay the price for it. Gino is generous, but you do not want his generosity. How is he supposed to feel?'

'How is he supposed to feel? However he feels, he can tell us himself. But he does not seem to be able to. Bicocca took him; then you got hold of him, and you have ruined him.'

They had reached the first of the temples as this was said.

Traiano laughed.

'I can only suppose that you are trying to provoke me,' he said. 'You are saying something you know to be untrue. Your brother was already ruined, as you put it, before he met me. His going to Bicocca was nothing to do with me. Alfio was – is - his great friend, but Gino made his own decisions; no one forced him down the path he has taken. And if you think I encouraged him to drink, to take prescription drugs, to put on weight, to marry whom he married, to behave the way he does, you are very much mistaken. I do not drink, I do not sleep with anyone apart from my wife, but Gino, Gino is different. He is riotous; less so that don Renzo, more so than Alfio. I have told him, I have told them all, but they do not listen to me. And why are you so disapproving? Isn't this what men like them do? Isn't this what men like you would do, if you could? You are a hypocrite. Someone should break your jaw.'

Corrado heard this in silence.

'I am sure you could break my jaw, if you chose to do so,' he observed quietly.

Traiano laughed.

'You do not seem to be afraid,' he observed. 'Most people are afraid of me. What is the matter with you?'

'Perhaps I am a fool. Perhaps I am just stubborn. Perhaps I am an idiot,' said Corrado. 'But I love my brother and I hate what has happened to him.'

'I understand that. I have children. I have relatives, well, my wife has relatives. I would hate it for any of them to go to Piazza Lanza or Bicocca. When did you find out we were staying here?'

'The day before yesterday. When I came back from Noto. Why?'

'Did you tell anyone we were at the villa? Did anyone ask?'

'No.'

He believed him.

'If you are worried about your brother, and I have to say even I am worried about your brother, the person to speak to is his wife. She is clever. She could perhaps get him to change his ways. He respects her.'

Corrado sighed.

'I have spoken to her. She denies there is a problem. Before we spoke, I got the impression she did not care for us, his family. After I spoke there was no doubt in my mind. She did not value my intervention.'

Traiano was thoughtful. He understood what Corrado was saying. Gino's wife did not love him. Well, he knew that. But it was sad, sad that Corrado should know it too.

'Why the hell did she marry him?' asked Corrado.

'She was pregnant,' said Traiano. But he did not add 'with someone else's child.' 'Look, this is the way the world is. Gino did not have the best start in life, being thrown into Bicocca. He's violent, and, if you will forgive me saying so, not the brightest. He likes all the wrong things. But he has done well for himself. He has lots of money, he has a wife, they are having a child, people like him, some people do. For a man like Gino, it is a good life. You have chosen a different path, and he has chosen his. Accept it.'

'I can't accept it.'

'What sort of man cannot accept the way things are, the way things work?' he asked. 'Look, maybe you should come to Catania; if you work all over the place, why not get a job near us, and be close to your brother?'

'It is too painful to see him the way he is. When he was young, when we were both young… The memory of how he used to be, that torments me.'

'You mean, when he was ten years old? Well, children grow up.'

'Do you want your children to grow up like that? Tell me, how many men has he killed?'

'Don't be ridiculous. You are letting your imagination run away with you.'

'I don't think I am,' said Corrado.

'You must have a very low opinion of me,' said Traiano.

Corrado did not answer.

'Come and work for us. Come to Catania. Bring your parents.'

'We are happy here.'

'But you are not. Look, Corrado, don't be stupid. One day you will want to ask me a favour, so you had better not be so standoffish now.'

'What have you heard?' he asked.

'Heard? Nothing. But I may have guessed something.'

They walked on. They spoke of the temples. Then Corrado asked him when the latest baby was due. He was surprised that this interested him. He replied that the baby was due very soon, more or less in the first days of September, and more or less on the same day as Catarina and Gino's child. He spoke glowingly of his wife. This exceptionally hot summer had been a real trial, and he hoped that the next child, whenever that happened, would be born in midwinter. It was surely easier to be pregnant in the winter than in August.

'I remember your wife Ceccina,' said Corrado. 'She is very nice. I met her at the wedding, Gino's wedding.'

'That was a strange occasion, Easter Monday. Our boss had just married his new wife that morning in Palermo. It was all a secret, being so soon after his previous wife's death. I got back for the reception, so joined the festivities rather late. And it was that night that Renzo got together with Elena and Alfio with Giuseppina. By this time next year, we will all be married, and there will be more babies. Or so I hope. Children are good.'

'Children are good,' said Corrado.

'Then you should get married,' said Traiano.

'I hope to, and soon.'

'You have got someone?' he asked, knowing already what the answer would be.

'Yeah. Now I have this work in Noto, I am at last able to save. So…'

They walked on. The sun was high in the sky, and the heat building.

'At the wedding, Ceccina and the others all said how much they liked you,' said Traiano. 'They noticed what a different character you were to Gino. I can't say that Gino is my sort of person, you know. He is too wild. I know that you and I are on different paths as well. But… while we cannot be the very best of friends, we can be brothers-in-law.'

They paused by the gateway. Corrado seemed about to say something, but hesitated.

'I will come to the baptism of Gino's child,' he said at last. 'Have people been talking?'

'You are almost as secretive as I am. Of course they talk, who likes whom, who is going to marry whom. A man like you comes and they all wonder about you, and they all assume that you are interested in someone. But I have to say this. No one has been talking, which is unusual. Both you and Pasqualina have been acting stealthily, which does the opposite to what you intend; it makes you stand out. You should have given it more thought. As it is, I suspect you of having a wicked purpose. But come for the baptism. And my own child's baptism will be at more or less the same time, so perhaps you will stay for that too?'

Corrado said nothing in reply, but only smiled. They shook hands and parted.

'You came,' observed don Calogero di Rienzi, that same day, two days after the funerals, in a not unfriendly manner.

'I could not resist the invitation,' said Volta in a level voice. They were on the roof terrace of what would soon be the new flat that Calogero would move into. 'When the person who once tried to have you killed asks you to meet, generally speaking, you accept. After all, no use provoking your enemies. One wants them to leave one in peace.'

'I am not your enemy,' said Calogero. 'What on earth gives you that impression? If I were your enemy... Do you still wear the stab proof vest? Not in this hot weather, I imagine. But it is a good idea, wearing one, and refusing a police escort; posing as a marked man, a warrior for justice. You know, Volta, you are an egotist, a publicity whore. That is why I like you. I like men with weaknesses.'

'Is that why you invited me here? To tell me you liked me?'

'Don't be so petulant. It's rude. Besides, both of us need to get on, so we must be polite to each other. Ah,' he said. 'I don't believe you have met my mother. Mama, this is Fabio Volta who once came to our house the day my father's death was discovered. Remember him? No? Ah well. Volta, what will you have to drink?'

The signora had come up with a very well stocked tray. Volta accepted a beer. Calogero, after a longing glance at the whiskey bottle, settled for a beer too. It was seven in the evening. The sun's rays were getting less fierce, and the panorama of the city was bathed in the delicious golden light of early evening.

'Such a lovely view,' said Calogero, while his mother withdrew. He watched her go. 'I wanted to talk to you about the state of the municipal cemetery. I have heard bad reports. I did ask about the state of the Confraternity tomb at the time my wife - my first wife - died. It seemed the obvious place to bury the dead family. No one has been buried in it for some time, and I soon understood why. My late wife is in the Church vault, thank the Lord, and that is where we put them as well. The state of the cemetery is a disgrace. There are smashed up graves everywhere, I am told, even bones lying around. And the place has a terrible reputation for robberies and for criminality. The next mayor will have to sort that out. If we cannot look after the dead properly, what chance have we with the living? Spending some money on restoration, which private firms will want to help with, and having proper supervision, that will be very popular. It should be the first thing on the new mayor's list.'

'And who is going to be the new mayor?' asked Volta softly.

'A local man, a man born in this city. A man married to a woman from this city, a man who will stand up for this city and for Sicily against the thieves and scoundrels of Rome. A fearless man, a man of the greatest moral rectitude. A man not too closely associated with the discredited former regime. A man who perhaps has fought injustice for many years. A man who will be on the side of the poor, and a man who will be approved by the Church. And a man who will know what is what. A man of competence.'

'You left out the important bit: A man who knows the right people.'

Calogero nodded. They sipped their drinks in silence.

'How is your wife?' he asked. 'And you child? Wasn't your wife a friend of Colonel Andreazza?'

'She knew his wife, who has left him. The Colonel, or ex-Colonel, is in jail, or so I assume.'

'Was in jail. They never charged him with anything, you know. The latest I have heard, and it is the very latest news available, is that the Colonel, no ex about him, has been released from custody, and is now on holiday, and his wife has been invited to join him; indeed, she is with him now. The Dolomites. Lovely in these hot days. They are reconciled. You see, she is not stupid. Someone has intervened on the Colonel's behalf, and he will be returning to Sicily and he will be promoted, to assuage the injustice he has suffered.'

'He must have powerful friends,' observed Volta. 'But as you said, you like men with weaknesses.'

'I have never met him,' said Calogero. 'I feel sorry for the poor wife. And your wife, how is she?'

Volta shot him a look of murderous hatred.

'Don't take on so,' chided Calogero. 'It is a friendly enquiry, though you are right to suspect I know the answer to the question. How do I know? Not by tapping her phone, hacking her email, or getting people to overhear things when she pours out her heart to her female friends over coffee. Those sorts of methods, we leave to the police. Rather, I know what your wife thinks because I have a knowledge of human nature. She worries about your safety. She worries more than ever now that you have a child. She fears that next time you may not be so lucky. You survived one assassination attempt, and she is not to know that no one is planning another. She assumes that the danger is ever present. And I am sure she has begged you to leave Sicily, to go somewhere else, to get a safer job. And I know this too: that she has begged you to swallow your pride and meet me, and, well, make peace.'

Volta was silent.

'Every now and then, every man has to do something to please his wife. I speak from experience. My first wife.... And now Anna Maria. I try my best to please her. And, you know, she is an excellent wife. She has been speaking to Rome. Rome has been speaking to her. She was incensed when our esteemed national broadcaster put subtitles on my little piece to camera, translating me into words everyone could understand, implying that the people of Catania do not speak properly. She is getting those responsible sacked. Well, I do not care. But it is a great local advantage when the Italians despise you for being Sicilian. The door, my dear Volta, is wide open. The consensus is that an independent candidate for mayor would romp home, especially if he stood on an anti-corruption ticket. The left, the right, the Greens, would not stand a chance. Indeed, the masters in Rome have given the hint, if I can put it that way, that if an independent candidate stands, he is not to be opposed too heartily. Of course, it will look like a proper election, but.... And the money, which is so very necessary, is guaranteed; it will be through hundreds and thousands of small donations, but if these are not forthcoming, Anna Maria will take care of it. She knows everyone. She just has to ask. The door is open for you; you just have to walk through it.'

'But there is a price,' said Volta.

'Of course. There always is. A political price and a personal price. Being mayor will be hard work; and there will be many favours to repay. There always are. And there is a personal price you have to pay, Volta. You have to drop your longstanding hatred of me. That is difficult, but it is possible, and it is also necessary, and above all, it is in your interest to do so. When you first saw me, I was a youngster of sixteen and I got the better of you, but now you have to forgive and forget. Yes, it is difficult but it can be done. I have done it, and so can you. You did your best to turn my beloved brother against me, and you succeeded. The only person I have ever truly loved, and you took him away from me. But I do not hold that against you; what is past is past; I forgive. And now, I am offering to make you mayor of this city. I can do it. You are the perfect candidate. You are already well known, already a popular hero. With me behind you, with all our friends behind you, with the Archbishop behind you – he speaks very well of you; we have discussed you. And I know you will say yes. I know you will do this for your wife and your child; that you will do this for yourself, because you love the attention, you love the thought that you can be one of the great men of our island; but there is something else you have resisted for so long, and can resist no longer. Me.'

There was a long silence.

'The Archbishop spoke wonderfully at those funerals,' said Volta at long last. 'I am not a believer, but….'

'Neither am I.'

'But what he said made perfect sense. This idea that in the midst of disaster we must seek hope, and that our city can rise again from the depths to which it has sunk. It was as if he were laying out an electoral campaign.'

'He was,' said Calogero. 'An election that will take place next spring.'

'It is hard not to feel inspired by what he said,' said Volta.

'Indeed. I am glad to hear you say it.'

Volta stood. So did Calogero. He held out his hand, and Calogero took it. He pulled Volta towards him, and held him in a tight embrace. Then he kissed him. From now on everything would be perfect.

Later, as darkness fell, Traiano came to him, as he knew he must. Looking out at the glimmering lights below, surveying Catania, he asked how Agrigento had been.

'The Valley of the Temples is lovely. The villa we stayed in was very pleasant, out in the country. It was useful. I discovered all I wanted to know about this Pasquale Greco; he has weaknesses; we can work with him.'

'And the other man? Ruggero whatever he is called?'

'Ruggero Bonelli? He has debts; he needs money, lots of money. Ruggero is a good person to work with. He loves cocaine. He is close to his sister. No wife. The sister, you remember her. She wants to make herself agreeable, hence this introduction, which he needs more than us, perhaps. He knows my stepfather; he's educated.'

'Middle class people,' said Calogero thoughtfully. 'We are rising in the world. We are washing not just lots of money, but our reputations as well. That ruse of having to build a platform under the new church to support the foundations, a platform that no one will ever see, or ever know, does not exist. Oh, what a beautiful farce that is! And now the art business. You are clever. And all the other problems, they are solved?'

He handed over the envelope that he had been given. Calogero took it, and studied the contents. He was silent for some time. He asked how the envelope had arrived, and Traiano explained, hazarding that it had come from Rome, via one of the local men in Agrigento, or via don Carmelo perhaps. The envelope had been sealed.

'And this was the work of…?' asked Calogero.

'Muniddu and Tonino,' answered Traiano.

'A pair of original thinkers,' said Calogero. 'Do not mention to them that you know. They have not mentioned it, have they? They have a degree of savagery that leaves me wondering. We will keep these in the safe and then release them to someone at the moment of maximum impact. I think I know when that will be. Volta knew them. This will win him the election. He is going to win it anyway. But this will make it certain. The Italian state must have connived at the murder of these two innocents. How else were they found? Someone betrayed them. Already it has created a stir, but when it comes out that the woman was doubly violated, and the boy violated too, that public anger will be harnessed against the government. You watch. Just as with the gas explosion. Their credibility is ruined, and will be ruined more. Reward Tonino. Reward Muniddu.'

'I was thinking of giving Tonino complete control over the sale of illegal prescription drugs on behalf of Doctor Moro. And Ruggero Bonelli has this flat full of art works that he has just inherited and which he intends to use as a showroom. Someone needs to live there to make sure it is safe. He and his mother; she can keep the place clean.'

'Who else did you see in Agrigento?' asked Calogero.

'Corrado, Gino's brother, and their parents. Nice guy. Very upright, won't take a penny from us; the parents live in poverty. He will be coming to the baptism. He is interested in my sister-in-law Pasqualina, and she in him.'

'We should watch him. But if he were a spy he would try to fit in more, wouldn't he?' said Calogero. 'But never say anything in front of him. How was the holiday, how were our men?'

'Alfio is sensible. He did not sleep with any of don Carmelo's prostitutes. He did not take any drugs. He was very cautious, and a bit on edge. I think he is clever enough to see that things are changing. Perhaps I overestimate him. Perhaps he is just frightened of getting beaten with my belt again. As for the other two, different whores each night, barely sober the entire time, and plenty of white powder and pills, the pair of them. But Alfio behaved himself, as he is getting married soon to Giuseppina. Gino said that was the reason he should misbehave. I think he would have liked to, but he saw that I was watching him. Gino said he needed to enjoy himself before the baby was born. As for don Renzo, he was just enjoying himself as he always does.'

'Did you give him a taste of your belt?'

'He is not marrying my sister,' said Traiano. 'I leave that to you.'

'Let's hope that Elena does not find out. She must suspect, but she wants to marry, and she wants to marry him. Poor girl. Does Catarina know about her husband?'

'The drugs, yes. The whores, probably. One reason he gave is that ever since she announced her pregnancy, she has not let him touch her. So he is entitled to the whores, he reckons.'

'Thankfully he is too stupid to realise that it is not his child. Though he may one day. Catarina must despise him. She is a clever girl. Drop them a hint that I want to be godfather to the child when it is born. It is my nephew or niece, after all.'

'Will do, boss.'

He left, to go back to Acireale, where his wife was waiting for him. Within half an hour he was there, and he found the house in silence, all of them asleep. He let himself into the house, went upstairs, looked at the sleeping children and then undressed and got into bed with his eight months pregnant wife. She stirred and drew him close to herself. She murmured a question about his trip to Agrigento, and how pleased she was he was back. In a few moments they were both asleep, and the house was entirely at peace.

The boss left to drive to Donnafugata along the quiet roads, in the middle of the night. When he arrived, it was very late, and he slipped into the house and one of the spare bedrooms lest he wake his sleeping and pregnant wife.

In the stifling heat of Purgatory, in the tiny flat he shared with his mother, Tonino lay awake in bed. It was hot and uncomfortable, but he had never been happier, not that he would have admitted this to anyone. Inside him, his ambition burned.

In the cool Dolomites, Colonel Andreazza lay in bed reunited with his wife, their child asleep nearby, thinking that he had made the right call. Far to the south, Volta slept on, knowing that he too had made the right decision.

There was darkness over Sicily now, and if Etna stirred, only a few scientists paid attention. Under the Church of the Holy Souls in Purgatory, the family of Amilcare lay at rest, and not far from them lay the boss's first wife, Stefania, in her expensive coffin. As for Beata and her son Paolo, they lay in a government mortuary in a suburb of Rome, their final resting place still unknown.

Author's Note

None of the office holders in this book are to be identified with real people. This is a work of fiction. All coincidences with regard to names and places are just that – coincidences.

Printed in Great Britain
by Amazon

Printed in Great Britain
by Amazon